CANINE

Kaitlin Bergfield

Dedicated to my steadfast crew of editors, reviewers, and supporters whose tireless efforts improved this work infinitely. Thank you.

Special thanks to Ludo for the use of lyrics from their song, "Air-Conditioned Love."

CHAPTER 1

"Berto…" Mia calls from the kitchen, her voice soft and gentle in a suspicious kind of way that sets the hairs on the back of my neck on edge. You know that tone, the one women use when they know they're about to ask far too much of you? It's *that* tone. There's something wrong in it.

At first I'm not too worried. She speaks this way more than I'd like, and it could mean any of a dozen mildly aggravating things – I love this girl but she's so, *so* very needy. Eleven months since I moved in with her and I'm still waiting to get more than a few hours to myself in this one-bedroom apartment that's just far too small for the both of us. And far too tidy and chic for someone as shabby as myself. Right now I'm trying to decide whether to bother getting off the bed to see what she wants this time.

"Berto, come here," Mia calls again, louder. I can't tell you how much I hate hearing that name from anyone but her with her irresistibly seductive accent. Alas, the name's never up to me. "Berto, querido, where you hiding?"

…Wait, hiding?

'Hiding' is not a word I want to hear, 'hiding' means she wants something big. When you can't communicate back and forth with people, you have to read a lot into whatever they're willing to tell you. *Should* I be hiding? And where the hell might I manage to hide, I wonder?

I really wish it didn't have to be this way, I wish I could just ask her what she wants and move on. I wish I could talk to her and tell her how deeply I care for her and how thankful I am to have met her and how bloody annoying it is that she speaks almost nothing but Spanish around the house and when she does practice English with me it's halting and terse and I can barely work out her real meaning. But that's not the game. She doesn't

1

know and she can't know how much easier life could be for the both of us if only she knew the real me. At least I'm starting to learn a second language, I guess.

"Berto!" Mia snaps finally, an uncharacteristic frown wrinkling that flawless brow of hers as she peers around the corner to find me now cowering on the far side of the bed trying to work out what's going on and how to get out of it. It's not often she raises her voice like that. She's glaring at me in exasperation. "Hey, vamos, we're going to be late!"

My stomach sinks a little more with that new information. Late to *what*, exactly? I can think of very few appointments she and I would have to attend together. And none of them are good. Maybe if I sink down and look pathetic enough she'll drop it. I put my head down on the blanket, halfway under a pillow, and she smiles sympathetically and crosses the room to sit with me. *Not* good.

Please don't do this, Mia. I don't like this. Whatever it is you're planning, please let's just call it off and pretend it never happened, yeah?

"It will be *fine*, puppy," she assures me, bending to kiss the top of my head, perfectly manicured pink nails scratching me behind the ear. "No te preocupes, okay?"

Don't worry? Oh God, time to panic. I hate this, I hate jumping to conclusions but I don't have a choice. That look of hers is too pitying and that tone is too nice and those words can only mean one thing when she's talking about being late... Because you don't make an appointment with your dog anywhere except the vet. *Why* does she want to take me to the vet? She doesn't have the money for a regular checkup and I'm not sick—

I have to get out of here. I can't believe I'm about to lose another one over *this*. Please, please, *please*, Mia, tell me what this is about, tell me it's only a checkup, tell me we're meeting up with friends at the park. Just say *something*, anything. Give me an excuse not to leave. I like you, I thought we had something good going here, I don't want to leave. *I don't want to start over yet...*

"Vamos," Mia says again, tugging at my collar. I have to give in. We're not at the very last second yet, and I can't be absolutely sure what she intends here. There's still time to work it out...

That thought's repeating over and over as we head into the kitchen — *there's still time, there's still time* — but the seconds are ticking by and Mia remains maddeningly silent as she gets her purse and roots through it for her car key and the house keys and her mobile, taking care as she always does to make sure she has everything with her. I love that about her. I don't want this to be the last time I watch her conscientious routine. She throws her purse over her shoulder and grabs my lead off its hanger by the door.

She's about to clip it onto my collar when suddenly her face lights up in recollection.

"Oh!" she cries, dropping the lead on the table and smiling wide-eyed at me before she darts off into the front room to get something. She's already coming back with that ratty old blue blanket she gave me as she explains sweetly, "I hate to think of you waking up after surgery without even your favorite blanket for comf— Berto! Hey, get back here! *Berto!*"

But I'm already clawing my way out the kitchen door. Mia's shouting grows quieter behind me as I break free into a warm late spring morning, bolting off down the alley and around the corner out of sight. I don't stop running for a full half hour.

And that's the end of Mia, my sixteenth roommate.

There's no way I'm ever going back to that apartment, not if she has designs on relieving me of my manhood. Who waits *eleven damn months* to fix her dog anyway? I thought I had a bye on this one! What changed her mind? Did I do something wrong? I can't believe how close I came to losing it — usually I overhear the call to the vet or something, I have time to escape discreetly. But *this...* this was way too close. If she hadn't given it away like that I might have actually gone under the knife this time.

Why, Mia? Everything was going so well! Sure the place was small, and she was around more than I'd have liked, and we didn't speak the same language most of the day... but she came home *every day* at lunch to hang out, and she was generous with the table scraps, and she was just so gorgeous and kind and compassionate...

3

But I can't go back there. Not even Mia is worth getting maimed for.

And I was never really her type anyway, I tell myself as I finally calm down enough to walk, trying to shrug off this persistent nauseous anxiety. A girl like Mia needs something more like a Pomeranian, or a Chihuahua, something she can carry around in her designer purse. She doesn't need me, some big ugly stray she thinks she saved, some monster wolf-style mutt who should have known it could never end well with a responsible girl like her.

I spend the morning meandering around town, at a loss for what to do next. I didn't expect to get railroaded like that. I've never had this little warning before, I need more time to think this through and plan my next move. I'm terrible at planning in this form.

The way things stand right now, everything is impossible. I don't know where the hell I think I'm going to sleep tonight. If I had more time I could have arranged an apartment, maybe, or a bus ticket to some other city. But then what? It's getting harder and harder to find a job anymore and I don't have much more than a few hundred dollars left in a safe deposit box down at the bank. Maybe I could get to it today and that'd give me a chance at a cheap hotel where I could kiss half my money goodbye straightaway...

In any case I've got to find some clothes, first. The last clothes I owned were bulldozed into oblivion over a year ago when the empty lot I buried them in became a car park for the adjacent shops. Besides, too much more time out here in the open and I'm going to get dragged back to the pound by some well-meaning cop or upstanding citizen, and this collar and tag will have me shipped right back to Mia by closing time.

Suppose I could always try calling the family...

Ha! Sometimes I crack me up. Forget it. Someone's got to have clothes around here somewhere, right? I take off running again, off to find some podunk suburbia household with an open back door.

You wouldn't think it'd be that hard to do, would you, find

4

some free clothes? If only people still dried their clothes on outdoor clotheslines – that would significantly expedite this process. As it is, I spend the better part of two hours passing carefully by house after house in a run-down neighborhood near the freeway before I finally find one that has a running washer and dryer sitting out on the back porch.

I creep carefully up to the back fence, listening for sounds inside the house. Someone's playing loud music in the front room, far from the back door. Can't tell much more than that but it's a comforting sign. I look around to see if anyone's watching me, this loose dog sniffing around someone's back gate. Jumping the wall into unknown territory is too risky – I've got to have some hands for this operation.

It's the work of four seconds to transform, reach over the gate to lift the latch and revert back to being just a dog before anyone's the wiser.

But that doesn't mean it's easy. I'm not used to going from wolf to man back to wolf again so quickly – with each transformation my body wrenches violently from one form to the other, stretching, snapping, contorting painfully as every bone and muscle and organ warps to accommodate my alternate shape. Volleying forward and backward again in a single fluid transition, one that still incorporates an efficient opening of the gate, takes a measure of control I'm barely able to muster even after a lifetime of practice.

I take a second to breathe and refocus, and then I nose my way carefully inside and duck behind the first big object I see: a kids' playhouse. From the playhouse I can make a quick dash for the bushes near the bedroom window and then creep along until I'm almost at the porch. I really need to be canine for as long as possible, slinking around this backyard. Dogs go to the pound, humans go to prison.

My heart's pounding as I inch forward to peer through the window and check the kitchen for any sign of life. Nothing. The kitchen's dark and I can see the lights on in the living room beyond. The music is toddler music, something with kazoos and a xylophone, and I'm picturing Mummy sitting on the floor playing with Junior, maybe coloring or something. It's perfect.

The dryer's still running and I move over to it, tucking in next to it against the wall out of sight of the house.

Please, please tell me Mummy's drying a load of Daddy's clothes right now.

This is it. I can't wait any longer. I take one last breath and transform again, yanking open the dryer and rooting around frantically for some clothes. Bingo. Daddy's got a pair of jeans and a shirt he's going to be missing. I shut the dryer as quickly and quietly as possible, reaching up to turn it back on before Mummy can hear the difference. The clothes are damp but not wet, and I make a quick pass at folding them into some sort of workable package.

Then I drop them on the ground and transform in an instant, grabbing the pile up in my jaws and making a break for the gate. My adrenaline level's through the roof when I reach up again to close it and transform one final time to sit there on four paws, trying not to breathe, listening for any sign that Mummy realized something was up. If I've got to run I can't afford to do it human, I'm too drained to outrun a fellow primate.

I think I'm going to throw up. Six transformations in a row is *way* more than I've done in a long time, I'm exhausted and the world's still spinning no matter how I try and shake it. I'm anxious to get going, but at the first wobbly step I have to claim defeat and sit crouched next to the gate for a few more minutes to recover.

Finally, *finally* the vertigo fades and my muscles stop twitching in protest and I can stand without falling down again. I grab up the clothes and drag them around the corner behind a dumpster for transformation number seven. The dumpster gets a fresh addition in the form of a dog collar with rhinestones on (bloody *rhinestones!* Oh Mia, Mia, why did I stay…?). And then I stroll out casually, just a regular bum, barefoot and carefree wearing a pair of trousers about three inches too short for me and a green shirt.

As I'm walking out the other end of the alley I look over and see an honest-to-God clothesline, in easy reach, laden with men's clothing.

I hate being human. I *hate* being human, dealing with humans.

6

I'm no good with people, not in this form. It's this repeating mantra in my head as I stand here outside a corner store begging enough change off old ladies to buy a ninety-nine cent pair of flip-flops.

Shoes, unfortunately, are an aggravating necessity. Shoes complete the look, they render me decent enough to hoof it down to an old roommate's house to dig around behind the back fence for my safe deposit key and then head to the bank for my life savings of three hundred forty-two dollars. No shoes, no service.

But see, *dogs* don't need shoes. They don't need money. They don't have to save away for a rainy day. They don't need to act gracious and meek and downtrodden and humble just to get a break, they don't have to work out a convincing story that explains why they're sitting barefoot outside a store in the middle of a weekday. The amount of manipulation required to convince people they ought to follow the golden rule is so much higher when the one doing the asking is their fellow man...

Sadly, dogs also don't have a lot of recourse for getting safely and quickly out of a city. Mia was a definite sign – it's time to leave Philadelphia. I knew better than to stay in one city two roommates in a row. It's time to get moving again, time to trade in some of those dollars of mine for the next bus ticket to the next Anywhere, USA. Somewhere nice and hot, maybe. And no Mias this time – no needy homebodies, no foreign speakers, no one who'd think to get their new stray pal neutered. I'm narrowing down what it is I want out of the next roommate. I think I'm going to find that elusive Right One soon. I can feel it.

The longer I stand here the more I think about Mia and how disastrously misguided I was to stay with her. I first caught sight of Mia outside a yoga studio. If you saw Mia leaving a yoga class you'd follow her home too, believe me. And you'd blind yourself to her obvious logistical faults like I did. You *cannot* be in my situation and not know the language. Picking up on what the roommate is saying is half the job. And as sweet as she was to take me everywhere with her and come home throughout the day to be sure I wasn't feeling too cooped up in that apartment, those moments of guaranteed autonomy are what I live for. And she was absolutely right to be worried about me — that place definitely couldn't handle an animal my size. I thought I'd learned that lesson after my second roommate's studio. What was I thinking, staying with Mia?

I knew the moment I set eyes on her she was a stopgap, not the solution. I lost sight of the goal. Settle down. Stop running for a while. Find anyone I can stand to be with for more than a few months. A place to sleep and some food and not too much hassle, that's all I want — is that so much to ask? It's not really freeloading, it's not. I'd like to think I give something back in the form of a well-trained Man's Best Friend, an existential comfort and an ideal sounding board. It's a fair trade. I've just got to find the right conditions.

The shoes take me about fifteen minutes because old ladies are stingy, but I'm such a charmer, I've got that genuine smile down pat and such a delightful British accent they can't help but imagine I've just accidentally fallen on really rough times. I don't even have to make up a story, just lay that dying old accent on thick and ask for a couple pence — they love it, the word 'pence' — and two old ladies later I've got exactly one dollar and thirty-three cents for my footwear.

I don't say much to these ladies at all, but even that first "Excuse me?" is more than I've said to anyone in over two years. It doesn't matter how many times I do it, every reentry into humanity feels like a weird culture shock.

I get green shoes to match the green shirt. Why not? You think werewolves have no fashion sense?

Dane is the guy I'm going to go see, meaning that I'm actually not going to let him see me at all and in fact am simply going to unearth my only real belonging from behind his duplex. His place is about six miles from here and I don't have it in me to beg for bus fare as well, so it'll take a while to get there.

Dane... man, it's been a while since I've thought about Dane. Dane's a great guy, and if things were different I wouldn't have minded hanging out with him on a Friday night after math class finished down at the university, going out for a couple of beers like friends are supposed to. I know him really well, better than maybe anyone else in this world does, but we're not on a first name basis. Dane knew me as 'Andy' – not particularly inventive, but I've had worse. You have to expect boring names with guys anyway, they're always way worse at naming dogs than girls are. It was a girl that gave me my favorite name: Lupus-Sapiens, Lou for short. Oh, Sophie... No, I can't get thinking about Sophie. Not now. Sophie's over and done, Phoenix has been checked off the list.

Even going back to Dane is a risk, but I don't have a choice if I want that key. This is my first time ever going back to an old roommate's place. I know better than this. But I won't stay long, I just have to get that key and I'm gone. I will not linger, I will not try and hover out of sight and catch a glimpse of this old friend of mine, I will not convince myself it's a good idea to make sure he's still doing all right in my absence. I've gotten over being worried for him – he stopped needing me long before I left.

Dane was really great, incredibly cool and laid-back, very personable and very good at concealing a whole host of seriously depressive tendencies that always made me nervous. Best comfort in the world is a dog, though, and I was a damn good dog. I always am. Dane told me every single thing that was ever on his mind. He used to remark all the time how crazy it was that it seemed like I was actually listening, like I really knew what he was saying, and what a relief it was to be able to talk to someone who wasn't a shrink and wasn't trying to fix him. That's what a dog's for, canine therapy.

I had a great time with Dane. If he hadn't started dating that psycho dog-hating girlfriend I might still be hanging at his place.

So here I am in Dane's alley almost a year after I left, and there's a frothing terrier mutt barking his head off at me while I go digging right next to him on the other side of the fence. This is ridiculous. I didn't expect the girlfriend to lose out to a damn *terrier*. When I left I was trying to play the gentleman, I snuck away quietly before the situation forced poor Dane to a difficult decision – but knowing that in the end Dane chose the dog, and that *this* is the dog he chose in my absence... that stings. I got Mia and Dane got a terrier. It's wrong, that's what it is – it's just

9

wrong.

The sick sense of regret washing over me at this realization is only amplified by a mounting aggravation at the incessant shrill yapping just feet from my face. The last thing I need right now is the attention of frustrated neighbors. I'm digging as fast as I can, damn these flimsy human fingernails, and I'm finding absolutely nothing. I know I've got the right spot. I *know* it. So where the hell is my key...?

And then the worst thing happens. The back door of the duplex slams open and there's Dane himself, eleven-months-older Dane shouting at the mutt to shut up – and then he sees me. By now I've straightened, praying to God he's not keen enough to notice I've been digging this hole, when I know already he's keener than that by half.

"Can I help you?" he asks me suspiciously, eyeing the hole and my appearance – the wrinkled clothes, the tousled hair and beard, the fine layer of dirt. I can't help it, looking like this so close after a transformation, I haven't had time to properly shower and shave – and it's always a real eye-opener to me to see how people choose to react to a stray man. Talk about an utter lack of fraternal goodwill.

I smile, turning on the charm again.

"Is this your dog?" I ask him, gesturing to the mutt who's still barking like a maniac. It's the first time I've ever spoken to Dane. It's so weird to see him like this, my good buddy Dane, to know him and know everything about him when to him I'm a total stranger. He nods shortly at the question. "What's his name?"

"Drew," Dane answers, and then shouts the name at the dog, "Drew! Get inside!"

I have to suppress my grin at the name, Andrew the Second. Not remotely inventive – Dane hasn't changed at all. Drew agrees to the command only reluctantly, chancing a few last warning growls at me before turning and skirting past his owner's legs into the house. Dane turns his attention back to me the moment the dog is inside.

"You looking for something?" he asks, gesturing to the hole in the ground.

"I lost a key," I admit sheepishly, beginning my fabrication which will be close enough to the truth that I won't seem like I'm lying. "Well, not *lost*, exactly – I buried it to keep the girlfriend from finding it and that's a good thing, in retrospect..."

Dane frowns, not sure he believes me, but he seems to think it's safer to keep me in his sight than to head back in the house and let me snoop around by my lonesome.

"You want help?" he asks.

"No, that's all right," I assure him, shaking my head and turning my attention back to the dirt. "I'm sure it's here somewhere – if you don't mind me looking, that is?"

Dane shakes his head.

"No, take your time," he replies hesitantly, and pauses for one agonizing moment before he accepts that there's no way around it and he'll have to head back inside so as not to seem like a jerk. I breathe a silent sigh of relief and go directly back to the dirt the minute he's out of sight.

It's got to be here somewhere. That's more than three hundred bloody dollars I'm out if I can't find this key. Three hundred dollars and all I have in this world, save a stolen pair of jeans and shirt, a legally-purchased pair of flip-flops, and thirty-four begged cents. I absolutely cannot get by as a human without any money, I don't do homeless gracefully. Every shelter and soup kitchen feels like a trap – I'm stuck constantly looking over my shoulder, worried that someone's going to start questioning this bum who can't seem to strike the last vestiges of an English accent, asking why he's got no ID and wondering if he's here illegally and whether he needs to be brought to the attention of the local authorities or immigration services so he can be sent back where he came from... I don't have the fortitude to deal with that kind of human interaction yet. If I can't find this key I'm sleeping on the street tonight.

I'm still digging, losing all hope in the dwindling daylight, when the door opens again and Dane steps out a second time. He's got a bottle of water in his hand, and for that I want to fall at his feet in gratitude.

"You sure you don't want help?" he asks, handing me the bottle over the fence. "How long ago did you bury it?"

"Few years," I reply. Dane raises a skeptical eyebrow. I

11

explain further. "It's a safe deposit box, see, the emergency stash." I gesture behind me to the house opposite his across the alley, the rental house with an endless cycle of tenants Dane has never once bothered to meet. "I used to live here. And then I moved in with the girlfriend, and then it all got ugly and this morning she literally threw me out, I didn't have time to grab anything useful. So here's me digging for my old spare key." I sigh for effect. "It's been a day, let me tell you."

Dane smiles, probably against his better judgment. "What's your name?"

"Andy," I reply without hesitation. He doesn't pick up on the not-coincidence.

"Dane," he introduces himself cordially, shaking my hand. "I'd offer you a shovel but I don't have one."

"No, no worries, thanks—" I say quickly, but he interrupts me.

"Seriously, let me help you look, eh?"

I nod, feigning reluctance even though I'm desperate. I have to find this key.

So Dane comes around to my side of the fence and we start digging. Pretty soon we've got a fair trench, him working one way and me working the other.

I find it oddly disorienting, sitting here with the guy as he strikes up a conversation asking me more questions about this girl I've made up to look like Mia in my mind. The world is so *different* from a human perspective – all I'm thinking about while we talk is this one night, ages ago now, where he came home all messed up from the bar obviously depressed and sat down to watch TV, and after a few seconds he burst into tears and there was no one but me to comfort him. I'm sitting here now digging this stupid trench, and I can't get it out of my head that I bloody nuzzled up against this guy for an hour while he cried into my neck. I didn't particularly mind at the time but I am, to say the *very* least, extremely weirded out by that now.

And then my fingers strike gold.

"Ah!" I cry, prying the key out from the dirt and holding it aloft. *Eureka!* "Found it!"

"Awesome," Dane says with a grin. He stands up, shoving the

dirt back into his half of the trench with the side of his foot. I try and do the same, and manage mainly to cover my foot with more dust when it pours over the lip of my flip-flop. I can't help thinking this whole operation would have taken me about three seconds as a wolf.

"Thanks for the help," I tell Dane, who shrugs it off.

"No problem," he says. "Take care, eh? Good luck with the girlfriend."

"Thanks," I say with a grateful smile, and before I know it he's back on his side of the fence, waving goodbye and stepping back inside.

I can think of a thousand things I want to blurt out just before the door shuts, and I'm thankful when it does shut that I didn't say any of them. I'm not that stupid anyway. I head back the way I came, meandering off to get my money, and realize only when I get to the bank that it's already closed for the night.

It's an unusually warm pre-summer night, and I'm thankful for that because I'm sleeping out under the stars tonight. It was dark by the time I got back to Dane's place and reburied the key right where I found it. And it was past midnight when I finally made it back across town to the other house, where I left Daddy's clothes inside the dryer. I didn't dare root through the dumpster for Mia's collar, but I left the flip-flops, with thirty-four cents nestled carefully in the ball of the flop, sitting on the ground next to it.

So I'm back to square one. I've chosen a nice bridge to sleep under, and I'm sitting here curled up on a flat bit of concrete covered in bird shit, trying to doze with cars thrumming by overhead. If I get sleep tonight I certainly won't feel it when I wake up, but I'm too tired to change my locale.

I'm already kicking myself for putting back that key. If I'd been thinking for half a second I would have realized that the bank closure wasn't exactly the end of the world, nor was it a sign from God that I ought to go just one more round as a dog before attempting humanity again and moving on. I know better than this. I know better. *Why* am I staying canine right now…?

I wish this were an atypical mode for me. As I sit here I can

13

practically hear my older sister's voice float up out of the depths of memory, nagging at me to quit being such a mindless stupid mutt all the time. I never listened to her – she didn't know anything, she's only a human, she can't understand how much better and easier life can really be for me this way. But I'm beginning to wonder if maybe she wasn't right, if choosing a canine form for the majority of my time hasn't in some ways drastically eroded my uniquely human critical thinking skills, because it seems I spend a lot of my life doing things which seem fully brilliant at the time but which I end up deeply regretting later.

All of today is beginning to seem like a perfect example. First the fiasco with Mia, the drawn-out search for clothes, the decision to waste time walking instead of begging for bus fare, and finally the total absence of pause to consider what time banks generally close. And the all-too-ready leap to the conclusion that going backward in the face of momentary defeat somehow made more sense than continuing to push forward, this evening. I have plenty of time now to contemplate just how many ways I could have done today differently in order to have achieved that end goal of cozy hotel bed and dinner, because concrete isn't at all as comfortable as it looks, and sleep continues to elude me well into the early hours of the morning.

I must drift off eventually, because I remember dreaming. I dream about Drew. Drew's a good dog, and loyal, you can see it from the way he defends so violently and obeys so readily. I dream Drew's sitting on the couch watching American football with Dane. That's the entire dream, really, and it's a wolf dream, which means vision takes a back seat to the other senses – scent primarily, sound secondarily. There's a smell of barbecue crisps and Miller Light, that absolute piss excuse for a beer which was more or less the only thing I ever couldn't stand about Dane.

The game is Green Bay and Dallas, and Dane's cheering his head off for the Packers because he grew up in Appleton. I never could get into football, I didn't see whatever it was he saw in it. But I could definitely get into hanging out on Dane's couch watching football with him again. Drew can't possibly be appreciating it as much as I would.

A semi blaring its horn overhead wakes me up with a start, and I realize I'm starving. I've got barbecue crisps on the brain. It's time to find me a new roommate.

CHAPTER 2

There's a method for finding a roommate. Step one, head to the suburbs. Step two, park yourself out of sight. Step three, check out the passers-by.

You can tell a million things about a person in those first few critical moments of people-watching. Clothes are a fair indicator, but face is vital. You want someone contemplative, friendly, someone animated without being manic. Someone who's not got a crazy gleam in his eye. Someone intellectual.

And when you've finally got your man, you follow him. Carefully. You *have* to see where he lives first, before he notices you're interested. You have to be sure he's able to care for a dog but doesn't have one already. You need to see how his place is kept. You need to check out the size of it, the yard, the presence of a car out front and the make and model if there is one. I prefer houses that use bikes as the primary mode of transportation – if I'm going to make life as a dog work I have to spend it with someone active.

That's really important, actually – this is your life. The whole of your everyday experience. Keep in mind at all times that you are gauging what type of person you're about to live with for a potential span of years. This is a very intense selection process.

Which is why I'm pretty appalled at myself when I catch sight of a guy out jogging less than an hour after dawn and start following him immediately.

I suppose you could argue that I have a sixth sense about roommates by now, but my recent epic failure with Mia ought to be weighing more heavily on my mind. My stomach's beating my head into submission, really.

He looks like a nice guy, I tell myself as he passes and I slink out of the bushes a few paces later to follow him. He's pretty short, he's really sort of scrawny actually. He's got light-colored

16

hair, and it's spiked forward but it's so long it looks kind of shaggy. He's not got glasses on but he looks bookish and pale, so I'm guessing he's wearing contacts. Which means he's smart, in the proper sense of the word. He's clean, he looks after himself. He wants to look good.

These are not the world's best signs for a potential roommate. I like a girl to be smart, but I like a guy to be a bit scruffy. Smart-dressed girls are more attentive, scruffy guys more adaptable to sudden change.

What else? This guy's got gold-and-blue running shorts on, which screams college affiliation to me. I have no idea what school it could be. But he's probably educated. He's not got a ring on either hand. Probably not married. He's wearing an iPod on his right arm, the latest one that came out a few months ago. So he's either tech-centered or superficial.

He finally notices in a rather comical way that I'm following him, hearing me clicking along behind him when the music pauses between songs, then turning halfway around and half-turning back before his brain kicks in and he turns all the way around, stopping dead in his tracks, startled.

I stop too, putting on my best curious dog impression. He's wary – and rightfully so, because I think even on all fours I'm maybe half his height. Maybe a third. That's still a monster-sized dog to have following you. He's not moving, and I'm not moving. He waits a few more seconds to see what I'm going to do.

And then he turns around cautiously, resuming his jogging. I resume my pursuit.

A few seconds later he turns his head again, very much aware I'm still there and still following him. He turns full around to face me.

"What do you think you're doing?" he demands of me, and I have to say I'm impressed. I *really* like this guy. I like a guy who wastes that sort of precious jogging breath to say a full sentence to a dog. I was expecting him to stamp his foot and yell, "Git!" – easily my very least favorite American saying.

He's sizing me up now like I'm sizing him up, he's trying to work out why I'm following him. He's checking out my neck like

I did his hands – wondering who owns me, like I'm wondering who owns him.

He gives up after another moment, turning back around and beginning again to run. I begin again to follow. He knows I'm doing it. He puts a hand up to his iPod to turn the volume down so he can attend better to me. Turn it down, but not pause it. He likes his music, this guy.

He turns right at the next intersection and I'm right with him, trotting along a respectful distance away, my head bowed low. This is the game. You look uninterested, look blasé, look harmless. I get the feeling he's buying it. He's certainly not all that worried about me anymore, though he keeps turning his head to catch sight of me in his periphery, to assure himself I'm not too close, that I'm still there.

This lack of a negative reaction is a good sign. He doesn't hate me. Please, please don't let him already have a dog.

I don't smell any dogs, though. He smells like sweat – like two types of sweat, the running type and the just-got-out-of-bed type. But he also smells faintly of cologne, a really rich, sort of herbal, very faintly fruity sort of scent, like ginger maybe, like sage. I get the feeling I'm only getting sage from that combination of cologne and stale sleep. This nose of mine can break down a scent in no time flat, eh?

Whatever this cologne is, it's not cheap. But last night was a weeknight. I wonder if it was a special weeknight – he must have gone out, he's got that smell of hard alcohol on his breath. Maybe he just likes to party. He's probably got someone special to go out with, if he's using cologne. Or he's looking for someone special to go out with.

His trainers look expensive. They're new, and based on the picture I'm building of this guy I'd imagine that's because he's careful to get new shoes every six months or three hundred miles, whichever comes first. First glance I'd have said it's because he's trendy, but... I don't know, the shaggy hair and relative pallor are saying something to me. And he's out this early in the morning. He must really want to run.

I'd kill to know what's on his iPod. Music is one of the best personality indicators you can get. I'd peg this guy as... jazz at home of an evening, classical while working, techno while running. I could survive that. I'm listening really closely to pick out the music in his ear buds, but from this distance all I can make out is a lot of bass and a few loud high notes.

He stops abruptly when he comes to the next intersection, waiting to cross the street to our left. I stop too, a few paces away, and I'm wondering why the hell he didn't just continue jogging across the street – he could easily have made it before the SUV coming over the hill even came near him.

And then to my surprise he holds a hand up to me as if telling me to stop, still watching the SUV. He turns to look at me, still raising his hand, making sure I'm not moving, and then turns back to watch the SUV as it passes, and then he puts his hand down and starts jogging again.

"Okay," he says, almost under his breath, and if I could smile I'd be doing it. I'm in, I know it. Pausing to make sure the dog doesn't do something stupid? That's an in if I've ever seen one.

He jogs halfway down the block, a tree-lined little nothing of a street like all the rest in this neighborhood, crammed with tiny houses built mere decades ago but crafted so shoddily they look more like they've seen centuries. Halfway down the block he turns, glancing both ways before heading across the street. He jogs right up to the front walk of a little white house, grey shingled roof, well-manicured lawn, tidy bushes under windows with drawn curtains. The back yard is fenced from view, but I'm not seeing any dog-related items lying around out front. He stops at the walk and turns again to me.

"So you've followed me home," he begins with an ironic smile, watching me in an incredulous way. "You think you're going to keep following me inside?"

I don't answer, obviously. I'm just watching him. I start panting, that lazy pant dogs affect when disinterested.

But I hold his eye. People like when a dog holds their eye, it makes them think the dog is a pretty smart beast. When a dog attends to human faces it makes people think he sees something familiar in them. They seem to think it draws two beings cosmically together, man and dog, watching each other's faces. Don't ask me why people get all philosophical about this. It's just instinct, really.

The guy grins, shaking his head.

"Go on, go home," he says. Standard operating procedure. He's got to attempt a shove at some point. It seems halfhearted to me. He knows I've got nowhere to go, and I only wish it weren't so true.

I take a step forward, bowing my head again to sniff at his feet the way dogs do in that curious initial foray, the investigation of a novel human. The trainers smell *very* new, there's only one scuff on the big toe of the right one.

He doesn't back away from my advance. He takes the opportunity to yank his ear buds out, and before he turns off the iPod I'm shocked to hear a lot of really loud guitar and the tinny melodic shouting characteristic of a punk band lead singer. It isn't a song I recognize, but I'm suddenly anxious to hear what else he's got. I bet I like most of his music.

I'm studying his face in part because I'm trying to determine how old he is. I'm guessing late twenties. He's got some serious crow's feet, and a couple of faint lines in his brow, but I'm taking that to signify animation of speech rather than accumulation of years. He's got sort of luminescent brown eyes, to match the hair. He's not got any piercings or tattoos. He's about three days beyond a clean shave. He's got teeth so straight I'm sure he's had braces, and they're very white. There's no way this guy doesn't have a girlfriend. I'm hoping the girlfriend likes dogs.

"You even got a home, bud?" he asks me, still studying me as intensely as I'm studying him. I've gotten pretty good at American accents, but I can't place his. He's got a bit of a Southern drawl the way he asks that, 'y'even got a home', and the way he said 'go on'… but the rest of it sounds pretty lofty, really, and in a way it reminds me of home. And he said 'okay' like an Aussie. The whole thing is very odd. I need to hear more to work out where he's from.

He sighs, looking up at what I assume is his front door, and looks back at me.

"I bet you're hungry, at least," he remarks, watching me for a reaction. I perk up at the word, half a tail wag to let him know I understand. 'Hungry' is a great domestic dog word – pets tend to pick that one up pretty quick. I can't afford to let him think I'm some kind of wild animal, he needs to know I'm house-trained. He's looking at me, searching my face. My stomach happens to rumble loudly at just the right cinematographic moment. He grins.

"Fine," he sighs, scaling the two steps up to his walkway and gesturing for me to follow. "Come on inside."

He doesn't need to tell me twice. I follow nonchalantly.

Twenty minutes later I've died and gone to heaven. He starts with a bowl of water, and then gets right down to business searching for food, growing more and more frustrated trying to find something 'suitable'. If I were able to speak I'd tell him that more than half the stuff he's discarded is perfect.

But then he gives up and roots around in the fridge and grabs out a whole pound of ground beef, ripping off the packaging and dumping it into a frying pan, turning the stove on with a match. And then he pulls out a Chinese leftover box of white rice and a full crown of broccoli, ripping it up and adding it and the rice to the beef already sizzling delectably on the stove.

He chuckles quietly, muttering half to himself and half to me, "I don't even cook this well for *myself*."

After a few excruciatingly long minutes waiting for it to fry and then to cool, he finally pulls down a mixing bowl from a top shelf and dumps the whole mess into it for me.

I'm already practically finished, and I think I'm going to be sick from eating too fast but I don't care. He's poured himself a bowl of granola and he's leaning against the counter, watching in amusement as I lick the mixing bowl halfway across the tiles in an effort to leave no grease stain untouched. I haven't eaten this well since I was last properly human, and I know it's my first and last shot at it because if he does decide to keep me around he's going to go buy some dog food, but forget savoring this. It's too good not to wolf down.

"You were pretty hungry, eh?" he asks me rhetorically, and I do the proper dog thing, licking my chops and looking up at him plaintively. I could definitely eat more if he's got it. He grins, shaking his head.

"Hell no," he declares, "You wait until that settles, bud, and then tell me if you're still hungry."

I keep looking, and he stares back. Dog-human interactions are full of such silent studies. He smiles again, taking a heaping bite of his cereal. That smells good, too. He turns his attention wholeheartedly to the bowl, as intent on it as I was on my own meal, and finishes it quickly. He stares at the milk a moment – he filled the bowl practically to the brim, he's definitely a milk drinker. But he's wondering whether to give me some. He compromises, putting the bowl to his lips and slurping down a couple mouthfuls before he sets the bowl down on the floor with a clunk and heads out of the room. I can hear the shower turn on in a bathroom somewhere as I lap up the rest of the milk, all sugary and maple-flavored.

I stand in the kitchen for a moment afterward, trying to decide what to do next. There's sleuthing to be done, after all, but I do still have a modicum of human decency and I can't go wandering about anywhere I please. It's about respecting a roommate's privacy. I feel that if my roommates knew what I was then they certainly wouldn't walk around the house naked, they wouldn't have sex with the door open, and I aim to respect that. Within reason. I mean you can't blame a guy if he's maybe had a few female roommates he didn't mind lounging near when they were trying frantically to get ready for a date, ripping clothes on and off and asking their oh-so-helpful doggie which dress looked best. As if I could tell them. I just liked the show.

So when this guy leaves the bathroom door open I assume it's so he can hear if I crash into something, and I don't care to offend him. I park myself respectfully in the living room, milling around, sniffing things and studying the place, waiting politely for him to finish. The living room is very nice, very clean. I'm shocked this guy wants a dog in his house for even a few minutes. I'm obviously filthy, possibly feral, and this house is immaculate. Correction: this front room is immaculate. He likes a good impression, this guy.

The room has wood floors with boards that creak in a quiet, melodic way. The drapes are floor-length, the walls are fresh eggshell white, and he's got one large painting over the sofa and

22

a smaller matching one on the adjacent wall. They look like original modern art pieces, oil-on-canvas, and they look bizarre through canine eyes. Honestly, most of human art is lost on dogs when they basically fail to see half the full rainbow. I resolve to give these two another shot when I get around to seeing them properly.

The sofa is dark leather and so is the recliner in the corner of the room. The other furniture is all a deep, rich mahogany with clean, slim lines, and it all matches. The rug under the coffee table is oriental. And finally, as if to throw everything off altogether, smack in the middle of the couch – propped prominently and with a touch, one thinks, of humble irony – is a lace-edged pillow stitched in meticulous needlepoint, depicting the words 'God Bless Our Home' in block letters surrounded by a blotchy floral print. I grin inwardly and head over to check out the titles on the bookcase.

This is personality test number one, and it's a critical one. I will go absolutely mental if I get stuck in another house like Mia's, full of nothing but Spanish-language paperbacks and all the latest fashion magazines.

I've got this To-Read list, see, I'm trying to teach myself everything I ought to have learned since I skipped out on school a good dozen years ago. Try teaching yourself everything you ought to have learned since you were sixteen when you've got nothing but someone else's reading preferences at your disposal and see how far you get. It feels like ages since I've had a roommate with anything better than a few trash fiction novels, and it was a miracle if I could glean anything truly useful from whatever college textbooks I found lying around.

But *this* house... this house is phenomenal. There's no order to the titles, and I find Tolstoy next to Stephen King, Poe and Austen nestled together cozily in one corner, two versions of the Bible resting at the bottom of a precarious tower of seemingly unrelated fiction and textbooks. I love this guy's style. This is my actual dream house.

The shower shuts off abruptly when his mobile rings on the bathroom counter, and the guy can be heard wrenching a towel off the rack. It takes another two rings for him to dry himself, and when he finally answers he sounds rushed.

"Hey, puppy, what's up?"

Ah. I knew it. 'Puppy' means there's a girlfriend. A girlfriend who certainly doesn't live here, I'm sure, or he wouldn't be so happy about her calling at seven from somewhere else. And this house screams bachelor pad, there's not a feminine thing in sight other than that incongruous pillow.

The guy emerges from the bathroom with a wide grin on his face, still dripping wet with towel thrown around his waist and gripped tightly in one hand. I make a halfhearted attempt to listen in from across the room, but he's got that mobile glued to his face and I have to content myself with just his side of the conversation. He doesn't give a damn that I'm listening. I'm an animal, what could I possibly be listening to? But he does catch sight of me, and grins wider, and after a moment he says into the mobile,

"No, actually I can't do lunch out, there's been a change of plans – no, no, we can still do it together, it's just I've got to come back home because this dog followed me home and now I've got no idea what to do with it – him – it – I don't know." He grins, still watching me, and chuckles a little.

"I know, I know! Of all people. But I like him." He laughs. "No, you're still my puppy, love. You're going to seriously love him – he's exactly your type, he's a monster… I don't know, some sort of mutt, Shepherd-style." He pauses, and then speaks immediately, "No, do *not* bring Bonks over, I don't know if this dog likes other dogs."

He pauses again, and looks at me critically. "I don't think so, he doesn't have a collar or anything. It's really crazy, he followed me all the way home. I'm going to try letting him out before I go, obviously, I don't want to keep him against his will…" He grins brightly, and lets out a dramatic sigh. "All right, baby, but he's going out back and if he jumps the fence it's not my fault. I don't know what I'm going to do with a damn dog… you think I ought to take him to the Humane Society…?"

Oh God, no – anything but that. I *really* wish I could hear the girlfriend's recommendation right now. The guy doesn't respond right away. He's had this grin on his face the whole time he's been talking to this girl, and I can't help but think this is a very new relationship because no man in his right mind would look this starry-eyed for this long in any other relationship scenario. His perma-grin has only wavered in degree as he speaks, and now he's mugging manically again.

"You haven't even seen him and you want me to keep him. Look, I'm going to put signs up and that's final." And now I'm in love with his girlfriend. I'm with her a hundred percent on this one. The guy smiles sweetly, and looks away at the wall to say, "Okay puppy, I'll see you at noon, all right? Just meet me back at the house, I can be back by then. I love you too. I'll see you."

He hangs up and stares down at me for another moment, remnant of that grin still lighting his face. I am so in.

"Well," he says with an air of finality, setting the mobile down and running one hand through his dripping hair, shoving it out of his face. He looks at me again, me who's now trying to seem interested in sniffing a bookshelf, and subconsciously wraps his towel more neatly and tightly around his body. Fantastic.

This is a man who's never had a dog before, obviously, and never wanted one. A man who's uncomfortable being naked around a dog because he's never really been around one enough to know how damn dumb they are. A man who thinks of dogs as fellow sentient creatures. Is there anything about this guy I don't like? I admit I'm not looking forward to meeting Bonks, whoever that is, because dogs really don't take well to werewolves. They can smell us, they know it's a façade. They know we'd snap their little necks in a heartbeat if they crossed us when the moon was waxing full…

That's a problem for later. Right now I'm concentrating all my effort on not screwing this up.

The guy leans in toward the kitchen to check the clock over the sink, and does a bit of a double-take before rocketing off toward the staircase, dashing up them two at a time with a thundering racket and crashing about in drawers trying to get dressed. I head back into the kitchen to see that it's two minutes to seven-thirty – *man*, this guy has an early start.

So I spend some time investigating the kitchen while I listen to him throw on his clothes (rustle of garments, clank of a belt buckle, practically silent pause for socks, clump-clump for shoes) and dash into an upstairs bathroom for what sounds and smells like deodorant application and teeth brushing. There's a fairly long pause before he comes stumbling down the stairs still buttoning his shirt. He glances into the kitchen to make sure I'm still there and sees me lapping up some more water.

He yanks open the front closet and pulls out a corduroy coat, and I think to check out his wardrobe: scuffed brown brogues, dark-colored jeans, brown belt, short-sleeve striped shirt, worn-out corduroy jacket that clashes fantastically with everything else and apparently gets used often as a sentimental favorite jacket. This is an academic if I've ever seen one.

He dives into a small side room which must be an office, because he's got a messenger bag slung over his shoulder when he comes back in, throwing the bag carelessly behind him as he stoops to pick up the bowls and throw them in the sink, then thinking the better of it and filling the larger bowl with water.

"Come on, bud," he says. I follow him as he heads through the doorway on the other side of the kitchen into a second living space, in which I am absolutely delighted to find an ancient blue bicycle with wire basket and shiny new old-fashioned bell on the front.

He opens the door to the back yard and I follow him outside. The yard is fairly spacious, and I can smell one ancient Bonks remnant in the far corner. A massive tree stands off to one side with a swing hanging from the largest branch, and there are vines crawling all over the wooden fences. A little concrete path heads in a direct line through the grass from the porch to the back gate.

The guy (God, let me hear his damn name already! – sometimes this process takes ages, working out a roommate's name) sets the bowl of water down on one side of the porch before running back inside. Clanking metal and the clicking of gears just precede the appearance of bicycle and man on the porch, and in a flash he's pulled a key ring out of his pocket and locked both the doorknob and the deadbolt. He takes a breath, and turns to me.

"Be good and stay here, okay bud?" he commands, and after usage number four, now, I have a feeling I'm going to be hearing the name 'Bud' for quite a while. "I've got to go teach – but I'll be back at noon, all right?" He hefts the bike down the three steps into the yard, and as an afterthought he turns to me and adds, "And I'm sorry if you don't want to stay. I'll make it up to you, yeah?"

That 'yeah' warms my little doggy heart. That's a British-ism, first-rate. I've heard enough to make a better diagnosis, now, and I'd call him Southwest States with enough time spent abroad and on the East Coast to start picking up a lot of little linguistic quirks. That variety seems kind of fraternal, in a way – I'd apply the same verdict to my own accent and lexicon, which get steadily less pure with every year I spend in this country and in this unspeaking form. After almost half a lifetime away it's a complete mess, and it's heartening to hear a fellow mutt.

I sit back on my haunches as if to say I'm parking it for good, and he smiles and waves and disappears around the gate. I listen until I can't hear his bike anymore.

I wander around the yard for the next hour or so, and that's stretching this yard's investigative appeal to its limit. I spend a lot of time around the porch searching carefully for some spare key hiding place, but find nothing.

I'm not particularly interested in hanging around for three more hours of mind-numbing solitude, but the very idea of getting caught out wandering *now*, when I've finally found the perfect roommate, is simply out of the question. I can't help but laugh a little at the notion that I've become a proper house pet again so quickly. I have to remind myself I really don't know this guy at all. I've got to see this girlfriend, and Bonks, and the rest of the house even before I can make a proper judgment.

So I give up and get another drink of water, and lie down on the porch to catch some of the morning sun beating down on one corner of it. It's so hot, that sort of cozy warm, just-edging-into-summer breezy midmorning heat that makes you want to crawl into a hammock and sleep the day away. And the food's finally hit my stomach, and it was a hell of a lot of food even for me. Before I know it I'm passed out in the sun, oblivious to everything.

CHAPTER 3

Next thing I know the back gate is opening, and I wake with a start to see the roommate candidate grinning at me and walking his bike up toward the porch. He's obviously gone and looked over the fence before opening it, seeing me sleeping.

"Have a good nap?" he asks me, and unlocks the back door. He takes the bike inside and I follow, and he closes the door behind us.

He sighs, running his hands through his hair, obviously relieved to be home. He sloughs off his jacket and throws it over the basket on top of his messenger bag, leaving it all standing next to the door and stepping past me to head directly into the front room.

I've barely had a chance to glance at this back room, and I take a moment now while he's gone to survey it. It's got a TV on the wall, and there's a DVD player and an Xbox on the table beneath it and a massive sound system flanking them. There's a couch here, too, but it's old and sagging with plaid fabric fraying at the seams. And there's an ancient recliner, brown leather. Bookcases fill every free inch of wall space, and they're all filled beyond reasonable capacity with books. God, if I can just manage to stay inside some days...

"Hey, dog..." I hear the guy call questioningly, and I follow the voice immediately. I can*not* mess this up. He smiles when I enter the front room – the drapes are drawn back and he's thrown the needlepoint pillow on the recliner and sprawled himself out along the length of the couch. He thinks I can't understand him as he comments idly, "Makes me nervous when I can't see what you're doing."

I put on my good-lazy-dog show, approaching the couch one slow step at a time, head down, lying at the foot of it as if there were no possible other trajectory I might have taken and no other goal I might have had in mind. And then I yawn, long and whining, one huge-jawed yawn that feels really great after a three-hour nap, and rest my head on my paws.

And then, on cue, his hand comes down tentatively onto my neck and he pets me when I don't react against it. First contact. He's stuck now, even if he doesn't know it yet. My whole job is to judge character, and everything about him screams 'dog-owner'. The petting is the point of no return.

We sit like that for a few fleeting minutes before there's a commotion outside, a car door slams and he darts up, checking out the window and practically jumping off the couch when he sees the driver outside. The girlfriend is here.

I don't bother to get up. He's run into the bathroom to check his appearance, and I can hear footsteps approaching on the walk and clunking on the porch step just as he comes running back out of the bathroom and yanks open the door.

"Hey puppy," he calls happily.

"Hey, lovey," a voice replies – a *man's* voice!

Damn it. I *knew* this was too good to be true.

I don't want to say this is a complete deal-breaker, because it's not. It's not like a roommate's orientation affects me personally or anything. It's just that when you've seen the kinds of things people are willing to do in front of a dog, you get a little more cautious about what kind of people they bring home. You never know what the hell you're going to be unable to avoid seeing. In the past thirteen years I have *seen things*, things I desperately wish I could un-see. And two guys pawing all over each other is not something I particularly want to add to my list.

I don't know yet what kind of person this boyfriend is, but if the pet names and flirty tones are any indicator I could be stuck here with a couple of honeymoon-phase exhibitionists. This house isn't exactly a mansion and I don't know yet what rooms I'll be allowed in – I can picture a whole host of scenarios that put me inescapably in at least hearing range… I don't know if I can handle this.

Before I can react the guy has come back inside, and he's followed by another guy even shorter than him – I think we're now edging closer to five feet than six – who looks like a quintessential gay. I don't know how to describe him any better than that. He's a waifish boy form of Mia. He's got short hair that he bleaches practically white and parts on the right, slicking it in front of his forehead with more hair gel than a man should sensibly go through in a full year. He's got a lip ring, and an eyebrow ring, and thick earrings in both ears. He's wearing murderously tight jeans and cheap black dress shoes and a form-fitting green thermal that matches his green eyes. He gasps when he catches sight of me.

"Is this him?" he asks, hands fluttering near his face in a parody of overexcited hyper-femininity. At least his nails aren't painted.

"What else would that be?" my now much-less-potential roommate asks sarcastically, smiling. His boyfriend slaps him playfully on the shoulder.

"Shut up," the boyfriend says, and moves forward instantly to pet me. I stand and steel myself in anticipation.

"Careful, Sean," the guy warns him, and Sean glances over his shoulder in reproof, but checks his behavior appropriately when he turns back around and approaches me with at least a modicum of caution.

"Don't you dare try and teach me how to handle a dog, Galen," Sean remarks haughtily, putting extra snide emphasis on the name – the name, finally, the name! The guy looks like a Galen. I imagine he got some pretty nasty taunting as a kid, given his apparent orientation…

Sean is fast approaching and I brace myself for the attack, which when it comes is not half as bad as I'm expecting. Sean's not a total idiot, he holds out a hand for me to sniff before he reaches out with both hands to scratch me behind the ears. He pets my neck and my shoulder, talking to Galen.

"He's absolutely *gorgeous*," Sean gushes, and I can't help but cringe. Lucky for me wolves don't cringe in quite the same way people do. I just look nervous, really, tensing up and hunkering down a little. Sean thinks only that I'm scared of him and backs off, still stretching one arm out to pet my neck. "It's okay, boy, I'm not going to hurt you. Poor sweet thing… You said he followed you home?"

30

"Yeah, I was out running and he appeared behind me out of nowhere," Galen replies with a smile. "Ghost dog."

"Baskerville," Sean says playfully.

"Anubis, more like," Galen says, undoubtedly referring to my appearance. At least they're well-read gays.

"If you keep him you ought to name him Anubis," Sean tells Galen.

"That's the gayest name I've ever heard," Galen says disdainfully.

"Like I said," Sean replies lightly, and Galen grins. "He's going to scare Bonks to death."

"I don't doubt it," Galen agrees. "Come on, pups, let's get some food started. I'm starving."

He closes the door, and I'm trapped. It's a knob door, no way to open that without a proper thumb. I'd have to transform to get it open, and two seconds per transformation is the best I can do. Four seconds is a long bloody time, there's no way I'd go unnoticed.

I sigh inwardly, resigning myself to at least another hour with these guys. I have to remind myself that this is not over yet. Maybe it won't be all that bad. Sean's over the top, for sure, but Galen's so normal even I didn't pick it up until now, and I'm usually pretty good. Galen seems like the kind of guy who'd rather die than let the dog watch. I just have to wait and see, I have to study how they interact in my presence.

"So how's work going?" Sean asks teasingly, following Galen into the kitchen. I hang back for a moment, putting on the indifferent dog act, listening in from the living room.

"I'm going back to grad school," Galen mutters. "I can't take it anymore, these kids are driving me crazy."

"Public school," Sean replies with a mocking sigh.

"Yeah, well, there's no excuse," Galen snaps bitterly. "I've tried everything. I pulled my last stop this week."

Sean gasps dramatically. "Not *Catch-22?*"

Curiosity finally gets the best of me, and I have to peer around the corner to see Galen's reaction to that. I've never read Catch-22 but I've had it on my To-Read list for years, ever since Sophie raved about it to a girlfriend and then lent her the book before I could get to it. To think I'd forgotten all about the books…

It hits me again that Galen is the most literate potential roommate I've ever encountered. I have to remember I'm in bloody Alexandria at the moment, and I really can't afford to burn it yet. Galen sighs in amusement, obviously used to Sean's impropriety.

"I can't stand to watch that book desecrated, puppy, I really can't," he says, and Sean smiles.

I inch into the room, sniffing around on the floor near Galen's feet, because he's the one making the sandwiches while Sean pulls out plates and a half-empty bag of crisps from the cupboard. From the fridge Sean grabs a beer – I almost die when I see Chimay Blue. Actual Chimay, for lunch! That shit is like five dollars a bottle. I *need* to get a look at this fridge!

Galen sighs when he sees Sean with the beer. "Aw come on, not my Chimay, that's so cruel."

Sean grins. "You can have some."

"I'll get fired," Galen says.

"You want to get fired," Sean quips.

"I *want* to quit," Galen counters sternly. "Put it back, grab a Leffe or something."

Sean gives in and goes over to open up what turns out to be the Holy Grail of refrigerators: two entire shelves devoted to beers of all shapes and sizes and nationalities, and the rest filled with various takeout leftovers (half of which always end up in Dog's bowl, it's practically a rule) and fresh fruit and veg and… oh God, chocolate. My mouth actually starts watering when I see it, Pavlov-style.

I don't know what it is about chocolate – it's that forbidden thing, it's murder on the canine system but it smells *so* damn good, it's like heroin. And Galen, bless his bent soul, seems to keep a ready supply of the stuff. Galen *refrigerates his chocolate*. Oh man, even I could live with gays for *this*.

Galen's putting the sandwiches together, and I move back over toward him just as he drops a full slice of turkey not-so-accidentally onto the floor. Sean bursts out laughing.

"You pushover!" he cries with delight while I accept the offer greedily, and Galen grins at him.

"I'm still putting up signs," he says, "don't get attached."

"I ought to tell you the same thing," Sean replies pointedly. "When was the last time you even *petted* Bonks, huh?"

"Bonks is annoying," Galen complains.

"How dare you?" Sean demands gleefully, mock-affronted. "He's easily the sweetest Westie you've ever seen."

Galen thinks for a moment, and replies, "Only by virtue of being the only Westie I've ever seen."

Sean grins, shaking his head. "You – you creep! You've hardly known this dog one day and already you're feeding him table scraps."

"Yeah, well, he's... smart," Galen says unconvincingly, shrugging. "I don't know, baby, don't make me analyze it. I need to wind down, yeah, not up."

"It really sucked today, huh?" Sean asks, turning suddenly serious, sympathetic.

Galen nods, shoving a plate of sandwich in Sean's direction. Sean takes his plate dutifully to the table and Galen follows him, and I decide to lie down against the cupboard under the sink. It's the perfect vantage point – I can see the table from here, and I don't look like I'm begging. What a good dog I am.

"The book was a mistake," Galen says, and Sean smiles his understanding.

"Pearls before high-schoolers," Sean replies, and Galen nods.

"I just don't get it," he sighs. "How can anyone not fall in love with that book? If that can't catch them, nothing will. And it's so awful watching it get filtered through their dense little skulls – they're like sieves, like evil boorish sieves that irreparably defile anything that passes through them. It's filthy, it's vile the way they discard it all out of hand, it just... boils me, puppy, it grates so damn much..." He's speaking now through clenched teeth, reaching out with hands like claws, like he's wrenching the neck of one such student. "The anti-intellectual attitude in this country is utterly disgusting. I just want to kill all these damn idiots, they're choking the rest of us."

Sean's shaking his head, grinning. "You've got issues, boy. Quit being such a narcissistic elitist. They may be dumb as shit but that's the way the whole goddamn planet operates. Let it be."

Galen smiles, shaking his head. "I'm going back to school."

"What's the point of getting a Ph.D. in Lit, lovey?" Sean asks. "You wouldn't be able to stand undergrads for the rest of your life any better than you can handle high-schoolers."

"Maybe I'll do philosophy," Galen says, and Sean raises a skeptical brow.

"You think that's *better*?" he asks incredulously. Galen smiles.

"You did it," he points out, leaning across the table to kiss Sean on the cheek. I look away hastily. "Imagine that, an unending cycle of fresh young students just waiting to be educated in all the ways of the world, ripe for the plucking…"

"Hey, you ain't never gonna find better than me, honey," Sean says, affecting a Southern drawl that sounds remarkably natural. So that's where Galen's pulling it from. Galen smiles, and turns suddenly serious again.

"I need to do *something* different," he insists. He looks over at me suddenly, gesturing to me. "I mean look at me, I'm honestly thinking of taking on a damn dog just because I think he's smarter than my students! It's crazy. What am I going to do with a dog? I'm going crazy."

"Hey, come on," Sean says, "lighten up. Look at him, you're hurting his feelings."

I don't know quite how to react to that in order to give the impression that I seriously couldn't give less of a damn. I don't bother to try. People will think whatever they want to think, really, they project everything onto their pets – dogs are nothing more than an animate Rorschach test. Sean continues, oblivious to my inner workings.

"You're not crazy. Maybe a dog's good for you, you know?"

"I hate dogs," Galen says. I suppose I knew that, but I think we can all see that at least with respect to *one* dog, that's a bald-faced lie. "They're a massive pain in the ass."

"Oh, yeah," Sean replies sarcastically, "Yossarian over there's a real bloody burden, I can tell."

I don't get the reference, but Galen does, and he smiles.

"Now *that's* a proper dog's name," he replies, and peers at me critically. "He's a bit more Flume at the moment, though."

34

"He just needs a bath," Sean says, also watching me keenly.

Oh my actual God, I'm going to throw up. The idea of two guys soaping me up has about the same effect that idiot students seem to have on Galen. I can't handle it, I have to leave the room. Sean bursts into laughter as I get up and trot out around the corner back into the living room.

"Or not," he declares jovially.

Sean leaves after another half hour, and I'm thankful the lunch hour doesn't include any talk of a nooner. Instead they head to the Xbox after lunch for a couple minutes of first-person shooter before Galen checks his watch and decides it's time to get back to class. I've been lying patiently next to the corner bookshelves in the back room with them, checking out all the titles while they play, gauging their value against my hesitance to stay here. I haven't found Catch-22 yet.

Sean heads out the front door, and I let Galen kiss him goodbye or whatever he does on his own. I consider booking it out the back door before anyone's the wiser, but after an hour of adaptation and careful consideration of all the pros and cons, I've got my head on a little straighter again and I don't entertain the notion too seriously.

I can't deny this place has its draws – in fact if Sean were a woman I'd roll over now and stay here until I die. This place has everything, it checks every single box I've generated over the years. And besides, I don't think I've heard a more direct call for canine therapy than Galen's in a long time. I think I can swallow my pride for a little while longer. I've just got to embrace the canine mindset, I've got to detach and quit seeing people as anything other than overgrown monkeys...

Galen comes back in after a few moments, and he locks the front door before heading directly for his bike. He spots me in the corner trying to act unobtrusive, and he nods toward the door.

"Come on, buddy," he calls, "time to go outside."

Oh, hell no. If I can't stay inside then I know exactly how I'm going to handle this situation. I stay planted firmly on the ground. Initiate pitiful whine sequence... now.

He sighs in frustration at the first disgraceful attempt, and even I have to admit it's pretty cruel. The guy's got a nice house, and I'm a big mutt. He's undoubtedly contemplating just how massive a shit I can take on his oriental rug.

"No," he insists, shaking his head, "forget it. You're going outside."

I whine louder. He sighs louder. He looks at the time, and the sigh becomes a growl.

"Get outside, dog," he orders. Not going to work, I'm afraid. He knows it too. He moves toward me and I scoot backward, whimpering theatrically. I'm a master at this. There's chocolate on the line, here.

"I don't have time for this," he warns, starting to get angry. Don't get angry with me, Galen, don't do it. You know you like me. You know I'm the coolest damn dog you've ever known. You don't want to mess this up either. If you don't let me stay inside I'm leaving the second you're gone.

Finally he gives up. He's out of time. I bet the next class starts on the hour, and he's got ten minutes to get there now. He heads back to his bike and points an accusing finger at me.

"I swear to God, dog, if you mess up my house I'll wear your hide, got it?" He's glaring at me, and I stare back impassively. I understand not a word he's saying. I am a rock. I am Zen incarnate. There's beer, too, and a shower. There's a chance for punk music. Cave? I don't think so.

He throws his hands up to the gods and kicks the stand on his bike, sending one last iron-melting stare my way before heading out the door and turning the locks again. I wait until I hear no sign of him anymore before I get up to explore the house.

It's not until I have the place to myself that I realize I've become the modern Tantalus. I can't touch the chocolate or Galen will know. I can't get a beer or he'll know. Worst of all I can't even take a shower, because he and his boyfriend both called me a 'Flume', whoever that is. It's obviously a guy who doesn't bathe.

I transform anyway, because I can bloody well do that

36

without anyone noticing and I'm itching to at least feign civilization for a little while.

I take a moment to survey the lower floors again with my new set of senses. I revisit the paintings. Oh, *much* better now. They're a sort of bold splashing of reds and burgundies and golds with jarring swatches of bright lime green and striking broad black lines connecting everything, and gold foil flecking swimming like shoals of fish between the colors. I like it, I really like it. If they're really originals I want to know whose they are. They aren't signed. And that needlepoint pillow looks even more ridiculous now than it did through canine eyes – shocking pink lettering with garish primary colors for the flowers. I can't help but smile and wonder where the hell it came from, what it means. Fantastic.

Finally I head into the bathroom and wash my hands, my filthy disgusting hands, and take a moment to clean under the nails. There's a lot of white showing at the ends of these nails. I've got to find some clippers.

So I know Galen showered in this bathroom downstairs, but I heard him doing all the grooming upstairs. Time to discover the second floor.

It turns out to be little more than the bedroom and a rather large second bathroom. It's obvious he showers up here most days. There's a closet, too, a closet so massive it probably used to be a second bedroom, lined with more clothes than a straight man would ever own. True, I am biased because the last time I actually owned any clothes I couldn't have been more than twenty-three and I was making about six hundred dollars a month. I didn't have the money for finery. But I still think... sixteen, seventeen, *eighteen* pairs of shoes is a bit much. I admit it's all tasteful, some garments plain but none flashy, just an exorbitant straight wardrobe.

The bedroom is equally tasteful—

But I stop dead when I see the painting over the bed.

It's a picture of Greece, midday view of the island of Santorini as seen from the town of Oia. I crack a smile of disbelief at this familiar friend. It was Shawna from San Diego who had that print of Oia she'd bought at IKEA for ten dollars and shoved up above her piano – I used to sit there and stare at it for hours, contemplating how on Earth I could get myself over there to see it. It's impossible without a valid passport. Good old Oia, that unattainable place, constant reminder that I'm stranded in this country because expired travel visas are nothing but a fast ticket home. And I *really* can't go home.

I console myself yet again with the fact that I've got two continents latched together that I have yet to fully explore, and that ought to occupy me for a while. But Oia does look like a brilliant vacation destination. I can't help but think God's trying to tell me something, shoving Oia at me again in yet another roommate's house. I don't believe in signs but this is one of them.

This painting isn't a print, it's acrylic. I wonder if it's the same artist as downstairs. They're different techniques, certainly. But Galen doesn't seem like the kind of guy who fronts for expensive art. I guess he has a nice house. But tasteful furnishings don't necessarily equate with excessive out-of-pocket expense. And he's a high school teacher with a B.A. in literature. He rides a bicycle. How much money could he possibly have?

I stare at Oia a while longer, trying to work it all out and failing, and then I give this reminder the heavy sigh of acknowledgment it deserves and move on.

The bathroom is the key component of the upstairs, at the moment. There's a razor lying on the edge of the sink, so the shave gel must be... in the medicine cabinet? I love medicine cabinets – such an unobtrusive item can reveal so much about a person...

I open Galen's carefully to reveal row upon row of shelves crammed so full of lotions, creams, cleaners, toners, colognes, gels and pastes that if I didn't know better I'd have guessed it was a woman's. But no matter how I search the only drugs I come up with are multivitamins and mild painkillers – three different types, which might border on excessive – but... the guy's clean. Not a single prescription. I don't know why but I was hoping to see *something*, at least – anxiety or hyperactivity meds, maybe? But no, Galen is just a very healthy guy apparently looking to stay so – he's dedicated to self-maintenance. He's got absolutely everything anyone could possibly need for skin and face care. And yet the nail clippers have yet to be located.

I'm like a monkey in a banana plantation. First things first, I decide – I ought to wash my face. Galen won't notice a clean face. And I might as well try all this junk out, not like I can get my kicks any other way around here.

Galen's got an iPod player sitting on the back of the toilet, and I get the idea to go find that workout armband I saw earlier. The ultimate test of Galen's disposition is about to occur.

You've got to be careful in another man's house. It's been my experience that guys like Galen are meticulous, they don't own a lot of stuff and they know where and how they leave it. He's left the iPod in its armband in the downstairs bathroom. I memorize the look of it on the counter and then pick it up reverently and carry it upstairs, searching through the playlist as I go. The last song he was playing is a song I don't recognize, by a band I've never heard of. I scan some more artists.

I can't believe my eyes when I see them. It's all here, everything I've ever wanted to listen to. I'm seeing Sophie scrawled across every title – she had an appalling fondness for some really awful music. Punk and emo were her two favorite styles. I hated that shit before I met her, and I've loved it ever since. She played it all the time – My Chemical Romance, Fall Out Boy, Arctic Monkeys... and it's all here. It's all *here!* Some of the albums are new, which isn't surprising – of course all these bands have come out with more stuff since I last got the opportunity to hear them. Some have since quit music altogether. They're a perfect encapsulation of a beautiful moment in time, these songs, it's like being back in Sophie's bedroom whenever I hear them.

I plug the iPod into the player, cranking it up just loud enough for it to drown out all coherent thought but not loud enough for the neighbors to take special notice. I'm living in the music as I wash my face – and I don't think I can quite convey what a magical feeling that is, washing one's face. People take cleanliness for granted these days, but I contend there is no feeling more wretched than an unclean face. I hate it. And I hate not being able to shave.

This is one saving grace of werewolfism – one's level of hair growth in one state has no effect at all on the other state. I can shave my whole body as a human and I'm still going to have a thick coat as a wolf.

So every chance I get for a clean shave I take it, and I've got to say I'm back in heaven at the moment, clean-faced, clean-shaven, listening to some familiar MCR before delving into unchartered territory and finding that their recent stuff is even cooler than the old stuff. I'm imagining Sophie rocking out to it, seeing her pretty face so elated when she sings these new songs at the top of her lungs. I hope her husband makes her a very happy woman. I hope her new baby turns out every bit as gorgeous as she is. I thank God daily for Facebook, so I can stalk her tragically from afar and think whimsically about what might have been if I wasn't a bloody mutant.

After a while I've got to claim defeat and shut the iPod off before I waste too much battery. I drop it back off downstairs and head into the living room.

I'm on a mission now. Catch-22's got to be around here somewhere. I concede superficially that it may very well be in Galen's messenger bag, seeing how he's teaching it, or it may be that he's left his copy at school.

If I had to make a guess, though, Catch-22 is going to be a very difficult read for me. Galen's far too possessive of it to contemplate taking his own copy to school. He's probably got two copies himself. There's the torn and frayed one, the dog-eared one, the battered and bruised one he reads religiously and whose every fingerprint smudge he greets with warm familiarity... and then there's the other one, the untouched one, the one he might have read once but decided to save as a memento, the one that's remarkably pristine and particularly susceptible to defilement-by-perusal. He's at least got the former one lying around here, guaranteed...

And sure enough, I find it relatively quickly once I enter the tiny office – a frightening foil to all the other rooms of the house, an explosion of paper and junk that has if anything more books in it than all the other rooms combined. Catch-22 is lying there on a pile of papers on the desk, faded blue cover and first ten or so pages actually torn away from the binding and resting askew on top of it. I can't touch this book. It's too obvious.

This sort of thing is what makes life as a wolf a real bitch. Sometimes it's fun playing detective, figuring out all the little forensic games you have to play to keep from being suspicious. Right now, it's a serious pain in my ass. I'm really regretting reburying that key because I'm going to need some of my own money, soon. As it stands, if I want this book I've got to wait and work out Galen's schedule, then make a mad dash across town when I've got a reliable few hours, dig up the key, and keep from swallowing it accidentally on the run back. Then I've got to hide it, wait for another dependable few hours, and steal some of Galen's dirty clothes so I can get down to the bank and get my money. Then I've got to hide the money, wait for another few hours...

Ad infinitum. Getting my own copy of this novel could take weeks. The temptation to pick up the book right now and start reading is overwhelming. It's right there...

I pick up the cover between two fingertips like it's a Dead Sea Scroll, the Declaration of Independence, and place it gently to the side. I have to do the same for the next four loose sheets of paper before I reach text. This book is incredible, it's a veritable encyclopedia of Galenic history all laid out on a scant few pages. At least a centimeter off the corners on all these pages have disappeared. He's taped the first page together, and on the second page he's had to pen in a section in the middle of a paragraph that's become too faded to read anymore. If I had to make a guess I'd say he penned it in from memory.

The trouble is that I know an addictive book when I see it. This is one such book, and it catches me hook, line, and sinker. In a few minutes I'm picking through it more quickly, getting into the pages still glued to the backing and praying I don't tear another fragile sheet off by accident.

The name Yossarian shows up instantly, the second line, and I'm fascinated to see what kind of character Galen and Sean wanted to peg me as. The guy is... mad. In a good way. An astutely psychotic loner, totally convinced the entire world is out to get him — and with good reason, as far as I'm concerned.

Frankly, at least on a superficial level I find the correlation amusingly accurate. I'm touched.

It's engrossing enough that I actually lose track of time. I'm twenty-three pages into it when I hear the back door open and my heart stops.

Shit.

I put the pages back frantically, silently resting them as close as I can to their original state before I transform and bolt off to the back room just as Galen calls, "Dog!" a second time. I bound up to him, a picture of thrilled gratitude, muzzling up to his leg. He seems to appreciate the appreciation.

"You get lonely?" he asks, bending to pet me. "You probably need to head outside, huh?"

I don't, but I'll make a show of it, sure. This whole bit is something that you have to get really used to as a wolf, and I definitely gave up feeling humiliated by it years ago. Dogs have no shame watching people do their business – and unfortunately people don't have much shame going the other way, either. Before I took up this lifestyle I never realized some people think it's healthy to monitor their dogs' shit production. I'm praying Galen's not that type of owner because sometimes I do enjoy the more sanitary use of a toilet. He doesn't seem to want to know, and I stick it out in the back yard for a few blissfully solitary moments before he returns to open the door, looking both pleased and relieved. So he's checked the house and found nothing patently offensive. Good.

"Sorry I was gone so long," he says as I trot on past him back into the house. "Thought maybe I ought to attempt to treat you properly while you're here."

He's reaching into his bag, and he pulls out a lead and collar. My tail wags of its own accord. A lead can be a *very* good thing. And then he yanks out a massive can of dog food. Not quite the hamburger morning buffet, but it's pretty fair as far as dog food goes and frankly I'm up for anything. Beggars can't be choosers, you know?

"You want to go for a walk?" he asks me.

Yes. Wag tail, pant more, look excited. Absolutely I want to go for a walk. Get me out of this house.

"All right, first things first," Galen declares, and holds up the collar. He wants to make a show of it because he's not sure how I'll react.

It always takes new roommates a while to work out how calm I am. Really the only time they ought to be worried is on one, maybe two days out of the month – and it's practically a new moon tonight. I'm not feeling even the slightest bit agitated, save for the minor aftershocks of the stress explosion that was Galen's return home. Galen buckles the collar without incident, and he pats me appreciatively with the standard accompanying "good boy" commentary.

And then he gets up and disappears, and I'm stuck wondering where the hell he's gone. I follow distantly, and as I enter the living room he emerges from his office with a camera. Ah, I get it.

"Okay," he whispers. I stand still at the word, like I know he's thinking about doling out instructions. "Okay... um, can you sit, bud?"

Oh no, man, you're going to have to try harder than that. This guy part-owns another dog, for God's sake. No wonder he hates Bonks, he doesn't know how to control him.

Galen seems to get the hint, because after a moment he commands more forcefully, "Sit."

There you go. I'm such a good dog, sitting on cue. He smiles broadly when I obey him. I like that look on people, that stunned, impressed look they get when they actually do something right and the dog gets it. Galen needs that affirmation, and I'm a hundred percent ready to give it. I haven't met anyone this bewildered by a dog since Dane.

He snaps a few pictures while I do my best to look handsomely presentable, and then he takes the camera back to his office and starts uploading the pictures. He takes a moment while they're transferring to make up a quick poster: Found, German Shepherd Mix... blah, blah, blah. I can't help thinking how absolutely useless this entire procedure is. No one knows me in this neighborhood. This is a tragic waste of trees and there's nothing I can do to stop it.

Finally the pictures load and he picks what he thinks is the best one – I would have picked the one next to it, I think it gives me a more sophisticated profile – and then prints a couple dozen in fast draft color. Color photos, I'm flattered.

While the printer runs he heads into the toilet for a brief spell, and when he emerges he grabs the pages together and pockets a stapler and a roll of tape, and finally, *finally* he goes to get the lead and clip it on my collar, and we make for the door.

This is it – freedom! He opens the front door and I jump out onto the porch and down the steps, dragging him a bit. I wouldn't be a dog if I didn't, right?

"Whoa, whoa buddy, hold on," Galen's saying, yanking on the lead. I give in and wait patiently while he locks the front door.

The truth is that for a cognizant animal, there's more freedom on a lead than off it. You can direct your walker to follow you, and the walker gives you a measure of safety. As a wolf roaming alone I spend more time looking over my shoulder than anything else. It's taxing. I just want to *walk*, you know?

We head off down the street, and Galen makes me stop every so often so he can hang another sign on a telephone pole. I take the opportunity to scope out the neighborhood canine scene.

There're a lot of dogs on these blocks. Big, small, male, female, all types. And as expected, not the slightest hint of werewolf. For all my wandering, I've never come across another wolf in the States. I mean of course I'd never remotely consider seeking them out, but how exactly does one *avoid* that one-in-a-million chance of passing an unfamiliar werewolf on the street...?

There's only a few of us left anymore, and only a handful would ever be caught dead out wandering around in wolf form, but werewolves have a distinct scent that dogs instinctively recognize. These dogs might never have smelled a wolf before, but I can guarantee the minute they smell me they're going to be on edge. So I'm going to have to tread carefully for a while. A dog's favorite way of dealing with intimidation is to attack, and I really hate it when dogs bite me. It's happened far too much for my pleasure. I'm already waiting for Bonks to do it – it's coming if I stay here, mark my words. I have to be the most submissive damn wolf on the planet to deal with my canine counterparts. It's just lucky for us that humans have such useless noses or we'd never survive as a species.

Galen takes his time meandering around. He puts up the last flier better than half an hour later, and I'd say we've done a good half mile radius around his house. Fine. Nothing's going to come of it. I'm already counting the days until he comes to take them back down. He puts the last one up with a smile of self-approval and looks down at me, who looks up at him. I manage a halfhearted wag of my tail. Well done, Galen, good boy. You're going to Heaven now.

"Want to see where I work?" Galen asks.

I pretend not to understand. This is a skill, believe it or not, pretending not to understand. There's a reason Sophie called me Lupus-Sapiens – I knew her before I fully understood that dogs simply do not attend to one's every word. They don't actually respond to very much that humans say, not even subtly spoken commands. Galen's going to have to work really hard to get me to do any parlor tricks.

Galen apparently takes my silence to mean 'yes, certainly' – just as I was hoping he would. We head off in a direction opposite the house, and after a few blocks I can see a chain-link fence looming down the way on the other side of the street. Sure enough we cross the street half a block later, and in a moment he's leading me in through a side gate to the school's baseball field. I'm praying that he thinks to unclip the lead while we're out here alone in this fenced enclosure, and momentarily he does. He smiles benevolently.

"Go on," he says, "wear yourself out."

I take off running. I love running, I really do, especially as a wolf. And Galen's right – if I don't knock out some energy I'm going to be up all night. I run straight to the edge of the fence and turn hard right, taking off along the fence like it's a track. One lap, then two, then three… I glance Galen's way around lap four and see him lying in the middle of the grass, splayed out on his back staring up at the sky. Looks peaceful. I pull a full stop and turn one-eighty, and start running around the field in the other direction. My lungs are on fire by now, I don't get to run like this very often. I'm really hoping Galen picks up on how much his new doggy likes this treatment. Maybe next time he'll bring a ball or a Frisbee or something and he won't have to sit there bored out of his mind.

Who am I kidding? He's far from bored. Guys like Galen live in their heads – they only deign to come down out of the clouds for the rest of humanity. He's perfectly happy where he is, I'm sure.

And that's too bad for him, because I'm getting tired and I'm ready to work on some proper human-canine bonding. I slow down and turn, panting and wheezing, trotting up to him out there on the grass just behind shortstop. I fall at his side, sticking my cold-ass nose right up against his ear, all wet and gross with stinking hot breath right in his face. No dog owner actually likes this, I don't think. I don't either, really. But it's standard protocol. It's a dog thing. I practically *have* to. He recoils with a groan of disgust, shoving me away, but he's grinning.

"That's seriously gross, bud," he complains, wiping his neck with the palm of his hand and reaching out to smear it on my neck in revenge. Why do people treat dogs like towels? I roll out of the way before he can manage it.

He wipes his hand on the grass, and then his hand darts out and he gets a hold of the collar and snaps the lead back on. And then he goes back to lying down, though I notice he's sitting farther from me now. He still reaches out a hand to pet my shoulder. We sit that way for a long while, and I'm even back to breathing normally by the time Galen finally makes a move to get up and head home.

This is all part of the process. He's got to like me before he keeps me.

"So we'll get you some food and then I'm giving you a bath," he declares to me as we head back out to the sidewalk and begin the trek back home. He sniffs his hand, and his whole face scrunches in a grimace of total revulsion. "And I'm figuring out a way to brush your teeth."

I can't believe my ears. I've got a teeth-brusher on my hands! I've had only one other roommate who's ever even considered brushing a dog's teeth. Usually I have to stash a spare toothbrush somewhere and do it myself, whenever I get a moment alone. Galen, Galen, you're a godsend, an angel, you're Mother Theresa. You're a saint and I'll worship you forever, my friend.

That evening I get my pile of canned dog food, and Galen heats up some of his Chinese food and sits down in front of the television with that and a beer. I whine like a bitch until he finally works out what I'm asking and gets up to pour me a taste. I'll risk seeming cognizant for a taste of beer. It's better than nothing.

After we watch a half hour of awful primetime network television which Galen clearly appreciates only because he's making all sorts of fun of it in his head, the bath commences. Galen is the most dog-phobic gay I've ever met, and while I really don't get it I definitely appreciate it. He doesn't know how the hell to bathe a dog, and I've got way more fur than he's willing to use shampoo on. It looks like expensive shampoo, it smells like mint. He makes a sort of cursory pass over my neck, back, and sides, and tries his best with each paw, and that's about all he's willing to give it. Thank You for that, God. That's all I need. Tomorrow I can take a shower with impunity and no one will be any the wiser.

I'm a good dog, I suppress every overwhelming urge to shake myself dry until he's wasted a good towel on me and shoved me out back. He leaves me out there for a little while to dry off and goes into his office to work.

I'm thinking it's going to be just a few minutes, but slowly those minutes begin to drag on. I tour the yard again, take my time, mark some territory, but even I can't occupy myself for this length of time out here in this grass square of a yard. I head back up to the porch after what feels like close to an hour and bark. Just once, and that's all I need. Galen comes running.

"I'm sorry," he apologizes, "I got caught up, I completely forgot."

It's like he really thinks I've got a brain behind these blank blue eyes, the way he talks to me. He's such an anthropomorphist.

He goes back to his office and I park myself in the doorway,

47

trying to glean what I can about him from the floor. He's sitting at his laptop, and he's got Catch-22 next to him and a stack of papers in front of him.

He'll read a few lines of a student's writing and get bored shortly and check his e-mail, and then he'll throw a couple of marks on the paper and go on to the next, then he'll read a few pages of the book, and get distracted again and turn around to me, and grin at my attentiveness and maybe say something to me, and then go back to grading, and sigh heavily, and mark another paper and another and maybe even another before he grows bored again and stares off for a second, then seems to get some sudden inspiration and checks something on Wikipedia.

The first time he does this he looks up World War I, the next it's a list of Catholic saints, fifteenth century, the third time it's the word 'psychology' and he peers at that listing for only a second before he switches over to Webster and scrolls to the end of the definition – looking for etymology, maybe? Then he'll check his e-mail again. Then Facebook (I'm thrilled to realize he uses it as well). Then back to some grading, then more Catch-22, then he hops up and grabs a book off the shelf seemingly at random and I don't quite catch the title before he's rifling through it, searching for something. Then he changes his profile on Facebook, adding a quote from the book he's picked up. His list of favorite quotes is about a mile long.

Okay, Galen, okay, I give in. Staying in Philly is a mistake, and staying with a gay guy is a mistake, but you're too damn intriguing to ditch yet. I will give you a month, do you hear me? Let's see if I can still stand you after a month.

CHAPTER 4

Galen's schedule turns out to be very easy to pick up. He sets his alarm for five-thirty and hits the snooze button twice, then stumbles out of bed right into his running shoes and drags me on a morning jog that lasts anywhere from half an hour to an hour. Then he goes back home to get ready and eat breakfast. School starts at eight and he's got an hour off for lunch at noon, which he'll spend with Sean or at school and only rarely back at the house, and then he has classes until three and generally comes home after that to let me outside. Sean apparently works at some office until five, and three or four days a week they go out for dinner somewhere and end up back at Sean's house or Galen's house, and eventually Galen gets around to grading or lecture planning and stays up until eleven or so before heading off to bed to prepare for the next day.

This schedule gives me a guaranteed four hours in the morning and two in the afternoon to do whatever I please. After Mia, that feels like an eternity. I spend it all in human form and use my time to the fullest. The first day I take a proper shower and finally find the nail clippers, and charge Galen's iPod while I check my months-old e-mail (all spam) and check up on Sophie and my other ex-roommates and add Galen to my mental search roster. The guy keeps most things private but he's let slip with the profile pictures – but he's one of those guys who's only ever changed his picture three times, boring shots all, so I learn nothing new. I check up on my little brother and sister, too, both of whom have had Facebook profiles since the moment the site went public. I don't know why anyone needs a phone anymore, I really don't. I Google all my new important destinations: nearby liquor store, grocery store, bookstore. My mental map of this city is pretty complete, I'm sure they'll be easy to find. I'm careful to clear my search history.

I spend a lot of time reading, but I'm saving Catch-22 until I can get some money — that one copy in the house is too suspicious, I just can't. I watch some TV, too, aiming to take advantage of my human refresh rate as long as possible. Watching TV as a wolf always gives me a massive headache — when I'm canine the television no longer refreshes as fast as my eyesight does and the whole thing flickers on and off in this horribly disorienting way. I leave the remote exactly where I found it.

I get to meet Bonks the first Saturday, two days in — Sean brings him over to Galen's house because (and here I must applaud Sean's apparent forethought) Bonks is going to feel less territorial at Galen's house than Sean's, and they both know Bonks is the dog most likely to go ballistic defensively. The meeting is still a nightmare.

Galen and I are waiting at the window when Sean's car pulls up. Sean gets out, and on a Saturday his clothes are if anything more garishly feminine than on a given weekday. He's wearing this pink shirt that's got to be a kids' large at most, and the typical tight jeans — but these have some frightening white lace pattern creeping up the flared cuffs and he's got a wide white belt with rhinestones on, and his shoes are pink Converse. He's wearing eyeliner, and now his nails are painted black. And I imagine it's all going to go away again in time for work on Monday, and suddenly Sean becomes a kid of many faces — ambiguously straight by weekday, flaming gay by weekend. How disturbing.

Sean comes around to the other side of the car where a scruffy little white face is peering up at him excitedly, and the moment he opens the door Bonks shoots out and Sean is lucky to catch the lead in time. It's immediately obvious that Bonks is an insanely skittish animal. This is not going to go well.

"I'm sorry in advance," Galen mutters to me with an ironic smile, and my tail wags at the sentiment. Galen doesn't notice, still staring out the window in dreadful anticipation of the impending introduction. He's got me on the lead again, and he's holding my collar tightly. He chances a glance at me, studying my reaction to the white muppet-furred bottle rocket heading our

50

way up the walk. It's true that I'm watching Bonks keenly – what dog wouldn't? I'm intent. But I've got a plan.

"Please don't do anything stupid," Galen tells me, almost a prayer. He's so nervous he's practically shaking. He really thinks I'm going to kill Bonks – he's not too stupid to recognize that for all intents and purposes I'm still a feral animal and I probably think Bonks is an overlarge squirrel. In a way I appreciate that he really thinks it's no contest, that he's not too worried about what Bonks might do to me. That's what *I'm* worried about. I've already catalogued where the Neosporin is, for quick and easy access the next time I get the house to myself.

Sean knocks at the door and Galen calls to him that it's open. Galen stands and I wait patiently by his side, heeling admirably. Sean opens the door a crack and, seeing we're well on the other side of the room, opens the door enough for Bonks to come darting inside.

The second Bonks sees me he starts barking madly. He's putting his all into it, straining at the lead, growling, barking, frothing, wild-eyed with terrified fury. He's got me pegged, all right.

Me, I'm an island. I'm Stonehenge. I do absolutely nothing.

Sean is yelling at Bonks to shut up, and Galen's not sure what the hell to do with himself. He's clenching my collar so tightly I think he's cutting off circulation to both his hand and my brain. I've got to get him to lighten up.

I sit back on my haunches and slowly ease myself to the ground. Galen resists at first, and my vision's starting a fireworks display before he realizes what I'm asking and lets go of the collar. I inhale deeply, gulping in some air, and go down flat, belly to the ground, ears back and tail tucked under my legs.

This is so emasculating. I'm choking down bile lying here on the floor, submitting like a bitch to a damn West Highland terrier. Bonks doesn't even seem to get it until I go a step further and half roll over, inching my way toward him on all fours in a pathetic display of unabashed groveling. Bonks quits barking, standing tall all of a sudden with his little scruff tail pointed right up in the air, all puffed up and ramrod straight, finally catching on that he's not really got to try in order to earn alpha position, here.

If Galen has any mind at all he's seeing this as a cunning tactic on my part, he's throwing himself even father into the anthropomorphist court and starting to personify me more than he already did. If this strategy of mine isn't a dead werewolf giveaway, I don't know what is. Any self-respecting dog would have torn out Bonks's throat by now.

And instead here's me, lying belly up on the ground, offering up my own jugular to a pipsqueak rat dog and licking his furry little face. Trump card, that tongue action. That's a proper wolf submission. Short of pissing myself, I couldn't be lower on the pack hierarchy right now. Galen and Sean are lucky they tried this when they did, that's for sure. If we were *any* closer to the moon… well, all I can say is if this dog tries humping my head I'm going to snap.

Sean asserts himself again just in time, reminding Bonks that the alpha spot is still reserved for the humans when he yanks Bonks's lead back and orders him to heel. Bonks doesn't heel but he does relent, pacing back and forth at his owner's feet. I'm still lying on the floor, watching to make sure Bonks really has got the message through his thick skull. I don't dare move.

Sean's looking at Galen incredulously, shaking his head in disbelief.

"That was *not* what I was expecting," he says, and Galen nods quietly. He's watching me, I know it.

I'm watching Bonks, who's still studying me from afar but with a much less belligerent air. I roll back over, pausing another cautious moment before I finally get up and head back quietly to Galen's side. He unclips my lead instantly and Sean follows suit with Bonks. Now comes the proper intro, the posturing and the tail wagging and the sniffing, and I endure it with a degree of amusement – Bonks is such a small dog it's like watching a kitten investigating a horse.

Sean comes over in the meantime, crouching down to pet me and Bonks. "So does Dog have a name yet?"

Galen's not been trying particularly hard on that front. The signs are up but no one's called yet, and he's going to wait until next week to take them down. So until then I'm not really his dog as far as he's concerned, and he's not interested in getting attached. Formally. Emotionally, he's probably more attached to me than to his own mother.

"Not yet," Galen replies with a shrug. "Nothing fits."

I can tell you right now I'm going to get stuck with Bud, Buddy, Boy and Dog all at once. I think Galen's too embarrassed to think of a name. He thinks I'll think it's stupid. Give me a break. I got called 'Tinkle-winkles' for two months straight by a three- and five-year-old – nothing sounds stupid after that.

Bonks calms down enough to grow bored and get distracted by my food bowl, trotting off to the kitchen to lick at it with gluttonous abandon. Sean and Galen take that as a sign that the show's over, and head into the kitchen as well to make themselves a frozen pizza for lunch. I have no doubt that Galen would give me a slice if we were alone, but with Bonks around and with Sean grinning his I-told-you-so grin whenever he sees Galen getting all sentimental about a dog, Galen's in no mood for any displays of largess today. I resign myself to a lunch time of fasting.

Sean and Bonks end up sticking around overnight, and Bonks is on me constantly from moment one, clamoring for attention. It's driving me crazy. I don't like dogs, I don't like the way they pry. They're like annoying little siblings, and after spending four years tolerating a pair of annoying little siblings who also spent a day out of every month being actual puppies I think I'm well qualified to say that. I'm just glad I can call on those infinite reserves of big brother patience now to handle this mad little dog's attention.

Bonks and I are forced to head outside for a good two or three hours in the afternoon, and I spend that entire time trying to prevent any horrific mental imagery from leaking in, trying not to wonder what the humans are up to. The important part is, *I* am outside while *they* are inside. This is a good sign.

And Bonks actually turns out to be a fair distraction – he's decided he likes me now he knows he can walk all over me, and he offers up one of his toys (Sean brought over a whole basket of them) to play tug-of-war. And he doesn't mind later on when I take one of his bones to chew on. He and I spend a good long while in canine bonding, lying out there in the grass with our bones. Bonks notices every few minutes or so that my bone is in fact the one that he wants, and he trots over to take it impulsively from my jaws, leaving me to stand patiently and head over to start chewing instead on his, which was mine, which was his. Nothing like sharing dog saliva.

Bonks is only about the third dog I've ever been around for any appreciable length of time, he's quite the character study. He *really* reminds me of the twins, somehow. I think it's the size. And the jarring, jerky movements, and the impropriety. It's a nostalgia trip I'm not particularly keen on pursuing, and I find myself sinking into a weird sort of melancholy the longer Bonks and I hang out together.

As the sun begins to head noticeably lower in the sky, Galen finally comes to the door to call us in. He smells all sorts of wrong, and I try my damndest to breathe through my mouth, beyond disgusted – the whole house has got a subtle canine-level smell to it that I'm not going to be able to cope with. I *really* don't need this right now, this day's been rough enough already.

I don't have to pray too hard for intervention – Sean's already holding Bonks's lead and the little terrier's going wild with excitement as Sean makes a valiant effort to slip the choke collar over his muzzle. Galen grabs my lead, too, but makes no move to actually put it on me until Sean explains rather theatrically to him that Bonks is going to get jealous and then they're going to have an issue on their hands. Galen hates the very idea of an 'issue', and concedes to putting mine on as well. I couldn't care less, I just want to get out of this house before I puke.

I can't take this. I really can't take this, and as we head out the front door together I'm staring down the length of the street and it's *so* bloody tempting. I could do it. I could run. I've done it before. I don't know if I can abide this house – not if this is going to be a regular thing, me stuck in that outdoor cell with a maddening white-furred reminder of best-buried old memories while Galen and Sean go about defiling the very rooms for which I'm deigning to put up with all of this.

It's not worth it. It's not. But Sean's got the keys to the house and while he's locking up Galen walks with me toward the sidewalk, and I can't bring myself to break away. Galen's too good a person, and I *really* need a roommate, and I think I'm actually feeling something like guilt at the thought of ditching him just two days in. He doesn't deserve that. I don't know what the hell's wrong with me.

Sean has apparently decided that they need wine with dinner, so the four of us end up spending half an hour walking all the way down to their favorite liquor store almost two miles west of Galen's house. Galen waits outside with me and Bonks while Sean heads in to buy what turns out to be a bottle of wine, a bottle of champagne, and a full case of Chimay Blues, handing the box to Galen with a dramatic exhalation, a quick kiss on the cheek, and a bright, "Happy early three years, lovey."

Galen's beaming at the surprise – I don't think I've yet seen him look so pleased. He reaches a hand up to Sean's face and kisses him deeply, and I freeze up in wounded exasperation. There's no getting away from these two. Why, oh why can't Galen be *straight*, for Christ's sake…? Why does God feel the need to meter all my life's happiness with equal amounts of misery?

The beer and the champagne are cold, which means we've got to get a move on. I thank God when we reach home twenty minutes later that the lingering sex smell has dissipated, and I head directly for my spot next to the recliner in the back room to doze while Bonks rips into his favorite squeaky toy and Galen and Sean start on dinner in the kitchen. I don't know when this three years business actually happens, but I'm guessing it's probably tomorrow – they're both in giddy moods, and they're making some extravagant meal, and I keep hearing all sorts of kissing and teasing and playful banter and one high-pitched shriek when Galen pinches Sean's ass.

They make up for it in the end. Sean insists on making a proper meal for 'their dogs' as well, so while they dine on cheese fondue and fruit and sautéed scallops, Bonks and I get to chow down on chunks of pan-grilled steak with gravy. And then Galen secures his position on my pedestal by insisting that 'their dogs' split a beer as well, and when Sean adamantly refuses to get his own dog sick I get an entire Chimay to myself. I'm going to regret it later, but hell, with my current metabolism one Chimay's going to take the edge off this evening just fine. Galen pours it into a bowl and lets me put my front paws on the counter to lap it up, so Bonks can't see what's happening.

They make up a chocolate fondue for dessert and take it into the back room with the champagne to watch a movie, and Galen's so drunk he passes me more chocolate-covered strawberries than I'm sure he realizes. I pass out, sated, halfway through the movie, and spend the early morning hours on Sunday puking my guts out in the bathroom. I breathe a sigh of relief when neither human wakes to the sound of the toilet flushing downstairs.

That first weekend is an eye-opener. I need my money. I said I'd hold out for a month and I'm damn well going to stick it out a month, I don't go back on my word. But you can never be too careful and if this whole situation goes pear-shaped then I plan to be prepared. And I want that damn book anyway, right?

So as soon as Galen leaves the house on Monday morning I go rooting through his dirty wardrobe for clothes to make a little trip out to see my good buddy Dane again. Dirty is key, obviously, because Galen's definitely going to notice if his clean clothes smell used and he'll know if there's a sudden strange addition of clean clothes to the dirty clothes pile. I fish around for a suitable pair of trousers and have to settle for shorts, because I was right, Galen's got to be a good four inches shorter than me. And he's thin – I have to leave the shorts unbuttoned and throw on a long shirt. And I go with flip-flops again, with my heels hanging over the back.

I was going to go as a wolf, but I can't risk getting picked up, not without a license. Galen's my only real option at the moment, and if someone decides to help a poor lost doggy out on the street then I'm screwed – Galen's never going to think I was kidnapped, he'll think I just decided to go my own way again. And it's a long way to Dane's house, and you wouldn't believe how hard it is not to get noticed on the street as a dog, especially over that sort of distance. *Everyone* turns to stare at a stray dog, to wonder what he's doing out on the town, to agonize over whether to stop and do something about him before he ends up a big furry lump of road kill. So I'm going human instead, because no one cares what happens to a human.

If Dane's got the same job that he used to, he's there until at least four today. I'm pretty sure I'm safe heading back over there. I'm careful to leave the back door unlocked as I leave Galen's house and start walking over to Dane's.

It's got to be eight miles from here to Dane's house. I can't walk that far as fast as I need to. There's a bus that heads south in about the right direction, and I made sure to swipe some spare change from Galen's drawer before I started off. I make it to Dane's neighborhood in just over fifteen minutes. There's no sign of Drew in the yard as I enter the alley, and finding the key is the work of only a few moments' digging. This is going much better than I anticipated – it's still only eight-thirty – and I'm confident I can make it to the bank and back to Galen's with plenty of time to spare. I start jogging toward the bank.

The tellers don't give me any hassle, even. They like my accent. I have the key, anyway, and I give the right name. What are they going to do about it? (That said, it was an absolute bloody nightmare trying to get this money *into* the bank – had to steal a guy's wallet to get some fraudulent identification in order to open an account. And good soul that I was, I spent two of my precious dollars to buy an envelope and ship the wallet back to the address on the driver's license afterward.) A gentleman kindly leads me back to the box and I open it, grabbing out the entire contents: one hundred dollar bill, eight twenties, five tens, two fives and four ones. Then I lock up the box and head out.

It's only ten-fifteen when I get back to Galen's, and I take my time trying to find the perfect hiding place. I end up getting a Ziploc bag and a push pin, tacking the money up in the lower kitchen cupboard next to the fridge, out of sight behind a drawer. Galen will never find it. And then I go upstairs to drop the clothes back where I found them and kick the shoes off in the closet, and head back downstairs to read until noon.

It was too easy. These things generally are. I feel like maybe it ought to be a little more dangerous dealing in different personas, putting up these layers and layers of façade, but it's really remarkably simple – and that always puts me on edge. It scares me that I've held onto the same safe deposit box for two years. It scares me that so many places in Philly are familiar – because if they're familiar to me then I'm familiar to them. I can't afford to be familiar. I can't be recognized, not for who I really am, not if there really are werewolves wandering around this city somewhere. I can't risk one of my fellows sending some sort of suspicious-werewolf query out through the network, to be picked up by the British pack... And the longer I stay the more chance I have of that happening.

This is stupid. I'm just being crazy, I'm always kind of crazy when I'm in roommate flux. The truth is *no one* knows who I really am and no one ever will. No werewolf is going to find me. And Galen will never even suspect I'm not a dog. None of the others ever did. He doesn't come home for lunch today but he does come home at three-thirty, and we head out for another jog around the block before he leaves again to go see Sean.

The next weekend we – the four of us again, God save me – all pile into the car to head down to the dog park. Dog parks are always a bad idea for a werewolf. But this park near Sean's apartment happens to be the same one Dane and I used to go to and I've already worked up some sort of rapport with these dogs. I can tell Galen's still nervous about it.

Poor bastard. He didn't sign up for this, taking on a dog against which all the other dogs of the world seem to have a personal vendetta. He's witnessed me playing super-meek a couple more times since Saturday, whenever we go on walks and happen to pass other dogs. Easiest for me to roll right over and get it out of the way so we can move on, really, because even the sweetest Labs tend to bristle a little at my presence.

Tomorrow night's the full moon, though, and it's taking a substantial chunk of my concentration just to stay above the red haze of rage that's beginning to rise up like bad bile. Tomorrow it'll be worse, and I hope Galen and Sean don't think to repeat the dog park idea two days in a row. I can survive the dog park today, but tomorrow might be another story.

We get to the park in a few minutes, and Bonks is so excited he's squirming right out of Sean's grasp as Sean steps out of the car. I'm calm as always, and Galen's used to my attitude by now – he doesn't bother to try holding me back when he opens the back door for me. He grabs up my lead, and Sean sets Bonks down awkwardly on the ground, and the four of us head toward the run.

There're at least half a dozen other dogs there, four of whom I recognize instantly. Trevor, Scrum, Barclay, and Phoebe – all regulars. It's only as we reach the entrance that I finally recognize another dog with a sudden start – Drew. Drew's here. I start scanning the humans frantically, searching…

It's embarrassing, but sometimes the dog in me takes over.

There he is! Dane! Oh God, oh God, Dane! *Dane Dane Dane Dane…*

"Whoa, calm down," Galen's saying to me, and I'm not listening at all. I'm hopping up and down, whining, half-lunging, desperate to get free of the lead. My eyes are fixed on Dane. He's sitting at a table a little way off, next to an unfamiliar young woman. It's *Dane!*

Finally Galen unclips my lead and I'm off, breaking clean out of the gate and barking in thrilled greeting. Dane recognizes the sound immediately, and looks up to see me bounding toward him. He breaks into a wide grin.

"Andy!" he cries, jumping up from the table. I can hardly stop in time, almost bowling him over as I jump into his outstretched arms, standing on two legs and licking his face, tail wagging so fast it's a blur. I don't give a good goddamn what it looks like – dogs have a different way of communicating than people do, all right? And this is Dane we're talking about, here.

"Where the hell have you been?" Dane's asking me, ruffling my fur happily. He turns his head to address the girl behind him, "Leyla, check it out, it's that ol' dog I told you about!"

This new girl Leyla is grinning at the display, and she reaches out a hand to pet me, too. I get back on all fours, careful not to claw Dane unnecessarily, and let her pet me as well. I can't believe it. Dane's here!

I hate to admit it, but I've momentarily forgotten Galen entirely. It's Dane who notices my new collar and realizes I must have come here with *someone,* and he starts searching for whom it could be. He catches sight of Galen and Sean watching our reunion and starts walking over to them.

I follow, and my heart cracks a little when I turn and see the look on Galen's face – he's got no expression at all, like he's just been handed the news that his brother died or something. He thinks I've found my real owner. Dane seems to notice that look as easily as I do, and he's already prepared to do some damage control as I go and stand loyally by my new roommate.

"So you've got him now, eh?" Dane greets Galen with a smile, holding out a hand. Galen shakes it suspiciously.

"I... suppose so," he replies. "You know each other?"

Dane grins at me knowingly, and I wag my tail back at him. God, I love this kid. Dane nods.

"This dog's an angel in disguise, let me tell you," he says. "Just showed up out of blue one day, right when I needed him, and then disappeared just as suddenly a year later. It's great to know he's okay, really, I was kind of worried."

"So he's not your dog, then?" Galen asks Dane, who shakes his head, shrugging.

"No way, man – more like he owned me, you know?" Dane grins. "He's not really anybody's, I don't think."

A truer word was never spoken. I can't stop myself – I go up to get petted again, leaning up against Dane's legs, and he obliges.

"So how long have you had him, then?" Dane asks.

"Little over a week," Galen admits with a smile, watching the display. "I've still got posters up."

Dane grins, nodding in understanding. "I did too. No one called."

"Do you know his name?" Galen asks, and Dane shrugs again.

"Beats me," he says. "I always called him Andy."

At the moment I'm feeling kind of bad for Galen, actually. All my former roommates had no idea until the day I left that I was going to up and go. Now Galen's already drawing conclusions, making a prediction, and he's going to be counting the days before I leave him, too. I'm wondering if this ruins my chances for staying, if he's going to want to preempt my exit and kick me out...

I look over at the dogs across the field in time to see Bonks sniffing Drew's backside. There's something bizarrely poetic about that.

I pull away from Dane and head off to greet the dogs. Let the humans talk it out for themselves, I don't want to play favorites. I've only got to do a major kowtow to one Akita before I'm accepted in the dog circle as the bottom rung, the eighth wheel. It's pretty damn hard to fit in anywhere as a werewolf. I'd like to think I'm over being pissed off about that, but it's probably a lie.

I spend the rest of my time at the dog park out playing with the dogs, and I run a couple laps on my own to stay in shape and get my mind off current events. As the minutes drag on and I get over that initial unthinking canine excitement, those all-too-human doubts start creeping back into my skull, and I can't help but notice that pretty much the entire time we're there Galen and Sean are sitting in animated conversation with Dane and whatever-her-name-was.

This is not a good thing.

The very last thing I need in my life is continuity. I've been hopping cities for years trying to avoid it. I *knew* it was a mistake to stay in Philadelphia, damn it, I knew I was crazy to stay.

It's just that I'm starting to get really damn sick of running all the time. I've spent a dozen years now moving around, jumping from place to place, never settling down anywhere for more than a year or two at most. It was fun at the beginning, it was exciting heading to new places every few months, meeting new people, figuring out how one went about living entirely as a dog. But all the fun's run out of it recently. I'm tired of it, I'm tired of running.

It's like these two monumental opposing forces in my head anymore, the need to keep moving and the need for a respite. I'm worn out, I just want a break – but the second I start giving into that sense of complacency it hits me that I'm letting my guard down. Constant vigilance is the only thing keeping me safe.

And even if all Dane and Galen know of me is that I'm a

transient house bum dog, it's just… not good, for any of us, for my roommates to be on speaking terms. Because Dane's going to start telling stories, and Galen's going to relate some of his own, and maybe one or the other of them starts to think that there's more to me than meets the eye. Maybe they exchange numbers and start hanging out on a regular basis.

I am all sorts of ready to execute my escape plan if it turns out they make any arrangements at all to meet in the future. I can catch a bus out of town tonight if need be, now that I have my cash. And I will, too, don't think I won't.

Here's the thing, the real crux, the rub, the reason I'm still running and the reason I'm scared to death of the idea that these roommates of mine will get to know each other. Werewolves are very, *very* careful about the humans with whom they choose to associate. As a species we're instinctively cautious, but as a society we're even worse. History shows that when humans know of us, it never ends well for us. We're incredibly protective – violently so – of our nature, our anonymity and our secrecy. If any of my fellows finds out I've been associating with humans as a dog, I'm dead.

I don't mean that metaphorically. I mean they will happily drag me out and murder me.

So why the hell am I doing it? It's a question I ask myself daily, and I can't find an answer. There's no good reason, there's really only the fear that if I give up now it's going to come down on me sooner.

I don't know why I started running. I mean I do, I remember it perfectly well, but the reasons all seem so alien to me now as an adult, as someone who can see outside the myopic boundaries of a sixteen-year-old's self-possessed universe.

But back then all I saw – all I ever see when I sit down to consider it – was my uncles, my mother's twin brothers. Anthony and Thomas McCarthy. Imagine me saying those names like titles, because they practically are – my uncles enjoy the highest status in werewolf hierarchy as wards of the British pack. You haven't met an alpha male before you've met my uncles. It's moments like these I can't help but remember their angry, ugly faces, their remonstrations, their tirades…

I can still see that day so clearly, I can see Thom throwing his hands in the air in overwrought frustration, I can hear his strained baritone voice perfectly.

'This is beyond useless! You can't even hit him hard enough to knock any sense in.'

'You are going to learn this, boy,' Tony tells me. He's about two inches from my nose, red-faced with fury. 'We've only four years left to make a proper werewolf out of you and I swear in the name God Himself, if you fail our line I'll kill you.'

I'm silent, I know better than to reply. I'm not going to rise to it. My plan to become just objectionable enough for them to give up and ask permission to pass on their legacy to my baby brother – then only four years old, still young and impressionable and full of potential – is definitely not going as envisioned. I'm starting to wonder at this point if it's still worth fighting in my stupid underhanded sabotaging way. But Thom's back, stalking in again and getting right close like his brother is.

'You know we're the only reason you're alive, child. We *created you*, and this is the respect we get!'

'Do you remember that, at least?' Tony asks. 'Or do you conveniently forget literally everything we tell you?'

'I remember,' I tell him, suppressing a sigh of annoyance at his trademark transparent segue, because Thom's about ready to backhand me and I'm not too stupid to see that. I don't need to hear this story again, I've heard it so many times I can recite it cold, but Tony never shies away from a chance to tell it. And sure enough he starts right in.

'Our line lost too much influence keeping your mother alive,' he says, conveniently refraining from mentioning she's his sister, too, in that way he has of distancing himself from all the trials and tribulations our side of the family have wrought for him over the years. 'Associating with humans, *biting* one – it's a miracle we got the Council to agree to spare her.'

'And to spare my father and sister,' I add strategically. Adding to their tally of good works always appeases them. They like knowing they held my parents' and sister's very lives in their hands, that it was their begging only which saved my family from execution. They both nod stoically at the mention.

'Exactly,' Thom replies. 'You're lucky your father is the meekest wolf ever made. I've never seen one act so sane – we'll take you to see one someday, they're nothing but frothing beasts.'

'In six millennia how many made wolves have ever survived their first year?' Tony interjects quickly to quiz me.

'Ninety-six,' I answer. I'm done playing dumb today. I know it all as well as any trainee – more than ten thousand humans bitten in our history, and only ninety-six survived that first mad year of newfound werewolfism.

'Humans can't handle the transformation,' Thom instructs, and I nod my understanding though I want to interject that my father seems to do just fine. 'Born wolves are the only real wolves.'

'The more made wolves we allow to survive,' Tony adds quietly, 'the more exposure we risk. It was a huge risk sparing your father, allowing them to raise a human daughter. A *huge* risk. If your mother had any sense at all she'd have killed him the minute she bit him, and if we had any sense we'd have done the honor killing ourselves, get rid of the lot of them. You're lucky we're such compassionate men.'

It's almost too much, I almost go off at that statement. Compassion, my ass. If they had any compassion at all, I want to say, they'd have understood that when a woman is cornered alone in a house during a moon with a five-month-old daughter to protect, it's no wonder she attacks the first thing that moves. And it's no wonder when she realizes too late that it was her baby's father come to surprise her and apologize for shoving the kid off on her when it isn't her weekend, the thought of killing him seems abominable.

That's the story my mother tells, the one I understand. She got knocked up by a human and she did everything she could to follow code and keep my father in the dark until she could wean the baby and disappear forever. Werewolves beget werewolves only when both parents contribute equally – she had a human child, and the code required she abandon it to its human father and get on with accepting a lonely, anonymous existence as a wolf.

And what she got for breaking code and biting my father was a husband, a daughter she could see every day, three more born-wolf kids and a happy life. You tell me which one you'd choose, if you were her. Tell me how our bloody werewolf code makes any fucking sense at all.

This is what I want to yell at them. This is what I rehearse telling them all the time, every time this comes up, every time they insult my family like this. But once more, I bite it back and listen as they condemn me for deigning to exist.

'You *have* to understand this,' Thom tells me seriously, fervently, 'you have to accept this is how the code works if you want to be a ward—'

'I don't want to be a ward!' I shout, unable to control myself, and out of nowhere his fist comes around and gets me right in the temple. I go sprawling out of my chair – I'm clutching my head and my eyes are watering from the blow and the last thing I want is for them to taunt me because they think I'm crying. Tony is already shouting.

'You don't have a *choice!* Do you think we want you to be a ward, either? If we had *any* sway left to ask out of passing it to *you*—'

'If you don't want it, child, tell us now,' Thom says coolly, levelly, and I've heard that voice enough times before to know now is not the time to speak up. 'I'd like nothing better than to end you and try again with your brother. Just say the word.'

He never threatened my life before that day, not like that, not so I knew he really meant it. I don't remember now how I replied – my memory jumps forward to when I returned home from that lovely visit with the extended family and my mother caught sight of my black eye and did her miserable best to sympathize without actually castigating her brothers for the injustice. That was the night I decided to leave. I'd been planning it, I had it all mapped out, but that was really the last straw. I left without telling anyone and I haven't ever considered returning.

If my uncles knew where I was right now they'd kill me. This isn't because I deserve it – I've never broken the code, I've never bitten a human at all, and if I ever do then I could probably find it in me to kill the poor bastard. I think. The point is that I'm

65

constantly tap-dancing on the edge of disaster, living constantly around humans, a whole array of different humans, a myriad of potentially suspecting humans, all the time. The McCarthys don't know how to act like dogs, and they can't see how a werewolf could stay in his wolf form all the time and avoid getting noticed. I personally don't see how anyone can think that a human turning into an animal every full moon isn't a tad more suspicious than a dog seeming to know what one is thinking all the time. Alas, it's not up to me.

And I knew full well what a blatant show of disregard it was to leave, and I know how much worse it'd be if they saw me carrying on with humans like this. To think that a *ward's heir* would do such a thing, to imagine that werewolf-kind came that close to putting this idiot in power, to think a ward family failed this spectacularly at indoctrinating their youth… it's a proper scandal. My uncles would never see my self-imposed exile as anything but a profound, grotesque and very personal insult, and for that alone they'd happily hunt me down. I knew all of this before I left, of course, I knew it might very well end me, but somehow that seemed a good trade for the chance to escape their psychotic stranglehold and start living.

It doesn't matter what drove me to it. The decision is made and my options are closed. Now I *have* to run. I have to protect my roommates from harm. I'm not the only one in danger if my roommate somehow manages to have the right combination of keenness and credulity to put two and two together and label me paranormal. Even an errant comment to a friend could get passed along, joked about in the wrong crowd… you never know how it's going to catch a fellow werewolf's attention. My roommates need to see me as nothing other than a dog, and the only way to ensure that is to act dumb and keep moving along.

It's a positive feedback loop that drives me nuts, really: I have to move on to protect them, but then I have to find someone else to protect *me*, which only makes me that much more of a liability because I'm increasing the probability of getting found out. If staying put means I give a random human ample opportunity to learn my secret then I have to leave, but if leaving means trying my luck with even more humans then I ought to stay, but the longer I stay the more urgently I have to leave, but the more often I leave the more humans I encounter... it's infuriating. And this isn't even to mention the fact that I don't stay canine the whole time, that I spend half my waking day at risk of being discovered as a hominid...

Yeah, my uncles would kill me, that's all there is to it.

I head over to the table to start listening in when Dane calls Drew to leave. Dane pets me one last time while the girl holds Drew on his lead, and then everyone starts shaking hands goodbye. Dane says,

"Well, it was good talking to y'all."

Galen nods. "Yeah, you too. Good luck with the wedding."

"Thanks," Dane and the girl reply together, and grin at each other. Wait, *wedding?* Wedding! God *damn* it, I wish I remembered that girl's name if she's really the one Dane decides to spend the rest of his life with. How freaking long can he have known her, anyway? God, I hope he knows what he's doing... but I've never seen him looking so happy. Dane points to me. "You take care of that dog, Galen, you hear?"

Galen nods again, and grins. "I will."

And that's it. They exchange a couple of see-you-around sort of waves, and then Dane and the girl and Drew all turn and head toward the car park. I almost die of relief.

I do everything I can to shove the run-in at the dog park out of my mind the next day, to forget about the close call and all the reminders it brought with it. It's been a long time since I've allowed my fears to get the best of me, and I'm definitely not going to let them back in now. Not today. Bad things happen when I'm agitated around a moon.

Nine o'clock tonight, that's the peak of it, the fullest it's going to get, and I don't need any damn forecast to tell me that. I can feel it.

You can see it in a werewolf if you're watching for the signs – you might notice someone getting defensive, short-tempered, you might notice him looking sort of uncomfortable in the day or two before the full moon. I always find myself getting really anxious and oddly alert as the moon waxes, I start itching to move, go somewhere, do something, anything, I just want to crawl out of my skin. That's how it starts.

And then the rage starts to build. It boils up out of nowhere, for no reason, all of a sudden the whole world makes no sense and everything is wrong and it's so phenomenally frustrating and you have to force yourself to recognize that what you're feeling isn't real. It's taken me decades to cultivate the self-control required to combat that rage, and it's not something most werewolves strive to learn. When I was a kid, my family just accepted that anything said or done near a moon should be excused as unavoidable and left it at that.

But I've had to get really good at it since I decided to live around humans. The last thing I need is to be a danger to my humans.

Because the rage keeps building, mounting exponentially with each hour until all you're seeing is red and it's hard to focus on anything but the hatred, the explosive fury at anything and everything in your way – and we haven't even reached the actual transformation yet. Strictly speaking it's about twenty hours, ten before and ten after the peak of the full moon, in which a werewolf has no choice but to turn.

The timing is remarkable. You can feel it start to happen first in your chest, your heart starts racing and all of a sudden you feel hot all over, your skin is scalding and everything starts to itch like crazy and you really can feel things start to move, like worms writhing in your muscles. And in a matter of minutes it all rises to a crescendo, you reach some indefinable threshold and suddenly the pain rips out of your chest like fingers of cracking ice and it's like fire, like acid poured on open wounds. Your head explodes and for a moment you go blind, deaf, you're trapped in this blackness and all that's left is this enveloping torture. And though it lasts an eternity it's only a few seconds before you're coming out of it – and if the rage was bad before it's nothing compared to the madness that takes hold after.

I obviously don't experience the actual transition anymore, wolf that I am every day. And even when I do transform, doing it outside the moon always hurts less, and doing it intentionally provides a measure of control, and doing it as often as I do makes it feel like nothing more than a really big sneeze.

I do still get a sudden shift in perspective at the moment the lunar transformation is supposed to happen, there's this surge of fury that I've gotten very good at preparing myself for – if I sit in one place and close my eyes and tense up for a few minutes I can hold myself there until it passes. No one's ever so much as noticed I'm doing it. After that it's just a matter of breathing, working myself up into one of those Zen states where I'm impervious to everything and nothing can bother me. I can keep it up for hours, even as that full moon peak gets ever closer and the mania becomes almost too much to stand.

I never remember much afterward, coming out of a moon, I get this weird numbing sort of vertigo that feels kind of like a blurry drunken haze. But to the outside world I remain calm, composed, serene. I've even managed to sleep during full moons, in recent years.

I remember times when this was very much not the case. I almost killed my first roommate on my first moon in the States – it hadn't occurred to me that these people and their houses were nothing like the safety of my own room to which I'd grown so accustomed at home, and I wasn't prepared for the violent agitation I felt going through a moon in a new place. It was pure serendipity that she kept a baseball bat by her bed, and one good swift crack to the head was all I needed to realign and escape out the window and start considering very carefully what I should do differently with my next roommate.

I spent many long months abandoning my humans for a night to get through a moon, and every moon meant hours of arduous practice trying to regain control of my head. Hours. It was agony. And the futile impotence of it all was so overwhelmingly infuriating and every incremental increase in awareness brought more despair because it didn't seem to be leading anywhere except backward toward insanity...

Learning how to control myself was the hardest thing I've ever done. I wasn't sure it *could* be done. No werewolf would put himself through that if he didn't absolutely have to.

But it was worth it, incredibly worth it, because now I can spend an entire lifetime playing dog and the moon has become almost like just another day. It's a beautiful miracle having the moon be just another day. It's like I can breathe now, I'm no longer drowning. The defining feature of my miserable monstrous life has been removed, and I can't begin to express how phenomenal it is to be that much closer to normal.

And this moon's not any different. I spend the day meditating in the shade of the tree in the back yard and the evening on the floor in the living room dozing, listening to Galen type furiously away in his office before he calls it a night and heads upstairs at eleven, and I manage to fall asleep finally around two.

CHAPTER 5

This week is finals week at Galen's high school. I can't work out his new schedule at all, so I'm stuck being a dog for at least five days and probably into the weekend. I catch snatches of humanity every once in a while, when he goes over to Sean's house of an evening or when Sean calls just as Galen's heading out of the house and Galen explains that his students' exam will be over at eleven and he'll call back then. This does not bode well for the summer. I'm hoping he teaches summer school, or maybe he's got some sort of training to do, or at the very least maybe he's around a lot more and I can have someone here to occupy my canine hours. The hours of solitude, steeped in uncertainty over his return, those are the worst.

I'm beginning to really like having Galen around. Every moment's an education. He reads quite a lot, and a couple of times now he's let me sit on the plaid couch with him while he props a book open on his knee. He doesn't notice me reading along with him, trying ineffectually to squint away the dog-vision blurriness and focus on the words. It's infinitely frustrating trying to keep pace with his ludicrously fast reading, and I have to just sort of glance at the paragraphs to get the gist of them.

He reads in a disjointed manner, as the book organization seemed to suggest – he yanks a random book off the shelf and opens it in the middle and goes from there. I find this method hard to adapt to. I imagine he's read everything in this house before. He's got the Encyclopedia Britannica in the back room, and he sort of picks an article at random and starts reading it. I know now that his glasses prescription is rather extreme, and Sean once made a mention about a Lasik ad in the paper, not as if he was informing Galen of something novel but as if Galen's been looking for a while and he's just pulling together the cash for it. It's sort of heartbreaking, isn't it? That the passion for which his eyes are critical to him is the very thing causing his descent into blindness?

He talks to me all the time, too. He can go on for hours, sometimes, if he's in the middle of doing something comparatively mindless, like fixing the shelf in the hall closet. He uses me as a sort of Litmus test for all his thoughts and arguments, examining their validity in the vacuum of my silent non-reply, reinforcing and modifying and clarifying and outright rejecting as he goes. He speaks aloud to solidify his train of thought, and he speaks to me for direction. Pearls before canine.

Really, most of what Galen does is argue with himself. He's got bees buzzing in his head all the time, and they never stop. I sleep downstairs, but I can hear him tossing and turning sometimes for hours after he's turned off the light in his bedroom. He's one of the smartest people I've ever met – he remembers everything he's ever heard or seen or done, he catalogues facts and trivia like no one else, he thinks critically about everything he encounters. He loves logic problems. He does crosswords. He asks me for answers to some of the questions – invariably I can't begin to guess what the prompt even relates to, and he'll just stare at me for a moment, eyes half-closed, concentrating hard, and in an instant he'll declare, "Oh, Sisyphean, duh," and move on to the next one. The most incredible thing about all of this is that he's not putting on a show, not for a dog – he's not trying to impress me or anything. He just operates this way naturally.

I still don't have a set name, though I've had quite a few transients. He calls me whatever comes to mind, really. Bud and Buddy still crop up most frequently, but Dog has dropped off the list entirely and Boy is heading that way as well. He threw in Andy a couple of times after that day at the dog park, but he's obviously not fond of it. Beyond that I've gotten Beast, Rover, Dunbar, Shylock, Old Tom, Lucan, Tonto, Lassie, Rin Tin Tin, Cerberus, Cujo, Moses, and a whole host of other names – all somehow appropriate to the moment, none solid enough to stick.

It turns out that he does have summer school, of a sort – he's been tasked with teaching Health, since he's one of the newer teachers and he really can't get himself out of it. It's only for two weeks, but even I can see he might not last that long.

He comes home after work, leaves his messenger bag in the bike basket and without a word goes to lie down in the middle of the back room floor, as if his last reserves of energy have been utterly depleted and he can contemplate nothing but rest for the next half hour or so. I come over to lie next to him and he throws an arm over my neck, but he doesn't move and he doesn't speak, he just breathes and I'm comfortable with that. Sometimes a guy just needs to reset.

He's generally happy, anyway, I'm sure – this isn't anything close to the depressive states I've seen other roommates sink into. And he talks it all out later with me and with Sean, he goes ranting and raving until he turns blue and the vein in his forehead is throbbing. Sean and I have very different ways of dealing with him when he gets like this – I go grab my lead for him out of the basket by the door, and Sean takes him up to his bedroom. Funny how neither of us would ever deign to debase ourselves by trying the other's method.

I, for one, am selfishly pleased by the fact that Galen has to teach summer school. It means that for a couple more weeks at least, I get the house to myself for a few hours daily.

I still haven't gone out to the bookstore yet, and I'm absolutely dying to read this book that is Galen's Bible. I tell myself during finals week that it's the schedule, I can't get it when I don't know Galen's schedule, but even I know it's a lie. It's regrettable but I have begun to notice I'm developing a serious phobia about braving the outside world by myself anymore – I don't have any sort of identification on me at all, and I'm so used to being a dog that I'm convinced people are always keeping a suspicious eye on me, wondering what I'm up to.

I have to get this book. I have to. It's not about reading it. It's about me being able to be a complete person. I am not going to let werewolfish agoraphobia get the best of me and I am not going to try spreading this money of mine over decades so I don't have to play human ever again.

But Galen, damn him, doesn't give me an opportunity to

leave for a full half week after I work up the nerve. Sunday night he washes all his clothes – *all* of them, even the ones he hates wearing, even the ones that aren't too dirty, even the ones that require hand washing – and puts everything away neatly. This is not his normal style. Well, it *is* his normal style, in that his normal style includes a lot of not tending to menial tasks until he finally cracks and does it all at once on a whim. This is one whim I could have done without.

Monday he wears a pair of form-fitting jeans, and there's absolutely no way they'll ever fit me. Tuesday he puts the same damn jeans on. Wednesday he wears dress trousers.

And *finally* after work that day he comes home and changes into shorts so we can meet Sean and Bonks at the park for a round of, well, Frisbee for me and tennis ball for Bonks. Bonks does not fetch – he steals and gets chased around comically for five minutes before he forgets he's got a ball in his mouth and drops it. I'm a damn good Frisbee catcher, and Galen doesn't have to sweat overmuch in those shorts to keep up with my game.

So Thursday. Thursday I will buy this book.

On Thursday morning Galen leaves the house at eight-twenty, heading out a little early for his nine-o'clock class. I'm thanking God, because his class has a long break at eleven-thirty and he usually comes home for that. I want to be back with plenty of time to spare.

The minute his bike disappears out the gate I'm off to the cupboard to get a twenty and a ten from my stash. I set the bills on the counter and take the stairs three at a time to get some clothes on – the shorts, and Tuesday's button-up shirt, and the same flip-flops I used last time. I check the mirror in the bathroom, splash some water on my face and take a fair swig of mouthwash to get rid of any lingering hints of dog food. I stumble back down the stairs (damn these transformations, the inevitable disorientation!) and head back into the kitchen to stuff the cash in my pocket before heading out the back door—

And straight into my worst nightmare.

It's Galen, standing on the porch, hand poised in mid-reach to turn the knob, doing a stunned double-take at my sudden appearance in the now-open doorway.

Oh fuck.

I don't even know how to react to this. But Galen does – he's already reaching into his pocket for his mobile, backing away from the door. I panic.

"No, no wait, I can explain," I blurt out, holding my hands up in surrender. "*Please* don't call the police."

"Why not?" Galen demands, shocked and disturbed by my pleading. He's still backing away and he shoots a glance behind me, searching the house in rising panic, and in a quavering voice he asks, "What'd you do to my dog?"

I will look back on this moment and wish time had had the courtesy to stop for me, just for a brief second. I will realize that I said exactly the wrong thing and regret that I didn't have more time to think it through and plan an exit strategy. I will kick myself for not ever considering this eventuality in the hypothetical. But right now, I'm not thinking, I'm reacting.

"No, Galen – I *am* your dog."

My heart jumps into my throat the minute the words leave my mouth. I shouldn't have said that – I shouldn't have said anything at all. Damn it! Why didn't I *run?* My heart's pounding in my ears, my mouth is dry, palms sweaty, breath bated, head a total mess. I'm having a fucking heart attack and stroke and seizure all at once.

So this is what it feels like to break the code.

"What?" Galen asks, eyes wide in confused shock. But before I can elaborate he turns, ready to bolt.

"No, wait—!"

I reach out and grab his arm. Galen tries to yank it away but I'm stronger than him. I jump forward and grab him clumsily around the neck, covering his mouth with my other hand before he can scream. He elbows me hard in the ribs and I double over in pain – he almost squirms out of my grasp, but I catch him by the shoulders and manage to haul him backward into the house.

And then I stumble on the doorstep. We both go sprawling into the room, Galen landing on top of me and scrambling away. I grab his ankle and trip him back onto the floor. And before he can get any farther, I transform.

Two seconds drag on into eternity as everything reforms itself into its canine shape, and at the end of it I've got him pinned under me and he's staring up into the face of his familiar dog still tangled in his ill-fitting clothes. I don't ever want to know what this looks like from the outside. Neither does Galen, apparently, because his look is one of abject horror.

We stare each other down for what feels like an eternity. Galen is stricken, mouth agape, too overloaded to say anything. And I *can't* say anything. And in this form and this frenzied state I can feel the rage building, I can't control it, I'm starting to see red—

I transform back in terror. I can't believe I just did that. Letting anyone – even another wolf, even a dog – see one's transformation is anathema to a werewolf. I've never done it before, and in a few seconds of utter lunacy I've gone and *shown a human* my own transformations and proved beyond a shadow of a doubt that werewolves exist. I have to suppress a wave of revulsion as I realize my mistake.

Galen's frozen in place like he's having a heart attack, and I don't know what to say to calm him down. We switch roles for a second, and suddenly I'm the one talking to fill the void. I ramble incoherently.

"I'm sorry, I didn't mean – I didn't mean to steal your clothes or anything, and I have my own money, see, I was just going out to get – I thought you'd be out past eleven, I couldn't let you know, I couldn't – I'm not explaining myself well at all…"

I realize I'm spinning out on tangents, and take a breath to steady myself. And then I remember the word I have to say. I continue dumbly,

"I'm a werewolf. Your dog's a werewolf. I know it sounds crazy, but you've got to believe me. I'm not some madman come to steal your shit."

Galen continues to stare. I know he understands what I'm saying, he just doesn't want to believe it. Logic dictates that werewolves don't exist, after all, and Galen lives in a world governed by logic. He's trying to reconcile what he just saw.

"This isn't happening," he says finally, shaking his head.

"No, it's real – I'm really a werewolf," I insist, standing and backing away from him. I'm eternally grateful when he doesn't move – and then I remember I'm blocking his only real way out. I wouldn't move if I had a werewolf between me and the door, either. "I'll prove it again if you want—"

"*No*, no," Galen says immediately, holding his hands up in surrender.

"I'm sorry," I say, crouching down again and regretting it the second I do – why the hell can't I act like a bloody human when I need to, I've got to go all cowering like a bitch? Really? But I can't stand up again or I'll look like an idiot. I'm so nervous I'm shaking, my whole body's shaking and I can't get it to stop. "I know how crazy this is."

"Why are you in my house?" Galen asks me, still on edge, watching me warily for any sudden moves.

"Because I – I mean – because you – I don't know," I answer lamely, too unnerved to come up with a reasonable answer. Especially when there doesn't seem to be one.

Galen frowns at my pathetic reply. I can think of a million other reasonable unanswerable questions that he's already devising, but he seems to reject them all out of hand and comes up instead with one that seems far too aberrant for the circumstances.

"You're from England?"

I frown in confusion at the question, stunned that he'd be concentrating on my accent at a time like this. It is noticeable, I'll give him that – it always comes on stronger when I'm pleading. The way I sound right now you'd think my life was on the line. It *is* on the line. I nod.

"What's your name?" he asks.

I will never tell him my name.

"Toby," I lie with convincing rapidity, throwing out the first word that comes to mind. He doesn't buy it for a second, it's obvious from his skeptical look. I shake my head, holding up my hands in a plea for him to understand. "I really can't tell you. And I'm begging you, please don't tell anyone else about this, not even Sean—"

"How do you know Sean?" Galen demands suddenly. I don't

blame him for his momentary lapse – a man-dog-thing that has him cornered in his own house just mentioned the name of his boyfriend of three years, and that'd make anyone a bit blank-headed with anxiety. I sigh and sit down on the floor across from him.

"I've been living here the past month. Look, I'm serious – if you tell *anyone* what I've told you I'm a dead man. I'll go if you want, I'll leave you alone, I'll never step foot in Philadelphia again so long as you swear not to discuss this with another living soul."

"Oh, I definitely won't," Galen assures me too quickly, shaking his head, "I swear."

"I'm not going to hurt you," I say, seeing how scared he still is.

"Really?" he asks doubtfully.

"I *won't*," I insist, but that comes out more angrily than I intended and I know I'm not making my own point. "Look, I just needed a place to stay. That's all. If I had any other intention I'd have done it by now, right? Right?"

Galen doesn't reply immediately. He lets out a breath he's been holding, running his hands through his hair, trying to calm down. I don't know what to say and neither does he. We sit in awkward, wary silence for a very long while. Finally he composes himself enough to say, "You know that feeling when you realize you probably ought to have fainted by now to protect yourself from total overload...?"

I can't help smiling when I reply, "I'm living it."

Galen smiles, too – a sudden, fleeting smile that looks out of place in the rest of his bewildered expression. And then he resets.

"Wait, what time is it?" he asks, as if waking up from a bad dream. He starts looking around wildly for a clock, then looks to me for an answer – I've no damn clue what time it is. Galen stands and darts past me into the kitchen, and as I get up to follow him I hear him yell, "Shit!" and I see him go running into the office. When I finally catch up he's grabbing a folder off the desk.

Oh, wow, that's what's he came back for. I'd completely forgotten there was a reality outside this one, that Galen is supposed to be at the high school teaching kids Health and he just had to run back for something on his way into work…

He pauses for a moment in the hall, seeing me again and doing another sort of momentary jolt, trying to think, to work out something to say. I have no idea what he's doing, and stand there silent, waiting.

"Stay here, will you?" he asks finally, breathlessly, like everything's moving too fast for him and he's running to try and catch up.

"Where are you going?" I counter, watching him carefully, searching his face to learn his intentions. I'm no good at it, he's a wall to me. I don't know if I can let him go – how the hell do I know what he's going to do the minute he leaves here?

"To class, I'm late," Galen says.

"But you can't – no, I can't let you—"

"You have to let me leave," Galen insists quietly, that fearful edge creeping back in his voice even though he strives to suppress it. I *hate* that my presence can make a human sound like that. "You can't keep me here forever."

I raise my hands in surrender. "But how do I know you won't—?"

"You're going to have to trust me," Galen interrupts me.

I let out a long breath, frustrated, averting my gaze to the floor. I can't think, I don't know what to do. I have to *think*.

"I swear I'll be back by noon," he says. "If I'm not, you go right ahead and leave. You have to know me well enough to know I'm good on my word."

This is not a good idea. All of this is so *wrong!* I'm not prepared for this at all, I don't know how to reply. But if I hold him here things are going to get uglier, and fast. I can't think of any solution but to let him go. Galen's right – he's a man of his word. I just have to trust him. My stomach knots up at the thought.

My expression must reflect my reluctance, because before I can reply he adds, "Please? Please. I won't tell anyone. It's just I *really* have to go…"

I hold out for a second that nevertheless seems to both of us to drag on interminably, and Galen's already growing anxious when I finally nod my agreement. His second smile is genuine, almost relieved, and there's another awkward moment while he tries to decide the most appropriate way to excuse himself from the presence of a strange man who also happens to be his dog standing in the hallway. He doesn't work anything out immediately, just smiles tensely and darts past, skirting me and running for his bike.

"I'll be back!" he calls from the back room, and I finally find it in myself to call back,

"All right."

I hear him slam the door, and stand in the hall for a long moment, not sure what the hell to do with myself. I can't believe that just happened. I feel sick.

Noon. Am I really going to wait around this house for *three hours* hoping a guy who knows I'm a werewolf will come back and we can talk like normal adults about it? What the hell is wrong with me? *Why did I let him out of my sight?* For all I know he's calling the police right now and stupid me is going to wait around until they break down the door—

But he seemed so sincere. And he's right – this is Galen we're talking about. If I know him at all I know he's coming back like he said. If this was *anyone* other than Galen I'd be out the door right this second. But when it's Galen, for some crazy reason it seems even stupider to leave than to stay here. I'm trapped here. Three whole hours...

I can't cope with this. Eventually my brain shifts over into autopilot and I head into the kitchen to grab a random beer and a one-pound box of chocolates and head into the bathroom to start the water running and halfheartedly attempt to drown myself.

Galen returns quietly just before noon.

I don't even hear the click and grind of the deadbolt, and it's only when he shuts the door and calls, "Hello?" that I realize he's home. I'm sitting in the office reading Catch-22 to get my mind off my own life, reading it because nothing much matters anymore and I can fuck up this house all I want now that Galen knows what I am. I can fuck everything up. I already fucked everything up.

"I'm in here," I call. I don't particularly want to get up. I don't remember the last time I was this drunk. It might have been half a decade ago. And I'm halfway to vomiting because of all the sugar. I'm really in no mood for the ensuing discussion. But I'm better off now than I was sober.

Galen comes around the corner, catching sight of me immediately. He pauses in the hallway, unwilling to come closer, but he seems calmer. Unnaturally calm. I don't know what to make of it. I set down the book carefully so as not to upset something in the process. I'm not sure which desk edge is real.

"You're looking a little worse for the wear," he says. He knows I'm trashed. It's pretty obvious. I've lost track of how many bottles I've gone through. There's still one around here somewhere but I lost it, and then I realize it's in my other hand. That was probably his first clue, come to think of it. Along with the slurred speech and the inability to focus and the total lack of coordinated movement. They might have helped.

"A little," I concede. "You gave me a bit of a start, earlier."

"I daresay the feeling's mutual," Galen replies coolly. "So start talking already. What's going on here?"

I don't know how to answer that question. His tone's shifted entirely from earlier this morning. I bet it's because I'm wasted. No way I can harm him now, eh, not if I can't work out which one of him is him. I'm staring off at the far wall anyway, trying to look at anything *but* him. I don't want to deal with this.

"I'm not supposed to be here," I mutter, remembering the beer and finishing it.

"Okay, you're allowed to *be* drunk, just don't *act* it," Galen says. "Come on, wake up. What's a kid's bedtime story doing showing up out of nowhere and mooching off me for a month? How long were you really planning on staying?"

"Few years," I answer honestly, shrugging.

"That short," Galen replies sardonically. "What, you'd get bored?"

"No, you'd notice your dog's not dying of old age," I say. "And I'm not – I'm not *mooching*."

"You're wearing my clothes and drinking my beer and using

81

my shower," Galen says. "Please explain to me some way in which this isn't mooching."

"What, you don't like the myriad emotional and existential benefits of owning a dog? They lower blood pressure, you know. I'm doing you a favor."

"You're doing yourself a serious disservice, at the moment," Galen counters. "How old are you?"

"None of your business," I reply.

Galen stares at me for a long while. It's not a pleasant stare. It's calculating.

"Who wants you dead?" he asks.

I sigh. "No one, yet."

"Who would?"

"Any wolf that found out I told a human."

"And how might they find out you told a human?" he asks with a frown of confusion. "Are we being watched right now?"

I shake my head. "No, it doesn't work like that."

"Then how does it work?"

"It's just…" I start, trying to work through an answer, trying to imagine a scenario in which some other wolf *could* find out what I've done. I can't come up with one, but I can't bloody think right now. "You just never know, all right?"

"Are there a lot of you running around here?" Galen persists.

"Not a lot," I admit. I'd be shocked to find ten in Philadelphia. But I'll be damned if I give away more to him than I absolutely have to. I'm in no state to separate innocent trivia from incriminating evidence right now, not when Galen's the one doing the detective work.

"And do you talk to any of these other werewolves?" he asks.

"*No*," I said with an immediate shake of my head. "Absolutely not."

"Then I don't see what you have to worry about," he says simply, "if you're not telling anyone and I'm not telling anyone."

I just nod. I don't know quite what to say. I don't think Galen's really cued in to what's going on yet. His reaction is way too deadpan given the enormity of everything he's found out in the past few hours. He's *certainly* not going to understand how badly I fucked up in revealing what I have.

I'm a traitor. I ought to be falling on my sword, really, and I'm a coward for living, for staying, for keeping on as if nothing's different. I'm so low I'm pissing myself, that's how rotten I am at the moment. I don't need someone telling me I'm a damn moocher, too. I *do* need someone telling me he'll keep quiet.

"I'm twenty-nine," I concede finally.

"What's your name?"

"I'm not telling you. It's better if you don't know, believe me."

"So what should I call you?"

"Whatever," I reply, shrugging. "Anything you want, I don't care."

Galen smiles, nodding his acceptance.

"So, uh, how long have you been a werewolf?" he asks. He stumbles a bit over the last word, still trying to come to grips with the idea and undoubtedly feeling more than a little put off by the notion that he would ever be asking that question seriously.

"I was born one," I answer shortly. "I come from a long line of wolves. And I hated it, so I left, and I came to the States and I've been here a dozen years and lived in as many cities and half again as many houses. And I may be a freeloader but I'm a damn good dog, and that's all anyone really wants out of me anyway."

"And you're happy with that?" Galen asks. He sounds exceedingly skeptical.

"It's not so bad," I reply noncommittally.

Galen sighs. There's a long pause while he tries to think and I try not to.

"Forgive me for being dense, but I thought the idea behind werewolves was they're only a wolf but once a month," he says.

"We can turn at will anytime but at the full moon. It's forced then. I'm the only wolf I know who does the canine thing twenty-four-seven."

"Mostly," Galen says with an ironic half-smile.

"Mostly," I admit.

"And why are you the only one?"

I shrug. "The others see being a wolf as an unfortunate predicament. A curse, a sin, a loathsome unavoidable affliction.

They just scrape along – live alone, go to work, take time off every month, try not to let anyone too close for fear there will come a day when they'll discover the truth. It's not *living*, really. I thought if I was at least one thing every day out of the year it'd be easier to have a life."

"But talk about restrictions," Galen says.

"Yeah, well, I was sixteen," I reply. "I didn't know any better. Living with roommates sounded far less restrictive than living with my family."

"So why are you still doing it?"

"Um…" I say, ever-so-eloquently. I smile halfheartedly and throw my hands up in the air, shrugging again. He nods.

"You don't have a backup, do you?" he asks, and I shake my head.

"I've got three hundred dollars. I know I owe you, you can have it, I don't care."

"You care," Galen says. "I can only imagine what a few hundred dollars means to an Englishman stranded in Pennsylvania without even a pair of shoes to his name." He pauses. "You said you were going out, earlier. Why?"

I sigh, and point vaguely to the book now lying precariously at the edge of the desk. I'm not looking at the book when I point, I'm looking at his reaction, and he grins brightly. I explain myself sheepishly. "You'd have known, right, if I went reading this copy?"

"You think so?" he asks, his grin broadening.

"I don't know, I think you're detail-oriented," I say. "I think you're too clever by half not to pick up on some part of your book getting excessively worn out in your absence."

Galen shakes his head, frowning. "No way, I'm so far beyond absentminded it's pathetic. Have you ever read it before?"

"No," I reply, shaking my head as well. "I've wanted to read it for a while, though, just never got the chance."

Galen pauses for a moment in thought, and then a light turns on and he darts off to the other room. When he comes back he's holding a second, practically brand-new copy of Catch-22 in his hands. He holds it out to me, and I take it hesitantly.

"Look, I'll make you a deal," he begins. Already I'm nervous about where this is heading. I wait for him to continue. "You stick around until you've finished that book, and *then* you start thinking about what you're going to do next. And I'll pay for your board until then."

I frown. "Sorry, how is that a deal for you?"

Galen shrugs. "I don't want to kick you out on your ass. And I think you need some time to get your head in order. I'd like to think I'm dabbling in altruism by keeping you here rather than on the streets, for a while – and not just for your sake, yeah, for society's as well."

I smile. "You think I'm dangerous?"

"I don't know," Galen admits honestly. "I don't think so. I've never met a werewolf before, obviously."

"I'm not dangerous," I assure him.

"I believe you," he says. "Look, just read it – for me, will you? I can't remember the last time I met someone this desperate to read Catch-22."

I smile at the sentiment, and sigh again, trying to think. I fail miserably, and shrug my tentative agreement. "All right – so long as you keep the secret, I'll stay."

"I'll keep it," Galen agrees.

The party breaks up after that. I feign having to use the toilet (all right, I don't feign – there's only so many drinks a man can handle) and when I emerge I'm back to canine again. Best way to avoid continued interrogation. Galen smiles his defeat, recognizing my total inability to handle any sort of pressure gracefully, and lets it slide.

"But I'm not cleaning up after you anymore, got it?" he insists. "I expect that room to be occupied a hell of a lot more often."

I nod my agreement, unnerved by his calm attitude. It makes absolutely no sense to me.

My entire life I had this vision of how your average human might react if I ever told them I was a werewolf. That vision involved a lot more screaming, or at least a good many more terrified looks and certainly an impromptu attempt to attack me, throw something at me, drive me away – *something* reactionary, at least.

The fact that Galen seems simply to have reasoned it out in his head and arrived at some sort of tranquil acquiescence to an entirely novel reality in the few hours he was gone is… well, it's not normal, but I suppose in a way it is very Galenic. It's logical. It's methodical. It's perhaps irrationally objective.

I give up trying to work Galen's aberrant reaction into my own reality, and instead head into the back room to sleep it off. Six minutes later I'm back in the bathroom hacking up a mess of poorly digested chocolate and beer into my newly assigned toilet.

Galen, the saint, lets me sleep through dinner and into the night, though I wake up a couple more times to puke and wish fervently during every round at the bowl that I'd not thought to turn back into a wolf until everything I'd consumed was all well out of my system. I wake up the next morning to find that I'm lying on the couch, human, with a towel tucked tight around my waist. I don't remember it, but I hope this was my doing. Sunlight is streaming through the back windows and Galen's bike is already gone, and it takes me a moment to focus on the DVD player across the room and find it's already nine-thirty. I'm starving. The last thing I remember was bile, a lot of bile. I've got nothing in me after that sort of memory.

Breakfast consists of half a loaf of patiently browned toast – two slices dry, five with butter, three with strawberry jam and one with peanut butter on. I'm still feeling like hell. I crawl back to the couch to try falling unconscious again.

But my mind keeps drifting, tumbling over and over in ever-mounting peaks of doubt and terror. I'm replaying every second of yesterday, trying to see it for what it really was.

I let a human know. Right now, there's a human out there in the world who *knows* – and I told him. It's the very worst thing that could possibly happen. I don't know what to do about this.

I don't think I'm going to get myself out of this situation honorably. I don't think that's possible. Because I told Galen I'd stay. And I did it as much for me as for him – I can't show a human my fucking transformation and then walk out the door, I have to keep a careful eye on him now.

Damn that code! Werewolfdom says I ought to be killing him. I ought to be killing myself. And I spent way too long internalizing that to ignore it now. And now I'm sitting here on this human's couch and I'm thinking about my mother, about how narrowly she survived making my father a wolf, and I know if it was me in front of that panel right now I'd be dead. And the worst part is that no matter how far I run and no matter how I resist werewolf society and its insanity, this damn dog in me still knows I deserve it.

That hateful paradox rears its ugly head again as I try to work out what it even means to keep running now that I've let a human know. I *have* to stay here. A little while. I need time to think, to plan, to decide what to do and where to go next. But I *really* need to get out of here, and the sooner the better. No matter how much I want to I can't afford to stay. I can't reconcile this in my head, I can't, I don't know what in God's name to do—

Before I know it Galen's bike is jangling up the walk. I throw the towel on the floor and jump down in order to transform, because God only knows whom he could be bringing home with him.

The transformation itself practically kills me. Psychedelic purple and green blotches dance nauseatingly before my eyes as my head tries to catch up with current events and my stomach makes another sharp overture to divulging its contents all over the floor. The sound of melted toast and gastric acid splattering on polished wood coincides melodiously with the grind of the deadbolt.

Galen looks… disappointed, I'd say would be the best word to describe that look on his face when he sees me on all fours on the floor. Disgusted might also fit the data. He pulls his mobile out of his pocket and dials a number.

"Hey, puppy," he says to Sean when the kid picks up, "I'm going to stay home tonight, Anon's just puked all over my floor… No, he got into that box of chocolates, I'm sure he'll be all right. I just don't want to leave him alone… No, you stay home – or better yet, call up Jenny, she's always complaining she never sees you anymore… Yeah. All right, puppy, thanks. I'll see you tomorrow, then, I promise. I love you too. Ciao."

He claps the mobile shut and stares at me. "What do you want me to do about this?"

I don't know what to tell him. I haven't felt this bad since I was little more than a pup and I learned exactly what theobromine could really do to a wolf's digestive system after one fateful, blissful egg moon afternoon consisting of a massive pile of hollow Easter bunnies and Cadbury eggs. It takes all my willpower but I manage to transform one more time, fighting off a second round of vertigo and grabbing the towel up again to drape over my lower half.

"I've got this," I assure Galen in one pathetic, ragged breath. He pauses uncertainly before giving up, heading into the kitchen and coming back with a handful of rags. One is wet – I recall with sudden clarity hearing him turn the sink on just now, the memory of the sound registering only now in a bizarre aftereffect. A wet rag is apparently the ideal puke cleaning kit. I can only smile my thanks when he sets it all down before me, because I'm really in no state to speak.

Galen heads off to the bathroom and comes back out ten minutes later to find me in the kitchen, trying to rinse out the last of the mess from the rags.

"Don't worry about that," he says, "I'm throwing it all away anyway."

"I'm really sorry," I reply, dropping what I'm doing instantly and washing my hands. This is the first time I've ever had to clean up my own vomit, and off the top of my head I can't think of anything I've done more disgusting than that. The persistent nausea certainly isn't helping. It's taking a lot of strength just to stay standing, and my hands are shaking so violently I'm finding it hard to control them.

"You need to go and lie down," Galen admonishes.

I don't need telling twice.

He starts opening up windows in the back room to alleviate the acrid tangy-sweet smell of fresh sick while I go and curl back up on the couch. And then Galen leaves the room for a moment, heading first to the kitchen and then to the bathroom, and I'm halfway to passing out before he returns with a massive glass of water, a bottle of Pepto Bismol, and a thermometer.

"I don't have the first clue how to treat a sick dog," he tells me, "so this is what you get."

He throws me the thermometer and unscrews the cap to the Pepto. I put the thermometer meekly under my tongue and turn it on. I'm not about to argue with any sort of ministration. He sets the full medicine cap and the water on the table next to me and heads off again. I can hear him rooting around in the front closet. The thermometer beeps. I check it. One hundred and two... I can't do the conversion in my condition. Damn Fahrenheit.

"What's one-oh-two mean?" I call.

Galen returns abruptly, carrying a heavy wool blanket that's practically the same plaid pattern as the couch. He's glaring at me like I'm crazy, and holds a finger to his lips.

"You want people to know you're here?" he asks me quietly, gesturing to the open windows. Damn. I completely forgot. "One-oh-two is thirty-eight point eight."

Oh. Yeah, that's high. Galen the human calculator throws the blanket over me and hands me the cap. It's filled with pink. It looks awful but smells like ambrosia, and I have no choice anyway. I'm still shaking like crazy but I manage to toss it back and then take a couple big gulps of water. Galen's already in the kitchen washing the thermometer off in the sink.

"Okay," Galen declares after a moment, coming back in, "answer me a few questions: do you have a headache, and if so is it sharp, stabbing and localized or more like one massive, omnipresent cotton-padded vice? And do you feel at all achy anywhere else?"

"Why?" I ask, confused, remembering to speak quietly.

"It's between aspirin, ibuprofen and Tylenol," Galen explains. I *knew* he had some sort of convoluted formula for pain treatment.

"The vice," I reply. "And I'm definitely aching everywhere and dizzy and lightheaded and nauseated. Which drug's that?"

"That sounds like a three-aspirin job to me," Galen replies, and heads off up the stairs to get it. When he returns, he adds with an air of blithe condescension, "One never can afford excess inflammation."

I smile, and take my pills dutifully. Galen's become a perpetual motion machine – the minute he hands me the pills he's off on the other side of the room rooting through his DVD collection.

"You have any favorites you've been dying to see?" he asks me.

"No," I answer quietly. He pauses for a second, scanning titles.

"Ever seen Royal Tenenbaums?"

"No."

"Oh, *great* movie," he says, grabbing it off the shelf. "You'll like it. I think." He turns around, watching me critically. "Do you like Wes Anderson movies?"

"Dunno," I reply.

"Do you like sort of… I don't know, bizarre darkish comedy, with the caveat that 'darkish comedy' doesn't actually do it any sort of justice at all?"

I can't help but grin. "Yeah, sure."

"Good." Galen pops the DVD in and sets up the movie, and just as it starts to play he's off again into the kitchen. Energizer Galen. I can hear him clanking around in there, but he's obviously trying to be quiet. I'm riveted to the movie. Anything Galen suggests has to be good.

He returns fifteen minutes in with a bowl in one hand and a plate in the other. He sets them down to pause the movie, and I see rice in the former and toast on the latter. The sight of the toast makes me queasy again.

"Think you can handle either one?" he asks.

"Only the rice, I think," I confess. Galen nods assertively, shoving the rice in my direction and taking the toast for himself. He pops back into the kitchen to slather some butter on each slice before heading back into the back room, grabbing up the remote and settling into the recliner, crunching into the first slice as he starts the movie up again.

Later that night we talk.

Despite my best effort I managed to fall asleep three-quarters of the way through the movie, which was an hour after Galen had to leave to teach his afternoon class about the evils of cocaine. Galen was good enough not to wake me up when he returned, and only when I rose groggily from my slumber to attend yet again to nature did he acknowledge once more that I was there.

I emerged to find him already in the kitchen making some more rice, and I'm sitting here now at the table with this massive heap of it and some steamed vegetables and a couple packets of applesauce as well. He's gone out and bought the applesauce special for me, says it's good for queasy stomachs, and I can't help wondering why he's doing all of this. He's having something else entirely, he's eating macaroni and cheese with ham in.

"So Anon," Galen begins, and I look up, grinning at the name I only vaguely remember overhearing in his phone conversation earlier today.

"Is that my name, then?" I ask, and he shrugs.

"Good as any," Galen replies. "More appropriate than most, really."

I nod my acceptance. "Fine."

"So you're twenty-nine," Galen continues, unfazed by my interruption. I nod curtly and resume eating. "And you're from England."

"Yes."

"Anything else I'm allowed to know?"

I pause to think for a moment. "Like what?"

Galen shrugs. "I don't know. You as a person. Your favorites, maybe. Favorite city, movie, color, clothes brand, band, whatever."

I frown in confusion, thrown again by his apparent lack of concern. "What the hell is wrong with you?"

Galen grins and frowns at the same time. "What?"

"Do you know what I am?" I ask pointedly. Galen seems to understand what I'm getting at. He nods quietly, considering it, but he doesn't reply. So I answer for him. "I'm a *werewolf*. Every month when the full moon rises I become a wild animal and I can't stop it. I'm something that doesn't exist, do you understand? You cannot *ever* let *anyone* know you know what I

91

am. I don't understand how you're so calm about this."

"I don't understand why I wouldn't be," Galen counters, raising his hands in surrender. "I told you I won't tell anyone, and I won't." He must see my skeptical look, so he repeats it, "*I won't*. I swear. I just want to understand all of this. So tell me about yourself."

I sigh, giving in again to his weird illogical logic. "What should I say?"

"Like I said, start with something easy," Galen suggests. "Favorites."

"I don't go in for favorites," I say. "I like a lot of cities, really, they all sort of have their moments. Philly's great in autumn, for instance, Phoenix is useful in winter, San Diego's lovely—"

"You've been to Phoenix?" Galen interjects curiously, and I nod. "Where at?"

I pause, trying to work out why he's asking. It occurs to me how idiotic it is to list off all the places I've been to in the States...

"Around ASU," I reply shortly. Galen grins.

"I'm from Tempe," he says, and I cringe inwardly. Of course he had to grow up right down the goddamn street from Sophie's apartment. More continuity...

"Small world," I say halfheartedly.

I think Galen can see he's edging into dangerous territory, because he waves his hands as if to wipe the slate clean and says, "Anyway, enough history – what's your favorite music?"

"Music," I repeat skeptically.

"They say it's a great test of character."

Well, how can I argue with that? I shrug. "I've got at least a dozen favorite bands, but MCR's at the top."

"Really," Galen says, eyebrows raised. He smiles. "I definitely wouldn't have pegged you for emo music."

"Yeah, well, there was this girl," I say by way of an explanation. Galen nods in sudden understanding. "There's a nostalgia factor."

"And by girl... you mean girlfriend?" Galen asks. I shake my head.

"A roommate," I explain. He nods, and I feel the need to

clarify, "I mean a human, uh, companion or whatever. Dane was also a roommate."

"Oh yeah, Dane," Galen says quietly, remembering Dane with a look of startled epiphany. He sits and thinks for a long moment, and then he frowns at me. "He only ever thought you were a dog."

"So does everyone else."

"So this girl thought you were her dog, too."

I nod. "She and her new husband just had their first baby."

Galen frowns again, but this time it looks sympathetic rather than critical. "I'm sorry."

"Don't worry about it."

We both resume eating for a while, and I can hear the bees buzzing ever louder in Galen's head. He's staring at the grain of the table intently, brows knit in concentration, undoubtedly thinking through a million and one issues he's having with this situation we both find ourselves in. That said, when he returns to the conversation he doesn't seem to have meandered off all *that* far, because he asks,

"Have you... *ever* had a girlfriend, then?"

"Not in so many words," I admit with a shrug, "They're hard to keep."

"You said you spent some time as a human...?" Galen adds tentatively. I get what he's asking.

"One year spanning age nineteen, three months at twenty-one and a year and a half that ended at twenty-four," I tell him. "The money I've got now is from a job in San Diego, and you're right, I'm clinging onto that because it's hard to find a job in this country without any form of ID."

"You don't have anything?" Galen asks doubtfully.

"Any papers I had are gone," I explain, "and they were never much use anyway. Needless to say it's safer to stick with the dog thing than try and get by as a human."

"But surely you could get the documents replaced," Galen says.

"And get deported," I say. "And I can't go home. So tell me where you got that pillow in the living room."

Galen's thrown for a moment by the change in subject, but he recognizes clearly enough that it's time to shift the conversation away from my personal life. I'm not at all interested in discussing it.

"It's from Sean's mother," Galen says. "She doesn't exactly know she gave it to me – it's supposed to be sitting in Sean's and his wife's house."

Whoa, what? *That* statement's definitely thrown me for a loop. Galen sees my confusion.

"I mean his mother's a Catholic," he clarifies with an ironic smile. "She wants him to get married and settle down and give her lots of grandbabies, and the pillow is her blatant style of subtle hinting."

"But she must know he's gay." No mother could be *that* blind.

Galen shrugs. "She's hopeful, let's put it that way. She thinks he's going through some strange effeminate phase, and she *certainly* doesn't know about me – or any other guy he's ever had, really."

"Is that why it's been three years and you're still not sharing a place?" I ask. Galen nods and sighs, almost angrily. I appear to have hit a nerve.

"He's just a kid," Galen says after a moment of careful formulation. "He's all of twenty-three, and he only finished college last December… He's a good boy from a good, rich family and the parents are still paying his rent – and he's happy to keep up the deception in order to keep the money flowing. And I suppose I can't blame him for that."

"He's only twenty-three?" I ask, stunned. Galen nods. "How old are you?"

"Twenty-seven. Why, what were you expecting?"

"I don't know," I concede. "I guess that's about right. What's he doing still living off Mum and Dad at twenty-three, anyway?"

Galen smiles coolly. "Sorry, what? You're almost thirty and the way I see it, you've just conveniently replaced the phrase 'Mom and Dad' with 'roommate'."

"I've got complications," I say, teeth clenched. He's good at hitting nerves, too. "You tell me it's easy starting from nothing in another country at sixteen. You tell me how many nights you've

94

spent freezing to death behind a dumpster or sitting in a cage at the damn pound."

Galen pauses for a moment. The counterarguments are right there on the tip of his tongue. I can practically hear them. I know them all because I've made them myself, and I'm ready with a defense against every single one I know he's going to bring up. But tact prevails and he lets them drop for now.

"Yeah, well, Sean's always lived a pretty pampered life," he says, sighing again. "He just wants to keep it up a while longer."

"Doesn't he have a job?"

"He does. He's putting it all away. Look, I'm sure you know what Catholic mothers are like. They've got a stranglehold, no matter how much their kids hate to admit it, and Sean's not ready to cut off all ties with his parents and sisters yet, that's all."

"Is Sean still a Catholic?" I ask.

Galen bursts out laughing. "Are you kidding me? Crucifixes burn his skin, more like. He's a staunch antitheist."

"And you?"

"Atheist with a hope of someday finding agnosticism," Galen replies wistfully. "Or at least apathy. How about yourself?"

"God and I have an understanding of sorts," I say with a smile. "I know He doesn't exist, and He benevolently refrains from smiting me for it. Frankly it's hard to *be* something that doesn't exist and still feel at all certain about all the other ones."

"Sounds fair," Galen says, grinning.

"It's worked out so far."

There's a pause while we resume eating for a few bites.

"So you're feeling better?" Galen asks after a while, and I nod, smiling my gratitude.

"Yeah, much better, thanks," I reply.

"It wasn't the flu or anything, was it?"

I shrug. "I'd have to guess it was simultaneous theobromine and alcohol poisoning."

"Sorry, theobromine…?" Galen asks. "Is that in chocolate?"

"It's the chemical that makes chocolate famous for killing dogs," I reply. "Dogs don't flush it through their system as fast as humans do. Don't think I could have died off that little, though – although fever and convulsions are supposed to be sort of end stages. Maybe it's worse for wolves."

"I'm sure the booze didn't help," Galen says. He pauses. "So it's not true, what they say, then? You have to have a silver bullet to the heart and all that?"

I have to smile at the question and shake my head. "No, that only started up last century. We *are* notoriously hard to kill, we heal quickly from most things – you have to, if you want to survive the transformations."

"I guess that makes sense," Galen replies with a thoughtful nod. "So how does one kill a werewolf? Not that I want to, or anything," he adds hurriedly when he sees my look.

"Same way you'd kill a human, basically," I answer with grave reluctance. I don't know why I'm trusting him to know this. "It just takes more work, it takes longer, you have to run the brain out of oxygen for a really long time. It's usually *major* trauma that gets us."

"So no wolfsbane either?" Galen guesses, and I have to chuckle.

"I don't know how that one got started," I tell him with a shrug. "No, the only *werewolf*-specific poison I'm aware of is another werewolf's bite. It's much nastier even than it would be for a human, it takes forever to get over."

"Is it like an infection, or something?"

"Something like that. One good bite can turn a human into one of us, it's not surprising it has a weird effect on us, too. But other than that we're more or less… just humans or dogs. Quicker to recover, but still susceptible to all the same diseases, injuries, health hazards and toxins as any other human or dog."

"So… so you knew you were poisoning yourself," Galen says cautiously.

"…Technically," I confess, choosing my words carefully. "I was drunk, I wasn't thinking. If I was thinking I wouldn't have transformed."

"I'd really appreciate not having a repeat of that," Galen says. "You accidentally killing yourself is about the last thing I need."

"I know," I reply sheepishly.

"Seriously, what's so awful about someone knowing?" Galen asks me. "I don't get it."

"It's just… our kind will do anything to keep werewolfdom a secret," I try ineffectively to explain. "The second a human finds out then it spreads and we get hunted down, that's how it's always been. You learn it before you learn to walk, as a pup. It goes against everything I know to tell someone." I pause for a moment, thinking it through. "I don't know, maybe that really was a subconscious suicide attempt. It ought to have been a conscious one, if I was a proper wolf. It's… it's sort of one's duty, when one fails that fantastically."

"Seriously?" Galen asks, doubtful.

"How else are we supposed to keep the secret?" I point out. "You think a wolf's never gotten arrested before? It's his responsibility to break out or commit suicide before he gets caught behind bars during a moonrise. *Anything* but let humans know."

"Wow," Galen says, shaking his head. He looks up at me. "Look, don't do it, all right? Quit thinking like that. Nothing's going to happen, no one's ever going to know. You can stay here as long as you want – you've got at least a decade until everyone starts thinking you ought to be properly dead as a dog."

"I don't need your pity," I say, trying to sound humble. He seems to take it as such.

"I'm not offering out of pity," Galen insists.

"Then why are you doing it?" I ask.

"Fascination, I guess," Galen replies with a shrug. "I want to see what this werewolf thing's all about. It's crazy, you know?"

"If so I've been crazy my whole life," I say pointedly. He grins.

"It shows."

CHAPTER 6

Galen is so much weirder than I already gave him credit for. He really goes back almost instantly to treating everything like normal, like nothing happened. Well, he talks to me like I'm a person now. The next morning he goes to the trouble of asking me if I want to go for a run. But see, that's the thing. Not two days after he finds out I'm a mythical monster, we get up and go for a run like it's any other day.

Galen invites Sean over later that evening, and when Sean bursts in the house all full of sweet, vociferous sympathy for "poor sick doggy and look, Nonny, I brought you a bone just for you, 'cause your daddy doesn't take care of you like he should," I look over Sean's shoulder to see Galen grinning back at me, shrugging as if to say it's neither his fault nor his problem.

Oddly enough, right now Sean's style of interaction is an immense relief. I'm used to dealing with people like Sean, people who think I'm a dog and nothing else, people who pour their hearts out to me with no expectation of a response. I need to believe that to most of the outside world I'm still just an animal, a house pet, a voiceless mindless thing worthy of no suspicion whatsoever. Somehow I lost sight of that in the wake of this revelation to Galen: the world is still turning out there, oblivious to my transgression and my identity. Werewolfdom's secret is still contained within the walls of this house. And it's so important that *even Sean* doesn't know, Sean from whom Galen hides absolutely nothing – so long as Sean doesn't know, I can rest assured the secret is safe.

So for now I just have to learn what it is to interact with a human that knows I'm really a werewolf. I've dealt with people in my human form, obviously, that's not what I mean – I mean that until now the single human in existence who ever knew me as both a man and a wolf was my sister, and she clearly doesn't count. Galen is a complete outsider who's seen both sides of me and knows it, and that's not something I've ever dealt with before. This is going to be very, very weird indeed.

Galen's got Health through the end of the next week, and I spend this time with him out of the house renormalizing. I try to get back into my routine, but it's the little things. I no longer have to clear my search history, I can take a shower any time of day – because Galen knows. I can't get it in my head *he knows*. It's so weird... It's been *years* since I was around anyone who knew what I was. When I got on that plane to Chicago I was certain I'd never experience it again. I'd almost forgotten what it was like, how much easier it was. And... I'm not going to lie, it's tempting.

I have to leave. But I don't want to. I was almost to the end of my month and I was pretty set on staying here, and now that Galen knows I don't want to leave him behind. I need these hours alone to work out how to get back to myself, how I should move forward. Galen gets through his week of Health and after that it's just summer.

And it turns out to be the best summer of my life.

Sean's still got work most of the day, so Galen's got nothing to do all day long but hang out. But on that first Monday Galen still heads out the door early, waving goodbye with a short explanation that he's off to wish Sean a good first day as the sole breadwinner and that he'll be back later on toward afternoon.

I don't get it, but hell, I have no problem getting the house to myself for a full morning. I spend it all reading, though I have to admit I've momentarily put aside my main assignment. I tell myself this is because I need more time to think this through, but even I know that's a lie. What I really want is to get all I can out of this house before I have to move on.

Galen drops back home around two, and he's carrying a couple of bags up the walk from the car. Instinct screams at me to transform before he comes in, and it's both unsettling and oddly thrilling when I decide against it – it's easy to catch a view of the front yard from behind the drapes and he's definitely alone. He's grinning ear-to-ear when I unlock the door for him.

That means he's got something up his sleeve.

"What?" I ask him suspiciously. He holds up a bag.

"I'm tired of you wearing my clothes," he replies. "I pegged you for a thirty-four."

Wait – what? He got me clothes? I have clothes? Actual clothes? Suddenly I'm grinning too. "Are you serious?"

He nods, reaching into the bag and pulling out two pairs of shorts and three shirts and shoving them toward me. And then there's another bag with two pairs of jeans, an array of different boxers and briefs, and at least a half dozen different pairs of socks. And in the last bag... man, there's trainers *and* loafers *and* flip-flops.

"You can keep whatever fits," he tells me. "We'll find a place to stash it all."

I'm speechless. I'm just staring down like an idiot at the clothes piled up in my arms. This isn't cheap stuff, it's all designer department store fare. There's a grey and a navy t-shirt and a black-and-blue striped long-sleeve. The jeans are both dark – one blue, one a faded grey. One pair of shorts is standard tan and the other is a ridiculous plaid. The trainers are blue and black, the flip-flops are black, and the loafers are brown. Count on Galen to make the most out of a few garments.

"You don't have to keep any of it if you don't want to," Galen's saying, misinterpreting my silence as displeasure. "Or if you don't like the colors or anything, or if it's the wrong size, I can return everything..."

"I'm just trying to remember the last time I owned clothes," I tell him, still stunned. "You didn't have to do all this."

"Eh," he replies with a shrug and a smile. "Not every day I get to go clothes shopping. Go on, you've got to try it on and see how it all fits."

So I oblige, heading into the bathroom and throwing on the grey jeans and the grey shirt. When I emerge he's in the middle of plugging his iPod into the stereo. He looks up when the door opens, and grins.

"Damn, I *so* nailed that," he remarks, checking out the fit of the jeans like he's my mum and I'm thirteen again. And he was spot on, they fit perfectly – the right length and everything. I've never in my life managed to find a pair of jeans that fit right first go, and this guy just goes out and does it without me even being there…? Madness.

"Yeah, they're perfect," I agree.

"Great." He waves me off happily. "Go on, go try the rest."

So I go back in and throw on the blue jeans and the long-sleeve shirt as I hear the music come on through the door. These jeans don't fit quite as well, they're wide in the waist, and Galen frowns his disapproval when I come out.

"The shirt's good, though," he says, and I nod.

He's got the music on heinously loud, and it's something I haven't heard before. Suddenly he grins, and he starts singing along with the chorus in this strong, clear, natural singer's voice that's amazingly good at mimicking every nuance of all the songs he's in love with singing. I wait patiently for him to finish. There's no point interrupting him when he gets going.

"Have you ever heard Ludo?" he shouts over the next verse.

I shake my head. "It's good."

"Seriously, they're amazing," he says with a grin. "Go on, I want to see those shorts, I thought they were ridiculous enough."

So I head in and try on the shorts with the navy shirt. Everything's fitting a lot better than I would have guessed. I throw on the flip-flops for good measure. When I come out he's sitting at his laptop waiting for it to boot up, and he nods assertively at the fit of the clothes.

"Do you like it?" he asks, turning the music down. He's mouthing the lyrics anyway as I reply – I've had to get used to this over the past week or so, him being distracted by the music while listening to me. He's good at it, though, he can multitask well enough that he remembers what I'm saying regardless.

"Yeah, I do, actually," I reply. "I never thought plaid would be my thing."

"I like it," Galen says, shrugging. And then he gets fully distracted by another chorus, and he's off singing quietly again.

"So Ludo… like from Labyrinth?" I ask Galen, to drag him back into reality. His expression changes instantly into one of wide-eyed, gleeful disbelief.

"Oh my God, you *knew* that?" he asks, shocked. "Everyone

I've ever quizzed has no clue. You've seen the movie?"

"Of course, it was fantastic," I reply with a smile. Must have watched it a dozen times when I was a kid.

"So is this band," Galen tells me seriously. "They're totally awesome – they've got two types of songs, really, this kind of ballad-style song and then these amazing satiric sort of songs. You have to listen to all of them, seriously, every one's a gem. It's just got to be another homework assignment."

"Fair enough," I agree with a shrug. "I'll go try on the other shorts."

"Indeed," he says with an assertive nod, waving me off.

I spend some time unwrapping socks in order to try on the trainers as well. The fit of the trainers actually bothers me a little, because it's exactly right, and to have guessed my shoe size correctly is plain abnormal. He could have gotten lucky on the trousers. But the *shoes?*

"How did you know my shoe size?" I ask suspiciously when I emerge from the bathroom.

"Lucky guess?" Galen says, grinning. I frown at him, waiting for his real answer. "No, really, you're going to think I'm a creep. I busted out the ruler while you were sleeping off your accidental poisoning."

"Really?" I ask skeptically, and he nods. I'm even more confused. That puts this whole thing in a really strange perspective... And in a sudden epiphany I see our dinner conversation last week in a whole new light, his incongruous asking about favorites – one of them was clothes. He was fishing. He really has been planning this all along.

But before I can respond, a familiar word rivets my attention back on the music. I point to the speakers.

"Wait, what'd they just say?"

Galen's already grinning broadly as he quotes, "'The loneliest werewolf, I wander the earth.' Now tell me that didn't just become your anthem and Ludo isn't your new favorite band."

I manage a halfhearted smile at the lyric he clearly engineered for me to hear. The sentiment is heartening, that he went out of his way to find a musical expression for his view of my life's predicament – I don't like the word 'lonely,' but I can see how a human would see it that way. And in my darker moments I can't say it's inaccurate. But... his *delivery*...

He's treating this way, *way* too casually. Casual is not a mindset I can afford for him to be in. I have to address it.

"So... the same day you find out you've got a werewolf living with you you're trying to find his shoe size," I begin. Galen shrugs, and the smile's leaving his face as he recognizes my hesitance. "Why?"

"I don't know," he admits with another shrug. "I was just sitting there in that class trying to think what I'd want if I was in your situation. Seems like clothes would be at the top of the list. And frankly I don't want you stretching my stuff out."

He gestures in the direction of his clothes now lying on the floor of the bathroom as he says it, the one pair of gym shorts and oversize shirt he's allowed me to wear since learning what I am, and I can't help but smile in sheepish gratitude. "Yeah, okay, you're a creep."

"Glad you think so," Galen says with mock hauteur.

"It's just... I mean I appreciate it, I really do, but..." I pause, trying to gauge my words carefully. "I can see how from a human perspective I might seem like an amusing novelty or a fable something, but this is my reality and I take it very seriously and I get the impression you're not really getting that."

Galen's face falls again as I say it. He looks away, thinking, and nods quietly.

"Well, I'm sorry," he apologizes at last. "I didn't mean it that way—"

"I know you didn't."

"—But I do want to say that however lighthearted I might seem, I really do respect your position and I want you to believe your secret is safe with me. I don't want to have to say it again. I'm just trying to put you at ease here."

Somehow he always manages to make me sound like an asshole. I nod, looking down at the floor, at my new shoes. *Damn* him.

"So... now that's settled..." Galen persists, a hesitant smile forming again on his face, "I guess I'd better get the *truly* creepy part out of the way."

He stands up abruptly, brushing past me back into the living room, and starts rifling through the bags. He comes out brandishing an envelope. He's gone manic again.

"What is that?" I ask him slowly. And then he fans out another envelope from behind the first one, and I'm forced to correct myself, "What're those?"

"Well, *this* one," he says, opening the first one easily, unsealed as it is, "contains three tickets to the Warped Tour in July."

"*Three* tickets?" I ask doubtfully, staggered by the implication.

"Because *this* one," Galen continues impishly, ripping open the second envelope which is actually a proper mailed letter, "is a truly saintly donation from one Michael James Stark, my old college roommate. Check it out."

He reaches in and hands me the contents of the envelope. It's a Massachusetts driver's license. This guy Mike Stark is staring back at me, and even I have to admit his specs line up well with mine: hair black, eyes blue, six-foot-one, twenty-eight years old… the ID was issued years ago, so the picture is young but definitely close enough.

"You want to hear the *really* brilliant part?" Galen says before I can react. "He's an Essex boy, moved to Massachusetts when he was thirteen so he's got a mess of an English accent. So far as *you're* concerned, he's got a couple days off work and thought he'd pop by for a night on his way to see his parents in Florida, just so's he can catch up with his old college buddy in Philly."

"What…?" I ask, utterly overwhelmed. The guy got me a fake ID. An actual legal fake ID. I can't even begin to ever repay him for this.

"I mean we're going *out* tonight," he declares, grinning ear-to-ear. "Sean's already got about a thousand clubs lined up, he's dying to meet you."

"To meet Mike," I say, to clarify. My brain has not yet caught up.

"Exactly."

"Hold on, hold on." I hold my hands up to force him to stop. Time is still refusing to slow down, and it's everything I can do to work out what's even going on, here. "Is this seriously happening?"

"Oh, it's happening," Galen says, nodding vigorously. "We've already got dinner reservations at seven. But I've got to start filling you in on details now if you're going to make a convincing Mike."

"When did you start planning this?" I ask, wide-eyed.

"Oh, about last Friday," Galen replies airily. "I told Mike that one of Sean's friends looks just like him and could Mike *please* conveniently lose his ID so we can get this kid into clubs, and of course he jumped right on the bandwagon. And he really will be stopping by here, actually, but only for lunch tomorrow midday."

"What does he do?"

"Accounting."

"I don't know the first thing about maths," I protest. Galen shrugs.

"How much do you think Sean's going to be asking about filing taxes?" he points out. "If it gets bad I'll order him not to talk shop. Honestly, if I can get him to stop prying about your love life it'll be a bloody miracle."

"Is it interesting, then?" I ask, and Galen shakes his head.

"Nah, Mike's got a girlfriend but it's only been going a few months or so," he replies. "Just a warning, though, Sean's a whore for gossip and he thinks everyone's at least a little gay, so he'll be asking for war stories."

"And... are there any?" I ask hesitantly, not sure I want to know the answer.

"No, just one," Galen replies with a smile. That smile is far too nostalgic for my liking. "I, um, I kissed him once. Actually *he* kissed *me*, oddly enough."

"What happened?"

"Well, so this was before... well, okay, so we were both trashed and I sort of told him I thought maybe I was gay," Galen explains rapidly, becoming suddenly self-conscious, "And he was confused as to how a guy couldn't be totally sure one way or another, and as I recall he finally said something like, 'Well here, if *I* can't do it for you you're definitely straight,' and out of nowhere he just kisses me. Like... *properly* kissing, you know? Mind you, he was *totally* messed up at the time, we both were, but afterward I told him, 'Yeah, okay, definitely bent,' and he got all

105

grossed out and then started laughing hysterically, and so did I, and that was that. And that's about the gayest Mike ever got in his life."

"That's... pretty gay," I says, frowning. Galen grins.

"Yeah, I don't think he ever forgave himself for that lapse in judgment." He shrugs. "Oh well, c'est la vie. *Anyway*, let's check out his Facebook and you can get an idea what Mike's really like..."

It still takes me a while after that initial foray to work out what the hell Galen is thinking. It doesn't make any sense at all to me that he's gone and lied both to Sean and this guy Mike so I can get a fake ID. It doesn't make any sense that he's planning on passing me off to Sean as another person entirely. It doesn't make any sense why he'd go through all this just to help me get out of the house. But somehow it makes sense to Galen, and I'm a little put off as I learn why.

It turns out that this Mike character is Galen's good friend, they lived together for a few years in college, and recently they've drifted, as people do when they move cities and start living busy lives. Well, busy for Mike at least, who's spent the last five years working his way up through the ranks of some accounting firm – honestly, despite my best intentions I have to admit my mind drifts as Galen tries to explain it to me.

Galen, on the other hand, moved to Philadelphia in order to pursue a Ph.D. at Penn, and quit with an M.A. after three long years getting nowhere with a terrible advisor, a man upon whose faults Galen is eager to expound in a brief, vitriolic tangential tirade. It was at Penn that Galen met Sean, who was his student in that last semester and who convinced him to do anything else but keep going doing something he hated. And that's when Galen decided to give up professional learning and try out professional teaching, which he has now found he hates with an even greater passion.

And that's the history from Galen's perspective, except that's not quite the *entire* history, because it doesn't explain the pressing issue from *my* perspective: why the hell he's willing to help me.

Let's dissect Galen's psyche for a moment. Let's consider that

106

awkward revelation of Galen's earlier, when he admitted so self-consciously that Mike has had one gay moment in his entire life and that moment happened to be with Galen. Let's also note that it was apparently Galen's very first of many such moments. I'm not wrong in thinking that firsts always count for *something* – I think everyone remembers the first, for better or worse, and I am absolutely positive Galen's pretty pleased about this particular 'first'.

This Mike guy seems pretty profoundly self-assured, as I get to learning about him via internet stalking and Galen's own recounting – Mike fits Type A completely. One might call him affably obnoxious, in that he seems loud, confident bordering on narcissistic, agreeable, no-nonsense, and – this is important – up for just about anything. I think Mike's gay moment could be readily explained away as a moment of very trashed unthinking flippancy, if I can use that word to describe the actions of a very comfortably and securely heterosexual male. It was... an inelegant move. It was more self-aggrandizing than anything else. And in my personal opinion, it was particularly ill-chosen in light of his audience.

It's obvious, in other words, it's palpably and unmistakably clear that while Mike may have shrugged that moment off years ago with a laugh and a jovial, 'Well hell, what'd I do *that* for?', Galen has not yet in fact gotten over it. It's easy to see from the way Galen talks, the way he relates his stories, the way he keeps clicking through picture after picture trying to find this or that photo that really captures some Mike-like essence, that he's smitten. He adores Mike. And I'm sure Mike knows it, and that's okay because hell, they're friends, and Galen recognizes that too. They're still pretty close, they keep up on each other's lives, and they're both eccentric enough that when the one calls up and says, 'Hey, mail me your driver's license,' the other will actually do it, without a second thought, just for the laugh.

Here's the thing that gets me about all of this. Mike's tall. He's got really dark hair, and blue eyes. He used to be lanky, back when Galen knew him well. And he's English. It all lines up. I'm not an idiot, I can look in a mirror – I know this fake ID is just about perfect.

Galen's reaction to me as a werewolf, his practically instant acceptance and his insistence on allowing me to stay, has not made one ounce of sense to me until this morning when I learned about Mike. It may sound radically unobservant, but until today I swear I had not considered the possibility that maybe Galen's got his own selfish motives for keeping me around. This fact is one I'm not really ready to swallow, and the longer I sit here learning about Mike and his girlfriend and his college years… I finally decide I've got to say something.

"I'm not gay," I blurt out with trite abruptness during a brief lull, and instantly kick myself for saying it that way. It's not quite what I meant. Galen stops what he's doing and frowns at me.

"What are you on about?" he asks me suspiciously.

"I just want you to know, I mean, in case you're wondering," I stumble, miring myself in pathetic backtracking inanity, "I mean not even remotely, not in the very least at all gay," and I point to the screen, to the profile of Mike Stark, whom I've already diagnosed as concretely straight, "I mean not even that gay."

"I figured that one out," Galen says slowly, watching me like I'm deranged. "I'm asking you why you mentioned it."

"I just… I don't want you to think, I mean…" I give up, shaking my head. "I mean like I said I appreciate this, all of it, really I do, but I want to make sure there's no confusion about – about any of it."

"What, you want me to take it back?" Galen asks, his look one of quizzical disbelief.

"No, no, I mean… thank you," I say, frustrated at my own inability to describe what I'm on about without seeming like a conceited ass. I determine to drop the subject. Galen finally grins, broadly.

"Guess that means you're not paying me back in blow jobs, then," he jokes. I think I actually gag at the imagery. Galen chuckles at my reaction, shaking his head. "Get over yourself, Anon."

So this is how I end up getting all dressed up and heading out in Galen's car to meet up with Sean at his house before we all go out for a night on the town.

My heart's pounding out of my chest when Galen parks the car in Sean's apartment lot, and I force him to stop for another second before we get out. I think I'm actually halfway to a full-blown panic attack. This is all so far beyond illegal – I keep feeling like someone's watching me, I'm being judged, I'm going to get attacked without warning for this.

Galen sighs amusedly at my discomfort, because he still doesn't get it. He will never get it. And this whole insane gesture of his practically proves it. But he waits patiently for me to feel well enough to go and meet yet another human as a fellow human.

"I can't do this," I say finally, shaking my head, sinking down in the hope that he'll turn the car back on and go.

"We're already here," Galen protests. "Come on, no one knows what you are but me. Who's going to find out? You've spent plenty of time being human before."

"I don't go impersonating other people and trying to make friends while I'm at it!" I insist. "Please, can we go home – I can't—"

"Okay, *calm down*," Galen says, grabbing my shoulder when he sees me start to panic. "Look, I've been where you are and you have to trust me when I say this is good for you, got it?"

"You don't know what the hell you're talking about," I argue. "How can you think you know what this is like?"

"Because I spent half my life trying to hide who I was from everyone I knew, myself included," Galen says. "And all it meant in the end was that I wasted a lot of time being something I wasn't. And *you* – you've given up literally everything it means to be a person to hold onto your precious secret. You need to get out again and see what you've been missing and see that you can *have* your damn secret and still have fun too. Which is why I'm not going home tonight until you've at least had a proper meal out with us."

I pause for a moment. That almost made sense. "So… you're saying I've been in the closet."

Galen chuckles. "Something like that, yeah. Now get out of my car."

*   *   *

Sean yanks open the door excitedly when we finally arrive on his doorstep, practically throwing his arms around me and crying, "Mike! Oh, it's so good to meet you finally!"

"Good to meet you, too," I greet him with a smile. He pulls away, holding me at arm's length and peering up at me critically. Man, he's so *short*... I mean I always knew that, but it's an entirely different view of him from up here and I feel somehow as if I'm not even looking at the same Sean. He's grinning.

"You look *way* cuter in person than in your pictures, you know that?" he tells me coyly, and I can't help but smile at the unwitting compliment. I am *so* damn lucky that I do look a lot like Mike. Galen grins at the comment as well. I shrug.

"Yeah, I'm not photogenic."

"Well come in, guys, come in," Sean says, standing aside and ushering us forward. He spares a quick welcoming kiss for Galen. "I've just got to find some shoes, I've no idea what to wear."

"He's got more shoes than God," Galen tells me in a stage whisper. Sean shoots him a glare before ducking into his bedroom to rummage through the closet.

The delay gives me a moment to take in the apartment. The place looks like it fell straight out of a home decorating magazine: professional paintings, immaculate furniture, even fresh flowers on the coffee table. I don't know why I was expecting something a little messier, or more cluttered and disjointed – because of Bonks? Sean's age? – but this makes so much more sense. It's so Sean, so fashionable and artistic and meticulous. Galen gives an impromptu tour.

"Living room," he says, gesturing around us as we advance farther into the room. He points in a wide circle from right to left, "kitchen, office, bathroom, closet, bedroom."

Galen's tone has shifted entirely now that I'm supposed to be Mike. He's become frankly laconic compared with his regular, overly-verbose self, and he's even more sarcastic than usual. I take it that this is how he would act around Mike himself – I'm not sure whether this current display is conscious acting or subconscious reaction on his part.

We move in view of the back door to the kitchen, and sure enough there's Bonks. He catches sight of us and starts barking wildly.

"Bonks!" Sean shouts from the bedroom, "Shut up! Galen, shut him up, will you?"

Galen sighs, rolling his eyes as if to express to me the utter futility of an attempt to shut Bonks up. I know it all too well. Time to defuse yet another doggy situation. I head to the back door and Bonks is still barking, mad with excitement at the prospect of a new playmate. He doesn't recognize me through the door, able only to see but not smell me. I crouch down and open the door carefully to avoid attack, but my precaution is useless. He leaps up—

And does a strange canine double take when he smells me and realizes who I really am. Instantly he darts off to a corner of his miniscule yard and comes back with his tug-of-war toy, bounding up to me and knocking full force into my chest, shoving the toy toward me in an effort to play.

"Come on, calm down," I mutter, trying to dissuade him, grabbing the toy reluctantly. I can hear Galen laughing behind me.

"Sean, come look at this," he calls, and Sean comes out to see Bonks on one end of the toy and me on the other, with Bonks making his best effort to drag me bodily into the yard.

"Oh my God, Mike, you don't have to play with him," Sean scolds guiltily.

"Oh no, that's all right, I don't mind," I assure him.

"He likes you," Sean says with a smile. "He's usually such a bother around strangers."

"I'll consider myself familiar, then," I reply cordially. Sean smiles again and disappears back into the bedroom, still looking for shoes. I turn back to Bonks, trying ineffectually to get him to drop the toy, and mutter to him, "Seriously, man, not now."

Galen comes over and crouches next to me in the doorway. Bonks drops the toy instantly to get petted by Galen. This is a rare treat for Bonks, and he is beside himself with joy at the prospect.

"You know," Galen says quietly so as not to be overheard, "I can't even begin to imagine what sharing a chew toy with this guy must be like."

I smile. "Yeah, not thrilling."

"That... hadn't occurred to me until now," Galen says, grimacing. "All the myriad ways you must interact with dogs, I mean. You're like a dog whisperer or something."

"A very, very bad one," I reply. "They can tell what I am, I intimidate them."

"Oh..." Galen says, as if he's been handed information he hasn't considered before, information which makes a whole host of incongruous facts suddenly make sense.

"Okay," Sean calls, heading back into the room before Galen can reply properly. Sean's changed not just his shoes but his shirt as well, and they match – pale blue shirt with pale blue Pumas. I've seen worse, at least. Galen's checking his watch.

"All right, let's go then," he declares instantly, and fast as that we're out the door. As we head to the car I have a momentary pang of guilt for leaving Bonks alone in the house. I've been there.

"So you're going to visit your parents?" Sean asks me. He offers me shotgun with a gesture, and I take it graciously.

"Yeah, for a few days," I reply. "It's been a couple years since I made the trip."

"You're all from England, right?" Sean asks.

"My mother was born in Ireland," I tell him. This is my own truth – I have no idea what Mike's real story is. I can't tell if Galen recognizes I'm being honest or if he thinks I'm just adding fake detail. "But yes, I'm from Essex."

"I love your accent," Sean says. I smile. My accent sounds nothing like an Essex accent, but Americans don't know any better. I suppose the years in America and the Irish mother could account for any inconsistencies. Score one for that inadvertent ass-covering.

"Thanks."

"So you guys were roommates for what, two years or something?"

"Three," I correct him before Galen can. Galen grins at me.

Don't worry, Galen, I've got a fine memory for trivia. "Sophomore and junior year in the dorms and then senior year in this bloody awful apartment – you remember that, Galen?"

"The heating worked only sporadically, if I recall," Galen says amusedly.

"And your boyfriend here stole the big room," I tell Sean, turning around to address him directly. He's grinning at the story. "Seriously, we get out of the car that first day and he grabs his biggest box and plants it directly in the middle of the room, simple as that."

"Hey, it worked," Galen says with a shrug. "Not my fault you're a moron."

"I prefer the term 'gentleman'," I shoot back.

"You remember the next-door neighbors?" Galen asks me.

"Oh God," I sigh, rolling my eyes. As if I really do remember. You can't fault me for being a natural-born actor. "These two girls, they played this ear-splitting rap 'round the clock, had parties every other weeknight…"

"Which was fine when we didn't have anything going on," Galen adds.

"There were always plenty of ladies available for the odd enterprising neighbor," I say wistfully. I shake my head. "This is how Galen of all people justified his need for the better room – he swore he brought home twice as many girls as I did."

"So Mike kept a running tally," Galen says.

"And who won, man?" I point out, turning to Galen. Galen shrugs. "That's right, me."

"I brought home more guys than you did," Galen argues.

"*Definitely* not arguing with that," I say with total sincerity, and Sean chuckles.

"So you have a girlfriend?" he asks me, and I nod.

"Yeah, her name's Dominique."

"Why'd she stay home this trip?"

"I haven't known her long enough to have her meet the parents yet," I reply.

"You've never known any woman long enough for that," Galen says sarcastically, "not according to you."

"Yeah, well, the last thing I need is my mother going all

psychotic over my 'future bride' and all that," I say. "High school scarred me. And you're not one to talk."

"That's because my father would sooner shoot me than meet my boyfriend," Galen argues.

"Same here," Sean adds from the back seat.

"So *neither* side knows?" I feign incredulity. Galen already told me this back at the house – and damn it, I wish I'd remembered that when he was playing all high and mighty about coming out just now. I try to think of a way to bring it up. "So... there's still people you haven't come out to, then."

"Hell, if I ever talk to my parents again maybe I'll mention it," Galen says dryly. "And obviously Marissa and Theo know." Marissa and Theo are Galen's four-years-younger sister and two-years-older brother. Galen said Mike has met them both before. And I can't help but think Galen did catch my double entendre and he's addressing it directly when he adds, "The way I see it, anyone who's going to hate doesn't have to hear about it. I'm not going to go out of my way to bring other people's shit down on my head."

There's no easy way to argue with him right now, so I let it go and continue pretending to be Mike. "How long have you guys been together, again?"

"Three years, last month," Sean says happily, and Galen grins at him through the rearview mirror.

"That long, wow," I say, shaking my head in mock-amazement. "Jesus, I feel old."

"Almost a decade, man," Galen says, and I nod.

"I can't believe I've known you ten damn years," I tell him. He just grins, and I turn my attention back to Sean. "So where are you from, Sean?"

"Memphis," Sean sighs dramatically, the word coming out in one long, emphatic breathy drawl, as if Memphis really were the very bane of any thinking man's existence. This is standard Sean, hamming it up for a stranger – I've heard him pining after the very same city before to Galen. "Penn was a blessing, to say the least."

"And what are you doing with your philosophy degree?" I ask. Sean shrugs.

"Not practicing philosophy," he replies with a smile. "I work at a municipal office, just a regular paper pusher."

"Not exactly pushing the limits of his potential," Galen comments wryly, and Sean reaches forward to slap him on the shoulder.

"None of us are," I point out, and I'm sure Galen's caught that I'm speaking not just as Mike but as Anon when I say that. He smiles.

"Fair enough," he concedes.

We spend the rest of the car ride talking about Philadelphia and Cambridge, similarities and differences sort-of-thing. I lived in Boston for two-thirds of a year before catching a train down to Pennsylvania, so my lies aren't all as far-fetched as they might have been, and there's a nontrivial degree of truth to the comparisons I'm making. Galen seems shocked that I'm actually able to pull this deception off. Are you kidding? I make this look easy.

We arrive at this seafood restaurant with a minute to spare before the seven o'clock reservation, and in fact Galen has to drop Sean off at the door so Sean can go explain that the other two in his party are trying to find parking.

The food's absolutely outstanding. I can't recall the last time I ate proper seafood, and for my sake they order practically everything. Galen insists immediately that it's all on his tab. They start with a bottle of white wine and steamed mussels and crab cakes. Second course is clam chowder for Galen, lobster bisque for me and a caprese salad for Sean, but Galen insists that everyone try some of everyone else's and by now I get what he's doing. Give the poor doggy a culinary experience he won't forget. And I'm wholeheartedly grateful. We're all so stuffed by the next round that we end up splitting two entrees three ways, the filet and a two-pound Maine lobster, and top it off with a bottle of red. And if that wasn't enough, there's still cheesecake and crème brûlée at the end.

This exorbitant bounty of food takes well over three hours to consume, and we spend the entire time in a whirlwind of animated conversation. I'm four glasses into it by the entrees and having a fine time indeed, and I don't much care at the moment that I'm making stuff up at this point.

I'm pulling bits and pieces from everywhere. I make Mike's little sister out to sound very much like my dear older sister, as I imagine she might have been at twenty-five. Mike's parents are exactly like my own mother and father. Dominique gets to be more and more like Sophie as the evening wears on. And Mike's suddenly got this good friend at work named Dave, we hang out all the time and watch football, he's a Packers fan. My stories from Harvard (can you believe it – *Harvard University*, for God's sake, and look how far mighty Galen has fallen! Wasting his summers teaching Health to a bunch of barely pubescent children!) are a combination of my father's from Oxford and my old roommate George's from MIT.

Galen is all over it, too, he's throwing in as much reality as he can to make it all work and he's paying keen attention to everything I'm saying. I get this part of his game, and I don't care. I'm not using real names and I'm not pulling out any facts that might be traced back anywhere. But I'm one big mess of nostalgia, the whole night, and there's no better mood for me to be in for Sean to buy this ruse completely. He's lapping it up.

And I'm not the only one talking, obviously. I get all my lingering questions answered as the night wears on.

Turns out Sean is the one who painted those pictures hanging up in Galen's house – his darling mother thought him a sort of prodigy when he was a child and sent him to all sorts of classes, and he considers it the one good thing his mama taught him. He likes nothing better than to throw paint around of an evening in his office that's really more of a studio.

Bonks was a 'vain attempt at foppery', as Sean so whimsically puts it – he was a mall purchase, an oh-my-God-isn't-he-*adorable* buy, a regular Scottish gentleman's hunting dog. And then Sean spoiled the hell out of him and they got Bonks. I ask where the name 'Bonks' came from, and the answer is mostly that Bonks's darling puppy head made that sound whenever he'd crash into a cabinet playing with a ball on the slippery linoleum floors of Sean's kitchen.

For kicks I ask about Galen's dog as well, this 'Cujo-style

beast' I happened to meet when I arrived at Galen's house earlier this afternoon. Sean gushes immediately that Anon is easily the gentlest dog that ever did walk the earth, he's gorgeous and brilliant and just such a sweetie. Galen grins at my transparent compliment-fishing and Sean's innocent trample directly through my trap, and he adds,

"He's cunning, I'll give him that."

I grin. "I still can't get over you having a dog, you always used to hate them."

"Yeah, well, Anon conned me good," Galen replies coolly, still smiling. "He's a real charmer, that dog."

And I get a fair history lesson too, after that. I know Sean's story pretty well, but Galen manages to drop a few more references to his own childhood out in Arizona, a history I duly appreciate. They tell me about their recent trip to the Mediterranean, where Sean got the idea to paint Oia – Sean headed out 'solo' on a backpacking trip starting in Lisbon and ending in Cairo that lasted a full summer two summers ago, all on Dad's dime. Sean carefully selected the pictures that he showed Mum and Dad when he returned. Galen happens to mention – I'm sure for my sake – that he was amazed how many strays there were in Greece just hanging around like they owned the place. Yet another reason to travel there when I get around to it, Galen, thank you.

And Galen has also traveled to England – he and I apparently took a trip back to see my home town, in Harwich near the coast. In reality I've never been there, and luckily Galen doesn't persist too long discussing the trip for which I have to fabricate literally everything and mostly end up nodding and 'yeah'-ing my way through. I think he's trying to hone in on where I'm really from. It'll never work.

After dinner Sean and Galen both explain that the entire area around Rittenhouse Square is absolutely awful on a Monday night for any sort of proper partying, and I reply hastily that I have no problem maybe going somewhere lonely and getting a table and a couple rounds of beers on me. I've brought every penny I own to this dinner tonight. I owe these guys *something*. And I'm not a huge fan of clubs, and I'm getting less so with every passing year as a wolf. This social anxiety I'm developing is really not healthy.

So we walk through the square and sort of meander around aimlessly for a while, and I find it heartening that out in public Sean and Galen stay well enough apart as we walk – no touching, no hand-holding, and in fact often as not I end up walking in the middle between them. I really wish I knew whether this dissociation is their natural tendency when other people are around, or if they're both doing it in deference to Mike, or if Galen is doing it in deference to me.

We end up at a hole in the wall bar, and park ourselves at a corner table with a few beers. After about ten minutes Sean begs leave to hit the restroom, leaving Galen and me alone at the table.

"You're holding up better than I thought you would," Galen says with a smile.

I grin. "I would love to know what you were planning to do if Sean saw through me."

Galen shrugs. "I don't know. I really ought to have thought of a better cover story. Obviously it's going to be difficult for Sean to ever meet the real Mike, now. I don't know – I thought, you know, the ID and everything, I wasn't thinking it through when I told Sean that Mike was coming to town."

"Yeah, well, I think you're in the clear," I say. "If he starts suspecting tonight just say it's all been a joke, like a running bet between you and Mike and me and I'm really… I don't know, some other old college buddy or something."

"Fair," Galen agrees with a nod.

Sean reappears momentarily, and not long after that we decide to call it a night. There's a bit of confusion while Sean offers to sleep over so Galen doesn't have to make a detour to drop him off, but I can tell Galen's not at all keen to have Sean asking questions about where Anon's run off to or where Mike's luggage and car are, and he finally convinces Sean that Bonks can't be left alone like that overnight. So we drop Sean off and head home, and I spend the night human on the couch to sleep off the wine and beer.

*   *   *

I don't actually wake up the next day until almost midday, when Galen comes and shakes me awake. I'm too groggy to really work out what he's going on about, but I get the gist: Mike is coming soon and Galen doesn't want to explain away a strange man sleeping on his couch.

So I stumble up the stairs to throw my clothes in their secret hiding place under the bed near the headboard before I transform… and not a moment too soon, it turns out. I can hear a car door slamming shut outside as I lumber back down the stairs in canine form.

Galen opens the door before the real Mike makes it all the way up the walk. Galen dashes out to meet him and they hug there in the yard, exchanging excited greetings. Mike is exactly like I pictured him — self-assured, easygoing, sarcastic. It's been more than a year since they've seen each other, and Mike has a lot to say about Galen's 'ridiculous' shorter hair, and Galen remarks that Mike must have put on a few pounds, typical catching-up comments. And then Mike catches sight of me standing in the doorway.

"Are you kidding me?" he says dryly, shaking his head at Galen. "You got a house pet?"

"He's a stray," Galen explains with a shrug. "He just deigns to stay with me, really."

"Still," Mike says. He heads up the walk to greet me, petting me behind the ears. "What's his name?"

"Anon," Galen answers. Mike grins at him.

"You are such a poser," Mike says. "You conform to anti-establishment so seamlessly."

Galen shrugs, smiling. "Yeah, well."

"And look at this place!" Mike declares, looking around the living room. "Who are you and what have you done with the real Galen?"

"The office looks normal," Galen assures him, gesturing off to the left. "You want a tour before we go?"

"Oh, absolutely yes."

I follow them as they wind through the house and exchange

119

standard pleasantries: how was the drive, when are you planning on heading out, how is Sean, how is Dominique, how're the parents, et cetera. The tour is brief, and before I know it we're back in the living room and Galen and Mike are heading out the door.

"Guard the house, Anon," Galen calls to me, and with that he closes the door and they're off.

And that's the last of the excitement for at least a couple of weeks. When they come back three hours later Mike stays only long enough to use the toilet, and then he's off to Florida. Galen spends the rest of the afternoon at the computer before Sean calls around five and says he's off work, and in another hour Sean is over at our house with Bonks for another overnight stay.

The rest of the week passes uneventfully. I've had quite enough of being human for a while, and spend practically the entire time canine.

We fall into a routine, Galen and I. The day always starts with a morning run, and then comes breakfast, and then I head back to sleep while Galen heads into his office to while away the morning. Then Galen heads off to meet Sean for lunch and runs errands in the afternoon, or he comes home and we watch a movie, and then evening comes and Sean gets off work and either he comes over or Galen goes over there.

I love this routine. It's like a return to the status quo, to my normal life where I'm just playing dog again. It's comfortable. It's static.

The next week is more of the same, though I gradually begin to throw in more hours a day in human form. I don't venture out of the house. Instead I take up cleaning, as the least I can do to repay Galen for his monumental kindness. I vacuum, I scrub the toilets, I wash windows, I muck out the microwave. The microwave turns out to be one task too many, Galen hurriedly explains as he pours a can of broccoli and cheddar soup into a bowl and throws it in on high for ten minutes, because Sean loves to tease him about that particular bit of filth. Also off-limits now are the soap scum in the bath tub and any dusting whatsoever, both of which are perfectly all right with me. And in my off time I continue my reading assignment, and Galen lets me borrow his iPod so I can start memorizing Ludo songs. I have three weeks to learn every word.

The next Monday I overhear Sean telling Galen that he's finally settled on a date to fly back and see his parents – he'll be heading out on Thursday the seventeenth and coming back the next Monday evening. They've been discussing this trip for a while – or rather, Sean's been bitching about it for almost a month now. He really despises heading back down south to visit the family. He has decided on these dates because his sister and baby niece will be there at the same time, which will make the trip almost palatable for him. Galen assures him that Bonks can come and stay with us, we're not doing anything that weekend. We don't do anything *any* weekend.

The news of Sean's departure has somehow changed Galen's demeanor. What's odd is that he seems not depressed, but actually sort of excited about the prospect of Sean being gone for four nights straight. I think I know what that means – and Galen confirms my suspicion later the next day after Sean has left to go off to work. Galen corners me in a brief moment of humanity while I'm in the bathroom. I recognize the necessity to catch me while I can still reply, but I really wish he'd find some way to ask questions when I'm not in the middle of other pressing matters. When he knocks on the door while I'm washing my hands, I sigh and yank the door open a crack, barely enough to see him through.

"Yeah?"

"So are you up for going out, next weekend?" Galen asks me.

I shrug, smiling only because I already saw this coming.

"Sure," I say noncommittally. "What'd you have in mind?"

"I don't know, just clubbing or something," Galen says. "When was the last time you went to a club?"

"I can't dance," I inform him immediately, reluctant at his choice of excursion.

"Neither can I," Galen says. "Come on, it'll be fun, I promise. I know a few good places, lots of cute chicks..."

"Sounds great," I agree with a forced smile.

CHAPTER 7

Next week, though, becomes this week far too quickly for my liking, and Saturday becomes today with very little fanfare on the part of the outside universe – which seems somehow unfair given the circumstances. That today should dawn warm and clear and only slightly breezy, rather than with some fantastic cataclysm in the form of a volcanic eruption or meteoric strike or the sinking of Philadelphia into the sea, seems utterly unsuited to my current mood.

I've lived as a human. I have no problem living as a human. I have a problem with living as a human with a human, and I have a serious problem with going out *as* a human *with* a human with *another* human's fake ID to a club with a *lot* of humans and more than a few very *critical* humans peering at me to see just how closely my face matches another human face.

It's not helping that the full moon peaked at four o'clock Friday evening, which means that the very first time I can consider turning human again is this Saturday morning, and in the meantime all I've been feeling is agitated and desperate for a fight.

I spent Thursday night and all of Friday curled up in a corner of the house trying to shove down the worst lunar mania I've felt in at least a decade, my mind reeling in tumbling circles of alternating paralysis and fury as I considered the fact that it was only this bad because of my worry over the ensuing weekend, and how this was all Galen's fault, and how ardently I wanted to kill him for it, actually murder him – and then that I was a sick monster for even thinking it, how Galen was the best thing that ever happened to me, how utterly beyond salvation I was as a werewolf, and most importantly how wildly deluded I was that I would even consider going out and potentially getting myself thrown in jail just so I could get a few drinks and dance a bit...

I considered bashing my head against the floor a couple of times to knock myself into blissful catatonia. And when Galen came into the back room to see if I was all right after hours having to listen to my truly subconscious whining, it was everything I could do to growl a warning at him without also getting up and hunting him down until I'd opened his carotid artery with my teeth. Thank Christ he got the message and left quickly.

So on Saturday morning, when I wake up on the floor to find sunlight streaming through the window, warming a patch of fur on my left leg as the day creeps its way across the rug, I transform immediately and head directly into the bathroom to drain the hot water in the shower.

After nights like these last two I want absolutely nothing at all to do with being canine, and it occurs to me as I'm sitting here with my face ensconced directly in the strongest part of the stream that perhaps this is how all the other werewolves feel after every full moon. I'm thinking back to my childhood moons, to the rules my family had in place about staying inside and out of sight, and realize that even though I was just a kid then and not much bothered yet by the world around me, even then I used to feel relief coming out of a moon and getting back to normality. And my parents, ever-vigilant and careful as they were, must have felt such a profound sense of helplessness that I can imagine the rage only served to make moons a living nightmare for the pair of them.

This is no life for anyone, these inescapable transformations, this madness. And one more time I'm thankful as hell for doing it the way I did it, choosing to live as a wolf, learning how to control the rage by virtue of habitual practice. I'm mentally congratulating myself for that completely unexpected personal betterment.

The shower is a fair solace, anyway, and I take a good long time to get clean. I rinse and repeat, I soap the bottoms of my feet and between my toes. I stand in the water until the skin puckers on the palms of my hands and I begin to feel a bit like a drowning rat. I take my time drying off, and emerge in a cloud of steam to the smell of bacon frying. I head to the kitchen to investigate.

Galen's standing over the stove in a shirt and shorts, yawning, hair a disheveled mess, tending two frying pans full of bacon and eggs, respectively. He looks up and smiles when I enter.

"Good morning," he greets me pleasantly.

"You too," I reply. I gesture to the stove. "You want me to take over?"

Galen frowns. "You know how to cook?"

I grin sheepishly. "No."

"Then you stay away from my breakfast," he says adamantly. His smile fades, and he looks suddenly serious. "Look, Anon, we don't have to go anywhere this weekend if you don't want to."

"No, it's fine," I assure him quickly. Now I get why he's actually bothered to make breakfast. A peace offering. "I'm, um, I'm sorry I snapped at you."

"You did warn me," Galen replies, referring to Tuesday night when I had the presence of mind to explain the moon to him and told him in no uncertain terms to stay away from me for a couple days. "But... that wasn't anything like the moon last month – June was like nothing."

"Generally they'll be more like June," I say.

"Because going out *does* bother you," Galen says.

"It does," I have to admit. Galen's about reply, but I continue before he can, "But I've got to get over it. If I can't hack playing human then I'm no better than any werewolf that can't hack playing dog."

"'Playing human'," Galen echoes with a thoughtful smile. "You really look at it that way?"

I shrug. "Probably more so than the rest do. But we're *not* human. And we're not dogs. We just happen to mimic you."

"Yeah, well, you do a fine job at both," Galen tells me. He starts pulling strips of bacon out of the frying pan with a pair of tongs in his left hand while stirring the eggs with his right in a fantastic ambidextrous spectacle. "Anyway, if you want any of this you'd better get a couple plates ready."

That afternoon Galen insists we head out to the mall so I can get some proper shoes –neither the trainers nor the loafers nor the flip flops are apparently acceptable for Philadelphia's nightclub scene. I can't remember when I last went shoe shopping – properly, I mean, not just corner store flip-flops – but my overwhelming hatred of the entire process comes back in a flash the moment we step into the store and Galen starts scanning the shelves. He's not doing so visibly, but I know he's inwardly laughing his head off at me the entire time I'm sitting there with the attendant learning what my shoe size is and trying on far too many shoes and walking around the store like an idiot in all of them.

And he must be a sadist, because when we don't find any appropriate pairs at the first store he insists we head to a second, and then to a third where we finally find a pair of... I don't know what the hell you'd call them, but they're made by Adidas – that suits both my staid sensibilities and Galen's impeccable sense of style.

We eat a late lunch at the food court, my treat, since Galen insisted on buying the shoes. He knows I'm down to just over two-fifty and can't afford to waste my money buying shoes I'm not particularly interested in purchasing in the first place. I'm also not keen on having Galen buy them for me, but there's really no way out of it as far as he's concerned. We eat at a table near the windows, sitting with a couple of burgers and fries discussing the immediate and eventual future.

"So is there anything else you want while we're here?" Galen asks me, and I shrug, swallowing a mouthful of fries before answering.

"I really don't need anything," I reply.

"Nothing?" Galen asks skeptically. "I mean you're... totally equipped for all eventualities tonight?"

I grin, frowning my confusion. "What's that supposed to mean? What am I forgetting?"

"Well, like a box of... I don't know, never mind," Galen says, taking a massive bite of his burger.

"What exactly do you envision happening, tonight?" I ask him slowly, amused. Now it's his turn to shrug.

"I don't know," he replies after a while. "You never know, right? Just thought you'd want to be prepared in case you're not going to head home with me, sort-of-thing."

"I seriously doubt I'll manage to find a way home with anyone else."

"You say three words to any girl tonight and you're going to have to fight her off," Galen assures me. I smile at the compliment, but fail to reply. He continues anyway, "When's the last time you got laid?"

"By a human?" I ask quietly, careful to make sure no one else is listening to our conversation. Galen's eyes open wide in shock, and suddenly he's grinning.

"Whoa, are you serious?" he asks, incredulous.

I sigh. "We've been over this."

"Yeah, but... wow," Galen says, still grinning. "I just never thought... huh. Then yes, to answer your question."

I concentrate for a moment, trying to remember what year it is. Wow. This *is* sad.

"Six years," I answer finally.

"Okay, then you're *definitely* buying some," Galen declares. "You can never count on a woman to supply her own."

"Don't you have any?" I ask, almost pleading. I really don't want to have to go and buy bloody condoms. Galen almost laughs.

"No," he says, shaking his head. "Please. What self-respecting monogamist still uses condoms?" I guess I can't suppress my outward cringe, because he pauses for a moment, studying me, smiling in that offhand manner. "Sorry to over-share."

"No, that's – that's fine," I assure him uncomfortably. He grins.

"You know," he says, "it's always been my observation that the less experienced someone is the more bigoted he is."

"Hey, okay," I warn, holding a hand up to stop him, and I can tell he knows he was stepping over the line with that comment. He meant to.

"I didn't mean it like that," Galen lies. "I mean that I think you've got to start lightening up already. I mean look at you – you haven't gotten laid in six years, you spend practically every day of your life sitting at home, you never go out and do *anything*. What kind of life is that, huh? When are you going to go out and live a little and maybe dump some of your less-than-PC phobias along the way?"

"Look, now is not the time, all right?" I say, gesturing pointedly to the other tables around us, chock full of ordinary Americans eating ordinary mall food.

"Now's the perfect time," Galen says. "You're living in the dark, my friend. I'm going to haul you out of it if it kills me."

I can't help but look away at that statement, because it hit far too close to home for my liking. He knows that thoughts of death and dismemberment have been weighing heavy on my mind ever since we started this mess. I know that he understands how I took it, and I'm pretty sure the double entendre was calculated.

"You know I was perfectly happy doing what I was doing?" I say after a while.

"...Until what?" Galen asks, smiling because he's incredibly good at picking up on grammatical quirks like that. "Happy until I started making you feel like shit about it, right? Happy until you realized you've just been deluding yourself for a decade and some. Because I don't really believe you, Anon, I don't think you're exactly halfway in between *anything*. You're too clever for that, you know which side you ought to be on. You've spent far too long being something you're not, and the longer you go the harder it's going to be for you to get out of it."

"But I don't *want*—"

"Of *course* you want," Galen interjects. "You're just scared. You're almost thirty years old and you're still running scared. When's your birthday, by the way?"

I stare at him. He knows he's not going to get an honest answer.

"Christmas."

He smiles. "Why not Halloween?"

I grin, shrugging and nodding my concession. "Halloween would have been better."

"You know, Sean always dresses Bonks up for Halloween," Galen says idly.

"Oh, God," I sigh.

Galen grins. We go back to eating, chewing in silence for a

while.

"How far are you in Catch-22?" Galen asks me eventually. I shrug.

"Somewhere in the middle," I reply. "Why?"

"No reason," Galen says lightly. "I was thinking if you've got some spare time you could spend it buying and selling stuff online. If you study it enough you can make some easy money."

"Is that a fact?" I ask with mock intrigue.

"Why not?" Galen says, shrugging. I pause for a moment to think about it.

"Can I use your laptop?"

"Of course."

"Maybe I'll take you up on that, then."

We meander around the mall for a while after that. Galen convinces me to get a belt, and buys himself a couple of shirts and a few DVDs, enlisting my help to find enough titles to fulfill the Buy 3 Get 1 Free requirement, and for good measure he gets a couple games as well.

It's already getting dark by the time we get back to his house, and he offers me first shower so he can decide exactly what he wants to wear. I dart upstairs to grab a black shirt of Galen's from the closet – I'm already wearing tonight's trousers – and take my ten-minute shower downstairs.

I hear the one upstairs turn on only after I'm done, as I start to brush my teeth and arrange my hair into some sort of working order. The hot water doesn't like being split between floors, unfortunately. Galen takes twice as long as I did, and I'm sure the hot water must be running out by the time I hear it shut off. I've already taken the iPod from the office into the bathroom while I go about shaving and throwing on some toner and face lotion. God damn Galen for turning me bloody metro.

Galen says it's worthless to get to this club much before eleven, so we sit around and eat pizza and play his new first-person shooter until a quarter to before piling into his beat-up Civic to head into town.

The club is nestled in a pretty shitty neighborhood, but the parking is easy enough. The line isn't long yet, either. Just two groups of people later I'm handing my fake ID over to the bouncer, a big, ugly white guy with an unfortunate goatee and a lot of unfortunate tattoos, the kind of guy who waxes his head to mask his gratuitous male pattern baldness. He stares at the picture for a while, scrutinizing it under his black light, then checks my face. I'm halfway to a heart attack before he hands my ID back, but he doesn't question me about it and Galen and I get waved through.

We pass through a couple of entry rooms, the standard coat check and a sitting room, before we get to the main room. It looks dark and cozy, with a couple of bars and a dance floor off to one side. It's not too busy, though there are enough people here that it becomes immediately clear that in an hour or two this whole place is going to be packed. I'm all ready to park myself somewhere with a drink, but Galen keeps moving.

I follow Galen up a flight of steps into a second floor filled with people, a whole mass of people dancing in time with the steady thumping of some deafening techno remix, red-yellow-blue-green lights flashing everywhere in the relative darkness.

This place is jam-packed with gorgeous girls. Everywhere I look I see dark, blonde, brunette, ginger, tall, short, waifish, curvy, voluptuous, wearing pink and black and gold and green, tall heels and flat slippers, piles of jewelry, with liquid lips and eyes buried under layers of meticulously applied powder and gloss and glitter.

In one corner there's a massive flock of them, a gaggle of females all huddled together like castaways drowning in a sea of men's ill-executed advances. It's a hive of nurse bees surrounding their queen, the most magnificent black-haired, doe-eyed goddess you've ever seen – she's wearing a criminally tight black dress and a tiara, she's beyond plastered, she's the epicenter of a Hollywood-style bachelorette party. I don't have to catch Galen's pointed glance my way to know that group's going to be the easiest, that the girls on the periphery are like sick gazelles practically begging to be picked off from the herd.

Galen leads the way over to the bar and offers to buy the first round. I take him up on it reluctantly, and in a minute I'm downing a pint of some awful beer I've never heard of and trying to stay out of the way of what seems like a sudden excess of people all shoving forward to order drinks. And then the song changes, shifts fluidly into some new, equally loud techno song, but Galen's eyes light up when he recognizes the new melody.

"Oh hell, come on," he shouts, gesturing for me to follow him out onto the floor. I hang back. I *really* can't dance, and I don't want to have to prove it. He sees my hesitance and sighs dramatically. "Come *on!*"

"Next song," I call back, and he grins, shaking his head.

"Fine, hold this," he says, handing over his beer, and warns, "I'll be back for that."

"I'll only drink it if I finish mine," I shout, and he laughs and then disappears into the crowd. I think I catch a glimpse of him making his way toward a blonde Amazon dancing out in the middle of the crowd.

"Hey, are you from London?"

I look over to see a small pixie of a girl batting long black lashes in my direction. She's practically half my height, dyed blonde-and-black hair cropped short to frame a kittenish round face, purple strapless dress hanging loose and clinging sensually to the convex curves of her petite, perfectly rounded little figure. She's absolutely marvelous.

"No," I reply cordially, "but I am from England."

"I thought so," she declares with a sweet grin, her voice girlish, flirtatious. "I went to London last summer."

"Did you?" I reply. "And how did you like it?"

"Oh my God, it was *amazing*," she gushes, big brown eyes opening wide on amazing's second syllable, leaning in for emphasis. "I had the *best* time."

"I'm glad to hear it," I tell her with a smile. I shift Galen's beer to my left hand and hold my right out to her. "I'm Mike."

"Adrianna," the girl replies, her meticulously manicured hand shaking mine in that really annoying, limp-wristed way that pampered girls have. I can't tell if she wants me to do something hackneyed and gentlemanly like kiss her knuckles.

"Charmed." I pull away, gesturing to the bar. "Can I get you a drink?"

"Oh, no, I'm all right," she replies, holding up a cup I hadn't noticed. It's half full of ice and a quarter full of something hideously blue.

"So where are you from?" I ask, trying to speak loudly over the music, grasping for small talk.

"Do you dance?" she counters, gesturing out toward the dance floor. I sigh inwardly.

"Not well," I admit, plastering on a smile. She shrugs.

"Me neither. Let's dance."

I give up and let her take my hand again, and she drags me with cruel haste out into the fray. Luckily I don't have to do much, just sit there and move a bit in rhythm with her while she does all the work, gyrating wildly and grinding her ass into my trousers, then turning around and clamping a hand on my hip to lock me in against her while she straddles my leg and moves her way up and down the length of my body.

She smells like vanilla, her teeth are sparkling white and her purple eyelids are flecked with glitter. I can see the underwire of a lavender satin bra from my vantage point a foot above her head. She's not leaving all that much to the imagination anyway, in that outfit. Her breasts are small but perfectly shaped, and shoved so high they threaten spill over the brim of her dress. Her caramel skin is silky, unblemished, her arms rounded and supple. She's soft, and small, and erotically sexy. I'm wondering if the bathrooms have lockable doors.

The song ends a few minutes later, and I'm all ready to drag her back off the floor, but her reaction to the ensuing song is frighteningly similar to Galen's reaction to the previous. This song is slower, and I don't recognize it immediately, though the tune is lurking teasingly on the edge of memory. Adrianna sneaks an arm tight around my waist, pressing against me.

"Oh, I *love* this song," she breathes, smiling broadly, eyes half-closed in a gaze of utter lustful reverence. For half a second her look reminds me of Sophie, the way she looks when out of the blue she hears the first few bars of a song she adores. I've died to give in to that look. All of a sudden I'm perfectly happy to play the insert-male-body-here role, which is really all this look of Adrianna's is requesting. She rests her head on my chest and hugs me amicably for a brief moment before pulling away, arms still wrapped around me, swaying as she sings.

I still can't place the song when the chorus starts, but Adrianna is singing along blissfully. I spare myself an ironic smile. Standard top forty muck, that's this song, and I think I've got Adrianna pegged by now. I don't mind, and in a way I appreciate her taste. I definitely appreciate her body. She doesn't have to be brilliant, too.

She's really gorgeous. It's all I can think about as we dance, both with hands around each other's waist like we're at senior prom, her pulling me close and hugging me every few moments in a fit of gleeful bliss at the song, and hopefully at the company.

The song ends, and another fast techno song starts up. She pulls away, wrinkling her nose in disgust at the music.

"Think I could use that drink now, honey," she declares, grabbing my hand yet again and leading me benevolently away from the floor. I follow like a good puppy all the way to the bar, where she slurps down the rest of her blue concoction and leans heavily against the bar's edge, breasts pressing down into her arm to create that excess cleavage illusion. I lean over as well.

"What do you want?" I ask her.

"Vodka cranberry," she orders, and I oblige, flagging down the bartender after a moment and ordering for her. I give up a precious ten in exchange for a drink that's mostly ice with a hint of pink. When I turn to give it to Adrianna I see her talking animatedly with another woman, some tall ginger with half a million freckles and perfect dimples framing her toothy, pristine smile, wearing easily the sluttiest black nothing of a dress I've seen yet tonight. Adrianna's eyes brighten up at the sight of the drink, and she squeaks her delight when I hand it over. She gestures to her friend.

"Mike, this is my sister Lizzy," she says.

"Sister?" I ask doubtfully.

"Sigma Kappa," they announce together, and immediately turn to each other and giggle at their inadvertent simultaneity. Great.

"So you're college girls, then?" I ask with a polite smile, and they nod. "What're you ladies studying?"

"Communications," Adrianna says, and Lizzy adds,

"Marketing." Such laudable, *grueling* pursuits. Perfect for suntanning and husband-seeking.

"How about you?" Adrianna asks. I falter.

"I'm, ah…" not at all prepared for this eventuality, in fact. I fail to think fast. "I'm an accountant."

"Really?" Lizzy asks as they both frown their confusion. She grins. "But you seem so normal."

"Normal but for an inordinate fondness for numbers." And a tendency to chase cats.

Just then Galen appears out of nowhere, hitting my shoulder. I don't immediately recognize that it's him, and in that initial split second I'm wondering anxiously which of these fantastically sexy young ladies has a boyfriend I probably should have asked about. But then he speaks, and my brain kicks back into gear.

"You didn't drink mine, did you?" Galen demands, and I smile and hand back his cup. I gesture to the ladies and make the introductions both ways. Adrianna and Lizzy appear to approve highly of Galen, both fixing on him like kittens with a new mouse. I'm instantly regretting having admitted I knew him at all.

"And what is it you do, Galen?" Lizzy asks him.

"Ah, bit of a jetsetter, really," he replies, eyebrows raised in typical Galenic mock-arrogance. "And I dabble in high school English teaching – humanitarian style of thing."

Lizzy seems to think it's brilliant.

"Buy me a drink?" she croons.

Galen grins. "Absolument, ma belle."

Which leaves me alone again with Adrianna. She doesn't particularly mind. In fact, we're alone for only a moment before she catches sight of another woman a little way off gesturing wildly to her.

"Mercedes!" she cries happily, shouting practically across the room at the other girl, "Oh my God, girl, I *completely* forgot!"

"What's up?" I ask.

"Come on," Adrianna beckons, pulling me forward toward Mercedes. "I forgot I was on my way to a Jägerbomb, I'm sure they've already done it, oh well…"

And she leads me directly into the gaggle of girls I noticed earlier. I'm stunned – blinded, more like, by all the glitter. For the most part they're all amazing, this group of almost a dozen girls. Adrianna drags me by the arm over to yet another woman on the other side of the group, shouting her name repeatedly until she catches her attention.

"Lana! Lana, Lana, Lana, come here, girl! *Lana!*"

Lana – hourglass figure in cobalt blue, auburn hair, big brown eyes, milk white skin – finally looks up just as we get within reaching distance and flashes a full-lipped smile. "Dree, darlin', where you been?"

"La-la," Adrianna declares to her breathlessly (God save me, I'm so tired of the pet names!), "Girly, you have *got* to hear this boy talk."

"Oh?" Lana asks, perking up and giving me a good once-over. I'd give her one too if I didn't think it was going to ruin my chances. This one looks even more high-strung than the rest. Even so, I'm already grinning at just how accurate Galen's prediction was.

"She's got a thing for Brits," Adrianna tells me conspiratorially.

"Imagine that – I've got a thing for Americans," I reply with a smile. Lana's eyes light up when I begin speaking, and she shoots a look at Adrianna, who nods back in a way I'm sure she thinks is subtle.

"*Anyway*," Adrianna says, "I'll leave you two be for a while, I'm going to check up on Kitty."

"She and Trina are in the bathroom," Lana calls as she turns to leave, and Adrianna waves her acknowledgement before disappearing into the crowd again. Lana watches her go, and then turns back to me.

"You want to go somewhere else?"

An hour later I'm downstairs hanging out on one of the couches with Lana, trying to decide how much more conversation I'm supposed to make before it's appropriate to offer to let her take me back to her place. Even a blind man could see it's heading that way – she keeps begging drinks, I keep buying, and she just gets more and more infatuated and slutty and gorgeous with each one. I've told her my entire fabricated

134

life story, and she's told me twice as much of her real one. She keeps pawing on me – touching my arm, putting a hand on my leg, leaning her head on my shoulder – whenever she gets the chance. I can't deny I'm doing some of the same toward her. Right now she's telling me about how she thinks American guys don't have any idea how to kiss a girl. I'm neither too drunk nor too dense to see this is a clear invitation.

And then I smell it. Out of nowhere, all of a sudden there's this overpowering stench – of wolf.

There's a werewolf here. *There's a goddamn werewolf here.*

Lana's still talking but I stop listening instantly, looking around frantically for the source of the smell. It's so crowded in here, it could have come from any one of these dozens of people passing by all around us, and I can't very well get up and go after the scent without looking patently suspicious.

There's no one paying us any sort of attention right now – all I see is a lot of backs and very few faces. I'm kicking myself for not focusing better, not watching these people around us to see who's been listening in. I can't even tell if the smell is incidental or intentional, if I was meant to notice it or even if the owner of it happened to notice my own. I know I've got a better hominid sense of smell than any other werewolf I ever knew, and it's entirely possible I've gone unnoticed—

"Hey, what's wrong?" Lana asks, and I snap back into reality reluctantly.

"Nothing," I assure her, "it's just getting claustrophobic in here."

"You want to get out of here, then?" Lana offers with a sweet, coy, predatory sort of smile. I can't fully appreciate her direct attitude now that I'm lost in wolf-anxiety mode. I'm thanking God for her offer for more than one reason, now.

"Definitely," I agree without hesitation, putting on a smile for her. She doesn't waste any time – she gets up immediately, taking my hand and heading directly out the front door with me in tow.

We make it outside without incident, but all the while I'm scanning the club and the entrance and the car park for any sign at all of another wolf. It occurs to me that if the other wolf noticed me, I could be in for a serious confrontation in the next few moments – and I've just pulled the girl into it, too.

I breathe a sigh of relief when we get to her car and she drives off down the street without anyone paying us any attention.

CHAPTER 8

I wake the next morning to find Lana still asleep next to me, sprawled over the entire width of her bed with an arm and a leg thrust well beyond her side and into my territory. Sunlight is already streaming in through the windows. I rub my face to wake up, and then I inch ever-so-carefully out of the bed, careful not to wake her. This involves a lot of stopping and starting on my part, as I listen with bated breath to the ins and outs of her light snoring and pause every time her breathing does. I grab all my clothes up off the floor silently and head into the other room to get dressed. And then I head out the door and wait at the bus stop to catch a ride back across town toward home.

I resolve not to tell Galen anything about my night out of the house – and especially not anything about the real reason for me leaving the club without even having the decency to find him and tell him where I was going. I've successfully shoved it from my own consciousness until now, as I'm sitting on the bus trying to seem unobtrusive. It's been so damn long since I've smelled any wolf other than myself... I'd almost begun to believe werewolves didn't really exist in the States. I wish like hell I could have seen who it was. The other wolf could easily have gotten a very good look at me, after all, and here I don't even have any idea if it was a man or a woman. To be perfectly honest, now that I'm well out of it I'm not entirely sure it wasn't a hallucination – this nose is good, I've no doubt of it, but I wasn't forty-eight hours outside of a moon last night and God knows I've had weirder things happen in that post-lunar fog. It's possible it was a mistake, a reaction to the crowd, the claustrophobia...

I'm trying to decide how to respond, now. Instinct is telling me flatly to run. Ego is insisting that I'm probably safe, that even if it was real there's no way that wolf could know who I am or where I live or anything of the sort. Cold logic is agreeing, throwing out reassuring probabilities and convincing points about the nature of wolves and their general reaction to outsiders, which is instant and severe – if anything was going to happen it would have happened by now. Conscience is siding with instinct, though, pointing out gently that I can't possibly be one hundred percent sure I wasn't followed and I'm not risking further exposure by staying in Philadelphia. Fear is screaming for me to go. Hope is dead set on staying. Optimism and pessimism are at war, and it's turning ugly. Reason is wavering. I'm just trying to stay afloat.

The pros and cons of running begin to line themselves up before me as I sit staring forlornly out the window at the passing scenery. First con: I haven't finished my reading assignment.

The fact that this is the first con that comes to my mind, and that I thought of this con before any pros at all, gives me pause. Because it's not accurate, is it? Who gives a damn whether I read a damn book or not? I'll get around to it – if I play my cards right I've got another half-century ahead of me to read any bloody book I want to. The real con is that I'm not done with that house. In part I'm scared to desert a human who knows what I am. I can't monitor him from afar. I know logically I don't need to, but this unease about Galen's sense of restraint isn't ever going to leave me.

But even more palpable than my fear of exposure is my desire to maintain continuity. I like hanging out with someone who knows what I am. It's… a relief. No, it's more than that. It's fucking fantastic. I've spent a decade entrenched in a world that doesn't have any clue what I am. A decade! The first time in almost thirteen years that I can discuss my real existence with someone, and then a bloody werewolf comes along to ruin everything.

The pros of running are obvious. Safety, first. I can argue it all I want, but there is just no way to be *sure*, absolutely sure, that whatever wolf was in that club last night doesn't have any idea who I am. Maybe the other wolf saw us walk up, saw who I came in with, saw Galen's car. It's unlikely, even I'll admit that. But it's not guaranteed.

The much less intriguing pro of moving on is that I can move on the way I should have last time. I can get my money, move to another city, get a job where no one asks too many questions, and seriously sit down to work out a way to live human again indefinitely. I can have my own place, go out, eat real food, all the myriad things that make humanity more appealing than caninity.

But I'm getting all those kicks *now*. Galen went *way* out of his way to get me this ID so I can go anywhere I want to. And he's perfectly willing to let me eat whatever I can find in his house. And whenever Sean's not around, he's not at all averse to having a human roommate.

This is stupid. I can see what I'm doing. I'm just blinding myself to the dangers of staying because I'm desperate to keep Galen around, aren't I? That sounds bad. But it's true. He's the most genuine person I've ever met. He's a fantastic friend. Hell, he even calls me a friend. It hadn't really occurred to me to think about it like that, but he's really the first honest-to-God friend I've ever had. Even when I was a kid I was a loner, and I certainly didn't associate with my fellow classmates, not like kids are supposed to. What werewolf kid can really afford to have friends, living the kind of life he does?

So what kind of friend will I be, eh, if it turns out I'm wrong and a strange werewolf now knows who I'm staying with? Am I not now risking his safety as well as my own...?

No. It'll be fine.

Everything's going to be fine.

I arrive back at Galen's house a little after ten to find the door locked, so I knock and wait impatiently. Galen's grin is threatening to pull off both sides of his face when he comes to open the door for me, gesturing me inside.

"*Told* you," he declares, and I shrug, heading directly to the refrigerator to find something to eat. It's not got terribly much to offer, unfortunately – a two-week-old apple, a tub of cottage cheese, a couple of slices of last weekend's pizza and a head of lettuce. I give up and head for the cupboards. Galen has gone to the back door to let Bonks in, and the instant the door opens I've got whiteness zipping eagerly about my feet. I ignore him too. Galen comes into the kitchen and leans against the counter, grinning at me all the while. He finally realizes I'm not going to say anything, so he begins, "So? How'd it go?"

"Well," I answer, still searching. Ah! Cookie Crisp. Perfect.

"Oh, come on," Galen says. I head back to the fridge for the milk. Galen hates it if the milk stays out for more than a few fractions of a second – one of his many quirks. He's probably not going to be thrilled I've grabbed the milk out before pouring the cereal into the bowl. Ah, well. He can deal.

"It went well," I repeat finally. I'm in no mood at all for this sort of interrogation right now. I don't want to talk about it. I don't want to think about it. I just want to forget last night happened.

"She looked cute," Galen says. I remember that I last saw him as Lana was dragging me downstairs last night – he flashed me a thumbs-up.

"She was," I agree, nodding, pouring the cereal and then the milk. Out of deference to Galen I put the milk back before rifling through the drawer for a spoon.

"So you had a good time?" Galen asks. I sigh.

"Can I at least eat something?" I say pointedly, leaning against the counter with bowl in one hand and spoon in the other.

Galen agrees with a smile, heading to the refrigerator himself for something to drink. He emerges with the orange juice carton, unscrewing the cap and drinking out of it directly. He hates drinking orange juice out of a glass. Doesn't see the point, he says. He's just lucky no one in his life appreciates proper etiquette. He chugs half the carton down in one breath, caps it again in an officious sort of way, and clunks it back on the shelf before grabbing the apple. He takes one huge bite, and instantly spits it out in the sink with a grimace of revulsion. He tosses the apple into the trash, snubbing it disdainfully, "Mealy-ass piece of shit."

These diversions allow me to make it halfway through my first bowl before he starts in again.

"Just tell me you got some," he says, "and I'll stop."

"Why?" I ask, frowning. I take another bite of cereal, continuing around a mouthful of miniature cookies, "What's it doing for you, exactly? Will it satisfy your matchmaking wishes?

140

Your vicarious desires? Your sense of altruism? Or do you want to feel like a good owner for finding your dog a suitable bitch?"

"Hey, come on now," he warns, holding up a hand to stop me. "It's just good form to let a wingman know his efforts weren't wasted, that's all. No need to get hostile."

"They weren't wasted," I assure him. He smiles but refuses to reply, expecting more. I give up. "What do you want me to say? Positions?"

"Plural?" he asks with a grin. I sigh again and he laughs at my total disinterest in continuing the conversation, but to his credit he backs off. "Fine, fine. Glad you had a good time. You want to go out again tonight, then?"

"Yeah, sure," I say, forcing nonchalance. I can't seem weird about it, I can't let on what really happened last night. I don't need to worry anyone else with my psycho mess. Galen's right, I need to get out more if this is how I react to my first try. "Why not?"

I'm upstairs later that evening brushing my teeth to head out when I hear the door open downstairs.

I freeze. Galen's in his bedroom, which means...

"Honey, I'm home!" Sean's singsong voice echoes in the living room. Bonks starts barking madly, rocketing down the stairs to greet his master.

I panic. I dart into the bedroom, undoing my trousers as I go. Galen is already panicking enough for the both of us – he's gesturing me wildly into the closet, bolting out of the room to go meet Sean on the stairs.

"What are you doing home so soon?" I can hear Galen asking Sean breathlessly while I yank off the trousers and then the boxers, looking around desperately for a place to stash them. I settle for the hamper, stuffing the jeans and pants in among Galen's other clothes, and I transform.

If I thought the two seconds in front of Galen that first time dragged on forever, I was mistaken. This is torture, sitting here in the closet praying that Sean doesn't appear around the corner while I ooze with geological slowness from one form to the other.

But in a moment it's over, and I take a second to calm down before trotting out to greet Sean on the landing. He's made it all the way up the stairs by now, and he greets me with a smile.

"Hi, Nonny!" he cries, bending down to grab me up in a hug and kiss me on the forehead. Bonks is leaping ecstatically around us, barreling into me in an effort to win all of his owner's undivided attention. Sean's petting both of us as he looks up to Galen, continuing some explanation I didn't hear the beginning of. "I took it for about an hour and then I just left – like mid-sentence. Christ Almighty, it was awful."

"Sounds like it," Galen says sympathetically. "Well hey, I'm proud of you, baby. At least it's not hanging over you anymore."

"Yeah, that's so *awesome*," Sean agrees sarcastically, standing again. "Seriously, all I want to do is go to bed and never leave."

Galen smiles. "I think I can arrange that."

And that's when I book it down the stairs.

Bonks stays planted firmly outside the bedroom door upstairs for the next hour. I battle myself for a good forty-five minutes about whether or not I should join him. I can't really stomach the idea of heading up there. But I'd be a terrible dog if I didn't wait faithfully for my owner to emerge as well, and I've got to keep up appearances for Sean. Every step is murder on my ego as I grudgingly head up the stairs to take my own place at the end of the hall, waiting with Bonks for the dinner-preparers to appear.

This is how I'm able to hear a conversation through the door that turns my stomach to knots.

"Since when do you wear boxers?" I hear Sean ask curiously after a while, having undoubtedly headed into the closet to find something of Galen's to throw on. Galen *doesn't* wear boxers, he only wears boxer briefs. It pains me that I know that, but I do all the laundry these days. That question alone practically knocks the wind out of me, and I stop breathing in order to hear Galen's reply.

"Since I almost froze my nuts off this winter in bed," Galen explains, sounding amazingly blasé about it. "They're like the perfect combination of warmth and freedom of movement."

142

"I've never seen you wearing them."

"Yeah, well I don't need them when you're around, do I? You're a furnace. What're you getting dressed for, anyway?"

Sean's reply is too quiet for me to pick out, but it sounds coy, and I begin again to breathe. It's another half hour before the door opens again, and nothing more is said about the boxers. But Galen shoots me a look as he follows Sean down the stairs – it's composed mostly of relief, with a generous portion of mutual understanding and just a dash of accusation. I nod, my human nod, so he knows I get it. It won't happen again, Galen, I swear.

In the end Sean doesn't seem altogether too suspicious about the boxers. He's too preoccupied with other matters, really. He and Bonks spend yet another night, and as Sean and Galen prepare dinner and eat dinner and then hang out at the table for more than three hours afterward going through the second of two bottles of wine, I eventually hear a play-by-play of Sean's entire family vacation in anything but chronological order. Let's put it this way: if I had Sean's family, I'd kill myself.

It goes something like this. Sean arrives at his parents' house by cab on Thursday evening to find that his sister and niece are not going to show up until Friday because they missed their connection in Dallas, which means he's stuck alone with his mother and father for a span of at least three excruciating waking hours. Sean has to put up with his mother's tendency to retell every story she already told him over the phone in the past six months, and then there's the standard tour of the house to check up on all the myriad changes she's made to her empty nest since he last saw the place the previous summer. And each of his parents somehow manages to bring up his lip ring a minimum of four times. And his mother asks if he's really going to a proper church in Philadelphia. And his father asks if he's nailed any pretty girls at his job. And his mother warns him again that if he gets a girl pregnant outside of marriage she will personally disown him, and that's when Sean gives up and asks for a beer.

The next day isn't terribly much better. Sean's natural tendency while on vacation is to sleep in, but his father manages to clank about loudly enough in the kitchen on his way into work that Sean's forced into chugging down a couple cups of coffee and heading out with his mother at nine to go and pick up the girls from the airport. His mother decides that the car ride is the perfect time to start discussing family with Sean, segueing into it by explaining how adorable little Alicia is now, as if Sean hasn't paid any attention at all to the twice-monthly e-mails full of baby photos his sister Emma has been sending since Alicia was born nineteen months ago.

His mother remarks what a gift it is to have grandchildren. She tells him that he's not getting any younger, and he might consider looking around seriously at his church the next time he goes – or better yet, he can look around Sunday at *their* church, because there are plenty of pretty girls in Memphis and she's sure he'll be able to find a lovely young lady to settle down with, and if he wants she's got some friends with daughters about his age that might be interested. And wouldn't it be wonderful to move back to Memphis, to be closer to family so they wouldn't have to see him only once a year, and just think what a joy it would be to have a wife and a couple of sweet children, and not to push too strongly, dear, but your father is hoping for a grandson to carry on the family name... Sean remains resolutely mute throughout.

His sister isn't quite the savior he wants her to be, either. Emma is a sweetheart, and easily Sean's favorite of his three sisters, but she's getting all caught up in motherhood at the tender age of twenty-one and every time he sees his baby sister with a baby it just depresses the hell out of him. The four of them have a fine afternoon together catching up, and when Sean's father comes home from work Emma springs the news on everyone: she's pregnant again. All sorts of ado and celebration ensue, though all Sean can think about is how much more his mother is going to be on his case this weekend now that she's got babies permanently on the brain.

By day three Sean's about ready to snap, as every single thing his parents say seems somehow to grate and as the days draw nearer to Sunday morning which is always Sean's very least favorite part of heading back to see his family.

In and of itself, Sunday Mass isn't ever all that bad for him. Stand up, sit down, kneel, sing, pretend to pray, try very hard not to burst out laughing. But there are two things that bother Sean immensely about Mass. The first is communion, which he simply can't get out of and which weirds him out as being strangely cultish and hedonistic. The second is his mother, who gets really into the whole thing and inadvertently makes Sean's life a living hell both before and after Mass as she goes on and on about how wonderful are the works of God and aren't we all so blessed and oh, there's Cindy and Claire, I'll bet you haven't seen Claire since you were a boy, you know I hear she's getting a law degree... It's a trial of endurance, really, Sunday Mass, and not for the first time does Sean consider that ironically he becomes a bit of a modern Jesus around his family, constantly turning the other cheek and accepting others' discreet opinions and blatant criticism with a commendable degree of modesty and restraint.

Sunday morning happens in typical fashion right up to the car ride. Everyone wakes up and heads into the kitchen for the standard eggs and bacon breakfast, for which Sean is tasked with cooking the bacon because it's apparently the one thing he *can* do right according to his parents. (Galen cracks a joke agreeing that he's an expert meat handler.) And then everyone rushes off to occupy the various bathrooms in order to get ready, and Sean pulls out the one staid outfit he owns to go to church.

The car ride is what finally tips the balance, and it's the lip ring that starts the ball rolling.

Sean's mother has been asking him since he woke up to please take it out for church. He's refused, because by now he's thankful to have anything at all to subtly jab his mother with, and he's hoping it makes him just objectionable enough to keep her from presenting him to all her old church friends like she always does. But she starts to get really insistent about it in the car, telling him it looks silly, and unprofessional, and it's utterly inappropriate for church, and then finally she pulls her trump card. She says, in that quiet undertone of hers that somehow manages to trip every possible button Sean has in him, that the lip ring makes him look gay.

'Well then it's doing its job,' he snaps. His mother pulls a full one-eighty from the front seat to stare at him in suspicious disbelief.

'What?'

And then it all just pours out of him, and the looks of horror on his parents' faces ratchet up with every single phrase. In retrospect, he says, those expressions were genuinely priceless.

'I'm gay,' he tells her, 'I've been dating guys since halfway through high school and I've got a boyfriend in Philly who I've been with for three years and I'd be perfectly happy to marry him.' (Galen grins at this statement, and Sean can't help but smile as well. Even I have to admit it's a nice sentiment.) 'I've never been interested in women and I never will be, and I'm sick of listening to you guys go on about it.' And then, for good measure while they're still stunned, he adds, 'And the Bible is a freaking fairytale.'

Immediately his mother orders his father to turn the car around, because they're heading directly back home in order to deal with this situation. And that's what lands him in that hour-long argument I overheard him discussing earlier – they've got him cornered and there's no way out of what fast turns into a really ugly fight. In the end he realizes he's never going to get anywhere with these people, and he heads to his room to call a cab and pack his bags. And he catches the first available flight out to Philadelphia and runs straight back into the arms of the only family he ever wants for the rest of his life. As he says with an air of jaded finality, swilling the last dregs of his glass before holding it out for a dutiful Galen to pour another round, "I always knew that the minute they found out, I was dead to them anyway."

I can tell this has all made Galen's day. Don't get me wrong, he's empathetic, and really feels wretched for Sean and wishes he could make it all better. But there's not exactly a Band-Aid big enough to fix this sort of rift, so he sits quietly and listens like a good boyfriend should, and assures Sean he did the right thing.

Galen has regularly complained – to me, his dog, who will tell no one – that after three and some years he's getting frustrated with Sean's persistent attachment to family, his constant emotional vacillations and his paralysis over the idea of moving in together and acting like any couple really ought to. As horrible as this situation is... it opens a door Galen has practically given up on hoping for anymore. Galen doesn't once bring it up tonight, though, moving in together. Sean's obviously still stunned he called the Bible a 'freaking fairytale' in front of his mother. He needs some time to process what he's done. And in the meantime all he wants is some good sympathy.

Sean's lease will be ending a few months down the road in November, and on Tuesday night Galen finally gets the request he's been waiting for – Sean asks to move in when his lease is up. Galen agrees immediately, and spends the rest of the week on Cloud Nine.

His bliss manifests itself as superfluous goodwill, of which I happen to be one recipient. I eat steak for dinner four out of the next five nights. And on Thursday, Galen agrees to write out a check to get the dog license for which I've taken the time to fill out the application. (I endure his crack about getting a discount if he gets his dog neutered with relative good humor.) He even offers to drop the envelope off at the post office for me. The license arrives in the mail the next week – which means free sailing if ever I want to go out wandering by myself, no more waiting for Galen to come home.

There is a critical wrinkle to Sean's imminent permanent arrival, however, one I'm sure Galen's already seen – in fact I'm sure his generosity is in no small part an act of conciliation as well. Because when Sean moves in, that's pretty much the end of my humanity in this house. The kid can't know the truth, it'd be a disaster. Hell, letting Galen know was disaster enough – and it's an absolute miracle I got caught by the one person on Earth who can resist telling even his steadfast partner such a wild secret. But Sean's too much like the rest of humanity, too heavily invested in intrigue and too sure of the confidence of all the many, many people in whom he trusts. It only takes one misplaced comment.

So it's back to caninity for me, sneaking around the place catching mere moments of human life when Sean's at work. Just like going back to finding a new roommate. Like falling back into a coma after a few fleeting, glorious weeks of consciousness. I find it ironic that not one week after I made the decision to stay in this house no matter the cost, if only because I finally realized the full value of living with someone who recognizes me as a werewolf, the whole thing unravels in front of me so damn effortlessly.

I'm not going to lie – I've thought repeatedly about leaving now that Sean's moving in. I almost did, the morning after the news, I got halfway out the door before Galen came back downstairs from his morning shower and asked where I was going. And I chickened out. *That close* and I just couldn't do it, I couldn't give that place up. I said I was going to the store, and I went to the store. And couldn't help but think this was probably one of the last times I'd be going to the store for a very long while.

But the truth is… it's not quite starting over, if Sean moves in. I've still got Galen. He knows what I am and he doesn't care, and he'll still advocate for me. The way he's acting now proves it. He's still going to find ways to help me out, like no roommate of mine has ever been able to do in the past. And for whatever crazy reason, he's happy to do it. What kind of idiot would I be to throw that away because the guy's boyfriend is moving in?

Besides, I don't have much time to ruminate before I've got to prepare for another human experience the likes of which I'm unlikely to see after November: the Warped Tour happens that first weekend after Sean's return.

Galen has not yet bothered to mention the third ticket to Sean, and after the near disaster Sunday night he's determined now not to mention it at all. This means that I get to take the bus and tackle the Warped Tour on my own. This is a serious challenge for my social agoraphobia and Galen knows it. He's apologetic, but he's not about to change his mind. The morning of the concert Galen tells me all the bands he really wants to see, and I promise not to go to most of them, and he assures me that if I stay on the left side of any crowd then he and Sean can hang on the right side and it's likely our paths will fail to cross.

In a way the concert is a strange sort of salve, a minor epiphany that calms my fears about how drastically Sean's presence is going to change my next few years. I get on the bus without incident, I get to the place just fine, and I have a pretty good time by myself. But I can't deny the fear that's lurking just below the surface the entire time I'm there, as I try not to panic when I go to get a beer and get my ID checked yet again, as I fail to suppress a growing, wary hyper-vigilance trying to keep track of everyone around me while I work my way through all these presses of drunk and excited and potentially violent people. I keep thinking someone is going to confront me or knock into me or similar and it's going to attract the attention of security or the police or the paramedics and then I will end up somewhere I *really* can't afford to end up. I can't relax, I can't force myself to have a good time when everything around me feels like another potential disaster waiting to happen.

I hang around the edges of the crowds and I drink my beer in unobtrusive silence and I can't help but think that humanity isn't bloody worth it. It may be boring playing a dog, and it may be annoying living without certain human comforts, but if it's between that and *this*, well, I think I've made my choice. I'll get through this concert alone, and I'll avoid Sean today like Galen asked me to, and then I'll happily resign myself to seeing the kid around a hell of a lot more often.

Despite our best efforts, though, Sean happens to catch sight of me in the crowd at the one set that none of us is keen to miss – the Ludo concert. Oh, but it starts so well…

I show up early for this one, ditching my drink and making my way into the crowd, because I'm absolutely determined to enjoy this. Pathetic as it sounds, this is the first proper concert I've ever been to – twenty-nine years old and until now I've only ever headed out to a couple of small in-town things. I've never been able to sing along with a live band before, and I've got Galen to thank for this opportunity. I am, needless to say, adamant that I not screw this up by thinking about what could go wrong.

The anticipation in the crowd is palpable as Ludo takes the stage, and I'm shoved forward by swarms of infatuated screaming girls and enthusiastic followers all pressing toward the band. And then the first song starts, the radio hit that even the least interested fans are familiar with, and everyone in the crowd starts jumping and singing – it's deafening, it's claustrophobic, it's so much more phenomenally fantastic than I thought it'd be.

Ludo is in the middle of their second song when out of nowhere I hear a familiar voice shout, "Mike!" and suddenly Sean's worming his way through the crowd toward me with a reluctant Galen in tow.

My heart stops. I wonder wildly if I can still get away somehow, dive through the crowd and ditch the concert and pray Sean doesn't try to follow – but it's far too late for that now. They're way too close.

Galen's still engrossed in the music, shouting lyrics at the top of his lungs as he gets pulled along. It's hilarious to watch, but I'm sympathetic to his euphoria. I was doing the same thing before Sean showed up.

"Oh my God, what are you doing here?" Sean asks me delightedly.

Galen doesn't even bother to acknowledge me – this is his favorite song playing right now, and he'll be damned if he misses it in order to deal with a phenomenally awkward social situation. The bastard's going to let me fend for myself. I smile politely.

"Just catching Ludo," I yell. "Don't have time to see it when they come to Boston."

"Why didn't you call us?" Sean asks. I falter.

"Didn't think you guys were going," I say with an unconvincing shrug.

"Yeah, but…" Sean says, trailing off. He seems to remember himself and turns to shout reprovingly at Galen. "Gale! Say hello!"

"No, no, good song," I tell Sean, gesturing to the stage, as Galen still refuses to let his singing be interrupted. Sean sighs and gives in, and lets himself be dragged forward into the crowd to jump along with us to the music.

After Ludo finishes on stage the three of us spend the rest of the day in each other's company, and Galen finally makes an effort to seem ecstatically surprised by my presence in Philadelphia. Neither of us can come up with a very good cover story for why I'm here without bothering to let either of them know I was coming, so Galen and I both pass it off as another Mike-style idiosyncrasy. It ends up being all right in the end, and

I manage to bow out gracefully after the concert by saying I have a train to catch back up to Massachusetts, and when Galen arrives home in the early morning hours I'm already asleep in the back room.

Galen tends to vacillate back and forth after the concert over whether it's a good idea to associate with me when I'm human – he's not at all keen on having Sean catch him out on the town somewhere he shouldn't be. Few opportunities arise in which it's even possible for me to be seen in public in Philadelphia anyway, though Galen never ceases to insist that I go out and have fun on nights when he heads over to Sean's to sleep. He's desperate to make up for having Sean move in, and he wants me to get really damn sick of going out before I'm no longer able to. It's futile to attempt to convince him I'm already at that point. I've tried.

In the next two months I take him up on the offer only twice, and both times are sufficiently innocuous for my low social stress threshold: I head out to a bar on a Friday in August, the weekend before Galen's school starts, and I treat myself to a solo dinner out in mid-September. I'm not keen to do much more than that. And Galen and I go out once, on a Saturday when Sean's off in Trenton attending a former classmate's twenty-fifth birthday party. The evening is limited to a few rounds of pool, at which I turn out to be comically inept. Galen's not much better, and as he tries to instruct me how to properly hit the cue ball it starts to look a bit like the blind leading the comatose.

I'm perfectly comfortable hanging out at home of an evening, anyway, as long as I get to spend it human while I still can. I spend most of my time now on the internet, buying and selling as Galen suggested. It's not that hard to keep my commercial venture from Sean – the mailman always arrives midmorning and I'm careful not to buy anything larger than can fit under Galen's bed. It's slow going at first, but I'm persistent. I can stare for hours at bid wars, perusing item after worthless, precious item until my eyes burn and my head is spinning with more irrelevant factoids than it can readily accommodate. I'm getting the hang of it quickly, and I can see the future looking very bright indeed.

By the end of the first month I've managed to make two

hundred and forty-six dollars, which puts me well ahead of my financial standing before I met Galen. I can finally start paying him back what I owe him. I could get used to this lifestyle – surfing the internet and listening to music, doing housework when I have to and doing whatever else suits my fancy when I want to. I watch embarrassing amounts of television, I take a shower every morning and many evenings, I drink beer, I occupy myself in plenty of unwholesome ways. I read constantly in this house of books, trying to fill the glaring gaps in my shoddy patchwork education – whenever I try and argue my points with Galen my untrained ineptitude definitely shows.

But I have put my most critical assignment indefinitely on hold. This isn't to say I'm not desperate to read it, to see what happens to Yossarian and the rest. It takes a level of self-restraint I've never before mastered to put that book down once I pick it up. I'm constantly rereading the parts I've already gotten to, and I advance about a page every other day or so to satisfy Galen's persistent nagging, but I think he realizes why I'm delaying. He understands my peculiar rationale behind failing to finish Catch-22, which has come to represent the only official requirement tying me to this house. He thinks I'm being ridiculous. He's told me more than once I can stay as long as I want, and he's actually threatened to kick me out if I don't just finish it because he's aching to discuss it with someone new. I don't care. I'm taking my time.

CHAPTER 9

Autumn announces its presence early this year – climate change gone mad – and the beginning of October is marked by showers of amber leaves falling on all the well-manicured lawns in this cozy little neighborhood that I'm starting to call home now. As prophesied by Galen back in July, Sean has already gone out and bought Halloween costumes for himself and Galen and both of their dogs. I can't help but feel Galen must have had a hand in picking a particularly emasculating one for me, though he swears up and down that he had nothing to do with it.

Sean came over two nights ago with the most outrageous ladybug costume I've ever seen (a bloody *ladybug*, can you believe it? Bonks at least gets to be a bumblebee, for God's sake) and insisted on trying it on to see if it'd fit me. I was forced to sit there in the living room groaning my futile canine protest while Sean manhandled the thing on me, all the while gushing over how 'downright absolutely *precious*' I looked. Honest to God, Galen actually collapsed on the damn floor he was laughing so hard. Needless to say I'm not looking forward to Halloween.

This particular autumn morning is a rather important one for Galen, who has his belated one-year performance review just before lunch.

He's been bitching about it for days, now. He's scared to death, though God only knows why, and his agitated insomnia kept me up half the damn night last night listening to him pace fretfully about his bedroom. He stumbled down the stairs a full hour earlier than normal this morning to go running, and now as he's pouring his cereal I'm in the living room still yawning, recovering from sleep deprivation compounded by exhaustion brought on by dangerously early exercise.

A car door slams outside, and I head to the window to investigate.

It's Sean. Odd...

He's storming up the walk, and his look is anything but pleasant. Not good. I'm trying to work out what's going on, what's got Sean looking so angry, wondering if there's any way I can warn Galen before Sean bursts through the front door.

The answer to that last one is 'no' — Sean's already got his keys out and he yanks open the screen, and Galen and I both hear the sound of the latch sliding back and all of a sudden Sean is standing in the living room, glancing my way for only a moment before he turns his attention to seeking out Galen.

"Hey, puppy," Galen calls to him pleasantly, curiously, heading in from the kitchen unaware of Sean's black mood. "What're you doing here?"

"*Don't* even start with me, Galen," Sean says. He's like one massive fireball of barely-checked fury. Galen shifts his demeanor instantly into meekly humble.

"What's wrong?" he asks softly.

Sean's already stormed past him into the office. Galen shoots me a nervous glance and I stare back, unable to reply. I think we can all see this is very, very not good.

"Have you checked Facebook yet today?" Sean asks, more shrilly than I'm sure he intends. Galen heads slowly into the office and I follow, trailing cautiously behind.

"...No, why?" Galen replies hesitantly.

Sean doesn't answer him. Galen has already booted up his laptop this morning to check for any last-minute e-mails from work, and Sean silently pulls up the internet, logging onto his Facebook account. And then he clicks over to Galen's profile and points. Galen heads over to read it. I would kill to know what it says.

"Care to explain that?" Sean asks edgily, fuming.

"Um..." Galen says, but doesn't continue. He's floundering. I've *never* seen Galen flounder. What the *hell* does that message say?

"I can't even *begin* to describe how *creeped out* I am, right now," Sean declares. "And do you know I went and looked at his pictures again, Galen? It's not the same guy, is it? *What the hell* is going on?"

Oh. Oh shit. Oh, this is very, very, *extremely* not good.

"I can explain this," Galen says slowly.

"Oh, I would *love* it if you would!" Sean replies acidly. "I mean it's not enough that you cheat on me—"

"I am *not* cheating—"

"—But you have to pass him off as *Mike*, too, so I can *meet him*?" Sean rolls right over him, practically shouting. "Do you have *any* idea how unhinged that is, Galen?"

"Sean, seriously, it's not – it's not what it looks like," Galen says, desperate. He's going to out me. I know it. This isn't a train wreck, it's a goddamn atomic bomb. A hailstorm of them.

"Then what is it?" Sean demands. "Who is he? Who really owns those boxers in your fucking closet, huh?"

"I…" Galen begins. He's in agony. Sean's just glaring at him while Galen searches for the words to explain and finally finds… nothing. He lists into silence, and Sean shakes his head impatiently.

"That's it," Sean announces, throwing his hands up and stomping back out of the room. "We're through, you hear me? I can't *believe* you would do that to me."

"Sean, wait—" Galen calls after him, but Sean yanks the door open and slams it shut again so fast I'm shocked he doesn't catch his own heel on the way out.

We stand together in silence, the two of us, for a long moment. Galen's turned to stone, looking at the wall, listening along with me to the sound of Sean's car door slamming before the car peels off again down the street.

I don't know quite what to do. After an uncomfortable pause I head into the bathroom and transform, and come out wearing a towel.

"Why didn't you tell him?" I ask.

Galen's staring at the floor. He doesn't look up.

"This way I lose my pride and his trust," he explains shortly. "God knows what you'd lose if Philadelphia's biggest gossip learned what you are."

I nod quietly, accepting his rationale. The whole thing makes me sick with guilt.

"What does your wall say?"

Galen doesn't have to look back at it to recite it word for word, and says in a sarcastically upbeat tone, "'I'm in Philly for a conference on the twelfth, can I stay with you? And can I meet Sean this time?'"

"Ah." There's another long pause while I try to think and Galen tries not to. And then I get an idea. It's a small one, and a terrible one, but it'll do.

"I'm going to fix this," I tell Galen earnestly.

He frowns, shaking his head. "Don't bother."

"No, seriously," I insist. "You stay here and think of a good story. I'll be back."

I head into the kitchen and grab my collar, my safety belt, clipping it around my neck.

"Good luck with the performance review," I tell Galen, and he just smiles sardonically, refusing to reply.

I head to the door and open it a crack, and then I drop the towel and transform. In two seconds I'm nosing the door open and heading off toward the street. I don't look back, but I hear Galen shutting the front door behind me. It's probably the last time he's ever going to let me outside.

I shouldn't have stayed. I knew that. I knew from that first minute I was going to fuck this up, and if I wasn't such a selfish bastard then I would have spared Galen's happiness and left nobly that first day. I really can't fix this, I know that. But I can do my best.

It takes me the better part of two hours to make it over to Sean's apartment building on foot. I recognize that I ought to have made this trip human, and even now I'm kicking myself yet again for reacting before thinking. I ought to be making this apology to Sean myself, in person, not *quite* as my real self but at least as the strange Mike impersonator. I'm frankly the sole cause of all this mess, after all. But I'm not particularly adept at apologies, or any sort of confrontation for that matter, and in choosing to remain a wolf I don't have to deal with Sean's wrath. And I don't have to deal with making up some realistic cover story. I trust that Galen will know what to say better than I would, anyway.

I trot around back and leap the wall into the yard, where

156

Bonks is halfway to voicing his objection before he recognizes me. He's whizzing around me like a furry electron as I head to the door, praying to find it unlocked. Today is not my lucky day. I sigh and console myself with a halfhearted game of tug-of-war with Bonks. And then I drink some of his water and go lie down near the door, putting my head down and trying to clear my mind enough to sleep for a couple of hours.

It doesn't work. I have to claim defeat even before noon, and I go jump the wall again and head off down the alley. I break into a run after a couple of steps and sprint to the street, then stop abruptly and sprint back in the other direction. I do twenty laps before I get tired of counting, and I don't know how many more pass before I'm worn completely ragged. I barely make it back over the fence, and after that it's pretty easy to pass out for an entire afternoon.

I wake again well in time for Sean to come home. I jump once more over the wall and trot around to the front, parking myself in front of his door. I want to make a good impression. I don't know how long I sit there, but I know it's long after five when Sean finally arrives home. I just sit patiently by the door, watching every car as it goes by in anticipation of Sean.

The people-watching isn't great. I do notice more than a few apartment dwellers eyeing me with suspicion as they carry groceries to their doors or walk out to their cars to head off God-knows-where. There's one guy I see twice, first heading out to his car and then heading back from his car with a couple of bags an hour later. He's an older guy, short, burly, with sandy red hair, and both times he stares me down from across the lot like I'm some phantom he can't be sure is really there. It's pretty comical, but I feel bad – I know a lot of people are afraid of dogs, and I'm a dog-fearer's worst nightmare. He's probably scared I'm going to start moving toward him.

My sense of self-loathing couldn't be deeper at the moment, anyway. This guy's fear is just the straw that sinks me into a profound depression as I sit there, mulling over the state of my existence.

I really don't know what I'm doing here anymore. I'm utterly surplus to the world, a waste of everyone's time... and I always have been. There's no point to my existence. It shouldn't have begun in the first place. I don't deserve to keep breathing. I don't want to keep pretending my life is at all worth a shit, and it kills me that somehow I fooled Galen into thinking it was. He did more for me than anyone else in my life ever has, and this is how I repay him for it. I'm absolutely worthless.

Finally I see Sean's car pull into the lot. The sun set just under an hour ago. He doesn't catch sight of me at first, and he's already parked and taken two steps from his car before he notices me sitting in front of his door.

He stops, startled by my presence, and I do my best to look like Sweet Nonny, waiting like a good boy by the door but twitching like I'm dying to run right up to him. I whine for effect.

"Nonny?" Sean asks incredulously. He starts forward again. "What are you doing here, boy?"

I whine again, standing and trotting up to him as he heads toward me, and we meet at the edge of the sidewalk. This is my best Lassie impression. I need Sean to help me rescue his relationship.

"How did you get here?" Sean asks, surveying the lot quickly for any sign of Galen's car. He doesn't find it, obviously. He sighs, gesturing for me to walk with him. "Come on, let's get you inside."

So I follow him and wait patiently while he unlocks the door. He offers for me to head inside first and I oblige. I stand in the middle of the room while Sean lets Bonks in and spends a few minutes throwing dinner together for not just one dog but two. Bonks chows down instantly when Sean puts his bowl on the floor, but I don't move to eat the food he sets down for me. I whine again. It's time for him to call Galen.

This is the most important element of my plan, the part that necessitates my presence here, the reason that I am the key to Galen's salvation: if not for me, Sean will pointedly ignore every single explanatory call Galen attempts. He will never forgive him, and he won't let him explain. What I need is for *Sean* to call *Galen* about the dog. They're going to have to interact to get dear old Anon back over to Galen's house.

158

My plan works brilliantly. After a moment watching me Sean sighs, and pulls his mobile out of his pocket.

"Boy, Nonny, you're lucky I'm such a good person," Sean tells me grudgingly while he dials Galen's number, waiting for him to pick up. I can hear the two rings, can hear Galen's voice but not his words. Sean starts off belligerently. "What the hell were you thinking, dropping your dog off here...? Anon – he was sitting at my door when I came home. I know you know what I'm talking about..." Sean sighs impatiently. "How the hell could he find the place, Galen? He's only ever been here in the car."

Sean pauses for a long moment, frowning, then stares critically at me. He listens for another moment, then holds the mobile away from his head, addressing me.

"Go home, Nonny," he commands. I do nothing. He puts the mobile back to his head. "Didn't work... I am *not* going to shove him out into the night! What's wrong with you? You'd better come and get him, you hear me?" And then he hangs up, clunking the mobile down on the counter with a growl of frustration. He turns again to me. "Your daddy is such an *asshole*, Nonny."

I whine again. His look turns suddenly pitiful at my response. Because I know he's lying, and so does he. He thinks Galen hangs the moon, and he really doesn't get what the hell just happened to him. He's feeling crushed, cast aside, like second-rate goods. He's like a kicked puppy. I know where he's at. It's bordering on human sentience when I head toward him and push up against his hand in sympathy.

"I just don't *get* it," Sean mutters piteously, petting me briefly before heading to his couch. I follow closely, close enough for him to keep a hand on me the whole time. He sits, petting my neck with both hands. I reprise my role guiltily as the world's best sounding board.

"I mean what the hell, Nonny?" Sean continues. "Did you witness it happening, huh? Do you know what's going on? Because I really, really don't. I just... God, I feel so *stupid*..."

He's got tears brimming in his eyes, and before he speaks again they begin to spill silently down his cheeks.

159

"I mean what did I do to deserve this, huh? Do *you* think I'm worth cheating on, Nonny? You think I'm that worthless? Like I'm not enough damn lay for him, or something? I mean *Christ*... And after I went and told my *parents* about him, even! I just don't *get* it...!"

He's crying by now, hugging me close and crying on my shoulder. He continues to mumble miserably into my fur.

"I don't know why I had to *meet* the guy, too. How am I supposed to compete with *that*, huh? You think he was trying to say something, Nonny? Just throw it in my face sort-of-thing? That's all I can figure, really. I mean I *know* I'm not his type, I know he just falls all over tall, dark and handsome, but that's just... cruel. It's just cruel. I feel like such shit, Nonny..."

He falls silent, and his breathing is still ragged but he's not crying anymore. I'm really not sure what to make of this directed soliloquy. I would give anything to be able to speak to him right now. I want to explain everything to him, because as it is, even if I can fix the relationship I can't mend this wound. I can't make Sean understand that he's ridiculously off-base, that he's got nothing to worry about, that Galen adores him. And selfishly, I'd like to ask him some pointed questions as well about exactly what Galen's 'type' really is, because my previously unfounded suspicions about the guy's motives are definitely taking deeper root after Sean's admission.

We sit there in silence, Sean running mental and emotional circles while he pets me absently, both of us waiting anxiously for Galen to arrive. Sean lifts his head up to look out the window a couple times when a car door slams, twitching the blinds open to peer through them at the car park, but it's only on the fourth time that his head stays up.

"Your daddy's here for you," he tells me. I *really* wish he wouldn't call Galen my 'daddy'. It sounds all sorts of wrong to me, especially right now.

Sean gets up from the couch, and opens the door just as Galen knocks.

"Hey," I hear Galen say quietly.

"Just take him and go, all right?" Sean tells him, stepping aside to let Galen in.

Galen doesn't step inside, he just leans in the doorway to address me. He looks like death. He looks absolutely miserable. I have to pull this off, for his sake.

"Come on, let's go," he says. I don't budge. I'm a mountain. I'm Everest. You couldn't move this dog if you tried. He gets the message, turning suddenly impatient. "I mean it, Anon."

"Go on, Nonny," Sean adds gently.

Forget it, kids. I'm not moving.

"God damn it," Galen commands angrily, "It's not funny. Come on."

"Hey, calm down," Sean chastises him, his tone harsh. "It's not his fault you're an asshole. Maybe he doesn't want to go home with you."

The funny thing is, it *is* my fault he's an asshole. And I really do want to go home with him. But I can't.

"Sean, come on..." Galen sighs, still leaning in the doorway but looking at the floor, imploring Sean to show some modicum of compassion and shut the hell up. He looks up at Sean abruptly, pleading. "Can we talk?"

"What's there to talk about?" Sean asks coolly.

"Look, he's... he's an ex-boyfriend, all right?" Galen explains quietly, quickly, beginning his fabrication. So far I'm gravely underwhelmed. "From Boston. And I swear nothing happened. I *swear*. I just thought you'd freak out if I let an ex stay over on his way through Philly."

"And the concert?" Sean accuses.

"I don't know," Galen says with a shrug. "Total coincidence, honest. He means nothing to me, puppy, absolutely nothing. I mean it. He's just a friend. And if I thought it would blow up the way it did I never would have let him stay."

I know what that really means. And I accept that. I wasn't planning on returning, anyway. I don't even want my money. I'll just tuck my tail between my legs and slink on to some new city. Hell, maybe I'll stop running. Maybe I'll turn myself in at the embassy, get back into England and try to avoid my extended family as long as possible. Maybe I'll even accept what I've got coming to me, because I finally get why it is that we don't break the code. We ruin lives when we do. I deserve what I've got coming.

"What's his real name, then?" Sean demands. His conviction is wavering, just a little.

"Toby," Galen lies with convincing rapidity. Sean actually buys it, too.

It occurs to me that there will come a point in the very near future when this ruse, too, shall fail. Any small degree of cross-checking scrutiny on Sean's part will bust it wide open. Galen is going to run this relationship right into the ground, for my sake.

I can't let him do it.

I can't believe I'm really going to do this.

I whine loudly. *Really* loudly, and it startles both of them into looking at me. They're just staring quizzically – Galen doesn't seem to get what I'm asking of him. I can't think of a great way to express it, so I trot over to him and take the hem of his shirt in my teeth, tugging gently. Come *inside*, damn it.

Sean's smiling at the move. Galen looks to him for permission, and Sean grants it. Galen steps inside reluctantly. And then a realization strikes him.

"Leave the door open," he says quickly as Sean's halfway to closing it. Sean pauses, and I whine again in frustration. *No*, Galen, damn it! It's hard enough for me to maintain my resolve here without him going and delaying me like this. I know he knows what I'm trying to say, and he doesn't like it. As if to prove my point, he warns, "Don't be stupid, Anon."

"What is going *on* with you, Galen?" Sean demands. He shuts the door anyway. Sean, my savior.

I bolt to the couch and transform. The second I've got enough dexterity to reach out for the throw pillow I grab it to cover myself.

I'm watching Sean the whole time, terrified of how he's going to react. At first he's still glaring at Galen – it's Galen's look of appalled fury that finally forces Sean to turn my way a second later. Instantly his face changes, he starts to cry out in shock – but Galen grabs his shoulders, putting himself between Sean and me, frantic to calm him down before he can scream.

"It's okay, it's okay," Galen insists, holding onto Sean as he backs himself against the door trying to get away from me.

"We're fine, okay? Everything's fine—"

"*What the actual fuck* is going on?" Sean demands, wide-eyed with terror.

"Just – just let me explain," Galen starts, but by now I've got my voice and my bearings and I interject.

"I'm sorry," I apologize stupidly to Sean, "I didn't mean to startle you."

Sean's just staring at me, mouth agape, bewildered and horrified. It's clear he recognizes me, he knows my face and my voice. I'm thanking God that if nothing else, the gruesome metamorphosis he just witnessed was from a close family pet to a familiar acquaintance – that familiarity is probably what's keeping him this side of hysterical right now.

"The truth is that the guy, he's Anon," Galen tells Sean, gesturing over his shoulder back at me as he works to ground all of this in Sean's reality, "Our dog Anon. He's the guy."

"*What?*" Sean asks, still trying to catch up to what's happening.

"I'm a werewolf," I tell him.

At the word Sean's look flits instantly through a host of expressions, doubt and fear and suspicion and disgust and even a half-smile of overwhelmed incredulity. It's a big leap I'm asking of him, I know it, a mental leap and a leap of faith. And if anything Sean's even more disdainfully skeptical of all things extraordinary than Galen is.

"A werewolf," he repeats at last.

"I *know* it's crazy," I assure him. "I know. But it's the truth. It was an accident that Galen found out. And he was just trying to make my life easier with Mike's ID and everything. He's a perfect saint, honestly. This is all a big misunderstanding, that's all."

"You can't tell *anyone*, Sean," Galen warns him sternly. "Ever. You'll get us all killed."

He chances a glance at me when he says it. And suddenly I understand… everything.

Galen's even smarter than I give him credit for. He knows I failed to mention *all* the consequences – he knows he's in as much danger as I am, if any wolf finds out that he knows. They're not above killing everyone involved.

Galen wasn't trying to save *me* by staying quiet – he was saving Sean.

And I just fucked it up for him again.

"I'm leaving," I say quietly, absorbing this latest blow of self-reproach as gracefully as I can manage. "I don't want to cause any more trouble."

"Where are you going to go, Anon?" Galen rounds on me finally, furious. "You going to play dog for someone else? Risk letting more people know? Where's it going to end, huh?"

"I don't know," I admit. "I'm thinking of heading back home."

"You're not going anywhere," Galen says coldly. "You've got some serious soul searching to do before you get up and go again."

I think I catch his meaning, and I deserve it. I feel like he should be at least be kicking me out or something. And he's refraining, and that makes it even worse. I just wish he'd do *something* less than fantastically laudable in all of this, so I could feel better about ruining everything for him. In a way I deserve his kindness. It hurts more than his cruelty.

"What do you mean 'killed'?" Sean asks Galen in hesitant concern.

"He means that other werewolves will kill us if they find out I've let humans in on the secret," I explain quietly, grudgingly acknowledging Galen's suspicion.

"You've *got* to be kidding me," Sean says quietly, stunned. He turns on Galen. "What the fuck kind of joke is this? Is this for real?"

"You have no idea how much I wish it wasn't," Galen assures him stonily.

Sean looks back at me, and shakes his head.

"This is beyond insane," he mutters.

"I know," Galen agrees. "Pretty damn weird, huh?"

"No shit," Sean agrees wholeheartedly.

"Yeah, yeah, all right," I sigh. Glad to know I'm such a fantastic freak show.

"So you're… *you're* the guy I thought was Mike," Sean asks me, as if to clarify the situation for himself, still trying to wrap his head around the idea. I nod.

"And the dog you call Nonny," I add, to be totally sure he gets it. He cringes at the mention, though, and I'm wondering what I said wrong.

"Oh," he says quietly. "And you... you remember, um, like what goes on around you?"

I can't help but smile. I nod again. "Perfectly."

"Oh." Sean looks off for a moment, cringing again as he undoubtedly recalls every interaction we've ever had. But when he replies, it seems he's only been considering recent events. "I'm, uh, sorry about all that stuff I said earlier."

"Not a problem at all," I assure him. I can't even believe he'd try to apologize for that. Sean turns to address Galen.

"And you've still got a whole world of shit to answer for," he warns, and Galen nods immediately.

"I know," he replies, risking a halfhearted smile.

"When did you find this out?"

Galen cringes. "...June."

"*June?*" Sean cries, looking back and forth between us in renewed fury. "Fucking *June?* What the fuck, Galen?"

"I couldn't say anything!" Galen insists, raising his hands in surrender. He points a finger at me. "He's not supposed to exist, right?"

Sean's staring at him like he's deranged. "You've had another man *living in your house* for *months*—"

"I *swear* it's not like that," Galen protests.

"*Definitely* not like that," I add emphatically, and Sean turns to glare at me too. I make a pathetic attempt at defending my honor. "I'm just a dog, all right, I cheat my way into living as people's dog. That's it." I gesture at Galen, "He was just trying to help me get set up playing human again. Total altruism thing. I swear. You should hear the way he talks about you."

Sean looks at Galen at the mention, barely suppressing a fleeting flattered smile, but Galen's staring resolutely at the floor in embarrassment.

"You still should have said," Sean scolds him, and he nods. Sean points at me, "I can't believe you tried to keep *this* from me."

165

"I'm sorry," Galen says, looking up at his boyfriend imploringly. "I was trying to do what I thought was best. You *know* you're my life, right? You know I breathe for you."

Sean sighs in overwrought frustration. He takes a moment to formulate his thoughts, and both Galen and I are both on pins and needles waiting for his response. And then he shakes his head, waving his hands as if to remove himself from the situation.

"Look, just…" he says finally, "call me when you get home, all right?"

"Yeah, all right," Galen agrees quietly, nodding his acceptance. They're not exactly going to get any real privacy with me sitting around the apartment here. Galen turns his attention back to me.

"You want a ride home this time?" he asks sarcastically.

"I'm not going," I insist.

Galen frowns his disapproval.

"I'm *really* not going to argue with you right now," he tells me. His patience with me is about to break. "Get in the car. You at least have to get your stuff."

"What in the name of Jesus Christ did you think you were doing?" Galen demands the minute we start to drive off.

I've transformed back to wolf form for the ride home, so I can't reply, but that's fine with Galen. I stare out the window from the back seat while he continues with what I would consider an excessively venomous rant, and fight myself not to argue back the only way a werewolf knows how – by attacking him. It's a close call, in the end. I recognize that most of my violent defensiveness is stemming from the fact that, unfortunately, I know he's right. And that only makes it worse.

"I mean what the hell would possess you to turn in front of him?" Galen insists, practically shouting at me, looking in the rearview for emphasis every once in a while as he drives. "You didn't need to drag him into this, too – it's enough you decided to throw *my* safety out the window, I practically asked for it, I earned it, I accept that.

"But I know you're not too stupid to figure out why the hell I

166

wasn't telling him. And you know he can't keep his damn mouth shut. You know you've just thrown us all in a world of shit, right? And you don't even have the decency to actually inform me about it, I've got to figure out for myself what the hell you mean when you start going on about whatever danger you've put us in – you *owe* me, Anon, you owe it to me to start bloody talking, already.

"But no, we're going to get back home and you're just going to play dog again because you think I'm going to let it drop, you're too goddamn self-centered to think I could understand or something, you think as long as you hold all the cards it'll be all right! It's bullshit. You don't have quite enough wits about you for me to trust you with both my and Sean's lives. Mine, fine, but not Sean's.

"And I don't *ever* want to hear you talking about going off and fucking up even more people's lives, yeah? You're an *idiot* if you think this is the last time you go making this mistake – there will be someone else, Anon, you mark my words. There's going to be someone else who finds out about you and it's all going to come down hard on you someday. You're a ticking time bomb and you know it. You're going to fuck up big – bigger than you already have. And if I let you go then it's all on *my* head, isn't it? You owe it to me to stay and you know it."

And finally, *finally* he shuts the hell up, he runs out of steam and sighs his frustration and punches the button for the radio. We listen to a commercial for a full four seconds before he gives up on that too and shuts it back off again. We ride in perfect silence for a long while, both of us far too angry to break it.

The car ride isn't terribly long, but it seems to drag on forever as I move past my immediate reaction in the ensuing quiet and start to consider what he's actually saying. He's right, I know he's right. And pretty soon all my resentment is dissolving back into remorse, a sick, gnawing sense of guilt that won't go away. I'm sinking as we drive, I'm folding inward, I'm paralyzed by the idea that he's right and I've somehow managed to drastically affect the lives of two other people in a way I never intended. I didn't think I had any effect on *anyone*, I thought I was more of a transient thing, a phantom, a nonentity. I thought I left no ruinous aftermath. I don't want to think that I was wrong. I don't want anything to happen to Galen or Sean, and someday I'm going to have to face the fact that by staying, I'm putting them at as much risk as I'm putting myself.

When Galen parks the car in front of his house I can't get out. He opens the door but I can't move, I've gone rigid, I can't stand the idea of getting up and starting again. I think I left my cozy little reality back there somewhere on the road, and until it returns I don't see how I'm supposed to start moving without it. Whatever world is turning now certainly isn't the one I'm used to, it's not the same one I woke up to this morning.

Galen gives up after a few seconds and shuts the door on me again. He heads back into the house, undoubtedly to call Sean, and leaves me to my miserable rumination in the car.

I feel suddenly like everything I do is wrong, every choice I make turns out to be the wrong one, as I'm sitting here in the car realizing that it was sort of a five-year-old move not to get up and head inside. But there are no right moves, anymore. It's like those stupid choose-your-own-adventure books you read as a kid where you've got to make some arbitrary plot decision at the bottom of each page and then flip through the book to get to the next passage, and when you reach a bad ending and flip back and make the opposite choice you find out that *that* way was just as inevitably ruinous, because the *truth* is that your critical mistake was in fact so many decisions back that you've got to just start the book over to get it right. Only I can't start this damn book over.

As far as I can tell, neither of my choices now are good ones. I feel like I've already debated this before. On the one hand I can stay here, stay canine and wait for Galen to retrieve me as he inevitably will, and I can go inside and continue living with him. He'll undoubtedly forgive me soon enough, because I think he's too rational to hold a grudge. And I'll drift back into doing whatever I was doing, I'll keep earning money like Galen suggested, I'll start saving and maybe I could even stay a decade before anyone who knows Galen starts wondering why I'm still alive, and I could take my earnings and leave. And maybe nothing at all suspicious would happen. Maybe that incident at the club won't ever happen again, maybe no wolf will ever know I'm in Philadelphia. I feel like that's asking a little too much of God, right now.

And on the other hand I could leave, this moment, and be done with it. It's not that hard to open this door myself, and in a matter of minutes I could betray Galen's trust but save his hide and get myself the hell out of Pennsylvania. It wouldn't be that hard to run. It's true that if I leave this second I'd be out all the money, I'd have nothing at all with which to start acting human, I wouldn't even have the comfort of the fake ID. But hell, if I want to leave then now is the best time to do it. It wouldn't take me that long to find the opportunity to steal some more clothes, or some cash, and find a job somewhere and maybe start being human for good. As human as I can make it, anyway. And maybe Galen's wrong, maybe I'm not going to fuck it up, maybe it's easier than I remember to stay human for any length of time without someone looking into my credentials and realizing they're stolen. If only I could believe that.

So. Do I leave, escape and stumble blindly into uncertain disaster farther down the road? Or do I stay, wait for disaster to find me instead and prepare for its arrival?

Two hours later, Galen comes back out to find me passed-out asleep in the car. The sound of him opening the latch startles me into immediate, vigilant consciousness, and I let out a breath of relief when I realize it's only Galen. He opens the passenger door and sits down in the seat, closing the door again behind him before he decides to speak.

"So I talked to Sean," he begins, not turning to look at me, staring out the front windshield at nothing as he talks. "He thinks I'm being too harsh on you." Galen smiles sarcastically at his own statement. "I'd beg to differ, of course, but I've been told I'm not a very good judge. So let's assume I'm being too harsh, and I ought to try out sympathetic for a change." He pauses for a very long while, and then he chuckles. "I have no idea how to start."

I can't help but smile as well, half a tail wag to show him I get it. If he sees the move he doesn't acknowledge it.

"I mean I just... some days I want to kill you, Anon, I'm not going to lie," Galen continues, sighing. "But I suppose most days I'm just kicking myself, actually, because you wanted to leave from day one. I should have let you go when it made sense. So I'm sorry for that. And I guess in a way I feel sorry for you, though I'm sure you wouldn't appreciate that at all. I think you made a couple of really stupid mistakes when you were a kid and you're still paying for it now. And I don't think you realize it like you should." He sighs again, rubbing his eyes, running his hands through his hair like he's so frustrated he can't handle it anymore. It's like he's voicing my own mood as well. Eventually he says, "I do think you're a good person. You just have a lot of intensely annoying quirks. That's about the nicest you're going to get from me tonight."

I nod, and see that he does catch that motion – he nods as well, and finally opens the door to get out of the car. I get up halfway so he knows I'm coming too, and he opens the back door for me. I follow him up the walk and inside the house.

It takes me a while to finally get up the nerve to head upstairs for my clothes stash. I'm a little sorry for that, in retrospect, because when we enter the house Galen stands in the front room, waiting, and I can't bring myself to transform right away. So I turn and head into the back room instead. And he sighs, throwing up his hands like he knew that was going to happen, and stalks off to his office to slam the door and spend the rest of his evening alone with his music and books.

I feel terrible, but I really can't do it yet. I need to formulate some sort of speech first. I need to think things through.

So it's better than an hour later when I finally knock on the door to his office. A moment goes by before I hear the music turn off and Galen comes to the door to open it.

"Yeah?" he asks suspiciously.

"I'm sorry," I say. I assume that's an appropriate first line. He pauses, watching me, and finally he gives in and steps aside so I can enter. I lean against the far bookcase while he takes a seat again in his desk chair.

"What for?" Galen asks. The question makes me smile. I

know it's loaded. There are a thousand ways to answer that, very few of which he'll appreciate.

"For scaring you, primarily," I explain. "It's probably not all as bad as I make it out to be. You know me, I'm paranoid."

He doesn't reply, and I'm not sure if mine is an answer he wanted to hear. I plunge on anyway, as fair compensation for forcing him earlier to speak to a silent observer.

"And if it turns out I'm not paranoid, then I'm sorry for dragging you into this. You said yourself I didn't want to," I point out, watching as Galen nods his grudging acknowledgement. "It's just... See, ever since I was a pup I've been taught that the act of *divulging* the secret is the end game. It didn't occur to me that it was possible to tell a human without the other wolves somehow knowing, without instantly incurring their wrath. So I guess I keep thinking I'm living on borrowed time, you know?" I smile. "It's hard for me to wrap my head around the idea of keeping secrets *from* werewolves."

"So why did you tell Sean?" Galen asks pointedly.

I shrug, uncomfortable with the accusation. "He was going to see right through your story."

"There wasn't a better one," Galen tells me shortly.

"Except the truth," I counter.

"That's not *better*," Galen insists, turning angry. "If it turns out you're not paranoid then I'd much rather have him alive without me than dead with me."

"I worked that out about ten seconds after I transformed," I assure him. He can't help but smile at my failed sense of timing. "Look, part of it is that it's hard to think straight as a wolf. I mean just *thinking*, fine, I can do that, but ask me to play chess and I'm going to fail miserably."

"Too many steps ahead?" Galen asks, and I nod. That's exactly what I meant. And he knows it's true. He's laughed more than once at my sensory bafflement following my transformations, and he knows that my canine thought processes aren't as effective as they could be, when I come out of wolf form and fail to follow up on things he says he asked me to do. In fact, living with Galen has been an enlightening experience for me at least as much as it has been for him – I didn't realize quite how bad I could really get.

"I know that's not an excuse," I add.

"Certainly not," he agrees.

"And you have every right to be angry."

"I should hope so," Galen says with a smile.

"And it's not harsh," I continue. "You seriously couldn't kick a dog harder than I'm kicking myself, I swear."

"I'm sure," Galen says, sighing again. "I know that. And I think I've done a fair enough job impressing upon Sean the dire need to shut his legendary yap on this one. I don't think you've got anything to worry about."

"Thank you."

"No problem."

A pause ensues. There's more I want to say, more speech I have to give, but suddenly one question seems far more pressing.

"So... did it work out, then?" I ask, and Galen frowns at me for a moment, not understanding the question.

"Oh – you mean with Sean?" he asks, and I nod. "Yeah, of course. Just a misunderstanding, right?"

"I guess," I concede, not fully agreeing with him by any means. I can't say that I can put myself in Sean's shoes exactly, but if I had a girlfriend, say, who pulled something like this... I don't know. I would have thought Sean might still be angry.

"Sean told me all about tonight," Galen says idly, and for a second I think he might have read my mind because he's exactly on topic. He's smiling like he really can tell it's where my thoughts were headed. "He seemed a bit shell-shocked by the idea that you were actually *listening* to him the whole time."

"Yeah, well, that's the way the game goes," I say uncomfortably.

"I just want to make it perfectly clear that whatever he said was *Sean's* opinion, yeah, not mine," Galen tells me. "That's not at all what I was about, here."

"I assumed as much," I lie. I think he knows it's a lie. I think he knows about my suspicions.

"Fine," he concedes, letting it slide. There's another moment of silence while we both decide how to continue.

"Oh, how was the performance review?" I ask. I'd completely

forgotten. Galen shrugs.

"Fine," he says. "Funny enough it wasn't the biggest thing on my mind, this morning."

"I'm sorry."

"Quit apologizing," Galen says, frustrated. "I mean I'm still pissed, don't get me wrong, but it's at least as much at me as at you. And seriously, Sean's not an idiot. It'll be fine."

I don't like that phrase, 'It'll be fine'. It's a cover for a grave doubt, it's hackneyed. And it's often wrong. But Galen's right, just worrying about this isn't going to get anyone anywhere. I know Sean's not an idiot. I have to trust him. It'll be fine.

"So… can I go back, now?" I ask, sensing the conversation's over, and Galen grins.

"Yes," he sighs dramatically.

Thank God. I book it out of the room.

CHAPTER 10

It's a few days before I see Sean again. And in the interim Galen leaves me alone at the house every night to head over to Sean's – on the second night he doesn't even come home, he just shows up the next morning to change before heading off again to work. He doesn't say and I don't ask what he's up to over there, but I have a feeling his earlier declaration that everything's worked out between them might have been a slight overstatement. He nevertheless reassures me repeatedly – and with ever-growing impatience each time I ask – that no, Sean has not told anyone, my secret is safe, I can stop worrying and quit bugging him about it already.

I can't help it. Galen I can trust – Galen was willing to self-destruct to keep even Sean from knowing what I am. But he's a total anomaly. And just a few days ago he held the same conviction I did, that Sean should be kept in the dark at all costs. I imagine his call to Sean that first night involved a major dressing-down from his boyfriend about trust and integrity which has since changed his mind, but as with everything else Galen refuses to talk about it. So whatever my profound reservations, I have to let go and learn to trust Galen's judgment too, his new insistence that Sean is just as ridiculously dependable as he is.

Sean finally decides to come over again on Saturday night. Galen's been over at his place since Friday after work, and I'm surprised when Galen's car pulls up outside to see both Sean and Bonks in there with him. Sean pulls his dog out of the car and heads determinedly up the walk, and Galen follows meekly behind with a bag of takeout.

It feels like a confrontation, because that's more or less what it is. The moment they get inside Galen tells me to go up and get dressed, and I don't dare try and get out of it. I slink upstairs to change, and come back down to find them already waiting at the kitchen table now piled high with Chinese food.

"Sit down," Sean tells me, but I'm stunned and grateful to hear the amiable tone he uses to soften the command. He smiles. "I figured I ought to properly meet the guy my boyfriend's been hanging out with these last few months."

And so the interrogation begins.

In the end it's infinitely more pleasant than I expected. Sean asks more about me as a person than he does about my werewolfism, and whenever the questions get too personal or confidential he actually accepts my apologetic refusal to answer. But every time I shake my head Sean invariably shares a look with Galen, and it's easy to see from their interaction that they've already discussed the werewolfism exhaustively these past few days – including my infuriating obsession with concealment, or whatever Galen calls it. As disturbing as it is to have that confirmation they've been talking about me while I'm not around, I have to admit it does simplify things for me this evening. We stay up talking well into the morning, until finally Sean's exhausted enough to declare he's satisfied and the pair of them head off upstairs to bed.

I don't want to say that after that things go back to normal. No, in fact as the days post-revelation turn into weeks, things spiral even farther into what for me still feels abnormal – and it is *fantastic*.

Sean knows what I am. It was an eventuality I wanted to avoid, but there's an undeniable silver lining, here: *Sean knows*. I am living in a house soon to be occupied by two humans who accept that I'm a werewolf, who put up with both my wolfish and human sides, who prove all my paranoid fears more unfounded with every passing day. Sean's moving in here won't destroy anything. My humanity is back.

My clothes have moved out from under the bed into the closet, and it's actually quite difficult to keep Sean from trying to augment my meager wardrobe – I have to thank Galen for forcing him to take back half the stuff he hauls in whenever he shows up of an evening. Sean finds the very idea of watching me eat dog food nauseating, and he insists I eat with them as a human for every shared meal – he's even taken to making Bonks's dinners from scratch, and he pesters me constantly for tips on how to be a better owner to his dog. And he practically insists that I go out nights, trying to drag me out with him and Galen to dinners and movies and bars and whatever other hangouts suit Sean's fancy.

And I'll give Sean this – he's crafty. He's got this way of convincing people into the most insane situations, and they never see it coming. These hangouts start small, but it takes practically no time at all for Sean to get brainstorming on *all* the places he wants to show me and working out how we're all going to get to D.C. and Yellowstone and Cancun and the Mediterranean... the list goes on. Somehow at the end of this I find myself sitting in a vet's office getting a whole host of unnecessary vaccinations and even a bloody microchip implanted in my back so I'm legal to take abroad. *Abroad*, for God's sake. Sean's already looking up flights to Rome next summer. I'm just glad the chip barely shows under my human skin.

My protests about going places are becoming feebler by the day. It's fast becoming a routine thing – Galen and Sean are like a crutch, really, they're people I can converse with in lieu of dealing with a world full of strangers. And that world of strangers is becoming less and less daunting with each repeated exposure, because it's no small relief that should I find myself in trouble I have someone waiting to bail me out. And so much more importantly than all of this, all these mad extreme lengths to which these two humans are actually willing to go for me, every single time we go out marks another time I've failed to notice any sign of werewolves in this city. It's getting easier to recognize that one time at the club as a fluke, even if I never want to head back to that place as long as I live. I'm able to breathe, to relax and actually enjoy myself in a form in which I've long felt wholly uncomfortable for fear of discovery. I think I'm learning how to be a real person, again.

Sean begins to come over more often than usual, now that November and the end of his lease are fast approaching. Galen's getting all weird about it.

It's not often that I see him acting particularly gay, but damned if Sean's imminent cohabitation here hasn't gotten him all effeminately emotive and bubbly. He's like a little kid waiting for Christmas morning. Out of nowhere he'll bust out grinning like a maniac and say something like, 'Just two hundred twenty-six hours to go!' and actually jump up and down in the bloody living room. It's pathetic. He knows I think it's pathetic. He doesn't give a damn. This is apparently the very best thing that's ever happened to him – he certainly tells me so at least twenty times a day. I find myself wondering if I've ever cared about anyone in quite the same way Galen cares about Sean. Even Sophie never got me acting quite like this.

Sean's stuff starts showing up toward the end of October, and I'm tasked with hauling boxes around and organizing while the two of them are off at work. There's a lot to go through, and I don't rightly feel qualified to be sifting through all of it. The kitchen stuff is easy enough, and the clothes all go upstairs, and Sean's toiletries take precedence in the top bathroom because Galen gets up earlier than Sean does and Sean has painstakingly explained that if Galen so much as attempts to disturb Sean's daily morning beauty rest by banging about in the room right next door then Galen is in for a world of pain the likes of which he has never before experienced.

All these items I have no issue moving. But Sean's art supplies will be taking over half of the back room and I have no inkling how to set all of it up, and his painting seems like such a personal pursuit that I don't dare drop anything or move a single brush out of place. And Sean's got a few books, but I can't begin to think where to put them in this house already overflowing with them, because Galen can get touchy about his books and he's already less than keen to have Sean's romance novels even cross the threshold, let alone take up residence near any of Galen's precious tomes. And then there's the Box, the one I would never have opened had I known a priori what it held, the one that was left unmarked at the base of the stairs and whose placement there could only have been Galen's idea of a practical joke. Galen already had an impish grin plastered across his face when he came home and found the box missing, and he cracked up when

I told him, "It's up under your bed, you bastard."

The Saturday before Sean makes his permanent arrival, I finally get a much-deserved break while Sean spends the evening packing up the rest of his stuff across town and Galen organizes all the personal effects I didn't feel comfortable touching. I've ensconced myself in the back room next to the couch, strategically out of the way of the disaster area that is Galen's undiagnosed hyperactivity disorder. It's currently manifesting itself in simultaneously copying all of Sean's ancient CDs onto his computer, messaging his sister in California, cleaning out all his desk and file drawers, excavating a miniscule space on one shelf for Sean's books, and figuring out how to shove half his wardrobe into the downstairs closets. I doubt he'll finish any of those before dinner.

There's a knock at the door, and I get up and dart into the living room to see if I can see who it is. Whoever's standing on the porch step is just out of view, so I have to wait for Galen to come and answer the door. Galen grins at my blatant hyper-vigilance, shaking his head at me before he finally opens the front door.

There's a man standing there, and he smiles at Galen pleasantly. He looks familiar, somehow, and I'm trying to work out where I might have seen him before.

And then I smell him.

I start growling even before the man starts speaking.

Galen looks over at me, confused, and the stranger looks at me as well. He knows. I know he knows. He can't *not* know. And I know he's one too, and he knows that.

This werewolf smells different than the one I smelled at the club, and I'm concocting a million simultaneous scenarios, ways they might be connected, or not – trying to work out how this guy's managed to just appear out of nowhere. How the *hell* did he find this place...?

"Can I help you?" Galen finally asks the man.

"Ah, yes, I'm a member of the Firemen's Association of the State of Pennsylvania..." the man begins. He pauses. I'm already halfway to attacking him, I can't control the sudden blinding rage that's come over me at his presence, and he can't ignore my growling anymore. He looks at me directly and tells Galen, "Nice dog you've got there."

"Yeah, he's a good boy," Galen replies, acting brilliantly casual though I'm sure he knows there's something wildly wrong with this situation. He turns and looks at me too, smiling. "But he's a bit weird around strangers."

"Seems like it," the man agrees. "Have you had him long?"

"A few months," Galen replies with a shrug. "Just picked him up off the street, really."

"Oh yeah?" the man asks, sounding more curious than he ought to, but covering it well as a solicitor trying to make friendly conversation in order to ingratiate himself. "What's his name?"

"Anon," Galen answers. "So... what is this about firemen?"

And that's the moment I recognize the man, when he turns back to Galen and his look turns more serious as he gets down to business. The smile was throwing me off. Instantly I recall the sandy red hair, the bulky stature, the flushed, full face...

Sean's place. This guy lives at Sean's apartment building. He drives a yellow Toyota – I chance a glance out the window, scanning the street, and see it parked halfway down the block. It's the same car – I have a vision, a memory clear as day of him closing the door, arms laden with bags, turning to stare at me from across the long car park...

Oh, Jesus. This can't be happening. This isn't *happening*.

I can't take it anymore, I snap – I bark and lunge forward, teeth bared, perfectly ready to tear this other werewolf limb from limb.

"Nonny!" Galen shouts, using the nickname he's never deigned to use before in an inspired effort to play it off like he thinks I'm just a dog, just his pet. He grabs me by the collar before I can leap past him out the door. "What the hell, boy?" He turns back to the man, who has retreated to the walk in startled haste. "I'm sorry, I don't know what's gotten into him."

"No, that's all right," the man assures him. I'm straining against Galen's grip, still growling, and I know the stranger gets the message. I'll kill him if he comes back here. Galen's yanking me back into the house, trying to shut the door.

"I'll be sure to donate something online," Galen tells the man,

179

who smiles and waves, and then Galen closes the door and it's over, he lets me go.

I dart over to the window to watch as the man makes his way down the street to his car. He turns and looks back at the house, seeing me in the window and watching me for a long moment before he unlocks his car and gets in. I wait until he's driven out of sight before I turn away.

"What was that about?" Galen asks me as I head directly past him into the bathroom to transform.

"He's a wolf," I say when I emerge. "And he lives at Sean's building – I saw him there when I went over, I didn't know what he was, he was too far away—"

"He lives at Sean's?" Galen interjects belatedly, stunned.

"I have to kill him," I say immediately, beginning to pace the room, trying to think. I look up at Galen, who's watching me like I'm crazy. "I've got to get over there and kill him."

"Okay, calm down," Galen advises.

"No, I've not got the time," I argue. I head over to the stairs, taking them two at a time. I've got to get clothes. "You stay here—"

"You're not going anywhere," Galen tells me matter-of-factly, following me up the stairs and into his room. He stands in the doorway, blocking it. I head for my clothes anyway. "You don't have any idea he even knows what you are."

"Give me a fucking break," I reply sarcastically. "He knows, all right? He *knows*. He knew before he came here. I've got to kill him before he does anything about it."

"How are you planning on doing that?" Galen asks.

"I don't know," I admit. I don't care. I've just got to get over there, and now.

"Okay, calm down and *think*, please," Galen says. I have to pause, frustrated, waiting for him to continue. He's right, I'm back to not-thinking again, and maybe I need a little clarity. My voice of reason starts his reasoning. "You don't have any practical means or any justifiable motive for going and *murdering* a man because he showed up on my doorstep. You know that he knows what you are, and you suspect that he came here already knowing you were here. But does he know *who* you are, or can

180

he? Does he think I know what you are? Did you give him enough warning, do you think, that he won't consider coming around a second time?"

"But he knows where Sean lives, he knows I'm not from around here – honestly, if I don't get him now he's going to get me later," I insist. "That's the way this game *works*. Kill or be killed. I don't want him jumping me in an alley somewhere."

"You at least need to plan this out a little better," Galen points out.

"Look, aren't you worried about this?" I ask him, unable to comprehend how he's not panicking as much as I am, right now. Galen shrugs.

"Sure, of course I am," he replies calmly. "But I also don't plan to be an accomplice to murder. I think we've got to wait and see what's really going on here. And I think in the meantime you can think more proactively about what we ought to do in an emergency."

I stare at him in undisguised incredulity for a good long moment before answering. And in the end I concede, and stand down. "I'm not happy about this."

"I can tell," Galen assures me. "Go on, get some clothes out anyway – you might need them later."

The next day we're hanging out in the back room, watching another movie. I'm not paying attention at all, I'm back to canine form so I can hear better, in case there's something I ought to be listening for.

This is not my best day. Yesterday was my worst day. I can't wait to see what the next moon is going to be like. In the meantime, as Galen has suggested, I've got a duffel bag sitting in the hallway with a change of clothes, all my cash, my fake ID, and Galen's pocket knife because he convinced me after a very long argument that a butcher knife doesn't travel well. Galen has added a few of his own things to it – passport, Social Security card, and as much cash as he could get out of the bank before it closed yesterday afternoon. He called Sean up as well and carefully explained that *without* looking suspicious, Sean should attempt to compile a similar stash.

And after that, Galen just went back to hanging out like he always does. I don't know how he does it.

My mind is in no sort of order to start accepting the prospect of normality again. I'm thinking only of every possible thing that can go wrong, going in mad circles trying to work out what the ginger knows and wondering if it matters. But there's been no sign of anything unusual, and I don't know if maybe I'm not going wildly overboard with my suspicions.

The worst part is that this fear of mine no longer has anything at all to do with my own safety. I pretty much gave up on myself the day I told Sean the truth. I've finally come around to admitting what the rest of werewolf-kind has been drilling into me since day one, that I'd already wasted my first chance at redemption simply by being born, that all I ever manage to do is cause trouble, that not a soul on Earth is any better for having ever met me. It's just that until recently I never met any soul I felt bettered by, either, so it seemed like a pretty fair deal either way.

And now I'm sitting here, frankly convinced that the whole world is about to come crashing down, and I couldn't give less of a damn what happens to me at the end of it. All I'm thinking about is my two humans, because I wouldn't be able to forgive myself if anything happened to Galen or Sean.

There's no way to argue that this whole thing isn't entirely my fault. I dragged them into this, I'm the one who's potentially shoved two innocent bystanders directly in the middle of a wolves' confrontation. And there's no one on the planet I'd rather have spared from it.

This fear of mine is a much uglier beast than any drive for self-preservation, it's far more terrifying to know that someone else's fate – a friend's fate – is in my hands. I'm suffocating under the weight of this combined guilt and self-hatred and frantic, impotent desperation, and I'm not quite sure what it's going to take to make me snap. It won't be much.

The house phone rings halfway through the movie. Galen leaves the movie playing and heads into the kitchen to pick it up.

"Hello...? No, I'm sorry, you've got the wrong number." He

182

hangs up and heads to the refrigerator for a beer before coming back into the back room. I'm looking up at him curiously and he shrugs, explaining as if I didn't hear him earlier, "Wrong number—"

The phone rings again. He sighs, and heads back into the kitchen.

"Hello? No, I'm sorry, still wrong number," he says. Now I'm nervous. One wrong number is excusable, but two... two is always suspicious. I get up from the couch and trot on into the kitchen to see if I can listen in. "*No*, ma'am, no one by that name lives here... Well I'm sorry, I don't know what to tell you..."

And then Galen pauses, and a strange look comes over his face.

"Hold on," he says, and covers the phone carefully before turning to me and whispering suspiciously, "Christian?"

Shit.

Oh, holy shit...

I transform immediately.

"Who is it?" I demand in a whisper, and he shrugs, handing me the phone. I take it quickly, my hands trembling. "Who is this?"

"Is this Christian Talbot?" a woman asks hurriedly, obviously agitated. And then I recognize the voice.

"*Mum?*" I ask, stunned. Galen's jaw drops when he hears me say the word.

"Oh, Christian, thank God—" my mother begins on the other line.

"How did you get this number?" I ask. There's a brief pause.

"Your Aunt Cynthia," she replies finally.

"Oh, *shit*," I whisper. That means my uncles know where I am. I'm a dead man.

"Christian, listen to me. You've got to get out of there, you've got to go *now*—"

"You couldn't stop them?" I ask, my voice rising along with my rapidly mounting alarm. "They're coming *now*?"

"Tony and Thom are both on a plane to Pennsylvania," my mother explains. "Sweetheart, please, hang up the phone and go."

"I can't just *leave*," I insist. "God damn it… is it just Tony and Thom? How many are there?"

"I – I don't know—"

"*Mum*," I growl, practically in hysterics. She couldn't have gotten me some *useful* information? *What the hell am I going to do…?* "What the hell am I going to do?"

"Run," she tells me. I can hear her voice cracking. The first time I speak to my mother in more than a decade and this is how the conversation goes. She's already convinced it's the last time she ever talks to me, too. Maybe it is.

"I'm not running," I inform her. "I'm tired of running."

"Christian, *please*—"

"So how's Dad?" I interject pointedly. She sighs, trying to compose herself.

"He's fine," she assures me. "So are Keira and Paul and Lara. And Keira got married six years ago, you've got a niece and a nephew."

"I saw that," I tell her with a smile. "I've been keeping up. Look, Mum, thanks for the call, all right? Tell everyone I love them, wish me luck."

"Good luck, sweetheart," she tells me emotionally. "I love you."

"Love you too, Mum."

I hang up to find Galen staring at me, silent. I sigh, looking back down at the phone. Logically I recognize that call just happened. Emotionally I don't think I've caught up yet. I've gone numb.

"So it's on," I tell Galen. I sigh, slamming the phone back down on the receiver. "God *damn* it, I *knew* I should have taken care of this…"

"What do you propose we do?" Galen asks coolly.

"We've got to get to Sean," I say, trying to kick my brain into gear. "As soon as possible. My uncles are flying in from Ireland, and I'm sure their henchman is around here somewhere."

"That redhead?" Galen asks, and I nod.

"And I don't know how many others."

"And after we get Sean?"

"I don't know," I admit. "I guess… first things first, we act like nothing's happened. You're just taking me out to see Sean. That won't seem suspicious."

"He could meet us at the dog park," Galen suggests. "It's public, at least."

"Not a bad idea," I agree, nodding while I mull it over. "Just... just give me a second, I need to think..."

"No, Christian, you need to talk," Galen tells me sternly, "and fast. Then *we* need to think."

It's so strange to hear my real name spoken aloud, to hear someone else call me by it. It's sort of surreal. This whole thing is. So I start telling him everything, and fast.

"So my name is Chris Talbot," I explain, "I'm from Birmingham. My mother is a born werewolf, and she bit my father and made him a wolf, and that's why I was born a wolf. My mother has two brothers, Thomas and Anthony McCarthy, they live in Dublin – they're the wards of Great Britain and Ireland, they're like pack leaders. They're on a plane to Philadelphia right now, and I don't know what they intend but I obviously have a suspicion. This ginger must know them, he must have tipped them off, and when my Uncle Thom told my Aunt Cynthia where he was going she told my mother, and my mother called me. And told me to run. And that's all the information I have."

"Okay, how many of you are there?" Galen asks patiently. "Do you know numbers, names? How many could be in Philly? Do you have any idea where the redhead is? How do they go about hushing people up, is there some sort of process? Some honor code, something? *Think*, Christian. I don't know the context, here."

"There is an honor code," I affirm with a short nod. "When you confirm the code's been broken you kill the offenders. Quietly, in proper werewolf style. No guns, weapons, poison, anything like that – just... straight confrontation. As for how many wolves we can expect in Philly... I don't know. There are just over sixty of us in the entire UK, and my family makes up twelve of those – we're the largest family. So in Philly... maybe half a dozen?"

"Six werewolves," Galen repeats frankly.

"And my uncles."

"All after the three of us."

"Maybe we could shoot them?"

Galen frowns. "Where are you going to get a gun?"

I sigh, throwing up my hands. "I don't know. Dane has one."

"You can't bring another human into this, you really can't."

"I can't kill eight wolves with my bare hands," I point out.

"You can't kill eight wolves anyway," Galen counters. "The second you do there'll be eight more, and eight more, and eight more…"

"Yeah, well, I've got to do *something*," I sigh, growing more frustrated by the second. Every minute we stay is another minute closer to death.

"First we get Sean," Galen says calmly, after a moment of silence. "Then we'll do as your mother suggests, and run."

"Where?"

"I don't give a shit."

I sigh, nodding my acceptance. "All right."

Galen heads over to the other side of the kitchen, grabbing my collar off the counter and coming back to hand it to me. I take it reluctantly, clipping it on while Galen reaches into his pocket for his mobile.

"Hey, Galen," I say before he can dial Sean's number. He looks up at me expectantly. "I, um… I want you to know that if I thought it'd help you guys I'd stay behind and wait for it. I really am tired of running."

Galen smiles.

"I know," he assures me. "But you're right, we're really going to need you."

"I know."

"We'll figure something out," Galen says seriously. "I promise."

"Just don't… don't do anything stupid, all right?" I ask him, knowing I'm not getting across what I really mean to say and praying he understands me anyway. "Let me do all the stupid shit, all the risks. Don't cover for me anymore."

"I won't," Galen replies. "Can I call Sean now?"

I take a breath. "Yeah."

*   *   *

Twenty minutes later we're pulling into Sean's car park. I'm in the back seat, but I can see the ginger's apartment window clearly. There's no sign of life.

And then I spot him. He's camping in the driver's seat of his parked car, that battered yellow Toyota I recall perfectly from the night I sat stupidly in front of Sean's door for hours looking patently suspicious. He's obviously waiting for us. His eyes are trained on Galen's car, and I'm staring right back at him. Fuck him. Galen does a phenomenal job at seeming not at all interested, though I'm absolutely positive he saw the guy even before I did.

Sean opens his front door, exiting with Bonks in tow the minute he sees Galen's car through the window. Galen parks and waits patiently while Sean throws Bonks in the back seat with me and gets in himself, strapping his seatbelt on and turning on the radio by force of habit.

"So what's the real reason for the impromptu dog park trip?" Sean asks cheerily, as Galen pulls back out of the spot as neatly as he pulled in.

"You got your passport? And the cash?" Galen asks him, sounding nothing but congenial. Sean nods. Galen glances in the rearview mirror, and continues speaking in that very conversational tone, "Whatever you do, do not act like I'm telling you anything strange right now."

"Okay," Sean agrees lightly, so casually I'm not sure he even heard Galen correctly, then turns around to look at me and Bonks in the back seat. He makes like he's just turning to pet the both of us, and asks me in his baby-chatter voice, "This is all to do with you, isn't it?"

"We're being followed," Galen explains to Sean. "You've got to help me figure out how to get out of this city."

"And go where?"

"Anywhere."

"This is a werewolf following us, then?" Sean asks, to be sure he understands the situation.

"Yeah," Galen says. "Anon's real name is Christian – his

187

uncles have been informed of his presence in Philadelphia and are on their way now to take care of him."

"Don't you mean 'us'?" Sean asks.

"I'm… not sure, actually," Galen admits.

Being a wolf is no way to go about this endeavor, because it means I can't talk. I'm dying to join in the discussion, to see what Galen's thoughts are, because undoubtedly he's thinking a hell of a lot clearer about this than I am. But I know a lot more than he does.

"There are a few scenarios," Galen continues. "Christian, you bark once if they're plausible and twice if they're not. First, this guy following us knows only that you're here in Philly, but thinks Sean and I are still in the dark."

I consider it, and bark once, quietly, barely above a punctuated growl.

"Second, he thinks I know but Sean doesn't."

I bark again.

"Third, he thinks we both know."

Another single bark.

"If it was the first then maybe we humans could still walk away from this," Galen tells Sean. "Maybe. Otherwise we've got to stick with Christian until we can figure out how not to get our throats torn out."

I can't stand this forced muteness. There's nothing for it. It doesn't matter anyway at this point. I hunker down real low in the seat and transform.

"You're in danger no matter what," I tell them, holding a terrified Bonks still by the scruff of his neck with one hand and reaching into the duffel bag at my feet with the other for my clothes. "At the very least you're collateral damage, or you're ransom. Or you might have information they want to pry out of you. You're not safe anymore, none of the four of us is."

"Train station, then," Sean says brightly, pulling out his mobile. "Let's try and lose him. I'll call ahead about trains."

"Try and find ones that leave close together," Galen agrees.

"Times *and* platforms," I add. Sean nods, and dials a number.

"Yeah," he says after a moment, "when is the next train for New York…? Okay, and I also need Chicago, D.C., Boston –

you know, could you just tell me the major cities in the next half-hour...? Okay... Uh-huh... And what platforms are all these on...? Okay, perfect, thank you.

"Boston, New York, and D.C.," Sean declares, hanging up.

"Then let's aim for Boston," Galen replies. "New York second."

"Boston leaves first," Sean counters. "I doubt we'll make it there in time."

"How long do we have?"

"Sixteen minutes."

Galen sighs, and that sigh turns into a growl as the light ahead of him turns yellow and the car in front of us begins to stop. Galen yanks hard on the wheel, gunning the engine and diving into the right-hand turn lane to make it through the light. He glances in his rearview again, and smiles.

"Think we can lose him," he says, taking the next right. At the next block he takes a left. He goes two blocks before turning right again, and then dives into a parking garage. There's a subway station across the street.

Galen parks quickly, slamming on the brakes as he enters the spot so that Bonks and I both go flying into the seats in front of us. I have a feeling that wasn't entirely unintentional. After a moment I manage to right myself, yanking my shoes out of the bag and throwing them on quickly while Galen and Sean both get out of the car.

"What about Bonks?" Sean's asking Galen as Galen heads toward the trunk and Sean opens the door to grab his anxious little dog, pulling Bonks close to his chest. "The train won't allow—"

"Put him in the duffel bag," Galen says shortly. Sean's about to protest, but Galen interrupts him. "We *really* don't have any options here, pups, just do it."

I dump everything out of the duffel bag and hand it out to Sean. He takes it reluctantly, setting it on the ground so he can work out a way to put Bonks inside it.

Bonks looks unhappy at best at his owner's choice of transportation – he struggles valiantly to get away, worming his way out of the bag every time Sean's close to shutting it.

Eventually Galen has to go over and help while I get out of the car, pocketing the knife and grabbing up the cash and ID, and I stand by and watch impotently while they struggle with the dog. In a moment they've managed to trap him and Sean hefts a squirming duffel bag up over his shoulder, grabbing it around the middle with one arm to keep Bonks from moving. It's disturbing to realize this really is the best we can do.

"Don't suppose you know any sort of doggy hoodoo?" Sean asks me, entreating me to calm his dog down, and I have to shrug an apology.

"No way he'd listen to me," I reply, and Sean sighs.

"Let's get a move on already," Galen calls, already on his way out of the garage. Sean and I both have to jog to catch up with him.

We're all looking both ways very carefully before crossing the street. There's no sign of the ginger or his Toyota. We move as one to the subway entrance, heading quickly down the stairs into the station. Three minutes later we're on a train headed toward 30th Street Station, and Galen's checking his watch with ever-mounting agitation as Boston threatens to slip from his grasp.

When we get to the station Galen makes a beeline for a vacant express ticket machine, punching buttons and cursing less than quietly every time he hits a wrong one. We have four minutes, if the train leaves on time. I'm already scoping out the platforms and checking Departures, trying to determine the train's status.

It's still sitting here, thank God, and in a moment the tickets are printing, Galen watching each one clunk into the slot while Sean croons quietly to the bag that so far has been, for the most part, mercifully still. Galen grabs the tickets and we make for the train.

And then I see him, standing at the base of the towering World War II memorial statue with arms folded like he's waiting for someone, just as he sees me – a man whose gaze is riveted to our trio the moment he lays eyes on us and catches me staring back at him. I don't recognize him, and from this distance I can't be sure he's a wolf.

For a moment he doesn't react, he's just watching us from

across the long hall as we start to move to the train. I don't bring him to Galen and Sean's attention, not yet, because I don't need to rush them any more than they're already going.

But as we approach our platform he starts moving, heading toward us. We're well in the lead – when we make it to the bottom of the steps there's still no sign of him at the top.

We get to the train without a second to spare. It's about to leave, and the security personnel closing the door of the nearest car aren't keen to let the three of us on. Galen makes a successful hurried plea for leniency, and as I'm climbing onboard I look back to see our pursuer shoving his way past a family of tourists crowding their way down the stairs. He's not got a chance. I dive for a window seat to see him running toward the car just as the train begins its departure from the station.

CHAPTER 11

I wait until we pull out of the station to tell Galen and Sean about the werewolf. Neither of them looks at all pleased when I mention it.

"Are you *kidding* me?" Sean whines angrily, slumping into his seat.

"What's he look like?" asks Galen, the only reasonably calm person left in our group. I shrug, trying to remember. All I got were glimpses, really.

"Dark hair, dark eyes, early twenties maybe," I answer. "I can't be positive what he is, even, I didn't smell him or anything."

"But you said he followed us," Sean says, giving up shortly on brooding to attend to his dog by making a slightly wider opening in the zipper of the bag tucked safely now on the floor between his feet. A little wet nose peeks its way out of the hole, but Sean is careful to hold the zipper tightly to keep Bonks from making it any bigger.

"He did," I reply. "He was watching us the whole time. I'm sure he was looking for us."

"So they're talking to each other," Galen comments. "He must've been stationed there – I don't think the redhead could have guessed exactly what we were up to, do you? You think he could have made a call back at that intersection and directed someone to the station that fast?"

"It's unlikely," I concede.

"How connected are all the, um, your family?" Galen asks me, keenly aware that this car we're in isn't exactly empty and that anyone could be listening in on our conversation. "Do they talk to each other?"

"Yeah, they all get together a couple times a year, and they all know how to get in touch," I explain, also trying to speak ambiguously. "It's frankly abnormal to be as far off the grid as I am."

"Are you the only one who is?" Sean asks. Galen's looking off, undoubtedly thinking a mile a minute, and he nods thoughtfully at the question. I get why they're asking. If I'm the only 'unregistered' wolf then werewolves worldwide already know exactly who I am by simple process of elimination. It could explain how the ginger contacted my uncles so quickly.

"When I was a kid we had a list of maybe a half dozen to look out for," I admit quietly.

"Is anyone in your family a cop?" Galen asks. "Or in the government, or anything like that? Or a credit company?"

"You're asking about their ability to track people," I mutter, to clarify. I don't want to be heard, but I want to be sure I understand the question. It's one I'd have asked.

"Exactly," Galen agrees.

"Not... like that, not in my family," I answer, mulling it over. "My father is a banker—"

"Okay, see, that counts," Galen sighs.

"No, he's not got that sort of authority," I insist. "And he's not going to help them anyway."

"Christian," Galen reproves, frustrated, "we can't afford to make any assumptions here! At the very least we know of two people who know what we're up to, and we're positive they've got at least some sort of connection to your uncles, right? And one of them just watched us leave on a train to Boston."

"We have to get off this train," Sean says instantly. "They'll call ahead, they'll have someone waiting in Boston."

Galen nods. I can't help but agree.

"...But they could have someone waiting at the next stop, too," Sean continues his thought, turning suddenly morose. "If we get off they'll just get us right there."

"No, whoever it is would be getting on the train, for sure," Galen points out. "To come find us before we get to Boston – they'll try to corner us on the train. We have to be off this thing before that happens."

"He saw what car we got on," I add. The other two are standing along with me even before I finish, "Let's get to the front of the train."

"What's the next stop?" Sean asks absently, holding the duffel tightly while we make our way up the aisle. Lucky for us, no one seems to notice it squirming as Bonks scrambles for purchase in the shifting bag.

"Trenton," Galen replies. "It's like twenty minutes from now."

"Is that enough time for them to get organized?" Sean asks. I make it to the door first, and as we pass into the connection Galen grabs my shirt to stop me from moving forward to the next door. The three of us pause for a moment between cars to confer.

"Well, how long do we think this guy was waiting there?" Galen answers Sean with his own question. Sean shrugs.

"It had to have been a while," I say, agreeing with Galen's earlier assumption. "There's just no way he could have come from somewhere else in that short of a time."

"So do we think there's someone already stationed in Trenton, or are they scrambling to contact someone right now?"

"They've got to be scrambling," Sean says. "30th Street's kind of a giveaway, really, but there's like a dozen routes out of the city…"

"So do we think they could get someone down to the station *and* buy a ticket in time?" Galen asks. I find myself wondering what the hell he's doing, asking all these questions, because I'm sure he's already got answers to every one of them. Maybe he just wants confirmation.

"It's not likely," Sean replies.

"It's not impossible," I counter.

"So let's say it's possible – do we get off or stay on?"

"*He's* definitely going to get on," I say. "They're going to be piling up as many as they can on this train."

"But do we have to get off right away?" Galen persists.

"Why wouldn't we?"

"Because I want to make it as far as we can to Boston before we have to get off," Galen explains. "Because the minute we get off the train we're stranded. Show of hands for wanting to be stranded in Trenton."

Sean and I get the point.

"But it's an hour to Newark," Sean protests, "hour and a half to New York – we're never going to make it that far. And God knows how many of them there are in New York."

"We can't stay on to New York," I add, agreeing wholeheartedly with Sean. New York has to be crawling with wolves, there's a big family in the area. I certainly never wanted to set foot there.

"Can we make it to Newark?" Galen asks. Sean cringes his doubtful reply, and I have to admit I don't know whether it's worth the risk. Galen turns to me. "Come on, you're the resident expert at running, here."

"I've never been bloody *chased* before," I insist, raising my hands in surrender. "This shit is way beyond me. I mean I don't know, I guess... I guess we can take our chances with Trenton. I can at least get off while it's stopped and see what I can smell."

"How good a test is that?"

I shrug. "I don't know, it's – it's probably *okay*, as long as he's passed by that spot in the last five minutes or so. If it was my other nose I'd smell him practically for hours."

"How the hell do you *smell* a... one of your type anyway?" Galen asks, momentarily sidetracked by the lure of an intellectual diversion.

"There's just... a smell," I explain poorly, shrugging again. "I don't know how to describe it – you people are all practically odor-blind as far as I'm concerned."

"Anosmic," Galen corrects me absently, already off in some other logical world, probably calculating likelihoods about the length of the platform, the range of my olfaction, the movement pattern of the prospective Trenton werewolf...

"What about Bonks?" Sean asks suddenly. "Could he smell one?"

"Much better than I can right now," I answer him, catching onto the idea. I hadn't thought of that. Bonks could be a fantastic sniffer...

"How the hell are we going to know if he smells one?" Galen points out, coming back out of his introspection cloud. "He didn't smell the last one."

"Okay, let's forget the smell thing, all right?" I insist, frustrated. We've got fifteen minutes at best to work out a strategy for Trenton. "Just run through the scenarios. There's either zero or one or many of them waiting in Trenton. He or they either do or don't get on the train, and if it's plural then they'll probably split up."

"So zero's no problem, we stay," Galen continues the thought. "If one stays off, we stay on. If one gets on..."

"We'll have to get off," I tell him. "I'm not fighting anyone on a fucking train. In fact if *any* of them gets on, we get off. No question."

"Fine. So tell me how we know if one gets on," Galen counters.

I pause. There's no real answer to that. There's no way to tell visually – really the smell is the only difference between us and humans. And we've already run the circles on that argument. Galen jumps on my hesitance.

"I say unless you actually know for sure one's gotten on, we stay on," he says. "And we'll get off in Newark regardless."

"And then what?" I ask. "What's so important about getting to Boston?"

"Mike," Galen replies simply. "We can crash with Mike for free – if we get hotels we're going to burn through all our cash in no time."

I'm not the only one underwhelmed by the proposal, I can tell by Sean's sudden dismayed look. I can tell you already contacting Mike is going to be a bad idea. For us, for Mike, for everyone involved. I've already got two humans and a dog to worry about, I don't need to be dragging more people into this mess.

Galen notices our hesitance. "Fine. We'll discuss that later. Let's get moving."

We push forward. I'm scanning all the seats as I pass, trying to remember faces. God knows the platform in Trenton is going to be crazy enough without me having to scan every single face and decide whether it's getting on or off the train. The cars aren't all that full, and I've got everyone memorized by the time we get to the front and find a group of four free seats on the left. Sean and I both move to get in, but Galen stops Sean.

196

"No – you're with me, over here," he insists, pointing to the next set of four seats on the right. He turns to me. "You check that side, we'll take this one."

The ulterior motive isn't lost on me. I get it. I make a halfhearted attempt to listen in as they sit down and begin to talk in rapid, hushed voices, but I give up shortly to respect their privacy. I could probably make up the conversation with a high degree of accuracy anyway – I love you, I'm sorry, don't be sorry, I swear everything will be okay, and if it's not, I love you. At one point Sean's voice rises sharply, "*No* – forget it, I'm staying with you," which means Galen's trying his damndest to convince Sean to find some way to get away from us.

I find it oddly heartening that Galen means to keep running with me rather than ditch me to fend for myself. He probably thinks I need him to think for me, that I'm a goner for sure if he abandons me. Which may be true. Or maybe he's got some sort of guilt complex, he's convinced himself he owes me for making me stay. Which is *absolutely* not true. Or maybe he thinks that because I was living with him, the wolves are just as adamantly driven to kill him as me, so we might as well stick together. I only wish that weren't true. But it is. They'd love to kill him, too.

I spend the rest of the ride trying not to over-think, which proves to be monumentally difficult. I want only to plan, to think clearly about anything at all, but instead my mind keeps churning over and over with all these doubts and fears and nagging uncertainties and for the most part I waste my precious minutes of calm solitude trying to shove everything away in order to consider properly what's happening here. The best I get in the end is a solidification of my pathetic plan, my flow chart of eventualities at the Trenton stop. I'm ready for everything – except, as it turns out, for what actually happens.

The train pulls into the station right on time, and as the car comes to a halt I'm watching every person whizzing by on the platform outside my window, searching for likely candidates. I have no idea what I'm looking for. All I can say with impunity is that none of the people I manage to focus on seems likely to be a werewolf, for various reasons of luggage or company or class,

197

but that's saying close to nothing.

Before the train stops I feel a tap on my shoulder, and I whirl around to see Galen gesturing for me to head over to the car's exit with him and Sean. I follow instantly, and the three of us go to wait in the space between cars along with a couple other passengers, a woman in a business suit with a single black rolling carry-on and a couple of guys in jeans and light jackets joking stupidly about how wasted their mutual friend got last night. I'm not listening, I'm waiting impatiently for the train to stop and the doors to open.

I find myself staring at the door handles, silently willing them to open, and that sense of frustrated anticipation peaks acutely when the car finally shudders to a halt and the businesswoman waits a fraction of a second too long to reach over and open them. But after that moment her brain seems to kick into gear with a start and her hand strikes out, and the doors open and she and the two men get off and Galen gives me a pointed look. It's show time.

I step off the train and peer off down the line, scanning the passengers getting on and off the train. It's a mess of people, and I can't get a handle on anyone who might look suspicious. And I can't smell a thing. There's a middle-aged couple on my left jostling to get on, and I step out of the way to let them up the steps into the train. Galen pokes his head out the moment they disappear around the corner.

"Well?"

"I can't see anything," I admit reluctantly. "I really think we should get off, though—"

"No," Galen says. "We stay on. Come on back up."

I pause a moment longer, anxious and totally unwilling to follow his direction. But in the end I have no justifiable reason to leave the train, and Galen's right – the farther we can get from Philadelphia, the better. So when the last passengers make their way onto the train I get on too, and we all go back to sitting in our car.

The two newcomers to our car have decided to take the two window seats in my section, but Galen whispers to me to sit back down with them and I do. The woman of the couple looks up at me rudely, apparently feeling that there are plenty of seats available elsewhere, but the man doesn't seem to mind when I sit next to him and I take that as a sign of welcome. They're quiet company, the woman pulling out a book as the train begins its journey again while the man hits play on his mobile and settles in. I sit back and try to relax, occupying myself with trying to work out what the song might be based on the readily discernible backbeat in his ear buds.

And then I feel a tap on my shoulder. It's not Galen.

Three things happen at once: I look up to see a man staring down at me, I smell that he is a fellow werewolf, and I sit impotently by while he smiles and takes the empty seat across from me. He bumps the woman in the process.

"Hey, come on," she chastises, looking up from her book to castigate him for his choice of seat. "The whole car's practically empty."

"We'll move in a second," he assures her, smiling coldly again at me.

He's oldish, mid-forties, with sallow skin and greying black hair and grey eyes and a grey button-up shirt that all put me in mind of a ghost, or a corpse or a zombie or some other such phantasm that seems altogether too creepy to be real but also seems strangely fitting given the circumstances. He's just staring at me, watching me impassively, and I don't dare chance a glance over to Galen and Sean's section of the car because I don't know the status of their and the werewolf's reciprocal acknowledgement. I don't know if they've seen him or if they know what he is. I don't know if he knows to be looking for them, and I'll be damned if I'm the one to give them away to him.

"So what do you say, kid?" he asks me finally, and I realize that I've just been staring him down for God knows how long, now, "Shall we get moving?"

"Where?" I ask shortly.

"Let's find an empty seat. And kid," he adds as I'm already standing, my mind racing at a million miles a second trying to work my way out of this. I pause, watching him carefully, and he smiles again. "No need to hurry, eh? Take it slow."

I get the hint, and though I don't see a weapon immediately on him I don't doubt that he has one. I stand – slowly, as suggested. He stands as well, and he gestures for me to turn around and start walking toward the back of the train. I do as I'm told, though the hairs are standing up on the back of my neck the moment he disappears from my sight and I find myself paying attention to every other sense I have in order to gauge his movements.

It seems he's just following me, walking as I'm walking, and I don't think he knows about Galen or Sean. The relief I'm feeling about that is almost enough to combat the terror clenching me at the thought of my own immediate fate.

I open the door and step through as slowly as possible, attempting halfheartedly to distract him with the anticipation of the door closing on him. I'm listening intently, trying to hear over the pounding of the blood in my ears, waiting to sense his next move. The sound is subtle, and beautiful – his footstep on my side of the door, just before the door whooshes shut. *Behind* us.

Yes.

I whirl around to face him, and I have a fraction of a second to gauge the aim before my fist connects with his face.

It's an inelegant hit, a glancing blow just below his right eye, but it's enough. He goes reeling, crashing into the wall directly behind him and bringing up a hand to protect his face – but I'm already on him, punching him again and again, slamming my fists into any part of him I can reach.

He's trying to throw me off but he doesn't stand a chance, not with my adrenaline pumping the way it is. He slumps to the floor under the onslaught and I bend to punch him a couple more times for good measure, knocking him unconscious with a nice right hook that smashes the back of his head into the wall.

And suddenly there I am, crouching in between cars, propping up this dazed stranger and studying him carefully while blood drips from his nose and mouth and he makes no further move to fight back.

When I'm absolutely sure he's unconscious, I start looking around for a place to stash him – and find the bathroom door, complete with the most glorious lighted 'vacant' sign I've ever seen. I drag him over to it, shoving him inside and kicking his feet in behind him. I shut the door on him quickly and turn back to the car door. It whooshes open again but I stay put, and call to Galen and Sean.

"Guys," I say, and both of them look up – Sean hoisting himself up to see over the seat and Galen craning his head around to look at me. I don't have to say any more than that. They both stand without a word, and Sean grabs the duffel, and in a few moments they've joined me in the space between the cars.

"What happened?" Galen demands, gesturing to my hands. There's blood on both of them – streaky smears on my right hand and dark rivulets down my left forearm. I don't have time to answer him before a sudden deceleration throws me into a new state of alarm.

"Why are we stopping?" I ask, looking around wildly. There must be a camera or something, the conductor must've seen what happened, security's going to bust in here any second, I'm going to get arrested—

"Oh! Metropark!" Sean cries, slapping his forehead when he remembers. "There's a stop."

"And we're getting off?" Galen guesses, still watching me carefully. I gesture to the bathroom door, behind which my former assailant lies slumped on the toilet seat.

"One got on," I tell Galen and Sean. "He came into the car."

"No wonder Bonks was going mental," Sean mutters. "Could you hear him whining? It was everything I could do to shut him up."

"The guy's in there?" Galen asks, gesturing to the door.

"I didn't have a choice," I insist quickly, "I think he's out cold."

Galen nods, looking about as unnerved as I feel, right now. This is not going as fucking planned.

"Did anyone see you?" Galen asks.

"I don't know," I admit, checking around the car and beyond the doors into the cars on either side of us. No one seems to be paying us any attention. It's just possible that it happened fast enough for nobody to have seen…

"All right, then, Metropark it is," Galen declares, and Sean and I both nod our emphatic agreement.

The deceleration is stronger now, and Sean has to grab hold of a handle to keep from stumbling. Galen and I follow suit. Galen reaches a hand into his pocket and grabs out a bit of napkin, passing it across to me. I'd laugh at the absurdity of the gesture, but I find it oddly sobering. This is the best we've got – bare hands and bits of tissue.

"Thanks." I take it gratefully, trying to wipe the blood from my arms. It's not nearly enough, and it sponges up the blood so quickly that I achieve only a less obvious smearing than what I started with. I stuff the tissue in my own pocket just as the train comes to a full stop. Galen punches the door open quickly and we get off, making a beeline for the closest platform exit.

An hour later the three of us are standing in a sort of huddle in the middle of a dingy, overpriced hotel room while our fourth member goes sniffing about the bathroom in his sixth excited round of investigation since we entered the place five minutes ago.

The place is small, with two undersized double beds and a minuscule desk crammed into a space obviously not designed to accommodate them. It's poorly lit and remarkably cold and it reeks of cigarette smoke. But it was available, in an unobtrusive hotel in a quiet part of town. It's almost exactly what we need.

The only problem is it doesn't allow dogs. Sean miraculously managed to coax Bonks into doing his business on the walk over from the station, so we've got at least a few hours before we have to worry about what to do with him. We're all praying he doesn't find anything to bark at.

"I still think this is a stupid idea," Sean insists to Galen, throwing up his hands in exasperation and stepping away. He's talking about the hotel phone Galen's got in his hand, the number he's already in the middle of dialing.

"Give me a better one," Galen retorts, still punching buttons. Sean remains silent. I'm no happier than he is about this, but I've got as many alternative suggestions as he does.

There's no dissuading Galen from calling Mike. We've been arguing about our next move since the train station, and we keep going round in circles. There's just no other way to get out of here without paying a shitload of money, using a credit card, or providing someone with some form of ID. None of which Galen wants to do, not if there's some werewolf somewhere in the U.S. who's got access to bank accounts or police reports.

He's being overly cautious, but I don't blame him. I'm more than slightly rattled after that encounter with the werewolf on the train. I've since washed the blood off my arms – it was the first thing I did when we got in here – but I still can't shake that nagging sense of terror, that unwilling recognition of just how close I got to getting caught. Getting killed.

Galen finishes dialing the number, and I take a seat on the bed to listen in while Sean goes to drag Bonks away from wedging his head permanently in the trashcan. After a few rings the other line picks up, and Galen smiles in relief.

"Hey, Mike, it's Gale... Oh, nothing, really – hey, when was the last time you were in Iselin, New Jersey...? For real? Well, hey, then I've got the opportunity of a lifetime for you... No, I'm – nothing, nothing. But you want to come...? Tonight... No, me and Sean. And the dogs. Hey, you know what – Sean's never seen Boston. Come hang out with us tonight and then we'll hang in Boston, yeah...? No, I'm being serious. What could you possibly have to do on a Sunday night...? Just take the day off... No, I can't, we left the car in Philly. No, I'm..."

Galen falls silent, frustrated, and tries a different tactic.

"Look, Mike, we need a ride. To Boston... No, we can't go back to the station, we had to smuggle the dogs as it was – it's a long story." He pauses for a long moment, and then sighs. "Can you just come here and I'll explain? Please. *Pretty* please, then... Thank you! Thank you thank you thank you! Yeah – and, um, wear a hat, will you? Just trust me... Um, that's actually a good idea – *Mike*, come on! I need help. I swear to God I'll make it up to you... Thank you. See you in a few hours – yeah, this number. Hotel. Thanks."

"So he's coming?" Sean asks hopefully when Galen clunks the phone back down on the receiver.

"Yeah." Galen lets out a long breath and stands, trying to think.

"What was the 'good idea' of his?" I ask.

"That he check to see if he's being followed," Galen replies. "Needless to say he's not at all keen on the idea."

"No shit," Sean says sarcastically.

Galen sighs. "Sean…"

"Yeah, all right," Sean gives in.

"So Christian," Galen starts, turning his attention back to me.

"Chris is fine," I interject awkwardly. "My mum's the only one who insists on using my full name."

"All right," Galen says. "So you're going to have to play dog for a while – if you don't mind."

"Sure." I'm obviously not unused to my other form.

"It's just that I don't want Mike to have any clue about werewolves, if we can help it."

"Then we're in perfect agreement," I assure him.

"So… you can finish any, um, human business before he gets here?" Galen asks. I nod. "Can you sleep on the floor?" I nod again.

"Actually, is this heater working?" I ask as an afterthought, heading over to it and flipping open the panel to test out the various knobs. I turn a couple promising ones, but nothing happens. Galen comes over after a moment to consider it as well, and turns the same knobs I did, and frowns at them in the same way I'm doing. I turn a knob one more time while Galen hits the side of the heater. Nothing.

"Are you serious?" Sean asks with a look of doubtful dismay when we both give up at once and turn to face him. "Can we call maintenance?"

"Can we hide Bonks?" Galen answers his question with a question.

Sean sighs, flopping down onto the bed, and peels back the covers next to him to see how many layers we're all working with tonight.

"Well, at least there's two blankets," he remarks stonily.

"And… you've got a fur coat, right?" Galen asks me hopefully. I watch him for a moment, considering all our various options and coming to the conclusion that the humans are probably going to need those blankets more than I am, before I give in with a reticent shrug.

"Sure." Sure I do, it's just I'm going to freeze to death in it. God save me, but that coat of mine isn't exactly the arctic suit humans seem to think it is. Maybe if I was more like a malamute or something, or an honest-to-God wolf… but I get the distinct impression my particular ancestry hails from a much warmer climate. Certainly my father's 'side' threw an unwelcome wrench into my carefully honed bloodlines. The point is I'm in for an uncomfortable night – especially when Sean turns on the television after a few moments and we learn that the forecast calls for near-freezing low temperatures.

Galen continues to set down ground rules as the afternoon wears on and Mike calls every so often to update us on his progress and get more accurate directions to the hotel. Galen decrees that we make no calls using either mobile, that we refrain from creating any volume too loud for the neighbors, that we leave the blinds shut, and that none of us leave the room until checkout tomorrow – not even for food, not even to let Bonks out.

That last request is particularly hard on both Bonks and Sean, who end up spending an hour together in the bathroom with Sean on the floor trying to coax Bonks to pee in the bathtub. Bonks manages to do him one better, and Sean very nearly breaks the volume rule with his vociferous disgusted complaints while he cleans up after his dog. I'm just thankful they leave eventually, because the last time I get to use this room will necessarily be before Mike arrives, and I need to make it count.

And beyond that it's just waiting – waiting and planning, which Sean and I have both decided to leave to Galen. He seems content to lie on the bed closest to the window, staring up at the ceiling while we watch television from the other bed, trying to wrap his head around everything that's happened since this morning when he and I were still sitting on his couch watching a movie.

It's a lot to take in. I'm still stuck wondering if it's really real, if we're actually sitting here in a hotel outside of Philadelphia trying to escape a pack of werewolves bent on our destruction.

If you'd asked me on Friday where I thought I'd be today, this eventuality would have been an unimaginably remote nightmare. Hell, three months ago I wouldn't even have believed I'd run across another wolf as long as I lived. I was convinced of my total isolation. Before that club, I'd almost completely given up on thinking I ran any risk at all of getting caught – I wasn't sure my past would ever come back to haunt me.

And now it's happening. I'm glad as hell to be off that train, really – and I'm wondering how long it's going to take the werewolves to work out exactly when we did get off. I can fool myself into believing that at least we weren't followed to the hotel. It's probably even true. I hope to God Galen's right, I hope we've got a whole night to rest up before we risk getting caught again.

The real Mike shows up outside the hotel door well into the evening. He's been driving for better than five hours and he's not interested in small talk. When Galen opens the door to greet him, the introductions are brief – "Mike, this is Sean, Sean, Mike, and that's Bonks and you know Anon" – and then immediately Mike gets down to business.

"So what is this you've dragged me into, here?" he asks Galen shortly, looking around the room, taking in the cramped quarters and us two dogs while he hands over the bag of fast food he's brought us.

"It's better for you if you don't know," Galen insists, shaking his head. "We just need to get out of Philly for a while. And we need a place to crash."

"What?" Mike demands, stunned by the abrupt and colossal request. Galen shrugs, lifting his hands in a plea for understanding. Mike stares at him for a moment in disbelief, and sighs. "You're not kidding, are you? This isn't a joke?"

"I wouldn't drag you three hundred miles for a joke," Galen assures him seriously.

"We're really sorry about this," Sean adds, eager to apologize. "We know we're asking a lot."

Mike smiles silently at him, nodding, unwilling to be impolite to a stranger. I have a feeling he'd be blowing up a little more if he were talking only to Galen. Galen capitalizes on his sense of decorum.

"It won't be long, I promise," he swears. "Just a few days, just until I can think things through. I haven't had time to think yet."

Mike grins at the statement. "You and your damn brain, I swear."

Galen grins too. "Yeah."

"Go on then," Mike sighs, gesturing to the food in Galen's hand. "Get yourselves some food. You haven't gone out?"

"Didn't want to risk it," Galen says.

He takes the bag over to the table, grabbing out piles of burgers and fries and splaying them out. Mike and Sean head over as well, grabbing for their own food while Galen takes the time to pry apart a pair of triple meat burgers into mushy, cheesy bite-size chunks. I can't say it's the most appetizing meal I could have envisioned, but Bonks is whining eagerly and I agree with him – I'd eat any damn thing right now, I'm not picky.

"So you're Sean," Mike is saying to Sean as Galen sets the food down on the floor for us and Bonks begins to attack his voraciously. I wolf mine down in a similar fashion, not interested in having Bonks attempt to steal any of mine once he finishes his. I'm in no mood for a canine confrontation. If he tries to touch *any* of my food he's going to wish he hadn't.

"And you're Mike," Sean counters him with a smile. "I can't believe I'm finally getting to meet you."

"Same goes," Mike says. "Your boyfriend here's been putting off a meeting."

"Yeah, the timing never seems to work out," Sean replies vaguely.

"Hey, how's your friend getting by with my ID?" Mike asks. "That work out okay?"

"It's, um, it worked, yeah," Sean says with a smile, nodding vigorously once he works his way through to an answer. "Thank you so much. It really means a lot."

Mike smiles. "No problem." He opens up the wrapping on his burger and takes a massive, contemplative bite, and fails to swallow before he asks Galen, "So why'd I have to watch my back on the way here?"

"Because I'm not sure if people know I know you," Galen explains. "I mean we were on a train to Boston, I've only got a few people I even know anymore in Boston."

"Then why would you come to my house in the first place?" Mike asks, confused at Galen's apparent disregard for his safety.

"I don't know," Galen admits hesitantly. "The likelihood is high that no one knows, I just wanted to be sure."

"Well, I didn't see anyone," Mike tells us. "If I'm being tailed it's below my radar. So what's the plan here?"

"We were hoping to drive up to Boston with you tomorrow morning," Galen says. "I don't know what time would be best to leave – there're advantages and disadvantages to rush hours. You've got the time off work?"

"I'll call in sick tomorrow."

"Perfect. Thank you."

"No worries," Mike replies, but he adds a warning, shaking his burger seriously at Galen, "I'd expect you to do the same for me."

"I would," Galen says earnestly.

"So… you're being followed, or something?" Mike asks, trying again to get some hint of exactly why Galen's asked him here. I don't blame him for having some serious reservations about this. If I were him I'd never have driven down in the first place, not in a million years. It really says something about him, and about his and Galen's friendship, that he was willing to.

"We are," Galen says carefully. "We had to ditch the car in the city and get on a train."

"How the hell did you manage to get Anon on a train?" Mike asks skeptically, looking at me. I'm about as easy to hide as a gorilla, after all.

"*Long* story," Galen replies, and Sean nods emphatically. Mike couldn't even guess the half of it, not if he tried. "Suffice it to say we can't keep going on trains, we can't use public transportation."

"I believe you," Mike agrees, sighing. "Well, fine. You guys can come to my place for a while. But you've got to be honest with me, here – can this come back on me, if I help you?"

"Not if you know nothing," Galen assures him.

That's a blatant lie. Galen knows he's throwing Mike in the crossfire, here. And to think *he* was the one to tell *me* we couldn't involve more humans... But I do have to grudgingly agree with Galen's assumption – we're not telling Mike anything about werewolves, and that's the real danger. He'll get out of this entirely unscathed, if we play this right.

Mike nods again, accepting Galen's answer. The humans resume eating in silence, taking their time with their dinner.

I'm kind of wishing I'd done the same. Those patties weren't the gentlest meal I've ever eaten – I can feel it all sitting heavily in my esophagus, and I have to head over to Bonks's water bowl to try washing it all down. Mike is the last to finish his food, and after the last bite he crumples up his wrapper loudly, takes aim, and shoots it into the trashcan. And then he glances at the clock, which changes to nine forty. He turns to the other two, focusing on Galen.

"Well. Shall we to bed, then? Because knowing you we'll be up at five."

Galen grins at his mock-elegant phrasing.

"Yeah, sure," he replies, and then asks Sean, "That all right, pups?"

Sean nods his agreement, standing immediately to get the first go at the bathroom. The other two stand as well, and Mike turns to address the heater with a critical frown.

"That thing work?"

"God save us, no," Galen replies, sighing.

"Great," Mike sighs. I agree with him wholeheartedly. The whole room is cold, with a nasty draft slipping in through the crack under the door – and unfortunately for me, cold air sinks. It's *really* bloody cold here on the floor next to the television stand.

Bonks has already ensconced himself on Sean and Galen's bed, curling up by the pillows like he does in Sean's bed at home. Galen protested about this earlier, but Sean let him know that if Bonks dies of hypothermia because Galen refused to let him sleep with them, then Galen won't have to wait for the wolves to find him because Sean will murder him personally. Which leaves me as the sole sufferer, here. And those burgers still aren't settling at all well, and to top it all off I already have to piss again and I'm in for at least ten hours before I can do anything about that. Tonight is going to suck.

CHAPTER 12

Tonight is one of the coldest in my memory. It's been a long time since I've tried to fall asleep without the comfort of a heater, and all I can think about as I'm sitting here huddled on the damn floor unable to sleep is how when I first came to Chicago and slept on the streets for my first blessedly miserable nights of freedom, at least I didn't have to pee, too.

The clock is glowing one fifty-three when I finally decide I can't take it anymore and I stand, pacing the room as silently as possible for a while, trying to work some feeling back into my legs while simultaneously ignoring the pressing urgency in my bladder. I'm dying, here. I can't stop thinking how if I wasn't a damn wolf right now I could head into the bathroom and take a piss, but the ergonomics aren't working to my advantage in this form. I know what Galen said about going out, but I'm in serious trouble. And the more I pace, the worse it gets. There's nothing for it, I have to wake him up.

I head over to Galen's side of the bed and whine, as quietly as possible. It doesn't work. My back paw is tapping the floor of its own volition, by now. I try again, a little louder. And finally Galen wakes up, but I hear Mike begin to stir as well. Rip Van Sean doesn't budge.

"What is it?" Galen mumbles quietly to me, sounding groggy and irritated. As if I could bloody answer him anyway. Sometimes I want to bite the bastard.

I whine again and head over to the door. Let me the hell out of this room, that's what I want.

Galen gets it – I see him shake his head in the dark.

"No way," he whispers. "You know you can't go out."

There's a hint of a growl in my next pathetic whimper. I can't stand it any longer. I can't tell whether I'm shaking more from the cold or my urinary desperation, but my leg won't bloody stop, I'm practically dancing on the carpet. I'm literally going to die if he doesn't let me do something about this.

"What's up?" someone else whispers. Mike. He's awake. *Damn it.*

"Nothing," Galen says quietly.

I whine again, louder because I can't control my own volume anymore. Necessity is overriding my judgment. Galen's glaring at me, silently willing me to shut up, but I really can't give a shit right now.

I can't get out of the room without help. There's only one other option. I bolt into the bathroom, at my absolute breaking point and unsure I can even make it. I kick the door closed and transform. The transition is agonizing given my current predicament, but two seconds later I'm in a state of perfect nirvana.

It's short-lived. I can hear voices out in the room, and the light snaps on under the door. I hear Galen's voice clearly – "No, wait!" – and a fraction of a second later, the eventuality I'd have done anything to avoid occurs. It's Mike who opens the bathroom door to see how Galen's dog managed to learn such a brilliant trick.

I can't find any appropriate reply in the few interminably infinitesimal moments that pass while Mike transitions from amused to shocked and then appalled and finally ends by slamming the door again with a loud, "*Holy shit* – what the *fuck?* What's going on, Gale?"

There's nothing I can do. So I finish my business and wash my hands and throw a towel on. The game's up. I might as well help with the explanation.

I emerge to find Mike still in a panic, cursing, stunned, and both Galen and Sean are shushing him, trying to get him to calm down and shut up. When I open the door, Mike gestures wildly to me and demands,

"What the *fuck* is that?"

Galen glances my way as well, and sighs. "That's the reason we're running."

"*He* is a werewolf," Sean explains to Mike, glaring at Galen, and I'm pleasantly astounded that he's actually defending me and my apparent humanity. "We had to leave Philly when these other werewolves found out we know what he is."

"I'm sorry we didn't mention it sooner," I apologize ineffectually to Mike. "And, uh, sorry for the shock. My name's Chris."

I reach out a hand in greeting, but he doesn't take it. He's watching me warily, ready to jump back if I try any sudden moves.

"It's... no problem," he assures me slowly.

"What the hell did you go and do that for, anyway?" Galen asks me, gesturing to the bathroom.

"What'd you want me to do?" I demand, "Piss on the damn floor?"

"You couldn't just hold it?" Galen insists.

"Oh, lay off, lovey," Sean argues with him. "The poor guy's freezing to death on the floor all night and you have the nerve to tell him he can't use the toilet."

"It's all right, I've lived through worse," I say before Galen can reply. And I turn back to Galen to address his earlier question. "And no, I really couldn't hold it. I'm sorry."

"Yeah, well, next time use the damn bathtub," Galen argues.

Oh. I hadn't thought of that. My face must reflect my sudden revelation, because Galen sighs, shaking his head in disapproving frustration at my persistent inability to reason while canine. But he lets it go, and turns back to Mike.

"So I imagine this explains quite a lot, yeah?"

"Yeah," Mike agrees, nodding emphatically, still watching me like I'm going to jump at him. He's frowning, trying to put it all together in his head. "But... how long have you, I mean, how – oh, oh wait..." He pauses for a moment, and looks at me with an expression of dawning clarity. "*You're* the guy who's got my ID, huh?"

"Yes," I admit reluctantly.

Mike turns back to Galen. "Are you shitting me? You gave my ID to a bloody *werewolf?*"

"I'm sorry," Galen apologizes immediately.

"No, no, that's... awesome," Mike insists with a bemused grin, turning back to me, shaking his head in awe. "That's crazy.

This is so cool."

"It's definitely *not* cool," Galen argues. "We already got chased out of Philadelphia and attacked on the train. We're in serious shit, here."

That silences everyone. Galen sighs again, trying to think.

"Well," he declares finally, turning to me, "Guess that means you're going human from here on out."

"You sure?" I ask doubtfully. We've already argued endlessly about whether I'm more recognizable as a human or a dog, whether our group is more obvious when I'm in one form or the other. And Galen's been of the opinion that the wolves anticipate me going human, they'll be watching for a group of three humans and a dog.

"I'm sure," Galen assures me, shrugging. "Mike complicates things."

"Why?" Mike asks.

"Because you look like Chris — they're looking for three humans that match our three descriptions," Galen explains quickly, gesturing to himself and Sean and Mike. "Now we have four humans. It's less obvious."

"Yeah, all right," Mike agrees reluctantly, clearly uncomfortable that he bears a striking resemblance to a wanted werewolf.

"So let's get back to bed, already," Sean argues, yawning loudly. It's past two in the morning by now, and the way we're going I'm sure we'll need all the sleep we can get. I have a feeling we're in for a tense few days.

"How's the floor treating you?" Galen asks me with a hint of a sarcastic smile, as Sean collapses back into their shared bed and yanks the covers up over his head.

"Fine," I lie with a shrug. I think they can tell it's a lie. We all know it's bloody cold in this hotel room, but there's nothing anyone can do about me sleeping on the floor. Fine. I gesture to the bathroom. "I'll just... go change back, now, if that's all right."

"...You want the other half my bed?" Mike offers hesitantly, gesturing to it. "I mean it's freezing out here."

"Um..." I can't say the idea makes me entirely comfortable.

But he's obviously not altogether too pleased about the proposition, either, he's just genuinely altruistic. He'd probably feel worse about me sleeping out in the cold than sleeping in a bed next to him, for all that it makes him uneasy. And I really am freezing. "Well, if you don't mind…"

"No, not at all," Mike assures me stiffly. It's his eyes that give him away. He's definitely still scared of me, and I don't blame him. I wouldn't want to sleep next to a werewolf, either.

Galen's practically laughing out loud at our parley – he thinks our mutual discomfort is hilariously ridiculous. He shakes his head and crawls into bed with Sean.

"All right," I concede finally, "I'll get my clothes, then."

"Oh thank God," Mike breathes, infinitely relieved that I have some to put on. Both Galen and Sean burst out laughing.

The next morning Galen manages to work himself up halfway to a serious traumatic fit over the exact time at which we should depart the hotel. He doesn't want to be on the road any longer than absolutely necessary, and he doesn't want to get caught in traffic in case of an escape emergency, but he also doesn't want us to be the only car out driving – it's easier to hide if we're in a crowd.

He goes round and round with this for a full hour while we're all getting ready, he paces and sighs and bickers with himself and even flips a coin best out of five for whether to aim for rush hour or avoid it. And then he immediately doubts the coin's validity. And then checks the weather channel for traveling conditions. And then tells Mike to go home and leave us all here to fend for ourselves. And then changes his mind and demands to leave immediately. And then looks at his watch and realizes it's actually fifteen minutes earlier than he thought it was and besides, at the moment he's still missing both his shirt and shoes. So he resolves to plant himself on the bed and refuses to move, a situation which lasts for about five seconds before he's up and pacing again. It'd be fascinatingly funny if I weren't so keenly aware of the fear driving him to act like this.

Eventually Sean gets tired of waiting, hands me the duffel now packed again with an irritated Bonks, and shoves Galen bodily out the door with Mike and me and Bonks following in their argumentative wake.

Galen goes to check out while the three of us pack the car, and neither event takes very long. Galen hands over the room key, and the three of us get in Mike's Volvo, and Mike turns up the heat and drives up to the lobby to find Galen already waiting for us. He gets in and Sean, sitting behind Mike, leans across the car to kiss his cheek in greeting before turning his attention to letting Bonks out of the duffel. As soon as Galen's buckled Mike starts driving, turning onto the street and heading toward the highway. And we're off.

The drive toward Boston is unexpectedly almost pleasant, I find myself thinking as we make our way north and then east into New England. Mike does all the driving, and the rest of us watch vigilantly for suspicious followers. We find none, though every once in a while Galen or Sean will remark that one car or another has been hanging around awhile and Mike dutifully changes his driving pattern to allow the other vehicle to pass on ahead. This 'once in a while' occurs at least a half-dozen times an hour, as we all find plenty of false alarms driving on a freeway in a unitary flow with scores of other vehicles. We're all fraying a bit at the seams, really, and it's all I can do not to panic every time someone points out a potential pursuer.

Thankfully, this sense of panic dissipates marginally with continued driving. The farther we get from Philadelphia the better, as if Boston is some magical safe haven and if only we can get there we'll be safe. As long as we don't stop the car, as long as no one's following us, we'll be fine. And I think by now we're all ready for any intellectual diversion we can manage, if only to bring the stress level down a notch or two.

So the conversation in the car turns briefly to autobiographical history, each of us informing the others about our own. It's reminiscent of the first time I did this with Galen and Sean, back in summer when I was still pretending to be Mike. It's intriguing to hear from Mike himself now, to find out how accurate my fabrications were. Sean actually remarks in confusion at one point that he thought Mike's mother was from

Ireland, and I have to remind him that that was what *I* told him – that I was really talking about my own mother. And then Galen has to explain to Mike that I pretended to be him for Sean, to justify the ID. Mike thinks it's fantastic.

We avoid much talk of our current werewolf situation, oddly enough. It's as if fleshing out a plan of action will serve only to make something horrible happen, as if by avoiding that conversation we can avoid the reality underlying our sudden exodus. I do spend some time talking about my family in greater detail, though, when Galen asks after them. He's trying to get a better understanding of our society, of the types of people he's dealing with here. I think he thinks we're like the Mafia, or a bunch of homicidal gypsies, and I don't try to dissuade him from that opinion.

I tell the guys what I remember of my uncles and grandparents, these people from my childhood who stick out in my memory only as stern, oppressive people we had to go visit at least twice a year. I wish I had better specifics to add to it than that, but I don't. I tell them about my parents, and how my close family is nothing at all like the McCarthys. I tell them about my sister Keira's kids, four-year-old Max and infant Sadie, both of whom I've only ever seen in pictures. And I describe my siblings as best I can, given that all my interactions with them are a dozen years out of date. I doubt Paul and Lara are the same people now that they were when they were four.

I take some time to describe werewolves as well, the very rudiments of being a wolf – what it's actually like being canine. I've described this all to Galen before, but the others have never heard it and Galen wants now to put it all in the context of our chase – what can the other side do that we can't? What advantages does this werewolf nature afford our pursuers? Galen goes back to my sense of smell, trying to determine what I can and can't distinguish, asking me all sorts of questions about chirality and functional groups and a host of other chemistry-related terms which he generally has to define in order for me to work out what the hell he's asking. Sean's most interested in my vision, because for the life of him he can't understand what the world must look like when one's entire system is built upon two

217

colors. I spend a lot of time playing a sort of road bingo, pointing out various landmarks and vehicles and objects and explaining what they'd look like through Bonks's eyes. And Mike wants to know about how well I can hear – how far is my range, can I hear things too quiet for people to hear, can I hear different frequencies like dog whistles, et cetera – and I think I impress upon him and the others how much they're missing in that department.

And then Galen starts asking again about the werewolf element in all of it, the transition from one state to the other, wondering how it can all possibly happen as fast as it does given this whole litany of various biological rate-limiting factors he starts listing off exhaustively. I don't have any idea how to answer him. And I find myself wondering, as I often do, why the hell he got an English degree if he's so clearly fascinated with science… and philosophy, and politics, and maths, and nearly every other field I can name off the top of my head.

"But *two seconds…*" he begins again a half hour beyond Hartford, his tone one of skeptical disbelief. "It's not possible."

"But it happens," I say again, for what feels like the thousandth time. "I mean like I said I'm fast at it, I'm probably approaching the limit."

"That's just too fast," Galen argues seriously.

"So there's your proof God really does exist, then," Sean snaps irritably, tired of hearing it. He points a finger in the air, waving it like he's reading an imaginary tabloid headline, "'Christian Defies Biology.' What a great double entendre. The creationists would be so thrilled."

"Oh, calm down, puppy," Galen tells him, smiling at his peevishness. "I'm just trying to figure it out."

"Yeah, well, don't go taxing my patience on an empty stomach," Sean says. "You know how annoying you get and you know I get headaches when I'm hungry. And I am *starving.*"

"Me too," Mike agrees with him.

"We can't stop, we discussed this," Galen warns them.

"Yeah, well I have to pee," Mike retorts.

"Me too," I chime in.

"God damn it, guys," Galen sighs. "Don't bother trying out

asceticism anytime soon, any of you – you couldn't handle it."

"I'm stopping at the next restaurant," Mike makes an executive decision, going over Galen's head to my and Sean's undeniable relief. Mike's the one driving, after all. Galen sighs heavily but he relents, falling to looking out the window again and pondering my werewolfish molecular makeup, or something.

It's another ten minutes before we reach an exit with food. Mike moves to the off ramp, and we have a brief, heated debate over which of three burger places to go to. I'm getting really sick of burgers. And finally Mike dives into an arbitrary lot and parks, and everyone sits for a second to reset.

"So we're getting it to go," Mike begins questioningly, and Galen nods.

"If that's all right, it's your car," he says.

Mike grins and shrugs his assent. "Like I give a shit."

Galen nods, and turns around to address Sean. "You don't have to go, right? We can leave you here to watch?"

"Yeah, that's fine," Sean agrees immediately. "Bonks and I will wait for you guys."

"What do you want then, puppy?" Galen asks him, as Mike and I move rather urgently to get out of the car, both with clear designs on the men's toilet.

"Whatever," Sean replies with a flippant shrug.

Galen smiles. I'm sure he already knows what Sean would order here, anyway – for every restaurant he dines at the kid has a favorite meal choice from which he never deviates. And it would be wildly un-Galenic not to notice that.

So we head into the restaurant, Mike and Galen and I, and leave Sean to sit in the car with Bonks. I hold the door open for the other two, and head off with Mike to use the toilet while Galen goes to wait in line. The place is surprisingly busy – there are three families in line ahead of Galen – and if we make it quick then we can duck back in line to relieve him even before he orders the food.

Mike makes it in before me and takes the urinal, which leaves me with the stall. Fine. We don't bother to speak. Mike is remarkably efficient, and he's already going to wash his hands when I emerge. There's only the one sink so I wait patiently, and after a moment he gets out of the way to grab some paper towels. He nods a silent goodbye and exits.

The door opens again almost immediately, and instantly my blood pressure skyrockets. I turn quickly to see a man walk in, but he just flashes me a polite smile before he ducks into the empty stall. He reeks of some weird musky cologne, but he doesn't smell like wolf. I turn around again, letting out a breath of relief as I go back to washing my hands. I pump out a couple handfuls of soap—

"Christian."

My heart stops. I wasn't listening closely, that's the problem – I have a flash auditory memory of a few too many footsteps and a distinct absence of a stall latch sliding shut. I turn around slowly to see the same stranger facing me, only now he's got a knife in his right hand. And I'm cursing another sense of mine as well, because now that he's closer I recognize the scent of wolf buried under that overpowering cologne. I raise my hands in surrender.

"What do you want?" I ask.

"I'm supposed to escort you to Boston," the man tells me. I'm focused on the knife, still poised in the air between us. I'm already envisioning what it'll feel like when he stabs it into me. It's not helping me stay calm.

"Why?"

"You know why."

"Well, no, actually," I try to stall him. Galen's got to be on his way. Mike's already gone back to the line, he'll take over ordering, Galen's going to open that door any minute now. Any minute now. "What have I done?"

"I really don't have time for this," the man warns, flashing the knife at me. I back away against the wall, arms still raised. I'm wondering absently why I never took a self-defense course. Of all the people on the planet most likely to need it...

And then suddenly, thankfully, the door bursts open—

And it's *Sean* standing there in the doorway, hand hidden in the pocket of his jacket with fingers pointing directly at the stranger holding the knife. And he's totally convincing – if I didn't know better, I'd think the kid actually had a gun. Sean

220

inches his way inside the room, shutting the door behind him.

"Put it down," he commands, stone-faced, gesturing to the knife.

The man hesitates. He's not sure he buys it. But Sean looks too serious, and too unlike a credible bluffer, for him to believe Sean's faking it. The werewolf sets the knife down slowly on the floor.

"Now back off."

The man takes one step back and I jump on the opportunity, snatching the knife up off the floor. So now we have one *real* weapon, thank God. Sean capitalizes on the man's credulity.

"Empty your pockets. Everything, you hear?"

And the man does. I'm shocked that Sean – *Sean*, of all people – is pulling this off. A wallet, key ring and mobile appear on the floor in short order, and I pick them up quickly while Sean keeps talking, his tone calm and perfectly reasonable.

"Now, we're going to head out to our car, and if I hear a goddamn word out of you I'm going to kill you. Understood?"

The man nods. Sean opens the door, exiting backward to keep an eye on the stranger. I follow closely, coming up next to the wolf and planting the knife between us, pointing it right up under his arm into his ribcage. My eyes are watering from the stench of his cologne. I'm pretty pissed at myself for failing to guess it was only a cover.

We make our way out of the bathroom to the lobby, and catch sight of Galen and Mike at the pickup counter getting our food. Apparently they didn't see Sean come in because they're shocked to see him now, and just as shocked to look past him and see the stranger we've appropriated. It's immediately clear to both of them what's happening. They move as one to the front door, Mike grabbing out his car keys while Galen holds the door open for us.

All five of us head to the car, and we have to pause a moment while Galen carefully opens his passenger door to catch an overly excited Bonks, tucking him under one arm in order to open the back door for us. The minute Bonks smells the stranger his demeanor changes – he starts to whine, struggling to get out of Galen's grasp and away from the unfamiliar werewolf. It's everything Galen can do to hold onto him as the stranger eases carefully into the middle back seat between me and Sean, who switch places to accommodate the positions of our various real and imaginary weapons. Galen and Mike get in as well, Galen allowing Bonks to dart under the dashboard and hide, shaking and whining incessantly, between his feet.

"So what do we do with him?" Mike asks, starting the car.

"Blindfold him," Sean says. He's still holding his hand like he's got a gun, and uses his left hand to tap Galen on the shoulder to signal for him to do it. Galen understands, immediately searching for something to bind over the man's eyes.

"There's a tie in the glove box," Mike tells him. Galen goes for it, though he shoots Mike a questioning glance. "Don't ask. I'm still not used to corporate life."

Galen can't help but smile, and turns around in his seat to cover the man's eyes as Mike drives back out onto the road.

"This isn't going to ingratiate you," the stranger tries uncomfortably, obviously still stunned at the sudden turn of events.

"Nothing would," I point out shortly.

"How long have you been following us?" Sean demands, transitioning fluidly into his newfound role as dangerous ringleader. He's clearly enjoying himself, despite the urgency of the situation.

"A while," the man replies vaguely. I'm in no mood for ambiguity. I press the knife sharply into his ribs, and he winces and adds quickly, "Since East Hartford."

"How many people know this license plate?" I ask him.

"Just me," he replies, and when he feels the knife again he jumps, insisting, "Really, really, I'm not lying! I wanted to be sure before I called."

There's a moment of silence in the car while the four of us try to discern whether we believe him. Sean definitely doesn't. Galen probably does. I can't see Mike's reaction. I don't know if I believe this guy, but I don't know what the hell I can do to get him to prove himself. I don't particularly care. I just want to get out of this alive.

"Who would you have called?" Sean asks. I'm already pulling out the guy's mobile at the mention, expecting him not to answer. He proves me half wrong.

"My ward," he replies, which isn't enough of an answer at all. But it is partly informative – he's answering to someone higher up, someone in the States, rather than directly to my uncles. They're undoubtedly at the end of this communication chain. I flip open his mobile and scan through the recent calls.

"Is that this Roger Armisten character?" I ask him. He's silent a moment too long, and I'm on it with the knife again.

"Yes," he answers instantly. I feel the need to give him a more serious warning, anyway.

"Do you think I don't have it in me to stab you?" I insist, leaning in and speaking in a low tone to impress upon him my total sincerity. "What've I got to lose here? Answer faster or you're dead."

"All right."

"Who does Roger call?"

"The Irish wards, what's-their-names, the McSomethings," he replies.

"McCarthys?"

"Yeah, the McCarthy brothers."

"Where are they?"

"I don't know."

"Guess," I persist, and this time I feel the knife break something – cloth or skin, I'm not sure, but his sudden loud yelp makes me think it's the latter.

"I don't know! They split up – I think one's in Boston, I don't know!"

"Why Boston?"

"The train, the tickets – the guy in Philly found a receipt."

Galen curses under his breath, and I can't help but crack a smile at his bitter self-censure. Luckily no one sees me. For a while after that we drive in silence, as Mike takes the initiative and gets off at a random exit, taking off in an arbitrary direction that I hope he's keeping track of in his head.

We start winding through back roads, heading out toward some unknown middle-of-nowhere destination where I think

Mike intends to have us drop this stranger. After a while Galen turns around to face me and I look up, not sure what he wants.

"Give me the wallet," he says.

I grab for it immediately, yanking it out of my jacket pocket and handing it to him. He opens it, scanning the various cards and even taking out one or two, peering at them before he speaks again, now addressing the stranger.

"So Travis," he begins in his unnervingly offhand way, that same cool tone I now recognize as the tone Sean was doing a fantastic job of mimicking earlier back at the restaurant. I *knew* I'd heard it somewhere – Galen's God voice, the one he applies mid-reproof with his deceitful students, the one he uses on his friends during a good rebuke. "We know where you live, we know what your family looks like – lovely pictures here, by the way – and we've got your mobile and your money. Ooh, and what a generous donation that is, thank you." He takes all Travis's cash, a small stack of twenties, and pockets it quickly. "In short we've got every possible means by which to make your life interesting. I wouldn't suggest that you go finding your way to a phone altogether too quickly, once we drop you off."

"Sure," Travis agrees immediately. "Whatever you want."

"How about here?" Mike suggests, and we all look around to consider the area. It's pretty agrarian around here, and at the moment we're at the edge of a large farm. We passed a neighborhood a mile back or so, and it looks as though there may be another one about a mile along. It's not exactly desolate, but this is probably the best we can do, and if the guy's got to walk a mile before he even reaches a phone then we can at least get back on the highway before anyone's the wiser. Sean and I both nod our agreement, but Galen looks reticent.

"You know," he comments idly as Mike pulls over, "if this was Arizona we wouldn't even have to look for a proper wasteland to dump him in."

"Yeah, yeah," Sean replies sarcastically, "miles and miles of intractable desert and all that."

"You wait – I'm going to show you someday, you'll see," Galen warns him. "You get out south of Chandler and the only thing in sight is going to be some abandoned RV park."

224

By now Sean has passed the lead up to Galen, who slips it over Bonks's scruffy little head, and everyone but me and Travis gets out. Galen hands Bonks over to Sean, who walks away a few paces to give the poor distraught terrier some breathing room. Mike opens my door for me and I pull Travis out with my left hand, still pressing the knife to him with my right. When we're finally out, Mike removes his tie from around Travis's face.

"We're going to be watching you until we're out of sight," Galen instructs Travis calmly. "Don't do anything stupid or we'll have to turn back around and run you over."

"I got it," Travis assures him. Galen watches him for a moment, and nods, and gestures for the others to get back in the car. Sean holds up a hand for a momentary pause, because Bonks is preparing nervously to mark some territory. Galen sighs, and he and Mike get back in the car. I plan to wait until the very last second to let go of Travis. I'm trying to decide why I shouldn't run him through right here. It'd probably be a while before someone found him, if we shoved him out of sight in these weeds…

But I'd like to make it out of this without killing anyone, if I can. I've never killed anything in my life, save a few accidental insects here and there. I remember when my brother Paul was all of three he brought a sparrow in from the yard during a moon, and Keira hollered at him until she was blue in the face over it. And the rest of us would've lit into him, too, if we'd had the voices to speak. I was, needless to say, raised a pacifist. All this kidnapping and stabbing and fist-fighting business is not my style.

Eventually Sean and Bonks get back in the car, scooting back over to their regular side so I can duck in easily on the passenger's side. Galen rolls down the window to address me.

"Come on."

I don't need telling twice. I back away from Travis quickly, still holding the knife, and duck into the car. Immediately Mike guns the engine, the tires spraying up dirt as he pulls a sharp one eighty and roars back down the same road we just came on.

"This is insane," he mutters, shaking his head, watching the rearview to be sure the werewolf is waiting for us to disappear before he starts moving. I think we all agree with Mike wholeheartedly.

"You think he'll keep quiet for a while?" Sean asks.

"Who knows?" Galen replies with a sigh.

"That was a fantastic stunt by the way, Sean," I say, recalling the past minutes' events. Sean grins brightly at the compliment. "How did you know to do that?"

"I saw him eyeing the car in the parking lot," Sean explains. "And then he went inside and I thought I ought to follow him."

"What happened in the bathroom?" Galen asks.

"That wolf just showed up out of nowhere with a knife," I say, "And then Sean here faked having a gun in his pocket and got him to drop it and hand everything else over."

"Jesus," Galen mutters, stunned. "Good job, puppy."

"Thanks," Sean replies with a tense smile. "What're we going to do now?"

I notice that Galen shoots a glance at Mike before answering, and I'm not entirely surprised when I hear what he's got in store for us.

"Did you get Travis's keys?" Galen asks us, and Sean nods while I pull the ring out of my pocket. "Good. Let's go steal his car and head back to New York."

"What?" Sean demands, startled. "Why would we do that?"

"Because we can't go to Boston," Galen says shortly. "They're already waiting for us there. New York's a surprise. We'll just take the car until we can ditch it for a bus or something."

"What about Mike?" Sean insists.

Galen turns to our gracious driver. "You think you can make it back to Boston okay?"

"Yeah, fine," Mike replies with a reassuring smile. "God get me out of this mess."

"Yeah, exactly," Galen says. "I think you can get there and we can get to New York before Travis gets his shit together enough to warn anyone."

"Two problems," Sean argues, and I think I have an idea what they are. I would have listed more than two. "He knows Mike's plate number, and the minute they find Travis's car they'll know we're in New York."

"But we'll be well out of New York by then," Galen assures him, "We just need one night to regroup and then we're gone. We'll figure it out."

"And I can apply for a new plate tomorrow, I'll report it stolen," Mike adds. "I can bum a ride off the girlfriend until I get a new one."

"Are you sure that'll be enough?" Sean asks him doubtfully.

"No," Mike admits with a shrug.

"Why New York?" I ask Galen.

"There's millions of people there. You got somewhere else in mind?" he replies pointedly.

I don't. He knows I don't. So I sit back, and so does Sean, and Mike keeps driving. He knows where he's going and we're back on the highway in no time, heading back toward the restaurant.

The car ride that had seemed to take an hour with Travis in the car has evaporated into little more than a fifteen-minute jaunt back in the other direction. We pull up to the car park we just left, and Mike parks while we all get out. Sean grabs Bonks and I grab our duffel and Galen gets the food that has gone uneaten in light of recent events. Mike gets out as well and pops his trunk.

"Are you guys sure you don't want any more help?" he asks awkwardly while we assemble on the passenger's side and Sean's surveying the parked cars to try and remember which one was Travis's. Galen shakes his head at Mike's offer.

"No way, man, get yourself out of here," he says. "I'm only sorry we dragged you this far into it."

"No worries, you couldn't know," Mike assures him. He opens the trunk fully, rooting around for anything that might be of use. "You sure you don't want like another jacket, or something? Flashlight? Oh, score, a toothbrush – and a water bottle. Seriously. Take it."

"Uh… sure," Galen agrees reluctantly, gesturing for me to open the bag so Mike can stuff whatever he feels is necessary into it. And then Mike closes the trunk and turns back to the three of us.

"Well," he says with an air of finality. He moves forward to give Galen a hug. "Good to see you, man." He hugs Sean as well, and shakes my hand, and gives Bonks a pat on the head. "You guys take care of yourselves, you hear? And I want a damn phone call. Daily."

"Absolutely," Galen agrees.

"I mean it," Mike warns, and it's easy to see he's sincerely worried for us. I don't find that comforting.

"Scout's honor, I promise," Galen replies with a smile. "Go on, get out of here."

Mike gives in and heads around to the driver's side, and pulls back out of the parking space. He waves one last time before he drives away, and we wave back. As easy as that, Mike's gone. We watch him head down the road for a moment only before Galen gets right back down to business.

"Where's the keys?" he asks.

I pull them out again and hand them over. Galen pushes the unlock button, and a white four-door down the way blinks a reply. We head over to it as one. I can tell the second I open the door that it's definitely Travis's car – that now-familiar stench of wolf and cologne practically gags me. I can't tell if Galen and Sean even notice it. Bonks does – he's not at all happy with Sean trying to shove him in the car.

"Hey, does anyone here drive stick?" Galen asks out of nowhere, and Sean and I both look up at him over the roof of the car, our hearts sinking simultaneously.

"Don't you?" Sean asks him.

"Not since I was seventeen," Galen admits grudgingly. "You can't?"

"Hell no," Sean declares. "Come on, you barely even let me drive automatic."

"Chris?" Galen asks me, his last hope. "You drive stick, surely?"

I shrug my apology. "I can't drive."

"What, at *all?*" Sean asks, incredulous. "Are you serious?"

"Never learned," I explain defensively, raising my hands in surrender. Sean's staring at me, appalled. It's apparently never occurred to him that *anyone* could live thirty years and fail to learn how to drive.

"Okay," Galen sighs, seeing that he's regrettably the best equipped driver in our pathetic trio. "Get in, I'll try it."

So we get in. Sean hands Bonks over to me, and I jostle him into the back seat with me while Sean takes the food from Galen and Galen starts the car. He manages that much just fine, but the minute he shifts the car into reverse and starts to back out, the car shudders and dies.

"Shit," he curses, slamming the stick back into neutral and starting the car again. The second time around he gets it and finally we're moving, and Galen makes it out of the car park without incident. Soon we're pulling back out onto the highway, heading back toward New York.

"I mean a plane's never going to work, right?" Galen asks out of nowhere. We've been riding in perfect silence for at least a quarter-hour, ever since we crossed the border back into New York State. Sean and I both drag ourselves out of our various worried preoccupations in order to focus on him. When he knows he has our attention, he continues, "There's too many ways we can get sabotaged. Too many security checks and everything. And there's the wait at the gate — we can get cornered, right?"

"We can't take a plane," I agree. "A car's going to be easiest."

"But we have to ditch *this* car," Galen remarks, and the question in his tone is obvious.

"Absolutely," I argue. I am not going to let him talk me into keeping a werewolf's stolen car. "This is the only thing we can be absolutely guaranteed the cops will be tracking."

"We can risk renting a car," Sean puts in. "We need to get the hell out of town, we've got to keep moving, as far and fast as we can."

"No, we've got to find some place to camp somewhere," Galen insists, "to regroup. As soon as we know we're not being followed I want to stop, yeah? Eventually we've got to get back to normal for a while — I mean Chris hasn't even finished his reading assignment."

Shit, that's true. I hadn't even thought about that. And I know what Galen means by it, anyway — somehow, eventually, we've got to regain normality. Whatever we do we've got to keep that end goal in mind, because otherwise what are we? Why would Galen and Sean ever want to take up my vagrant lifestyle, and how in the hell am I ever going to forgive myself for dragging them into it?

"What reading assignment?" Sean asks suspiciously. Galen just looks at him pointedly, and he smiles. "Catch-22?" Galen grins, and Sean shakes his head in amusement. "You're too easy."

"Sue me," Galen replies happily.

"So we'll find somewhere to stop," Sean says. "Eventually. But I'm serious, lovey, I don't want to stay anywhere too long. One night in New York and that's it, got it?"

"Of course, of course," Galen agrees immediately. "New York's a shit place to camp, for sure."

"So where are we ditching the car?" I ask. Galen's earlier comment has made me nervous. I want to make sure he's committed to getting rid of it.

"I don't know," he says. "We'll park near a subway station somewhere. Keep your eyes open."

"We're sure we're not being followed?" I ask, looking around again at all the cars surrounding us.

"We're obviously not good judges," Sean mutters.

"I haven't seen anything," Galen says.

"But Travis could have called someone as much as an hour ago," I persist.

"You don't think we scared him enough?" Galen asks.

"No offense, but we're not exactly terrifying," I tell him.

"He probably ran to call someone the second we were out of sight," Sean says.

"You turned his phone off, right?" Galen asks me for the thousandth time.

"*Yes.*"

"So we ditch the car, find a hotel, and move out tomorrow," Galen says. Sean and I nod our agreement.

I can't say that I end up paying all that much attention to our direction as we approach the city. I'm watching every other car, every pedestrian, every possible suspect to see if I can find a werewolf anywhere nearby. The problem with searching like this is that the false positive rate is through the roof – my damn heart's stopping and starting in halting spasms every few seconds when I see someone turning to watch our car go by, wondering if they're motivated by anything more than idle interest.

Sean's the one who's spent the most time in New York City, and he directs Galen toward some suitable neighborhood he seems to recall, caught up in trying to remember a specific car park he used to leave his car in that had a subway stop nearby. Eventually we find it, and Galen parks, and we all get out. By now Bonks is used to the duffel bag and makes no overt protest about heading back into it, but for his sake I ask Sean to give the poor guy a second out in the fresh air first. That car was perfect torture.

"Are we *sure* about this?" Galen asks doubtfully, staring at the car with an air of reluctant unease, still unwilling to give it up.

"Yes," Sean and I chorus immediately.

"It's not a choice," I add. "We're not keeping it."

"All right," Galen concedes finally, reluctantly. He waits until Sean's got Bonks in the duffel, then turns on his heel and starts heading off toward the subway entrance. "Let's find a hotel."

Our strategy on the subway goes something like this: get on any line, get off anywhere, and hope for the best. I'm the one in the lead on this expedition, and I'm on high alert – Galen's counting on me to identify any wolves in the area. Every sense I have at my disposal is working overtime, but I don't smell or see or hear anything that indicates we're being followed. When we get down to the platform we find it regrettably crowded – we've managed to hit the end of day rush. Galen almost loses heart the moment he sees how many people there are. It's hard to keep track of everything going on. But Sean and I convince him to get on the train, and to his credit he hesitates only a moment before he finally does.

When we get off the subway our choice of hotel is similar. Walk in any direction and take the first cheap place we find. We go for a total of five blocks before we find a suitable hotel, and less than half an hour after we left Travis's car behind, we've managed to secure a perfectly satisfactory place to hide out in New York.

When we get to the room we take a moment to savor the silence, to look around the place and get settled in and take a while to breathe again. I don't think my stress level has gone below critical for at least three days straight. I need a damn break. I drop onto a bed almost immediately, utterly uninterested in the room and wanting nothing better than to sleep for the next twelve hours.

As Galen and Sean keep moving, checking out the bathroom and the closet and the toiletries and everything else the room has to offer, I find myself thinking absently how like rats we all are, with our instinctive need to physically move about to investigate novel territory. Caged rats, that's what we are, the three of us. It's not a pleasant image.

Bonks is the next to drop, and surprisingly he decides to come and lie next to me, leaping up onto the bed and startling me with his sudden presence directly in front of my face. I let him lie wherever he will, and finally he chooses to curl up right next to my shoulder. Fine. I even give him a friendly scratch behind the ears. I need some canine therapy right now.

Sean's the next to go, sitting down on the other bed, picking up the remote and considering turning the television on for only a moment before he disregards the idea. He reads the channel menu and then the checkout card and finally grows bored and falls to sitting idly, mulling things over.

Galen doesn't stop. I could have predicted that from the beginning. He's up and walking, fidgeting, tapping his feet and running his hands through his hair, sighing, talking to himself. He's not going to stop plotting until he knows we're well and truly finished with all of this. The rest of us listen to him pace with varying degrees of interest.

Finally Sean sighs out of nowhere, staring off into the middle distance, and comments morosely, "My parents are going to say this is God's way of punishing the wicked."

Galen glares at him.

"We're going to get out of this, Sean," he insists, gritting his teeth. "The last thing we need right now is your fatalism."

232

"Yeah, well your optimism isn't bloody helping us!" Sean snaps back. "These *things* are bloody everywhere – how are we going to outrun them?"

"We just need to think," Galen repeats himself tiredly. "There's got to be a way out."

"They'll track us forever if they have to," I say tentatively. "Our best bet's to keep moving—"

"No, we can't keep moving!" Galen bursts out. "I am not going to spend the rest of my life running. I don't even know how the hell you kept it up as long as you did. Just give me a second to think."

"But Gale—" Sean begins.

"Shut up!" Galen shouts at him. "Just one bloody second, Sean! Jesus Christ, you two are driving me up the goddamn wall – just *shut up*."

So we both shut up. And Galen thinks. Sean shoots me a less-than-pleasant glance in the interim, and I get it. Yes, I agree with Sean, Galen's being an ass. And yes, it's all the werewolves' fault. Correction: the werewolf's fault. My fault. Eventually Sean stands, disgusted with the both of us, and goes into the bathroom to slam the door and take a shower. I sit in uncomfortable silence for a while, racking my brain for any way out of this situation. I can't find any. There is none.

I'm getting used to the idea that I'm probably going to die. We've encountered three werewolves in two days, and that's not even counting the first ginger on Saturday. That's a woefully depressing frequency. And two of them got way too bloody damn close for my personal comfort – it's true they wouldn't have been the ones to actually kill me, but I've no doubt my uncles, my executioners, are at most a few hours' drive away right now.

I'm regretting having hung up so abruptly on my mum, I want to call her and talk to her more seriously. But I won't, and it takes me a moment to realize why not – because calling her is giving up. Calling her is allowing myself to believe we're all dead. And I can't bear to do that.

"Hey, Chris…" Galen says out of nowhere, his voice distant, and I look up from my spot on the bed.

"Yeah?"

"Do a little mental exercise with me, here."

The request makes me nervous. "…All right."

"Why exactly are they after us?" Galen asks me.

"Because you know what I am," I answer slowly, frowning, not sure what he's getting at.

"No, no, take it further," Galen instructs, like I'm another one of this thick students and he's got to draw me out. "Why do they care about that?"

"Because… you'll let people know," I guess, throwing my hands up in frustration. "Come on, Galen, what are you playing at—?"

"But why do they care if the world knows?"

"Because you'll kill us," I explain shortly. "Because that's what humans do. They'll kill us again, just as they used to do, as they always have."

"You believe that?" Galen asks me doubtfully, looking down at me. "You think we've not moved beyond that?"

"*Maybe* you have," I reply skeptically. "*Maybe.* Maybe some countries would be tolerant. But maybe some countries still condone witch hunts. Maybe people still get hanged for believing the wrong religion, or gunned down for being the wrong color, or destroyed just for being in the wrong place at the wrong time. Maybe genocide isn't yet a thing of the past, what do you think? Maybe humanity won't take so kindly to another sentient species when it still despises even its own."

"To be fair, your species obviously isn't any better," Galen points out.

"I didn't say it was."

"But think about it," Galen continues, unfazed. "The three of us are only dangerous to them because we know something the world doesn't, right?"

I sigh, because I already know where he's taking this. "Yeah."

"So if the world knows what we know…"

"No," I tell him, shaking my head. "Absolutely not."

"But look, it's brilliant! We just need to get you to a TV station or the police or something—"

"*No*, Galen. I'm not going up in front of a bloody camera!

234

Forget it."

"Why not?"

"Because no one would believe it," I reply shortly, sitting up to argue with him. "And the minute people *do* start to believe it then I've got all the wolves' lives on *my head*. No. Now and forever no. Keep thinking."

"So you'd rather we all die, then," Galen says.

"You're asking me to kill my family!" I protest, trying hard to keep my voice down. It's difficult. "My mother and father and little brother and sister! They're *seventeen*, for God's sake!"

"That doesn't answer my question," Galen replies coolly.

"I'm not doing it," I tell him, standing up and wishing there was anywhere I could go to get out of here. I can tell already he's going to try and argue me to death.

"But it'll get them off our backs," Galen persists, right on cue.

"How are you so sure?" I demand, rounding on him. "You think they'll say, 'Oh, okay, so sorry we pushed you to it, we'll let you go now'? No way. You take werewolves public and they'll kill you as payback."

"But you just said the world would be all over them by then," Galen says. "Look, it'll go one of two ways, right? We tell the world, the world goes after werewolves, and that gets them off our tail. Or we tell the world and no one gives a good goddamn, and the werewolves realize your stupid code wasn't worth a shit in the first place. End of story. We just have to hide out until we see which way the wind blows."

"I'm not going in front of a camera," I growl at him.

"You don't want to because you're as bad as the rest of them," Galen shoots back. That remark just about kills me, and I'm halfway to punching him before I manage, barely, to stop myself.

"*Don't* compare me to them," I warn, taking a step forward and pointing an accusing finger at him. He knows I'm about to snap, I can tell by the way he leans surreptitiously away from me. "I'm *nothing* like them."

"You call it like you see it and I'll call it like I see it," he replies, and to his credit he does wince in anticipation when he says it. "You're just as interested in upholding that damn code as any of the wolves following us."

"I am not!"

"Then why are you defending them?" Galen demands, his voice rising right along with mine. "What the hell do you propose to do to get us out of this?"

I grit my teeth against a spiteful reply. "I don't know."

Galen sighs. "Look, I know it's not easy. But you've got to start seeing reality."

"But a bloody *camera?*" I ask. "It's... it's sacrilege. I can't do it. It's too much to ask."

"Maybe it is," Galen concedes.

"I mean it," I tell him. "You ask me to go in front of a camera and I'll be dead by the end of the week. No question."

"Fine," Galen gives in finally, frustrated. "But think about it, will you?"

"I'll think about it," I reply.

I don't plan to entertain it at all. It's out of the question.

...But the longer I sit in the intervening moments of silence, the feebler my arguments become. He's right. Eventually I might have to accept the possibility of doing something drastic. I just can't stand the thought of having it come to that, not yet. I keep trying to think of something to say to fill the conversational void, this uncomfortable brooding silence that's ensued while Galen falls back to looking off, probably contemplating another escape plan.

"Do you know what it is about people like Yossarian, Chris?" Galen asks out of nowhere after a while, still staring off. I look over at him, but I don't reply. I know a rhetorical intro when I hear it. "I mean he's so phenomenally frustrating to read, right? And there are moments when you want to throttle him – but when you look at it from his perspective you realize that in his weird, ostracized little world he's reacting perfectly sanely, you know? He's a first-rate asshole, but at least he's not a zombie sheep like the rest of us. *That's* what I really love about anti-hero stories – I like to live vicariously through those sorts of wildly egocentric self-serving maniacs."

"Am I supposed to take that as a compliment?" I ask, half smiling at his pathetically transparent rant.

"I don't know," Galen says. "Is it complimentary to call someone a self-serving maniac?"

"A wildly egocentric one," I remind him.

He smiles. "Well, when you put it that way... I mean yeah. Of course it was, um, if not a compliment then at least a conciliatory gesture."

"I appreciate it," I reply with a smile. "And for what it's worth I'm sorry."

Galen looks up at me with a disapproving frown. "What the hell for?"

"You know." I don't want to have to be explicit. "If I'd known what would happen I wouldn't have stayed. I swear."

"I know that," Galen assures me. "Look, what's done is done. No sense worrying about it. And I mean honestly... I don't think I'd have changed it."

"Serious?" I ask skeptically.

"Well, I mean obviously I'd rather Sean wasn't here," Galen says, and I nod my understanding, "but... yeah. We'll get out of this *somehow*, and before this weekend... I don't know. I mean I had a pretty good time, all in all." He grins. "Today, anyway. Ask me again tomorrow and you'll get a different answer."

"I'm sure," I agree.

"Well," Galen declares, taking a breath and standing. "I'm going to go apologize, then."

"Go right ahead," I reply, and he disappears into the bathroom to be with Sean.

That night's sleep is fretful, for all of us. Bonks is dreaming in scruffy grumbling nightmares, and Sean keeps tossing about all night, unable to rest while his dog kicks his side incessantly. Galen spends the entire night on his back, staring at the ceiling, arms folded behind him like he's lying out in the grass again watching the clouds go by. I'm not dumb enough to think he's idly musing. And I only notice because I spend all those same hours on my side, unmoving, watching the pair of them and wondering what I've gotten them into.

We got incredibly lucky with these last two attacks. I don't know how many more we can afford. There's got to be a way to escape this, but I can't see it. I don't care what Galen says – for the moment we've got to keep moving. We have to get off the East Coast entirely, and out of the country would be even better – we'll be harder to keep track of if we leave the States. I'm still partial to renting a car and just driving. We'll take shifts – well, they'll take shifts. Hell, I think I could work out how to operate a vehicle on the long stretches of nothing in those middle states. Just keep heading west. We could even steal a car, or steal a license plate, just switch them out and then there's no way the wolves could track us.

Actually... that's not a bad idea.

I get that idea just as dawn is breaking. Neither of the other two is asleep when I reach my delirious epiphany, so I sit up immediately and start talking.

"Let's rent a car and switch the plates."

"What?" Galen asks me, his voice not at all drowsy. This is probably not a good way for us to start a cross-country trip, running on nothing but adrenaline and a potential future caffeine load.

"Like Mike said – we steal a plate," I tell him, ignoring that unavoidable problem. "All we have to do is find a car that looks similar – switch the plates and they'll be looking for the wrong car."

"That's... not a bad idea," Galen admits, frowning off again while he mulls it over. If it can pass Galenic scrutiny, this idea is golden. After a second, he looks back up at me. "Yeah, let's try it."

CHAPTER 13

Half an hour later we're all dressed and ready to leave the hotel. Galen's been rattling off possibilities and instructions and plans since the moment he agreed to my idea, while we take turns in the shower and rush through our last opportunity for proper hygiene in the foreseeable future. Galen's already trying to decide whether we ought to aim for Mexico or Canada, and he's not planning on stopping until we get there. And he's not interested in delays. Bonks is already on the lead.

"Let's go," Galen orders, and we head out.

I'm out the door first as usual, and I check the corridor quickly. Nothing. Galen and Sean step out behind me, with Bonks trotting along beside them. We don't waste time checking out. We head down the stairs and straight out onto the street, and again I look both ways before giving the go-ahead. No sign of wolves – smell or otherwise – anywhere.

"So which way was that rental place?" Galen's asking Sean, who took the initiative and raced through the hotel tour guide earlier while Galen was in the shower and I was taking my turn with the disgustingly communal toothbrush. The kid's got a practically photographic memory when it comes to maps.

"It's going to be a left on Ninth," Sean answers shortly, waiting for the traffic to turn before we cross.

But suddenly I hear rapid footsteps behind us, and to my unthinking dismay I see Bonks tense up in fear at the exact same moment I smell wolf.

"Run," I have time to tell Sean and Galen before I turn to confront our attacker, fist raised—

"Try it and I'll shoot," the man warns with a smile, holding up a hand to stop me. He's short, almost as short as Sean, with brown hair and beady brown eyes that light up when he realizes he's got me cornered. There's no doubt that's an actual gun in his jacket pocket.

I put my hand down immediately. Galen and Sean are still here, there's no way they could have run anywhere. We're trapped. And the wolf knows it.

"Gentlemen," he says, smiling broadly, "I think you're coming with me."

He backs up a step, gesturing with one hand for us to move around him and start walking back the way we came. We do, edging carefully past and walking slowly down the sidewalk with the werewolf at our backs. I'm not about to risk trying anything stupid when there's an actual gun involved.

"Turn here," he commands, just as we approach an alley. There's a car waiting, already running. Which means they knew exactly where we were. They were just waiting to pick us off. God *damn* it.

"Care to take a ride, gentlemen?"

There's no choice. Sean picks up Bonks again and the four of us pile in.

I get shoved in the passenger's seat alongside the biggest damn werewolf I've ever seen, a hulking beast of a man crammed in behind the wheel. He grins maliciously. Galen and Sean and Bonks get in the back, and the man with the gun gets in behind my seat. This is starting to look suspiciously familiar. How long did Travis wait to call someone, exactly…?

"Where are we going?" I ask the two werewolves, as the big driver puts the car in gear and heads off down the alley.

"None of your damn business," the gunman says. "And let's get this clear right now – I want no funny business or I'm gonna shoot you, got it?" It's a gruffer, less refined request than before, but I'll be damned if he doesn't put me directly in mind of Sean and Galen's act yesterday.

"That's against code," I remind him, disgusted.

"Big talk coming from a dumb asshole like you," he snarls back. "You know, I never understood why we have to follow the rules to take care of assholes who can't follow the rules themselves."

"That's a very American opinion," I remark coolly. If I didn't have a gun pointed at my head I'd have a few more words for

240

him, but I leave it at that for now.

"You're just lucky they said to bring you in alive," the gunman retorts.

I don't have any interest in continuing this conversation. We ride in silence for a long while, driving past buildings I don't recognize, turning down streets seemingly without any logical progression toward a goal. I have a feeling that's intentional.

Out of the blue Galen asks our captors, "Why are you doing this?"

"Don't ask questions," the big driver warns him.

"But... we're not going to say anything," Galen persists. "We've had five months to say anything and we haven't. And we won't."

"You'll promise anything to get out of it now though, won't you?" the gunman says.

"But this is all being blown out of proportion," Galen argues.

"What the hell do you know about 'proportion'?" the gunman demands of him. "What makes you think you know a goddamn thing about werewolves?"

"He knows more than you do, you stupid prick," I tell him, and instantly my head explodes in pain when that stupid prick hits me with the butt of his gun. I give in and shut up. I'll bide my time. If I'm picturing my immediate future correctly, there will be plenty of opportunity to pay him back for that, anyway.

The gunman turns his attention back to Galen, his tone turning annoyingly patronizing. "Please. Continue. What do you know about werewolves?"

"Well, you've got a culture based on fear – of humans, of course, but also of your rules and your leaders and not least your own bodies, though I'm not sure most of you'd put it that way," Galen answers after a moment, and I'm impressed by his tone – humble, academic, pensive. God knows how he can manage pensive, under the circumstances. But he does. The patient silence during his subsequent pause implies I'm not the only one impressed. "As far as I know you're spread thin across the globe, and if I had to make a guess I'd say the only two things binding all of you together are the fact that you all change shape every so often and you all have a mortal fear of letting any human find out about it. But other than that your society seems strangely disconnected – a lot less cohesive than I'd have pictured, honestly. I'd imagine, for instance, that if you even know this man's name now you certainly hadn't heard of him before a few days ago.

"But now you're involved inextricably in his – and our – fate, and that's logical to you because he's a werewolf like you. That's enough. That's critical, really – I mean his father was made a wolf, so as far as any of us know *I* could actually be more closely related to him than you are. But if you pushed him to be honest he'd tell you that even if I was his brother you'd still be more like him than I am by virtue of your shared werewolfdom. And though all three of you would probably revolt against me for saying it, that similarity forces him to value your laws above all human ones. Just as you obviously value them.

"It's a dangerous assumption, though, isn't it, this notion that 'my' ideology supersedes 'yours' because it takes my experience into account – that human law doesn't incorporate the existence of wolves so it must be inferior in its entirety? That's practically a logical fallacy. Surely we have *some* common morality. And right now you're sitting here pointing a gun at a guy's head and you're perfectly willing to *kill him* with it, and the reason is that you think he told me what you are. Nothing more than that. You think he told someone, and you'll kill him for the offense.

"Now, I'll give you credit and concede that your lot probably subscribe to the utilitarian notion that killing one person now will save other lives down the road. And that would be noble, except that you haven't given humanity any say in the matter. You *think* exposure will end in bloodshed but you don't actually *know* how modern humans will react, because you refuse to even let us find out you exist – this fear driving all of you prevents you from learning if there even is anything to fear! From a human perspective I think it's all patently insane. But as Chris has pointed out to me, I have only the vaguest sense of what it is to fear for my life because of how I was made. I didn't grow up with your moral structure and I don't know your daily experience. Maybe it's perfectly sane, if you sincerely believe that speaking the truth to a human is a greater sin than killing a fellow wolf. Maybe we're all crazy, really. It all comes down to our ability to see outside our own isolated worlds and find a reality higher than our own."

I can't help but smile at his explanation. I get the hint clearly – he's talking to me as truly as he's talking to the gunman. One final effort of Galen's to get me to realize that I'm still mired in werewolfish myopia. What he wants me to do about it now I can't guess.

"Why you gotta get them talking like that?" the big driver asks the gunman.

"Yeah, yeah," the gunman replies sarcastically. "Don't listen to him, then."

That's the end of our conversation. We all fall silent, looking out our respective windows as the driver navigates his way toward our uncertain doom. I'm already lost, and I'm hoping Galen or Sean is paying attention to the route we're taking to our destination. I'm too focused on what we're going to find when we get there. It's not going to be pleasant. I'm trying very hard to force all these regretful visions of my wasted life from my consciousness, to keep it all from clouding my judgment. I'm going to need every faculty I've got for this.

After what feels like forever we apparently reach our stop, out in some deserted alleyway between a couple of warehouses. The driver parks and gets out of the car, coming around to my side. He yanks open my door and pulls me bodily from the car – I have to struggle to catch my balance. The gunman is prodding Galen and Sean to get out as well, still pointing the weapon at them while they walk around to our side of the car. The driver's still holding onto my arm, but he gestures with his other hand to the gunman.

"Put that away."

"Why?" the gunman demands. "We might need it."

"You know the rules," the driver insists. "No weapons."

They stare each other down for a long while, the big goon and the little one, and finally the gunman gives up and storms over to the passenger side door with a growl of frustration. He yanks open the door and then the glove box, and throws the gun in. Two loud slams later, he's back over between Sean and Galen.

"Don't even think about doing anything stupid, I'll kill you," he commands. He nods to me and the driver. "Check him."

Galen shoots me a glance as the former gunman moves over to him and starts patting his pockets and the big goon does the same for me. I know Galen's got the pocketknife on him somewhere, and I desperately want him to keep it. I'm trying to remember where the hell he put it.

Wherever it is, it's apparently a very good hiding place because the werewolf doesn't manage to find it on him before moving over to frisk Sean. Galen doesn't give himself away with a smile, but I imagine his second pointed glance in my direction is an indication the knife is still safely in his possession. I'm just hoping it's not so far out of sight as to be inaccessible.

When the gunman is done checking Sean, we all move toward an inconspicuous metal door at the corner of a massive warehouse. The big one pulls the door open without ceremony and shoves me inside ahead of him.

The place smells overpoweringly of wolf when we enter, and it's easy to see why: there are four men waiting for us in the middle of the warehouse – this big, empty, cavernous room of a warehouse – watching our entrance like predators surveying their prey. That means six on three. On four, if you count Bonks. I'm tempted to count Bonks as a negative. I study the men's faces, these fellow wolves of mine, and I'm shocked to notice my uncle Thom in the crowd.

"Christian," he calls jovially to me when he sees my eyes on him.

I don't reply. I know that tone all too well, and it's not pleasant. It's so strange to hear his voice, that familiar voice taken straight out of my childhood and dropped here in a warehouse in New York City a thousand miles from home. That voice is the voice of God, as heard from six feet off the ground whenever an insolent pup found himself wrenched up by the neck to come face to face with a pair of cold, malevolent grey eyes and a petrifying wrathful countenance that's still etched in my memory after all these years. But Jesus, he looks so *old...*

I've got to stop. Now's not the time to bloody reminisce. I've got to find a way out of this.

Thom is still smiling, clearly enjoying this. "Christian, my boy, why've you been running from us?"

"You know why," I reply shortly.

The big goon finally unlatches his hand from my arm, throwing me forward into the room when he does so. I stumble, but I don't fall. No way I'd give them the benefit. Galen and Sean follow close behind me, prodded forward by the former gunman. I chance a glance at Bonks, the most unpredictable member of our little group. He's terrified, trembling violently in his master's arms. Please, Bonks, for God's sake stay still just a little longer...

"You've broken your mother's heart," Thom tells me.

"It's been broken for a while," I retort. "Leave the humans out of this, they've nothing to do with this."

"Oh, but they do now," Thom counters. He sighs, shaking his head dramatically. I'm obviously a grave disappointment to him. I'm not exactly here to win his approval, but that sigh gets right under my skin. This man is precisely what's wrong with werewolfdom. He's all rules, precedents, obligations – bent on imposing human hyper-morality to stifle an animal nature he couldn't simultaneously deny and embrace in a more hypocritical way. He can't be human and he won't be a wolf, and after that all he has left is this broken, crippled werewolf code and he'll do anything to hold onto it. He'd rather kill his own nephew than look weak in front of a bunch of New Yorkers he's never met. "You know I don't want to have to do this."

"Of course you do!" I burst out, appalled by his condescension, by that damn smirk he can't seem to wipe off his ugly face. I want to wipe it off for him. "You've wanted me dead since I was born."

"Christian," he warns reprovingly. "You knew this was coming."

It's only as he says it that I notice we're being shoved farther into the room, that the other wolves are coming closer. We're about to be surrounded.

"I want precedence," I announce immediately. It's our only shot out of this. Galen's got his knife, sure, but he'd never be able to get to it in time and besides, Sean's got nothing and

Bonks is as good as dog food if the wolves go after him. If I can just focus them all on me...

"Are you sure?" Thom asks me, his smile broadening.

I nod. He knows what it means, what I'm asking. He knows I think the humans are useless against the other wolves. We both know I've gauged it correctly.

Precedence means the wolves kill me first, and go after the others only after I've been executed. Precedence usually means I'm taking the coward's way out, I want to go before I witness the deaths of my friends – but I'm thinking about it a little differently. I'm banking on being able to take out six wolves by my lonesome. The odds, I admit, are abysmal. But six on one seems somehow less risky than six on three, right now.

"What are you asking?" Galen mutters to me.

"Don't worry, I got this," I whisper. Not even the goons behind us can hear what we're saying. And then, more loudly for the benefit of the others and in keeping with the disclosure required by the code, I explain the rules to the involved humans, "If they grant precedence, *do not move* until I'm dead, understood?" They both nod immediately. "They stay on me unless you move. Once I'm dead you do whatever you need to do."

"Are these the only humans you've told?" my uncle asks me, his voice loud and official. And thus the Inquisition begins. I can't help but crack a smile, a nervous one, and turn back to address him.

"Has any wolf ever answered 'no' to that question?" I say. "I want precedence."

Thom smiles, grey eyes glinting with genuine delight at the prospect of finally, *finally* being able to dispatch me properly after all these long years. He nods shortly. "Then you'll have it. Which way would you like to start, my boy?"

I don't answer. I'm already unbuttoning my shirt so I can start in wolf form, because that's how they'll be starting. I'm trying not to fumble, but my hands are trembling. It's from nerves, sure, but my head is perfectly clear at the moment. I'm thinking a mile a minute by now, and while I undress I'm taking the opportunity to size up these other wolves.

They're almost all older than me – there's one kid on my right who can't be more than twenty-five, but he's small. He'll be easy. And the rest are out of shape from the look of it – they're fat, lazy, human-style werewolves. Comfortable with their humanity. And though I bet they're itching to get at the four of us, I also bet they're going to be no damn good at it.

That massive driver is definitely my biggest worry, at the moment. Unfortunately for me, he's one of the three currently in the process of undressing to fight me first, along with Thom and another man. God forbid we ruin our clothes in the endeavor of murdering people.

No – I can't be thinking that way, I've got to stay focused. I can do this. I've been a wolf for more days in any given year than these bastards have been in their entire lives. They've got nothing on me – I'm faster, stronger, better prepared. I know how to handle my wolf side, and I'm betting they've not the first clue. I can kill them, all of them. I've got to kill them. I can do it.

I know the code as well as any, know it by heart after years spent training to be a ward. I know the rules of execution exactly and I know that if I break them then all bets are off. With precedence the attack is limited to three on one. This is absolutely not to level the playing field. More than three starts to get confusing and messy, and it's always nice to have some intact witnesses around afterward to help patch up the executioners.

This is the beauty of the code, the sick dovetailing of justice and violence perfectly tailored to satisfy that rage, the bloodlust we force ourselves to suppress in all other aspects of our lives. These wolves are aching to kill me, longing to tear me open, and there's just that added thrill if they risk their own blood doing it. And with three on one they're not exactly risking death – as far as I know no condemned werewolf in history ever survived an execution in this fashion.

But if I *do* get lucky enough to kill or disable one of them, then the code dictates that another wolf steps in to take his place, and another, and another, until all of us or all of them are dead. If I jump the gun on transforming, or pull out a weapon, or turn and run, or if anyone else on my side steps in, then they have every right to go after us all at once.

So I wait patiently in the cold until the three other men are ready. And then a fourth wolf calls out,

"Three, two, one—"

And we transform, the four of us, and instantly it starts.

I'm faster than any of them at transforming, and before the big one's even finished I'm already on him, knocking him to the floor. The warehouse erupts in a cacophony of barks from the transformed wolves as I let the rage take hold, the red haze descending over my vision as I search for purchase around this first one's neck. He should have stayed human – he'd have had arms and hands to combat me.

It's a lesson he learns far too late. I sink my teeth into his throat and pull. Blood sprays up from his neck, a fountain of red spattering all over my face and chest and the concrete around us.

I feel a sharp pain in my side, and realize belatedly that what I'm feeling is teeth – one of the other two wolves. I turn and see the blood on the second stranger's muzzle. *My* blood. After that my mind shuts off as I'm fighting first the stranger and then my uncle and then the stranger again, scrambling to keep from getting pinned by either of them. And already there's another wolf undressing to fight while the rest go to help the dead man, and I'm finding myself in serious shit.

The world transitions smoothly into a phantasmagorical kaleidoscope of images and sounds and smells and pains – a neck, a leg, a tail, a flash of teeth, the stench of blood, a deafening roar of yelps and snarls and growls. And then Thom gets a hold of my shoulder, clamping down on it, and though the bite hurts like hell it gives me a perfect angle on his neck. I grab for it, searching for an artery, a vein, anything, tearing at him with teeth and claws and anything I can manage, when suddenly a cry rivets my entire consciousness—

"*Bonks!*"

It's Sean, and he's screaming, and out of the corner of my eye I see a wolf and a white ball of fur. The poor little bastard must have gotten out of Sean's grasp, to run or fight I don't know – he's defending himself now feebly against my third attacker, and it's abundantly clear he's got no chance at all.

And even as I watch, in the one split second that I manage to look up from my own personal catastrophe, I see the wolf dig right into the terrier's stomach and shed his bowels all over the floor. Bonks' yelp is horrific, and the sound is drowned out in a gurgle of blood.

"Bonks!" Sean screams again, hysterical. He jumps forward to save his dead dog, and Galen yanks him back by the shirt. A glint of light at his side lets me know Galen's not an idiot, he's preparing himself for a fight – but so are the other wolves. They're all moving to enter the fray.

All of them.

My heart stops. That's against code – they're not supposed to move all at once! They can't do this! *They're breaking the goddamn code*—

And then it hits me. Bonks. Shit, Bonks! The wolves counted him in. He's their perfect loophole, he broke the code first by jumping into the fight! All bets are off now—

I don't have time to think. I lunge at the third wolf, the one that killed Bonks, because he's now the one closest to my humans. I have to kill him before he realizes what Bonks has done.

He doesn't even know what hits him – I'm on him in an instant and I provide him the same service he did for the dog. I don't wait to see his last breath, I whirl around to face the other four wolves still standing. My uncle has retreated, he's nursing his neck wound.

That leaves three wolves. And three of us. The odds are better, at least.

The momentary pause isn't long enough for me to regroup. The wolf in the middle – the gunman – tenses, and we both move at the same time. My first thought is simply to block him, to block all three wolves from advancing beyond me.

It proves impossible. I'm faster than them, it's true, and I might have managed to defend against all three of them – but I wasn't counting on Bonk's killer.

He's not dead yet, the bastard, and he clamps onto my hind leg right as I lunge at the gunman.

You'd think it might hurt but I can't feel it, not on top of the adrenaline. I recognize only that I've been impaired, that I'm stuck, and the world grinds to a gut-wrenching halt as the wolf on my right capitalizes on my immobility and manages to leap around me.

I don't see it happen. But hearing it is worse. There's the growl, and the scream – Sean's again – which cuts off abruptly when the two collide and the impact knocks Sean's breath right out of him. They fall together, crunching onto the concrete, and after that... I can't bring myself to describe that sound. I'll never forget it.

I hear not a word from Galen, but suddenly there's a yelp so loud it echoes, and the wolf is snarling, and the wet sound of the knife pounding repeatedly into him is unmistakable.

I hear it all though I'm still battling the gunman, who just won't bloody die. It's all moving too fast, I can't focus on him, I can't find a way to get at him when the dying one's got me pinned. I finally manage to kick my leg free and suddenly the gunman doesn't have a chance. I pivot and throw myself at him and we go rolling across the floor. At the end of it I pin him on his back and promptly tear away at him. I want to make sure he dies—

Wait.

There was another wolf. *Where's the other wolf—?*

I know the answer before I turn. I'm still not prepared for it.

The final wolf lunges at Galen just as I turn to find him. Galen's got the knife out, and it goes directly into the wolf's ribcage as they fall. That's not going to be enough.

I'm already running. I barrel into the other wolf at the exact moment that he clamps his teeth on Galen's neck. He tears into Galen's throat as the two of us go flying.

CHAPTER 14

I can't even remember later how I manage to kill that last wolf. It's an instantaneous blank in my memory. All of a sudden he's just dead, just a corpse bleeding all over the floor. I transform back into my human form, frantic to get to Galen and Sean, to see if they're all right, praying that when I turn around they're still alive. There's a chance they're still alive.

The first thing I register is blood – a big indistinguishable mess of redness. And then the scene shifts, and I see Sean lying on the ground with a heap of wolf piled on top of him. He's not moving.

But Galen is – he's breathing, I can see his chest heaving. I run to his side, I stumble and fall next to him. Blood is pouring from his neck. His eyes focus on me for a moment when I enter his field of view. He attempts to speak.

"No, no, don't," I tell him. My voice cracks uncontrollably. I press my hands to his neck, ineffectually trying to staunch the wound. He swallows, choking, struggling for air. "It's okay, you're going to be okay."

He smiles ironically, and mouths the word, 'okay'.

And then he just... stops. His eyes roll up in his head and he goes limp, his head lolls to one side. I grab his face with both hands in a desperate effort to pull him back, to force some life back into his vacant face. Maybe he's just unconscious, maybe it's not too much blood, maybe, maybe...

"No, no, no," I can hear myself mumbling, choking on the words, "no, come back – Galen, *Galen!* I'm sorry, oh shit, I'm so sorry, come back—!"

I break down, grabbing Galen's shirt and shaking him, repulsed by the way his body flops around under my direction. I give up after a moment and collapse onto him, too overwhelmed to move away, too stunned to believe this is really happening and too horrified to imagine having to get up and accept it.

A voice brings me back to reality.

"Get up," my uncle Thomas commands, his voice cold and harsh and unbearably loud given the gravity of the occasion. To think I'd forgotten all about him. He's picked up Galen's knife, and he's holding it to my throat. The audacity of the move infuriates me.

I move too fast for him to react. In one fluid motion I stand, knocking the knife away with one hand and clamping the other around his neck.

I grind my nails deep into the gouges made by my teeth earlier, fresh blood spurting out between my fingers and coursing down his body. I don't have any words for this moment, as Thom stares at me in wide-eyed, terror-stricken disbelief and I stare back, unmoving, focusing all my strength on stopping his air supply. He struggles weakly, clawing at my arm, but our wolves' poison works fast and he's already crippled double by infection and loss of blood. His efforts are futile and he knows it.

I kick his legs out from under him and we go down together. I've got both hands around his throat now. I want to watch every second of his death, every nuance. I want to make him suffer.

He's trying to speak to me too, to say a few last words or to plead with me, I don't know which, but either way I can't bear the thought. I press tighter. His face is turning a horrible shade of purple. He's still struggling, kicking, but by now it's reduced to the last frantic jabs of a body deprived of oxygen.

I'm thinking back on every time in my life I envisioned this moment, every time I dreamed of killing my uncles for making my life what it was. The real thing is far less satisfying than I ever thought it could possibly be.

He stops twitching, and I let go. The whole place is eerily silent as I stand up and survey the carnage.

Four wolves, one dog and four men lie on the floor in varying states of bloody disarray. I check each wolf's body carefully to be sure it's not moving. My gaze flits guiltily past Bonks, because it's painfully obvious there's no helping him. I survey Sean's body for a long moment, willing myself to see any sign of life in him. He's just lying there, eyes closed, head to one side, like he's sleeping off a hangover. Whatever that wolf did to kill him is covered by the wolf's own body, draped heavily over Sean's torso. I don't dare move it to investigate.

Finally I turn back to Galen, who lies exactly as I left him. If I try hard enough I can almost trick myself into believing he's still breathing. His face looks so tranquil. It strikes me suddenly, in a profound moment of clarity, that this is the same face I saw out jogging at six in the morning just a few months ago. This is the same guy who took me into his house, who made me dinner and watched movies with me and laughed at my jokes and managed to move me deeply when he called me his friend. This is the only friend I ever had. And I repaid him by leading him and the person he loved most straight into a gruesome death.

I can't bring myself to move closer. I mutter again that I'm sorry, and I wipe away the tears that fall when I do.

After that I'm on frantic autopilot. For all I know there are other wolves out there guarding this place, waiting for word of the execution, and I can't stand the idea of any of them finding Galen and Sean before a human does. I dart over to the discarded mounds of clothes, fumbling in pockets for mobiles. I find one in a pair of jeans and immediately dial 911, listening impatiently through two rings as I search for more.

"911, where is your emergency?" I hear finally. I've already found another mobile and I'm dialing on it, too.

"There's been a murder," I explain quickly. "Please, a lot of people are gravely wounded and I need immediate assistance but I don't know where I am—" I find another mobile and dial, "I'm in some warehouse, there's a bunch of warehouses around here but there's a blue car parked outside this one with all the doors open. I don't know if you can track GPS or something but I'm calling from a bunch of mobiles."

"Okay, please slow down – you say someone's been murdered?"

"More than one, a lot of people were attacked, it's like a dog fight," I say. "Look, I'll leave the mobiles on but I have to go. Please hurry."

The dispatch's reply eludes me as I drop the mobile and go

back to the clothes, grabbing at anything suitable to cover all my various wounds. I've got blood all over me, and not all of it's mine. But under it all I can see a few ragged gashes on my legs and arms and one particularly sensitive one in my side, and I'm sure there are more that elude my initial cursory scan. I can't really feel them all yet, but I'm sure that's going to change soon.

I end up filching the kid wolf's turtleneck and my uncle's jacket, and I throw my own jeans back on and root through everyone's pockets again for cash, credit cards, whatever I can get. I find the car keys in the driver's pocket. I don't have a plan yet, so I'll just steal everything and deal with sorting it out later. The moment the last pair of trousers is discarded I leave the building, trying to favor my right leg as little as possible. It didn't take too bloody long for that wound to start hurting.

When I get outside I prop open the door to the warehouse, then unlock the car and open all the doors as promised. The key has a panic button on it, so for good measure I trip the security alarm. Anything to get the cops here faster, anything to keep whatever other wolves might be waiting around here at bay. Amid blinking lights and a deafening chorus of honking I stare at the keys for a long moment, wondering if I'm not being an idiot, but in the end I've got to drop them and walk away. Neither the car nor the gun inside it is any use to a fugitive who never learned to drive and can't afford to be stopped and questioned about a weapon.

I make it about two blocks before I throw up, staggering over to the wall for support while I puke up the entire contents of my digestive system.

There are a hundred possible reasons for it. I'm exhausted. I'm battered up. I just fought and killed people. But the only thing in my mind as my stomach wrenches into violent spasms is that I've got Galen's blood all over my arms. I'm seeing his corpse – that's the word, *corpse*, which tips the balance. I can't believe that it's over, that I failed and that because of my failure, my two humans are dead.

Galen's dead.

He's dead.

I puke up everything I've got until I can't breathe, I'm gasping against the side of the building and clutching the wound in my left side that went from merely painful to pure, ungodly torture in the process of hurling. It's too much all at once, I can't handle all the combined calamities and my knees buckle and I fall over. I already reek of blood and wolf and sweat, and the proximity of the vomit tips the balance again and I start puking up black bile all over the place. This shit's layering up like a bad allegory, and at the end of round two I'm lying on the ground in a fetal position, folding inward like a crippled spider with legs all cramped in and both hands pressed tight into my side to stop the flow of hot blood seeping between my fingertips.

I don't know how long I lie there before I hear the whine of police sirens overtake the incessant blaring of the blue car's alarm system. It can't be long, maybe even less than a minute, but there's no telling when every second feels like an eternity. My muscles are already seizing up in the cold as I manage to roll over and shove myself up off the ground and stumble onward. I don't know where I'm going. I just have to get well away from the warehouse.

I've got the room key. I've got my fake license. I've got dead men's credit cards and a fair amount of uncounted cash. I'd guess maybe a couple grand – some of these New Yorkers carried hundreds. It's all in my damn pockets. And my pockets are soaking up all sorts of vile fluid as we speak.

Pharmacy. I need some alcohol and some gauze and whatever else bleeding people need. Aspirin, a lot of aspirin. I wonder what Galen would prescribe for this sort of pain… I really can't afford to think about that right now. Just have to shove it down a little longer, a little longer. I need to get out of this situation. I'll go to the pharmacy. And then I'll head back to the hotel room and take a shower Macbeth-style and fail to wash all this blood off me. And then I'll get the hell out of New York.

I end up walking a long way to find a pharmacy, and by the time I get there my leg hurts like a bitch and my side is throbbing like my heart's decided to take up residence there. I did have the presence of mind to check my appearance in a window on my way here, and did my best to wipe off the smears of blood covering my face and mouth. I don't know how well I managed it. First stop: bathroom.

Thank God no one gives me a second glance before I make it back there and wash my face off in the sink. It's one of these one-toilet rooms, so I lock the door and take my time at the sink, rolling up my sleeves to get as much blood off my arms as possible. I make the same attempt with my hair and face and neck. There's not much I can do about the rest of it, yet.

I towel off carefully and take a moment to reflect on how to act natural, because I know myself well enough to recognize that at the moment just about anything could set me off in some fantastic tirade of hysteria. Bring on the Zen. Be calm. Collected. Now is not the time to go reacting to outside stimuli. The inside ones are hard enough to battle.

After that it's a matter of wandering the aisles. I pick up the gauze, and tape, Band-Aids, rubbing alcohol, extra-strength aspirin, a massive bar of soap, a roll of cotton, fresh socks, shampoo, a disposable razor, scissors, and a huge tube of Neosporin. That ought to cover it. I pay with cash, thankful that at least the one bill I pull out of my pocket to pay the gangly, pockmarked, terminally bored kid on the other side of the checkout desk doesn't have any obvious stains on it.

The cashier strikes me as odd, somehow. He's too uninterested. Too normal. I can't help but wonder how no one else seems to have noticed how far out of joint the world is at the moment. It literally stopped, back there half an hour ago in an empty warehouse near the river, and no one cares. No one knows yet what a tragedy has occurred today. No one can see how vile I really am. It's enough to drive a man crazy.

I walk out with my two plastic bags full of pharmaceutical products. And when I get out onto the curb I have to stop, because it's taking me a moment to get my bearings and I'm not quite sure where the hotel is from here. I'm not even sure whether to turn left or right. I wasn't exactly paying attention to navigation on the way here.

My momentary survey requires that I actually look around me to see where the hell I am and what I'm doing. And in the process of scanning the street, I immediately find something upon which to focus my undivided attention.

There's a woman across the street holding a microphone. More importantly, there's a man across the street pointing a video camera at her.

My eyes don't waver from the pair of them for a second. The traffic on this street is light at the moment, and I don't think twice about crossing the road to get to them.

The woman is talking as I walk up, but she stumbles over a word and sighs loudly, interrupting herself, "Wait, wait, hold on," and takes a deep breath before starting her sentence over. So whatever it is it's not live. Good. The microphone has the number four on it, as does the camera. The woman's in a suit. I don't give a damn what story she's trying to cover – I walk into the frame and interrupt her.

"I'll give you the story of your career if you stop what you're doing and talk to me," I tell her. She's immediately affronted that I'd interject like I did, and both she and the cameraman start telling me off even before I'm finished with the sentence.

"We're in the middle of shooting here, do you mind?" the woman demands.

"Get out of the damn picture," the cameraman adds, in case I didn't pick up that request implicitly from the woman already.

"Just give me twenty minutes, that's all I ask," I persist.

"No. Go away."

"Look, I don't have time to argue," I tell her, shifting one bag from my left to my right hand. I lift my shirt up gingerly, exposing the set of parallel gashes that run from my ribs to my hip bone. Both reporters cringe in revulsion. "I need to get this cleaned up."

"You need to get to a hospital, is what you need," the woman insists, already gesturing to the cameraman for a mobile to call for help.

"Not yet," I tell her quickly, yanking my shirt back down and holding up a hand to stop her. I have to stop her. "Please. Let me just... find a hotel room or something – I have to tell you this story. I owe it to someone."

The woman hesitates, and for that hesitation alone I want to kiss her feet in gratitude. If I were in her position the cops would already be here.

"Why can't you tell us out here?" she asks suspiciously.

"Because if I don't clean this shit up soon I'm going to faint," I half-lie. She'll understand the real reason in a few minutes, if she agrees to come. "And I can't show you everything I need to show you out here. Please. Both of you."

The woman turns to her cameraman, who looks reluctant at best. They share a look, and I'm ready to start begging again when finally the cameraman shrugs and the woman turns back to me with a hesitant nod.

"All right," she agrees.

"I'm Cynthia Reed, by the way," she introduces herself fifteen minutes later.

We're in a hotel room around the corner from the pharmacy, one I paid cash for downstairs. It's a small room, with a single queen bed and a little desk under the window. The cameraman is setting his equipment down on the desk, and I'm heading into the bathroom with my own equipment. I set my bags down on the floor and turn shortly to shake her hand.

"Christian Talbot," I reply. The truth is all I have room for, at the moment.

"So what is this story you have to tell us?" she asks, getting right to the point.

"Give the man a moment," I say, gesturing to the cameraman, who is currently fiddling with something on his camera. I take off my jacket and throw it on the bed, kick my shoes off, and then remove the turtleneck to address the above-the-belt wounds.

"Oh my God," Cynthia breathes, stunned by the carnage concealed under the black shirt. "What the hell happened to you?"

"I'm... going to need a moment to answer that," I tell her. I gesture to the bathroom. "You mind if I just...? I've just got to wash this off, it stings like a bitch."

Cynthia's frowning doubtfully, disturbed by the apparent extent of my injuries, and the cameraman doesn't look any happier about the matter.

"You're not going to call anyone, are you?" I ask them.

Cynthia shakes her head. "...No, go shower. We'll be here."

I watch them for a moment, trying to discern whether she's being honest with me. I don't have much choice. I grab the soap and shampoo out of the bag and head into the shower, stripping my jeans away gingerly behind the curtain. I don't close the bathroom door. I want to hear them if they start calling someone.

"Are you from a news station?" I ask Cynthia over the noise of the shower, unwrapping the soap. The water flooding off me is vivid crimson.

"Yes," Cynthia calls back, but she doesn't elaborate on which one. "I'm a field reporter. Troy's my cameraman."

"Nice to meet you, Troy," I call.

"Yeah," Troy replies laconically.

There's a long silence. I take the opportunity to inspect my wounds.

My right leg is chewed up below the calf muscle, though only a puncture or two go in more than a half centimeter. My left leg and arms have a few minor scratches. My shoulder and the upper part of my back both burn like hell, though it's hard for me to see the damage without a mirror. As far as I can tell my side is the worst of it – the cuts left by the two top canine teeth are at least a centimeter deep, running diagonally down my body. It's still bleeding. And it will for a good long while, unfortunately, until the infection from all these bites works its way out of my system.

"So what is this story?" Cynthia repeats herself after a couple brief minutes. I decide to cut the shower short there – she obviously won't wait. I can't afford to let them get impatient. I grab a towel off the rack and wrap it around me, and emerge still dripping.

"Can you have the camera rolling the whole time?" I ask them. Cynthia turns to Troy, who nods and presses a button. I take a deep breath before I continue. Here goes.

"I promise you I'm going to sound insane," I start, "but you have to bear with me. You're not going to be able to doubt me by the end of it..."

And I begin. I tell them everything. I tell them first that all my wounds are from wolves. I tell them that these were no normal wolves, they were werewolves.

Both of them are about to get up in frustrated disbelief at that word, just as I knew they would. I panic. I jump up, putting myself between them and the door, I show them the wound in my side again. An animal did this, it's obvious. They don't have to believe the werewolf part to know I've been involved in something outrageous and horrific and probably newsworthy. So eventually they concede, and sit back down. They think they're humoring a delusional vagrant in the middle of a psychotic episode.

As succinctly as I can manage I record my story for the camera – name, hometown, brief autobiographical sketch. I explain only vaguely what it is to be a werewolf, I describe our society – but with every word I'm picturing my parents, I envision what it will do to them to have these secrets laid bare. However badly I need this story recorded, I can't shake the terror that I'm making a huge mistake in telling it.

So I don't give names until I get to this weekend, the warehouse, the events leading up to this moment where I stand bleeding in front of a camera in a hotel room in New York. I give my uncles' names twice. I try to be as explicit as possible – I'm seeing this tape being played at a police station, I want to give them as much information as I can. I trip up only a few times in the telling. Every time I mention Galen I see his face, that motionless face against a backdrop of bloodstained concrete, and it's all I can do to pause and collect myself and keep talking.

I occupy myself all the while with mending – I toss back a small handful of aspirin, I cut away all the bits of skin hanging off me, I pour alcohol and slather Neosporin all over everything. I'll have to wait to put any bandages on until after I show off my parlor tricks. I point to each wound as I come to it in my description, explaining where this or that injury came from. It's the only thing I can tie to the reporters' reality.

By the end of it I think I've at least got them questioning, doubting whether someone truly insane could tell a consistent story so coherently. My explanation of the warehouse massacre has certainly put them on edge – however wild this story might sound, that part is something they can verify later. It's tangible and immediate and scary. And the visual evidence of it is right in front of them.

Finally I stop speaking, and for a moment we three sit in awkward silence. The reporters are trying to work out what to say. I'm trying to work out what they're thinking.

"So you said you called the cops?" Cynthia asks finally. I nod. "What did you tell them?"

"I said it was a dog fight," I admit, sure I know where the question is headed – and the glance she shares with Troy at the mention confirms it. They think I'm lying. They think I'm mad. They want this to be some twist ending where the crazy guy's 'cover story' is what actually happened. I struggle to remain calm as I explain, "I had to tell them something they'd believe."

"That makes sense," Cynthia assures me, her tone aggravatingly placating.

"I'm *not* making this up," I repeat, teeth set, and she raises her hands in surrender. "I really am a werewolf."

"You said you could prove it," she counters.

I let out a long breath, not exactly sure how to do this. They don't believe me, they aren't prepared to see me turn into a wolf. I don't know how they're going to react when I prove them wrong.

"Okay, first," I say quietly, looking back and forth between them, "I need you to *swear* to me you'll sit there and watch, no matter how unreal this is. I know you don't believe I can do it. I know that. So when it happens I don't want you to freak out. It'll take me two seconds to get there and two seconds back, and that gives you four seconds to react in a whole host of ways I can't afford for you to do right now. I *promise* I won't hurt you."

They're starting to look hesitant. It's like a skeptic preparing to see a magic trick – they know it's not real, but this magician's too confident to make them feel wholly comfortable with their conclusion.

"Can you swear you'll just sit there?" I repeat, and they both nod. I don't know whether to believe them. I gesture to Troy's camera and ask him, "Can you see the floor from that angle?"

He checks it, shifts the camera a little, and nods again. I take a deep breath. Now or never.

I get down off the bed and crouch in front of them, trying to minimize my appearance. I don't know if it'll help.

"I'm going to count it down," I tell them, "and this first time I'm just going to go there and back as fast as I can, all right? You ready?"

I'm heartened to see Cynthia tighten her grip on her chair. *That's* the telltale sign I needed – she's *not* sure, she's bracing herself. I need her to brace herself.

"Okay, here we go," I say, "Three, two, one—"

Their reaction is instantaneous – even as my vision starts to blur in the transition I see them leap back in their chairs, startled and terrified, like visitors to some haunted house on Halloween. The transformation itself is torture, battered and broken as I am already, and I can barely hold onto reality enough to hear their cries of horror in that dizzying volley in and out of wolf form – I'm sitting here helpless for four eternal seconds while they finally come around in the worst way possible to believing everything I said. And it means the fight was real too, it means I'm a murderer, it means they're trapped with a homicidal maniac animal covered in blood—

And yet they stay in their seats. I can't believe it. They're both cursing and shaking, but in their terror they remain frozen in place, unable to move around me to escape. And four seconds later it's just me again, this human person slumped pathetically on the floor, and frankly it's hard to be intimidated by an injured guy in a towel.

"I'm sorry," I apologize the moment I can speak, holding my hands up in surrender as I fight off the inevitable wave of nauseous vertigo, trying to put them at ease. "I warned you—"

"How the fuck did you do that?" Troy demands.

I stare at him. What the hell does he want me to say? "I'm a werewolf."

"Don't fuck with us," Troy warns, furious and still clearly terrified, and Cynthia struggles to suppress the quavering in her voice as she adds, "No *really*, how'd you do it?"

I sigh, looking down at the floor, channeling patience.

"I don't have another answer," I reply. "Look, I'll do it again, I'll go slow."

"*No*, no – hold on," Cynthia interjects, holding up both hands to stop me. "Just – just hold on a moment."

"Okay," I agree, sitting back while they calm down enough to really internalize what they've just seen. I take the opportunity to emphasize what I've already explained. "I haven't lied about anything. All of this is real, all of it happened. I *need* you guys to get this message out for me, blow it up as big as you can. I should have done it days ago—"

And again I have to stop. I'm reliving that argument with Galen yesterday, the one I was one the wrong side of as always. He was exactly right – *this* was our road to salvation. And he's dead now because I couldn't listen.

All of this is too little, too late, isn't that the phrase? Even when these reporters see me transform *right in front of them* they don't believe me. Why the hell do I think they can convince an entire planet this isn't some stupid hoax…?

"I have to make sure you get a good shot of this," I start again hesitantly, pointing to the camera. "Please. I need people to know this is real."

It takes them another minute to come around. I sit there self-consciously, grabbing a bandage from my bag and dabbing again at the fresh blood seeping down my body while they confer with each other, standard did-you-see-that-too discussion. And as they begin to convince themselves they weren't hallucinating, Cynthia looks at what I'm doing and realizes that I've told them a whole lot worse than the mere fact that I'm a werewolf. She asks me again – did it happen, the warehouse? Are my friends really dead? Where was it again, and when exactly? She needs facts, she'll want to confirm this. I can barely stand to give the information a second time.

Finally, *finally* she's satisfied with her interrogation, and she and Troy both agree they want to see my transformation again. They're ready to scrutinize my movements for any hint of trickery or illusion. I don't have any idea how they still believe I could be staging this.

This time I go slow, I push against the transformation as it happens, feeling each jolt and snap and stretch in renewed agony as I almost never feel it anymore. They watch carefully, tense and cringing all the while, and agree they see nothing that would suggest I'm faking it. Much as I want to strangle them for their unceasing doubt, I wait patiently and hold on to wolf form a long moment to give them a solid view before I return to humanity. They ask me *how* I'm doing it, physically, and I don't have a good explanation — I tell them what I told Galen, that it has the same feeling as coughing or moving one's arm, it just happens as I think to do it. How does one explain a thing that comes naturally, like kicking a ball? In the next round Troy stands to watch from another angle, near the window. By now they both agree that however bizarre this is, I must truly be what I say I am. Cynthia asks to see it again.

As the transformations begin to pile up I find myself sinking, overwhelmed by the vertigo growing exponentially worse with each transition, struggling not to vomit again. I'm losing my grip on this. Every inch of my body aches in protest as I try to hold the transformation sickness at bay long enough to give the camera plenty of proof of my mutant existence, and when my vision finally goes black for a few seconds upon returning to human form, I have to admit defeat. No more, I beg, I can't do any more. I just have to pray the reporters got what they needed.

Troy turns the camera off, and I ask them not to follow me when I leave. I tell them they're welcome to call the police, submit the tape to whomever they want — but make copies first. Make the story public. They agree to all of it, after they confer about whether or not they're going to be considered accessories now to any of the various crimes to which I've confessed. I can understand their point.

As for me, I'm not worried about getting caught. I'm not dumb enough to explain that Christian Talbot isn't the name on my ID, and I doubt that NYPD is going to have a clear idea of how best to tackle tracking down a presumed-mythical creature.

All the while we're going over these technicalities, I'm bandaging myself up as quickly and efficiently as I can, fumbling now against shaking, twitching limbs rendered practically useless in the wake of so many transformations. But I can't make the

264

reporters wait any longer. In a moment I've managed a serviceable wrapping job, and I throw on my jeans and stuff the rest of the gauze in my pocket for later. Then shirt, jacket, socks, shoes, and I'm ready to leave. Cynthia's already halfway to the door, and Troy's hefting the camera up over one shoulder. It's time to go.

"Thank you, both of you," I tell them, meaning it sincerely. "For everything. I really appreciate it."

Cynthia's look is sympathetic, Troy's impassive. They both nod their welcome.

"You take care, Christian," Cynthia replies with a sad sort of half-smile. "We'll handle it from here."

"Thank you," I repeat gratefully. Cynthia gestures for me to head out, and I do.

They plan to give me three minutes' head start. I don't waste a second. I stumble down the stairs and out of the hotel, turning left on a whim, heading anywhere. Away. I just need to get out of this.

I have no concept later of how long I spend walking. I can't get my head to cooperate, I can't think, I can't bloody think with all this shit in my head. Every step I take seems somehow worse than the last, the longer I have to contemplate the horrid finality of this whole situation. I don't know where I'm going, and I don't care. At least I'm not in the warehouse. And I can't begin to imagine what sort of place would be any better than here, anyway. I'm not running, not now. I need to think awhile. If only I could think awhile…

At one point I remember with a start that we didn't call Mike today, I wonder for a wild second if maybe I should – and then I realize he's going to find out soon enough anyway. No news is bad news, but it's better news than any I've got to give him. I'll let him believe a little while longer. They're alive a little while longer in his mind, and I'm not going to take that away from him. It's an excruciating, vile, ghastly, unspeakable revelation, this reality I'm facing all of a sudden.

I finally give up on walking and stop, resting against a street sign, unable to continue. There's nowhere to go from here, there's no escaping this devastation. The only thing I've got now is bodies, blood and bodies and gore. All I can hear is screaming and growling and the sick sound of flesh tearing. All I can see is Galen, lying in a pool of blood, his own blood. The vision still sickens me, and if I had anything left to give I might throw up again at the thought.

This sense of stricken self-loathing is suffocating, it's crushing me. I should have fought harder, I should have protected him, I should have saved him and Sean and Bonks. I can't live with this. I deserve to be dead. I'd give anything to trade places with any one of them.

After a while it occurs to me that I've been standing across the street from a church, staring absently at the doorway. Without thinking I head across the street toward it, and all these drivers slam on their brakes and honk at me. God, how I wish they wouldn't bother. Just keep going. Slam into me at forty miles an hour, I don't care. But they stop, and I continue, half-oblivious, up the steps and into the church.

The whole place is dark when I enter the foyer. The lights in the chandeliers hanging from the black recesses of the ceiling serve only to cast shadows, and the windows are stained by more than just the color of the glass. The carpet is threadbare, and I wipe my feet gently, afraid to tear it. There are holy water stoups on either side of the doorway, and I walk directly between them without touching my fingertips to either one. My hands would rot off if I did.

The place is mostly empty, though there are a few old ladies and one young family sitting up in the front pews, near the altar. Their whispered voices are too low for me to pick out any words, but the sound echoes eerily throughout the empty chamber like the muttered judgment of angels. I try to ignore them as I make my way around the rows of pews to the left, heading toward a side altar in which there stands a statue of the Virgin Mary, her face lit by the dozens of votive candles burning at her feet.

I can't help but feel pathetic and clichéd as I grab two candles from a container off to the side and light them, one at a time, first for Sean and then for Galen. I can feel the Madonna's eyes on me as I do, I feel that she knows I'm a fake, a fraud, a liar desperate to light these candles for my own solace rather than for any true sense of religious devotion. She knows that I'm a sinner lighting candles for atheists, and as I set each candle carefully in its place, I'm struck by a strange sense of terror that she'll bend down and blow them out in reproach. I need my two candles to stand there forever, as testaments to the men they're lit for, as symbols of my earnest prayer for their contentment in whatever afterlife they've just found themselves in, an afterlife I've sped them to far faster than they deserved. An afterlife hopefully far sweeter than whatever God's got in store for me now.

I watch the candles burn for a while, two tiny pinpoints of light glowing quietly, anonymously amongst their peers. I wonder if any of these other candles have quite as much pain attached to them as my two. The longer I stand there staring at them, these little flames, the stronger the urge becomes to blow them out again. They're not enough by any means, they're nowhere near the tribute I need. These candles aren't going to bring anyone back to life. This whole religious charade of mine is so damned idiotic, and I can't help but feel wretched as I stand here and wonder if Galen and Sean would even *want* candles lit for them. They wouldn't go in for this sort of thing. I shouldn't have done it myself. It's a shamefully useless tribute to their memory – listen to me, 'their memory'. As if they're long gone, as if they weren't alive only this morning! Just this morning they rolled out of bed like I did, they brushed their teeth and got ready for the day as simple as that, as easy as any other day...

And then today became the last day of their lives. I'm going to be sick.

I turn away from the candles, even more thoroughly disgusted with myself now than when I walked in here. I head over to a pew, and out of habit and deference I cross myself before sitting down. Memories from my childhood wash over me in waves, bringing back a thousand Sundays' worth of masses, of prayer and liturgy and dogma that always felt far too similar to the oppression of wolf code for me to appreciate it.

I'm regretting that now, wishing I had anything I could believe in, wanting more than ever to believe that death isn't an end, a turning off of that switch we like to call a soul, a simple and irreversible abolishment of consciousness. I'm trying to remember anything at all from the Bible that might comfort me, and I'm failing. The cavernous emptiness of this nave is nothing compared to what I've got gnawing away at my soul.

Before I know it tears are pouring down my face. The remorse and anxiety and grief strike me all at once out of nowhere, and suddenly I'm choking on the sobs, burying my face in my arms to stifle the sound, dreadfully aware of how jarring it is in the relative silence of the church. Some part of me recognizes it doesn't matter. They're dead. Galen and Sean are both dead, and nothing I do anymore can bring them back.

And they're not the only ones who died. I've got all sorts of blood on my hands, I killed six of my fellow werewolves today. Six men who were more like myself than all the rest of humanity. I even killed my own uncle. I clamped his throat shut and watched him die. And to think that that man used to sit next to me in a pew just like this one, on Sundays when I was a kid and we'd go back to Ireland to visit the family.

I killed them all, wolf and human alike, directly and indirectly. And I can't help but feel that with this reporter's tape, I've now condemned hundreds or even thousands more to die. And for what? For *what*...?

I don't notice when a woman comes to sit next to me. I only feel a hand touch my shoulder and I jump up, startling the woman who startled me first, glancing at her only for a moment before burying my face again. She's young, she's the mother of that little family up at the front, and I'm sure she just thought to comfort me. She can't help me. I don't even speak, too overwhelmed by disaster to consider having a conversation with anyone. I can't stop bloody crying. I don't particularly want to.

She sits for a long while with me in silence, listening to me carry on. She's rubbing my back in sympathy. I want to tell her to stop, to warn her that she's only giving solace to a monster, that she's commiserating with the Devil. I can't force the words out.

"It will be all right," she tells me gently, her voice soothing, her words agonizingly meaningless. "This, too, shall pass."

"Do you think so?" I manage to ask, horrified at her well-meaning use of such a stale banality to combat the entirety of my

268

worldly sorrows. My voice is muffled by my shirtsleeve, and I hope she fails to hear my sarcasm.

"Of course," she replies. "God will help you through it."

"I'd rather He killed me," I say.

She chides with honest compassion, "Oh, honey, don't say that."

"Why not?" I demand, my patience breaking along with my sanity. In a few moments I'm going to regret so wildly misdirecting all my anger at her as I continue, "Do you have *any* idea why I'm sitting here? Would you guess that I *killed people* today, six men and two saints, would you believe I watched their blood pool at my feet! What makes you think you can sympathize with that?"

The woman's eyes have grown wide with alarm as I speak, and I can see her husband getting up from the front pew, roused by my yelling at his wife, ready to drive me off. I've only got a few moments more before he arrives, and it seems cruel that my catharsis would have to have been interrupted in such a rude way, that my mourning would be cut short. I'm wondering if maybe the Madonna directed them here to drive me from her church, banish me for the sins I've committed.

"Did you really do that?" the woman asks, appalled.

"I did," I answer her coldly. "So what kind of God do you worship, ma'am, Who lets men like me enter your churches? What God would make a man like me, a man who watches his friends die in front of him! Tell me why you think I deserve to breathe, why He allows me to keep walking!"

"Hey, that's enough," the husband warns me. He's reached our pew, and he's coming down the way toward us. The woman has stood up abruptly, retreating farther from me with every blasphemous statement I make. I don't mean to say it, to spoil their evening. But they shouldn't have spoiled mine. I back off anyway, raising my hands in surrender and stepping back from the pew. I take one last look at the statue of the Madonna and my two useless little candles, my hopeless offerings, before I give up and head back the way I came.

The train ride back to Philadelphia is long, and slow, and

miserable. But for once I don't have a problem with going backward, retracing my steps and getting back to where everything started. I recognize that I can't actually reverse time, that when I arrive Galen's house will still be empty, that he'll still be in New York where I left him and Sean and Bonks. Getting scraped off the floor of the warehouse in which I abandoned them after I failed them.

There aren't enough words in the world to describe how fervently I want this not to have happened. I've just been replaying the warehouse over and over in my mind, trying to see what I should have done differently, how I could have gotten them out of it. I've picked apart every piece, every moment of the encounter seared so vividly in my mind, slowed down now in the frame of memory so that every moment I managed to miss the first time stands out now in cruel clarity – I've dissected and studied and analyzed and reanalyzed every possible angle of the wolves' attack.

There are so many things I could have done, so many things I should have said... So many ways I could have stopped it, long before it ever got to that point. *So many times* I should have left, so many times I stayed for no other reason than that I was comfortable, I was too goddamn proud and arrogant to go!

No – that's not the only reason. I was desperate to stay, because for the first time in my life I was perfectly content, I was honestly happy, and I can't help but disagree wholeheartedly with Galen – I'd have traded that happiness in an instant if I truly knew what it'd come to. No amount of contentment could possibly make up for this punishment.

My other uncle is presumably still in the States somewhere, pursuing me all the more adamantly now that I've killed his brother, but I can't bring myself to care. Let Tony find me, I'll kill him too. The idea haunts me. I keep vacillating back and forth, at first anxious to hunt him down in retribution and then immediately regretting the thought, sick of bloodshed, shrinking from the idea of ever touching a hair on my uncle's head until I remember again how I acquired this revulsion and want instantly to destroy every fucking person who ever had a hand in sending me down the path that ended in me standing impotently by while

Galen drowned in his own blood. I want to make the world pay for what happened to Galen. And I know there's no way to do that. The best retribution I can think of is already set in motion.

When I get off the train in Philly I head straight for an old friend's house.

It's the fiancée that answers the door when I knock, and I must look like a bloody wreck because she cringes when she sees me. I withhold a sigh of frustration at my persistent misfortune – I was hoping to see Dane first. Drew's here, too, he noses his way around the door and wags his tail at me in recognition. He barks a greeting.

"Can I help you?" the fiancée inquires.

"Is Dane in?" I ask her. She half nods, already turning to go call for him, and then thinks better of it and turns back to me.

"What's your name?" she thinks to ask.

"Andy," I reply.

"Ah," she says, and heads back into the house. She shouts up the stairs, "Honey, there's some guy at the door for you, name's Andy."

I stand at the door and wait, and Drew comes up to sniff at my feet. I let him sniff, but I don't bother to move. I'm in no mood to deal with dogs right now. Finally I hear the clumping of feet down the stairs, and in a moment Dane appears in the doorway. He breaks into a smile.

"Oh, *that* Andy," he says. "Didn't know who the hell she was talking about. What's up?"

"I'm a werewolf," I tell him bluntly, and in the face of his momentary surprise I plunge on, the words pouring out of me in a torrent, "It'll be all over the news soon, I'm sure – I'm a werewolf and I was your dog, Andy, and I really need you to do me a favor. I need you to take me to Greece. Now. As soon as possible…"

CHAPTER 15

Five days later I'm sitting on a beach in Santorini, alone, watching the sunset. It's a vacant, obscure little pebble beach, a short walk down from the town of Oia which sits at the top of the cliffs behind me. The sunset is gorgeous, all reds and yellows and purples as seen through human eyes, and the viewing is perfect – it's a clear, cloudless day, even if it's horrifically cold. I'm not really bothered by the chill.

I've been in Greece for four days, now. Dane was remarkably receptive to my request, and though he asked far more questions than I answered, he was perfectly willing to take an immediate trip out to Athens with 'his dog' in tow, stowed away in the belly of the plane in the biggest crate I could find at a pet store. And from there he graciously brought me to Santorini, stayed one night and left as abruptly as he'd come. The news of my existence had already leaked by then and he was going to be lucky to get home without people becoming suspicious about his travel arrangements – arriving with one massive werewolf-size dog, departing without. He understood the predicament. I thanked him profusely and he left.

I don't know anymore what brought me to Greece. I had a few reasons floating around at the beginning – I had nothing to lose anymore, I've been dying to get here for ages, I might as well see what the pictures were all about, I wanted to be the hell out of the States, I needed to keep running, I wanted to forget all about New York and everything that happened there. But all those reasons seem to have evaporated now as I sit here, meandering aimlessly about the streets of Fira and Oia and Perissa like a ghost, unable for any length of time to see past my own introspection and soak in the marvelous views.

I don't give a damn anymore about any of it, all these places and experiences I thought I'd never be able to survive without. I can't help but feel that every breath I take is another breath I don't deserve, and the guilt and loathing and self-pity are breaking me down with every damn day I spend here. And I can't help but feel that any attempt I've made to escape will never be enough anymore, anyway.

It turns out that humans are far more credulous than I give them credit for: the notion that werewolves might actually exist is sweeping the globe as we speak. I wasn't kidding when I said Dane needed to hightail it back – everything's snowballing out of control.

It seems Cynthia's tape and the investigation of the warehouse massacre in New York have at least served to get every major media station speculating about whether or not my story could possibly be real. I can't bring myself to watch any of it, but it's becoming increasingly difficult to avoid – televisions and newspaper stands everywhere are choked with news of this story. The headlines are ridiculous, and terrifying. I sought out only one myself, checking the Guardian online to find what my parents were undoubtedly reading. It waxed poetic, *Werewolves in Our Midst*, but seeing my picture, name, and hometown was acutely heart-constricting in the brief skim I managed before closing the window in revulsion.

And two days ago, a wolf in Los Angeles came forward as well to share in the notoriety. Another one in Germany today. Both given courage, they said, by my own initial bold move. The idea turns my stomach.

I don't know how the world is going to react to this, all these werewolves showing their faces all at once. I don't care to find out.

When the sun goes down over the water I sit for another moment staring out to sea, reflecting quietly in the gathering dusk. Finally I stand and head back up the path toward my hotel room, stumbling along carefully up the slope and cursing the persistent stiffness in my right leg. I don't know why I'm being cautious. I'm not living in this moment, I'm not seeing Oia as it exists in front of my eyes. Oia is still sitting in a painting hung over a bed, in a house I used to live in. It's something created by a true friend of mine, and it's something given to another, even dearer friend. Oia is something I stole from both of them.

When I get to my room I stand for a moment, blank-headed, looking about this hotel room that is my whole world at the moment. I have a sense of disoriented clarity, an epiphany of unfamiliarity as I take it all in again and wonder what possessed me to come back here tonight. These four walls seem strange, unnatural. This made bed, this unlived place, this miniscule pile of personal effects on the dresser – none of which are mine, none of which mean anything to me. This all means nothing to me, and suddenly I understand what I have to do. I see what I've been doing wrong.

I spent the first half my life trying to be human. I lived in terror and I obeyed. My life was measured in increments of twenty-nine and a half days, and everything, *everything* I could have been or done or seen or had was overshadowed by that. My sick secret. The shameful and despicable thing that was my other self, the half of me no human could see. I hated it. I hated my life and myself and my nature, and more than any of that I hated the society that had forced it all on me. I hated God, because then I still believed in Him and I could never forgive Him for making me what I am. And every day that hatred grew, it festered, until finally it became some palpable and overwhelming black thing that propelled me out of my house and my country and my human skin.

And now I've spent the second half of my life playing a dog, surrounded by humans and more alone than I'd ever been before. I went for years without speaking a word to anyone. And I thought I was happy, I thought I was free. Ha. I wasn't free. I was as scared and as stupid as ever. I was dedicated to my self-preservation, and I wasted more than a decade doing absolutely nothing in order to preserve my anonymity.

I realize now, as I'm sitting here in this useless hotel room on a desolate island in a foreign country, that I've been directed to this place, this moment, this utter dead-end completely by my own fears. I've been driven by fear my entire life. But I've no fear now. I lost it back at the warehouse, along with everything else that mattered to me. I've nothing left, and what little I possess I no longer want.

So this is it. I'm done pretending. I failed at being human, I failed at being a dog. Time to at least be honorable.

I have to admit I don't know how to do this gracefully. Grace is not something I've ever learned to do properly. And loss is not something I've ever borne. Without thinking I take off my shirt, and my trousers and my shorts and everything I own and lay it all neatly on the foot of the bed. And then I leave my room and head out the back door of the hotel.

The street is empty as I step out onto it, retracing my footsteps back out to the cliff face. I peer over its edge to see the waves crashing quietly on the beach below. The sun is gone now, the twilight dwindling. The whole world is hushed. Waiting.

As I stand there, alone, I think a silent prayer to Galen and Sean. This one's for you, guys – a proper tribute for your deaths, a real one-gun salute. A first-rate honor killing. An attempt to return the world to its proper order, because I shouldn't have been the only one to walk away from that warehouse.

I take one last breath, and jump.

EPILOGUE

Maya and Gregor were both exhausted. In retrospect, they shouldn't have started their honeymoon with a twenty-hour, two-layover flight followed directly by a long ferry ride. But they were here – finally! – in Santorini like Maya had always dreamed. And nothing was going to stop them from enjoying a walk out on their first night in paradise, even if they had just missed the sunset on the drive up. The hotel director gave them directions to the famous cliffs where tomorrow they'd come and see it properly, and they were off, strolling arm in arm through the streets of Oia.

And as they rounded the corner on the last leg of their walk, Maya let out a breath of surprise.

"...Hey, sweetheart?" she asked with a hesitant grin, nudging Gregor and pointing curiously, "Is that guy – is he naked?"

Greg looked where she was pointing, and he couldn't help grinning as well. "Uh... yeah, I think so."

They came to a halt simultaneously, amused and unsure what the hell to do with themselves – the man was standing right where they wanted to go, after all. They grinned at each other awkwardly.

"Well, we came for a show," Maya said, and Greg chuckled.

"This is not my idea of a show," he pointed out.

"Do you think we should just... keep walking, or something—?"

But Greg startled her into silence.

"Hey, wait!" he shouted suddenly, alarmed. She turned back to the cliff where he was looking – but it was empty. The man was gone.

"Oh my God," Maya whispered, knowing immediately what it meant.

Greg was already running to the edge of the cliff. She darted

276

after him, heart pounding in her chest. By the time she got there Greg had already glanced over the edge, and he whirled back around to face her, holding his hands out to stop her. "Don't look, baby, don't look."

"Is he – is he dead?" Maya stammered, searching her husband's ashen face.

"I don't know." He looked over the edge again, calling down, "Hey! Are you okay, can you hear me?"

But he got no response. He turned quickly back to Maya. "Go get help!"

And then he took off down the side of the cliff, scrambling down the makeshift path, kicking up loose rocks that went tumbling down the hill before him as he went. Maya watched him only for a moment before her brain kicked into gear and she turned, bolting back down the street toward her hotel.

"Help!" she cried as she entered the front lobby, and the same director looked up, startled. She rushed to the front desk, trying to catch her breath. "Help, a man fell off the cliff – we need a doctor!"

"Slowly, please," the director entreated, putting a hand on her shoulder to calm her, unable to understand her hurried plea. "Say it again."

"A man fell off the cliff," she said again, gesturing wildly, trying to pantomime something falling from a great height. "Please, call a doctor, a hospital, he's hurt, he's injured."

"Oh," the director said quietly, understanding at last. He picked up his phone and dialed a number. She waited impatiently with him until finally someone answered, and he spoke to them in rapid Greek. She couldn't understand any of it. But shortly the call ended and he slammed down the phone and darted around the edge of his desk, gesturing for her to come with him.

Together they ran back to the cliff, both of them out of breath by the time they reached it. They headed together to its edge and looked over. Maya was already cringing before the beach came into view, terrified of what she might see—

But it was only Greg, Greg frantically scouring the empty beach.

"Did you find him, is he okay?" Maya called, and Greg looked up to see her and the director both watching him. He threw up his hands.

"I don't know!" he shouted back, voice echoing off the wall of the cliff. "There's blood over there but I can't — I can't find him! He's gone."

The story continues in

CANINE: AWAKENINGS

As the human world learns of the existence of werewolves, the ones responsible for that revelation find themselves in a desperate fight for survival. Two men lie crippled in hospital, three siblings flee for their lives, and no one seems to know what's happened to the rogue werewolf who started it all…

About the Author

Kaitlin Bergfield is a neuroscientist with a longstanding, consuming passion for all things paranormal. She now writes fantasy novels while on break from caring for her latest and most fascinating neurodevelopment case study.

Made in the USA
Monee, IL
12 December 2021

84913147R00166